WAR OF THE WORLDS

ALSO BY DOUGLAS NILES
FROM TOM DOHERTY ASSOCIATES

Fox on the Rhine (with Michael Dobson)

Fox at the Front (with Michael Dobson)

WAR OF THE WORLDS

NEW MILLENNIUM

DOUGLAS NILES

A TOM DOHERTY ASSOCIATES BOOK • NEW YORK

WAR OF THE WORLDS: NEW MILLENNIUM

Copyright © 2005 by Bill Fawcett and Associates

This book is printed on acid-free paper.

Edited by Brian Thomsen

A Tor Book
Published by Tom Doherty Associates, LLC
175 Fifth Avenue
New York, NY 10010

www.tor.com

Tor® is a registered trademark of Tom Doherty Associates, LLC.

Library of Congress Cataloging-in-Publication Data

Niles, Douglas.
    War of the worlds : new millennium / Douglas Niles.—1st ed.
        p.   cm.
    "A Tom Doherty Associates book."
    ISBN 0-765-31142-9
    EAN 978-0-765-31142-9
    1. Human-alien encounters—Fiction. I. Title.

PS3564.I375W36 2005
813'.54—dc22

                                                    2005041759

First Edition: June 2005

Printed in the United States of America

0 9 8 7 6 5 4 3 2 1

To the men and women of the
Wisconsin National Guard—
and "Welcome home!" to the 232nd AG HHD

ACKNOWLEDGMENTS

This story would not exist if not for the bold and visionary genius of H. G. Wells, one of the true patriarchs of science fiction. I owe a debt of gratitude to him, and to all those, from Orson Welles to George Pal, who have relocated and retold his epic tale through the intervening century-plus.

Many thanks to Bill Fawcett, who made this exciting project happen. I am also grateful to Brian Thomsen, whose steady hand on the editing tiller helped to shape and nurture the tale. On the Tor staff, Natasha Panza shepherded the book through the publication process. Copy editor Sara Schwager intercepted more embarrassing authorial gaffes than I would care to admit.

A number of good friends, colleagues, and family members contributed their time to review the manuscript and offer many helpful suggestions and corrections during the writing of the book. Michael Dobson's critique was thorough and exceptionally helpful. Major General Al Wilkenning of the Wisconsin National Guard was gracious enough to discuss the A10 Warthog with me, resulting in the removal of at least one factual error from the text. Longtime friends in the Baxter family, including Betty, Fred, Ian, and the late Ivan Baxter, contributed engineering and computer know-how to the book.

My fellow members of the Alliterates Writing Society—especially Troy Denning, Rob King, Lester Smith, Don Perrin, Matt Forbeck, Tim Brown, and Steve Sullivan—provided excellent brainstorming assistance at several points in the writing process. My family contributed three generations of perspective as my father, Donald Niles, Sr., my brother Dirk Niles, and my son Dave Niles all read the manuscript and offered their reactions.

I owe each and all a great deal for their contributions. Their comments have improved the book. Any remaining errors or contradictions are my responsibility alone.

Douglas Niles
February 2005

AUTHOR'S NOTE

A War of the Worlds for a New Millenium:

When H. G. Wells wrote *The War of the Worlds* in 1898, there was yet to be a "world war," a military strategy using tanks, or even a practical exploration of rocketry as a means to penetrate the stratosphere. Yet all are clearly ensconced in the book's plot. It is true that the theories of rocketry are closer to ballistics, the tripod fighting machines more fanciful than practical, and the world that is referred basically pertains to the civilized world of Great Britain, making this "war of the worlds" rather parochial in nature.

In the end, Wells penned a classic that has spawned countless other alien invasion stories featuring such sundry invaders as little green men, the Snouts of Niven and Pournelle's *Footfall,* and the mutating virus from Robin Cook's *Invasion.* The story itself made headlines in the classic panic broadcast by Mercury Theater. In Ecuador in 1949, another broadcast of the play resulted in such distress that some twenty people were killed and the radio station burned down by a vengeful crowd of listeners who had learned that they had been panicked by a fictional performance.

On the silver screen George Pal placed the story in Los Angeles, and there was even an eponymous short-lived TV series that might have been more accurately called *War of the Worlds—The Next Generation.* Obviously such blockbusters as *Independence Day* and *Mars Attacks* owe their lineage to the Wells tradition, and the anthology *War of the Worlds—Global Dispatches* fleshed out what was happening elsewhere in the world during the events of Wells's original storyline.

. . . but what if the events depicted in the original short novel happened today?

. . . what would be different?

. . . how might the invasion proceed given our hi-tech weapons and media broadcasting, and knowledge of space travel and exploration? And how might modern techniques of storytelling refine the plot, characters, and scope of the story?

As always man/humanity will rise to the occasion with ingenuity, technology, and a bit of dumb luck.

The world of the new millennium plays by a different set of rules . . . and Wells might possibly approve. More probably, he would disapprove of us now as much as he did of those of his contemporary time.

There is one other key difference in the world of *War of the Worlds: New Millenium:* In order for the world to work properly, Wells must never have published the original *War of the Worlds,* making this new world much more deprived than our own.

WAR OF THE WORLDS

PROLOGUE

The image appeared crisp and lifelike on television screens across the country. It was animation, but it looked real.

Millions watched as the spacecraft struck the rust-colored planet at a shallow angle. Gravity pulled it through a long, flat arc as the parachute broke free. The clamshell housing snapped open, jettisoning the rover before the second impact nearly a kilometer away. The discarded outer container flopped to a halt, kicking up a blizzard of dust, while the package bounced again, and still a third time.

Each impact scraped away momentum, until the silver polygon was rolling along the rust-colored landscape.

Cushioned by an array of airbags, it finally halted, crouching on one long side, settling into place with a shuddering, nervous wobble.

Air gushed into the thin atmosphere, a long sigh as the bags deflated. Motors hummed, and the panels of silver metal began to move. The upper surfaces folded outward and down, bridging the flattened airbags, revealing the rover. The ungainly contraption that had been concealed within seemed to approach the alien planet cautiously. One by one the inclined ramps settled to the ground, until the rover sat atop a metallic dais, several feet higher than the vast, dry landscape, presiding over the planetary surface.

Only then did the reporter begin to speak.

"This animation, prepared with the aid of experts at the Jet Propulsion Lab here in Pasadena, is a fairly accurate representation of what is occurring right now, more than a hundred million miles from Earth." The image abruptly shifted to the rotund, beaming reporter. Jay Manstein was so visibly enthusiastic that he all but hopped up and down.

"Already that rover, the most advanced robot ever created by the mind and dexterity of man, is beginning to work. Watch, and you'll see what this baby can do."

Back to the animation: A small camera rose into position above the rover's body and focused on the horizon, looking around with a deliberate demeanor. Like a periscope above a cartoon submarine, it swiveled and absorbed.

"The lens is seeing, and the digital memory absorbing, picture after picture of the bleak, utterly lifeless landscape," Manstein exulted. "And never before have we humans dared to probe to such a dramatic portion of the Martian surface!

"To either side you see massive, stratified walls, miles away and still looming high. With imperceptible increments of movement the camera pivots through a full circle, the powerful telephoto lens zooming in on the distant crests, capturing frame after frame of the walls and rim. Then the aperture will dilate, the shutters expand, so that the lens captures a fish-eye look at the whole of the vast, dry Valles Marineris—the deepest canyon in the entire solar system!"

Manstein took a breath, knowing that his words were not just hyperbole. It was a rare moment for him, the pinnacle of a career spent educating viewers about the magnificent and unplumbed depths of space. He looked at his notes and finished the story, knowing he'd have only minutes to get to the briefing room for the upcoming press conference.

"In a mission of unprecedented precision and daring, the rover has targeted this rough and rocky gash for landing. Now it sends confirmation back home, a visual 'wish you were here' as the digital signals beam spaceward through the auxiliary antenna mere seconds after the camera records them. This low-power transmitter is barely able to reach the widespread antenna of the Mars Global Surveyor, one of two American satellites in steady orbit around the Red Planet. Since the main signals mast won't rise for another few hours, the rover cannot yet communicate directly with Earth. Instead, it employs MGS as a powerful transmitter, a relay switch on the interplanetary network sending a continuous stream of signals through more than a hundred million miles of space."

Ten minutes later, those signals were decoded and rendered into dramatic photographs by the computers at the Jet Propulsion Laboratory in California, along the West Coast of the United States of America, on the planet Earth.

"We did it!" shouted the black-haired technician, leaping up from her chair and clapping her hands, grinning as the whole control room broke into applause.

"Beautiful pictures—Carla, I could kiss you!" Bob Wolfe, Director of the Vision Rover Project, led the cheers. His ursine shape loomed over all the others in the big control room, and he enthusiastically reached out his big paws to embrace his favorite employee.

"Okay, Bob, but just this once!" The chubby little technician threw her arms around her supervisor and smacked her lips to his as, throughout the large control room, people whooped and shouted, cheered, embraced, and exchanged stinging high fives.

Carla Gonzalez, called "Speedy" by her colleagues, adjusted her blazer and her glasses, blushing slightly, and quickly turned back to her keyboard as the celebration accelerated. Two photography specialists did an impromptu jig past the huge, wide-screen images on the wall screens. A paper airplane curved over the front-row monitors, skidding off of Bob Wolfe's bald head, and he waved cheerfully at Derrick Whitten, the wizened mission specialist who was already folding another of his unique missiles in the back of the room.

Carla glanced at her boss and smiled slyly. "Well, maybe we can do it again, once we get the subplanar readings coming in?"

"It's a date," said Wolfe, wrapping a bearish arm around her shoulders. "For now, you get to watch the slide show—live! And I have to go talk to the cameras. When I get back, we'll see what we have to do before we can take this bad boy for a drive." He turned and addressed the more than two dozen elated scientists in the room. "Good work, people! Keep those pictures coming!"

The project director looked to be walking on air as he bounced out of the room and down the hall to the auditorium. The press conference was a lively scene even before Wolfe stepped to the podium. Print reporters were still filing in, and a bank of television cameras representing the national networks, a number of local outlets, and a few specialty organs like the Discovery Channel and *National Geographic*, were jammed into all the space along the edges of the room. They held their unblinking eyes on JPL's top scientist as, grinning broadly, he ambled toward the podium. As the project director approached the microphones, the questions were already flying.

"Dr. Wolfe—are you ready to call this mission a success?"

"What's the mood in the control room?"

"Do you have any glitches to report?"

"How soon before Vision starts to drill?"

"Ladies and gentlemen," Wolfe began, an avuncular smile coupled with a calming gesture of his hands lowering, as if by magic, the level of excitement in the room. His size was an advantage at times like this, and he had learned to use his presence to his advantage when dealing with the press, as well as subordinates and superiors. Now his expansive mood and clear air of delight seemed to inspire the normally sanguine journalists to mutual enthusiasm.

"I have prepared a brief statement, then would be delighted to take your questions." He pulled a crumpled piece of paper from his breast pocket— as always, he wore a white shirt, no tie, under a loose-fitting lab coat—and meticulously spread it out on the podium. By the time he had the page satisfactorily arranged and had cleared his throat several times, the room was mostly silent except for the electronic chirps and chimes of phones and recorders. Camera lights flashed, while people adjusted PDAs and all the other paraphernalia of digital equipment that enable modern electronic communication.

"Mars Rover Number Three, the robot we call Vision, has arrived in the Valles Marineris after what can only be described as a flawless landing. Naturally, after the unexpected—and still unexplained—losses of Rovers One and Two, we are only cautiously optimistic. But the initial signals from Vision have given us good cause for hope, and already represent a significant leap forward in our understanding of Martian geography."

"Dr. Wolfe?"

The director winced slightly as he recognized Josh Hickam from the *Atlanta Journal-Constitution*. Long a NASA gadfly, Hickam—naturally—did not wait for an invitation to continue. "Can you offer any assurances that Vision won't encounter the same kind of terminal problems that brought the Spirit and Opportunity missions to premature ends?"

"Now Josh, I'm sure you're aware that *both* of those rovers lasted significantly longer than their original mission specs required," Wolfe began.

"But each of them went off-line so quickly, under circumstances that were never satisfactorily explained," pressed the reporter. "Are you worried that the same thing will happen with Vision?"

"Those failures are not unexplained!" Wolfe argued, fighting for self-control as the bearlike director recognized that he had begun to growl. "They were natural progressions of entropy—dust building up on the solar collectors, temperature-related failures, that sort of thing."

Hickam scribbled away in his notebook, no doubt satisfied that he had provoked the reaction he was looking for. Bob Wolfe took a breath and forged ahead. He spotted Jay Manstein, long a friendly booster of the space program, near the front, and smiled at the reporter's enthusiasm. Remembering that this was an exciting story to most of the country, he directed his words to the CNN astronomy specialist.

"If you will look at the screens behind me, you will see the first of an extraordinary series of pictures. These shots show a view from the largest canyon in the solar system—five times deeper than our own Grand Canyon. The resolution is higher, the depth of focus greater than on any previous Martian pictures. They raise the promise of new observations, the possibility of exciting new discoveries. Already we have determined that the hematite surface that apparently extends through the entire canyon is water-based in origin. We can see strata in the walls of the cliffs that suggest billions of years of planetary history.

"Of course, we are all aware that the real potential in this mission involves the rover's mining capacities. That is, for the first time we will be attempting to drill through the crust of the planet. It is our hope that the resulting data will help us to determine how long ago Mars was host to free-flowing water, and also give us better understanding of just what, exactly, happened to those once-vast seas. . . ."

Over the next few days Vision adjusted its stance on the landing platform, poised like a dragster at the starting line. The powerful signals mast rose and deployed, then found the signals from the distant Earth. This antenna increased the rate of data transfer a hundredfold from the initial, chirping emissions passed along by the Mars Global Surveyor.

With stability and equilibrium ensured, Speedy Gonzalez instructed the six-wheeled robot to move off the platform and onto the rusty surface of the planet, earning her nickname with the unprecedented haste of the maneuver—at its fastest, the robot scooted along at nearly twenty meters per hour.

Of course, the driving operations were exceptionally tricky because they did not occur in real time. Gonzalez merely sent suggestions to the robot's powerful electronic brain, then the rover itself decided how to proceed. With the ten-minute signals lag between the planets, she could only give a general instruction, a destination. The rover was steered by its robotic computer, aided by fore and aft hazard cameras allowing for analysis of the ground. After study and electronic contemplation, it selected its own route and reported back as the job was done.

Once on the ground, the six wheels rolled easily across the flat surface of the canyon floor, with cameras meticulously recording each track in the dusty ground, every potential obstacle in the device's path. During the frigid, lightless nights, the rover sat still, conserving energy, maintaining just enough heat in the Warm Electronics Box to keep the most sensitive instruments from freezing up. With the Martian dawn, solar panels charged the rover's batteries, and Vision commenced a new round of research activities. With the exception of a backup radio transmitter in the photography module, every system checked out one hundred percent effective.

More days passed, the Martian clock advancing just a little more slowly than Earth's, one rotation of the Red Planet equaling twenty-four hours, thirty-seven minutes, and twenty-seven seconds on the Terran clock. Operating during daylight hours, Vision ventured farther from the lander, breaking the kilometer milestone on the eighth day of mobile operations. The machine's robotic arm scraped into dusty rocks, scuffed away the layer of iron oxide—the hematite—that covered the ground, collected pebbles, and crushed those same stones to analyze their mineral content. Other instruments bombarded the planetary surface with X-rays, infrared and ultraviolet light and, in a new innovation unique to Vision, radar signals directed outward as well as straight down.

At three weeks into the mission, the rover had covered an area of more than one hundred square kilometers with crisscrossing tracks, back and forth on the canyon floor, and was approaching one of the looming walls. Data poured from the powerful antenna as fast as the cameras, spectrometers, mini-TES, and other analytical machines could process the immense amounts of information gathered by the host of sophisticated instruments. The Mars Global Surveyor served as a reliable relay station, transferring the stream of binary code through interplanetary space. At the same time, the satellite took pictures itself, contrasting the surface viewpoint of Vision with the bird's-eye perspective from orbit.

Back at JPL—and across America, in the laboratories of universities and

the offices of NASA in Houston and Washington, DC—the data was ana-
lyzed, studied, cross-referenced, deconstructed. Bob Wolfe, to use his own
phrase, was tickled pink by the quality of the data and the performance of
the rover.

This was an audacious mission. Not only was the rover intended to ex-
plore the surface of Mars but, for the first time, an unmanned probe would
actually attempt to drill through the surface of the planet. Thanks to a telescoping drill mechanism, Vision had the possibility of probing as much as
thirty meters below the ground. Geologists, astronomers, metallurgists, en-
gineers, technicians, and even a few veteran oil prospectors studied the resulting information, debating the most crucial decision of the mission:
where to poke that hole into Mars? All of the arguments and counterargu-
ments, the pros and cons—and the cautions—came to rest on Bob Wolfe's
desk. For more than a full day he sequestered himself with Derrick Whitten in his private office, studying charts of the area mapped by Vision.

Finally, they chose a site. Carla guided the robot across the plain to the
selected location, moving at the unseemly, almost reckless rate of nearly
one kilometer per hour. The rover settled into the place with a rocking motion as all six wheels spun back and forth, giving the machine as solid a
stance as possible. For more than thirty hours it sat there, snapping another
series of photographs, confirming the X-ray and spectrograph readings.

The auxiliary robot arm extended with precise movements, unfolding
over the span of several hours until the terminus of that limb was pressed
against the planetary surface just a meter or so off to Vision's side. The
elaborate hardware moved into place, forming a metal stalk more than
three meters tall—twice as tall as the rover. Vision's appearance had often
been likened to a golf cart; now, it looked like a golf cart that was tethered
to an undersized telephone pole.

Within that telephone pole, motors pulsed into life. A sharpened bit, not
unlike a mason's drill, moved gradually down to the surface of the planet.
The hardened carbide tip came into contact with the ground, quickly penetrating the loose layers of dust and gravel until, forty-seven centimeters
down, it began to penetrate the solid bedrock.

The sound of the high-speed drilling would have been shrill and irritating in the sound-friendly atmosphere of Earth. Here on Mars, the noise immediately dissipated into the near vacuum of the thin, frigid air.

The sound carried much more effectively, of course, through the solid
surface of the planet.

"We've got good readings, seventy-three meters down," Derrick Whitten announced, reading the numbers as they flashed across his screen.

"How's the heat—do we need to back off for an hour?" asked Wolfe. The director paced back and forth behind his mission specialist's chair. The atmosphere in the control room was tense and quiet. There were no reporters there, and not just because it was the middle of the night in California. It was high noon in the Valles Marineris, and that was what mattered.

"Readings are all in the acceptable range. I guess that's one advantage of drilling into subfreezing rock. I think we can go another meter before we back off for the day."

"All right, Derrick. You're the boss—for the time being."

Wolfe turned away and started to pace. Predictably, he took only a few steps before he was back, peering over his old colleague's shoulder, squinting at the figures still streaming across the screen.

"What about a visual, Bob?" Whitten asked tactfully, urging the director to go somewhere else for a little while. "Are we raising a dust cloud or anything?"

"I'll check." Relieved at the excuse for action—or at least purposeful movement—Wolfe went over to pester the photography specialists. He saw the pictures of the drilling site, which was in fact raising a small wisp of dust, though not enough to conceal the ground from the hazard-avoidance cameras mounted on the rover's belly. Of course, like the data from the drill itself, he knew he was looking at information that had been collected ten minutes before. Likewise, any command they sent to the rover would take ten minutes to get there. With that in mind, he headed back across the room to Whitten and his team.

"Derrick, I think we should give it a rest for a little while—an hour or two. Let the data catch up to our progress."

"Okay, chief," Whitten said with a nod. He reached for his mouse, quickly clicked to a new screen, and started making adjustments to the drilling apparatus. "I'll back her down slow, so we don't catch the bit. Hard to find a plumber up there if we need a service call."

"Right."

"Dr. Wolfe?" The summons came from one of the photo specialists.

"What is it, Chris?" The project director hurried over to the specialist's station.

Chris Rasmussen pointed a well-manicured finger at her screen. "It looks like the dust is trailing away to the west, here. I wonder if we've got a bit of wind."

The picture came into view—the familiar red landscape of Mars, with a trace of dust rising from the low foreground, the plume extending away off the top of the screen. The camera was trained down, but it still caught the surroundings to about ten or twenty meters away from the rover.

"Raise the camera—let's see if we can get a look farther out in the direction. I wonder if the dust cloud is bigger than we think."

"Bob! Get over here, quick!" Whitten stared at the readouts of the drilling control. The tone of his voice brought Wolfe on the run, even as the mission specialist turned a dial and started tapping on his keyboard.

"We're heating up fast, now. Faster than I would think from friction, unless we hit something goddamned *hard*."

"Stop the drill!" Wolfe ordered, knowing that Whitten was already doing that. Never had the project director felt, so acutely, that crucial time gap between the rover's sending of data and the receiving of a command.

"What do you see?" he called across to Chris Rasmussen.

"Just the same as a moment—oh, shit! I've got a gray screen, nothing but snow."

Bob Wolfe looked up at the wide-screen display, where live photo images were continuously broadcast. That image vanished before his eyes, going to static. He wasn't even surprised when Derrick Whitten made his own scientific analysis of the data before him.

"We're screwed, Chief."

BOOK I
THE GOD OF WAR

ONE

April 20.

I look at that day on the calendar, and realize that it all started one year ago today.

April 20. It has become a whole story, in itself, like December 7, or September 11. You don't need to attach a year to it.

Later I learned that day was Hitler's birthday. It was also the date when Tim McVeigh decided to blow up the federal building in Oklahoma City, and, in a different year, when those teenage mass murderers shot up the high school in Columbine, Colorado. Last year it was my daughter's thirty-sixth birthday, though as usual I forgot to call her. This year, of course, we don't have any working telephones.

In point of fact, throughout history April 20 was mostly just another day. There was no glimmering of significance, no thought of the calendar in my mind as I decided to go outside that night. The pertinent inspiration was the first clear and balmy night of the year. (I had to settle for "balmy"; in Wisconsin, the nights don't get "warm" until June. But it was remarkably pleasant on that April 20.)

My name is Mark DeVane, and I am a retired professor of astronomy. Now I live in the country, writing articles and the occasional book, living by myself and liking that state very much. Spring fever had possessed me all day. I'd had no phone calls and no visitors, and Browne's dogs had been mercifully silent.

The sense of exhilaration didn't dissipate when the sun set. Energized, I disassembled my telescope and tripod from winter quarters in my upstairs study and put on my hiking boots and a light jacket. I started through the woods to my neighbor's pasture, relishing the lingering warmth of the day. It was a moonless night, so I carried a flashlight in my left hand while I walked the narrow trail. When I came out into the grassy field, I clicked off the light—the stars were brilliant, the dome of the sky bright with plenty of ambient light.

Plus, I didn't want Browne to see the light and know he had a trespasser in his upper pasture. My last conversation with him had been unpleasant, with good cause. His dogs had made a mess of my garbage can, and I had told him to keep the damned mutts off my property.

As for my going to his hilltop, I wasn't going to hurt anything. My boots got a little wet crossing the swale below the hill, but once I was on the slope the ground was dry and firm. It smelled like spring, a mixture of dampness, worms, and a little tentative photosynthesis left over from the sunny afternoon. The peepers were chirping like crazy in the marsh that curled around the far side of the hill.

I set up the telescope and quickly raised the lens to the southeast sky. My target, tinged that familiar red, stood out like a beacon among tea lights, surrealistically bright. Mars was unusually near to Earth then, the two planets' separate orbits approaching alignment on the same side of the sun. Here, on this grassy hilltop, I had a totally unobstructed view.

Removing my glasses I leaned over and, with a few sweeps to the right and left, located my target. The focus was close enough that a quarter turn of the knob brought the rust red disk into crisp detail.

The view of the planet was breathtaking, as fantastic as anything I have ever observed in the night sky. Transfixed, I stared in amazement. Famous features were outlined in crisp detail. The great, belt-line gash of the Valles Marineris—the largest canyon in the solar system—was a clear stripe across the rusty orb. The outlines of known craters were visible, and I even made out some shadows near the horizon, where the sun was setting on the Martian surface.

I had lectured about this view often enough, used magnified slides to try to capture the wonder for a hall full of bored underclassmen, but the tiny image in my scope was so much more entrancing than any image. The sense that this was the real thing, the actual planet before my eyes, carried a profound wonder that, even after more than a half century of life, I still found fascinating.

When my right eye began to tire I switched to the left. After another ten minutes I put on my glasses and walked around a bit, admiring the Milky Way that was even then beginning to show the promise of summer's glorious display. Only to the west was there a little blur, the light pollution from Madison forming a pale dome behind the horizon. I could still see Orion in the south, though he was nearing his seasonal disappearance. So clear was the sky that even the individual stars of Ursa Minor's tail were apparent to my casual inspection.

Even in the midst of that dazzling brilliance, Mars was the brightest object in the sky, unique as well in that little suggestion of redness in the midst of a million silver-white sparkles. Like a moth to light I was drawn back to my scope. With a minor adjustment it caught up to the planet that had orbited just beyond view of the lens. (More accurately, Earth's rotation had carried me, and the telescope, around just enough so that Mars was no longer lined up with the scope's path.) It was there again in a moment, brighter, warmer, more real than I had ever imagined. If time had frozen there, or events taken a different course, it might have remained that spectacular fantasy in my memory forever.

The flash was a jarring check against my pastoral, naïve delight. The yellow-white spark came from the equatorial canyon, the Valles Marineris. It was a brief pop of light, fading so quickly that, of course, I wondered if I had imagined it. But it had lasted too long to be some optical illusion, perhaps two seconds, maybe more. (Later, after study and analysis of the whole sequence, NASA would report that each flash lingered for somewhere between 1.8 and 2 seconds.) I stared at the planet, all but begging for a repeat of the phenomenon, for some clue that might offer an explanation. Unwilling to tear my eye away, I stared until my back grew sore and my legs started to cramp. That glorious, rust red orb taunted me with its inanimate reflectivity.

Was I going mad?

Browne's dogs started barking, and a few seconds later the coyotes replied, their yodels ringing out from every direction. A wind came up, penetrating my light jacket, reminding me that winter had not been long offstage. But still I stared, quickly shifting from one eye to the other when the strain got too great. Mars beamed back at me, red and desolate and distant.

Well, it was red, anyway.

I began to think that I was wasting my time—perhaps I could already sense that events were moving on without me. Packing up my equipment in some haste, I started back down the hill, stumbling along the woods trail even in the light of my flash. I approached my own house and, strangely enough, wished that I had left the porch lights on. Of course I hadn't, not when I was going out with the 'scope, but the dark windows, the silence as I opened the patio door, seemed unsettling. Quickly I went to my office and turned on my computer, then went around and turned on plenty of lights, before I came back to sit down at the glowing monitor.

There was the usual, interminable hissing and crackling of my modem making contact with my ISP. (I loved living far out in the country, but a patchwork web of tenuous, buried telephone lines linking me to the nearest town was a price that I had to pay. Cable hookups and DSL were for more urban people.)

I started with the official NASA Web site, but found nothing posted in the way of recent news. I went to Space.com, and there I saw my first confirmation, a news flash near the top of the page: "Anomalous flash of light observed on Mars, 10:55 EDT, April 20."

Relief was my first reaction—apparently I really had been worried that I had imagined it. At least someone else had seen it, too. Surfing now, I went to one of my favorite astronomy weblogs and was rewarded immediately.

DID YOU SEE IT? was the top thread on Starboyz.org.
EXPLOSION ON MARS! exclaimed another poster.
STRANGE FLASH. I SAW IT AT 9:55 CDT. PLEASE TELL ME SOMEONE ELS SAW IT TO! begged a spelling-impaired stargazer named Luna from Iowa.

She was rewarded by a host of eyewitness testimonials that pretty much mirrored my own experience, intermixed with a good number of skeptics accusing the posters of irresponsible falsehoods. A clear trend became apparent, however, as the number of testimonials increased dramatically over the course of ninety minutes. Also, it seemed like the skeptics were beginning to give ground. All except a few trolls—they continued to mock and declaim with increasingly vitriolic posts.

Looking over the names of the posters, I confirmed my earlier conclusion. The Starboyz site was still pretty much limited to amateurs. There were no addresses that indicated that anyone from a major observatory or university science department was weighing in on the matter. Of course, it was still the middle of the night, but there were other options.

I surfed over to CosmicCowgirl, anticipating some slightly more pithy analysis. Indeed, the Cowgirl had a good summary describing the event, and the beginnings of a thread of debate over what caused a sudden burst of light on the distant planet. I took the time to follow some of these posts and replies. Normally I'm not bothered too much by my connection speed, but I remember that on April 20 I fretted as each individual message took fifteen or twenty seconds to load.

Virtually all of the posters speculated that this was a volcanic eruption, brief but incredibly fiery. I had already raised that hypothesis in my own mind, as early as on the walk back to my house, but I was skeptical. How could it be so bright, and disappear so quickly? Wouldn't one of the Martian satellites—we Americans had two, and the Europeans had a third—have picked up some preliminary infrared or visual clues if such a massive eruption had been brewing? I had plenty of questions, lots of reasons for doubting the theory, but of course I had absolutely no idea of any other logical explanation.

It was one of the posters on CosmicCowgirl who first raised what sounded like an outlandish possibility.

Remember last fall, when Vision was still active? It started to drill and they got a few dozen meters down into the bed of the canyon. Then everything went all screwy. It was the end of the mission.

We all assumed that some technical glitch happened. But what if the Martians got pissed off about us sending all these rovers? What if they launched a rover of their own, one that's coming to get us?

I'm going to head for the hills!

—Orion2333

Immediately the thread attracted a lot of attention, including a couple dozen flames. I shook my head at some of them—I can remember my thoughts as clearly as if it was this morning, muttering aloud that people take this stuff too damned seriously. There were a few others who saw the joke and played along, but the line of messages fizzled out pretty quickly. The people who came to the Cowgirl's site, by and large, were not looking to enhance their senses of humor.

I clicked through a few other Web sites. The AP had picked up the story and already had a banner headline blinking on my home page. (That page was set to flash me on any space- or astronomy-related news.) That sent me to the television, where I checked CNN. After a few minutes they had a mention of the flash, and for the first time I saw a picture—obviously, someone had been shooting a movie through a telescope and managed to freeze out a single frame.

The flash was, well, just that. A tiny spot of light, coming from the depths of the Valles Marineris, just where I remembered seeing it. Somehow it didn't look so shocking when I saw the picture; the impression was more like a mistake, some sort of scratch on the image that came out as a fleck of light. By then it was two hours past midnight. I glanced at the phone, tempted to give Alex a call, but of course she would be sound asleep. And given the events of the night, I expected she'd be getting up fairly early in the morning.

So I would talk to her later. I shut down the computer and turned out the lights though—unusual for me—I left the porch lights on. "You're getting old, Professor," I suggested to myself, out loud.

Then I went to bed.

TWO

Alexandria DeVane groped for the phone that jarred her senses from the nightstand. She got her fingers around the handset, shook her head to knock away some of the cobwebs, even cleared her throat before she answered.

"Hello? This is Alex."

It still came out like the croak of a frog with tonsillitis.

"Alex? This is Bob Wolfe."

"Dr. Wolfe? I-I'm sorry. I was sleeping. What can I do for you?" Damn, she sounded like a nervous kid, when she really wanted him to know that she was pissed off about being awakened. She pushed herself into a sitting position with a mental sigh. There was no point in venting. Wolfe was such an übergeek, her anger would have gone right over his head.

"You probably haven't heard the news, then?" It was a question, but he didn't wait for an answer. Indeed, his enthusiasm was almost childlike. It might even have been endearing, at a much later hour. "We have an anomaly up there!"

She was fully awake, growing interested in spite of herself.

"In space? Or on the planet?" The "planet," to both of them, was Mars.

Wolfe was the director of the Vision Rover Project for the JPL. DeVane was the project management guru, special assistant to the NASA administrator. She was responsible for coordination between the Air Force, NASA, and JPL, tasked with keeping tabs on all of the agencies working toward the eventual manned mission to the Red Planet. That mission was still two decades away, but to Alexandria DeVane it was already a full-time job.

More than full time, she reminded herself, as she checked the digital clock—4:05

Wolfe was already describing the flash to her, his certain tone overriding her initial assumption that someone had simply made a mistake. "We have hundreds of witnesses, mostly amateurs, but a few of the big boys had their gear trained on Mars last night. I understand it was perfect sky for viewing on the East Coast—I'm surprised you weren't out there."

He *was* surprised, she knew. Bob Wolfe wasn't just a night person, he was a night-sky person. "I'm one of those humans who needs a little sleep," she informed him dryly, knowing that the irony was strictly for her own benefit.

"Sleep? There's lots of time for sleep—you can sleep all day tomorrow! This thing is big!"

She thought of the NASA administrator. Mike Koch used her as his resource for all matters Martian, and she knew she wouldn't be sleeping tomorrow. Still, Wolfe was right about one thing: this *was* big. At least, it would be in their circle; and it would probably warrant some mass-media attention, she guessed. He went on to explain, and discount, the volcanic theory, speaking at several hundred words a minute. Despite her grogginess, Alexandria was drawn into the web of his enthusiasm, though her role in the conversation was very much that of the listener.

And as she listened, she pondered. What in the world, in *any* world, could cause such an occurrence? She felt a momentary urge to call her father, to ask for his advice, opinion, even an educated guess. That urge passed quickly—she had learned long ago that, despite his vast knowledge of matters astronomical, when it came to her own tasks, she was on her own.

By the time Wolfe signed off—she felt certain that he had lots more people to wake up—Alex was fully alert. She padded around her apartment in a nightshirt and a pair of fuzzy slippers, and tried to think of all the things that might explain a sudden, brief flash of light on the surface of the Red Planet. There were not a lot of good possibilities: volcanic activity, a reflection of sunlight, or an explosive meteor or asteroid impact were the three that came to mind, and she could think of problems with each.

By then she found herself turning on the shower; obviously, she was up for the day. The stinging hot water brought all of her nerve endings to full alertness, and she continued to conjecture as she turned on the TV and had a bowl of Cheerios. She opted for CNN, winced at reports of a plane crash in Uruguay and the usual round of terrorist bombings in the Mideast. Finally, she saw a crawl on the bottom of the screen:

SCIENTISTS OBSERVE UNEXPLAINED FLASH ON THE SURFACE OF MARS.

There was no elaboration—the next item concerned a possible abduction of a teenage girl in Tennessee—but the level of attention was certain to increase as the country woke up. By then her cereal bowl was empty, forgotten on the small breakfast table. She didn't have the patience to wait around for more such tidbits, not when she had the chance to beat the traffic on her way to the office. Mike Koch would be demanding answers, and he would want them right away. Since she didn't have any of those answers ready to hand, she knew she would be spending some very busy hours this day seeking them out.

She dressed with her usual haste, though when she glanced in the mirror, observing her lean shape in black slacks and a red-and-white sweater, she thought she looked okay—though she took the time to rebrush her brown-blond hair before binding it, again, in the ponytail that was her typical "no frills" hairdo and rushing out the door.

Alex couldn't help but smile as the elevator doors opened in the garage and she spotted her classic Firebird parked amid the Caddies, Beemers, Volvos, and Mercedes that hauled around the building's other tenants. The fire-engine red color of the car brought a similar glow to her cheeks as she rumbled out through the automatic door. It was still dark, traffic just starting to stir, so in five minutes she was roaring up the ramp onto I-365. She drove at more than seventy-five almost all the way to the Potomac, slowing only slightly as she crossed the river. She only had to change lanes a few times before she downshifted and rumbled through the first exit in the District, wheeling around a few corners to the NASA Administration Building on E Street.

Five minutes later—it would have been thirty during rush hour—she was walking through the front doors of the block-long concrete-and-glass-fronted building, flashing her ID badge and a smile to the night duty officer. He glanced at the wall clock, arching his eyebrows in surprise.

"Don' get a chance to say good morning to you too often, Dr. DeVane," he said cheerfully—though he did examine her badge. "Trouble sleepin' last night?"

"You might say that."

She got to her desk before six and put the time to good use, clearing up some tardy e-mail, editing a proposal one of the interns had submitted, and frequently glancing at her phone. At precisely 8:30, it rang, and she was not surprised by the caller ID.

"Good morning, sir," she answered.

"Alex? You've heard about this Mars thing, I presume?" Mike Koch's voice was direct, though it sounded like his second cup of coffee hadn't kicked in yet.

"Bob Wolfe called me a few hours ago. I didn't see it, though. Did anyone get a picture?"

"CNN is showing something, snapped by some amateur taking a movie. Damned if our satellites weren't out of position, though. They didn't see shit. Anyway, *I* need to see *you*."

"I'm right downstairs—I'll be there in five."

Koch was waiting for her when she walked into his office, which was the nicest in the building, of course. His two windows allowed for a view of the Capitol Building and of the neighborhood where the White House was hunkered down amid taller buildings. The director had often remarked about how, with a few well-placed demolitions of some unsightly, albeit classic, structures, he could get himself a view of the two most sacred buildings in DC. Alex always chose to believe that he was joking.

Mike Koch—his named rhymed with "book"—was a very big man, a political appointee of the current president. He had been pulled from his senior VP position at Northrop Grumman, moving his office a few miles north and across the Potomac; and when he had moved he had brought his talented young director of project management with him. Alexandria De-Vane, Ph.D., now functioned as his special assistant, with an emphasis on the far-in-the-future Manned Mission to Mars—the MMM, to those in the know.

He smiled when he saw Alex, just like he smiled when he saw anybody, and gestured with a beefy hand for her to take the seat across from his desk. Leaning back in his chair, intertwining his sausagelike fingers over a belly the size of a beer keg, he squinted at her and shrugged.

"So tell me, what the hell is going on up there?"

"That would seem to be the question of the hour, boss." She outlined her three possibilities, her skepticism showing through as she discarded the ideas of volcanic activity and reflection. "My best guess is that it was one helluva meteor impact, possibly a good-sized asteroid. In that case, we should be able to see some sort of impact crater when we look at it closely."

Koch shook his head. "That's not it, then. I was on the phone with Wolfe just an hour ago—you weren't the only one he woke up, though I'm glad he called you first. By that time they had the Hubble telescope zoomed in on the place. There were 'no surface anomalies,' so far as those fellas could see."

The "fellas" were just as likely to be females as males, Alex knew, but she didn't bother to point that out to the administrator. For a sensitive guy, he was kind of thick about certain things. More important was the fact itself—it seemed to negate what she had concluded was the only plausible theory about the source of the flash.

"I guess I'm fresh out of ideas. But I'd like the chance to look into it some more."

"The morning paper is suggesting it was a volcanic eruption." He made the statement a challenge.

"Perhaps. But there would be some lingering IR signature that should help us get a handle on that. If it is a volcanic eruption, that's the biggest news about Mars since Professor Lowell claimed he saw canals up there."

"I don't think it was a volcano. Doesn't feel right." Koch shook his bullet of a head, then looked at Alex, a glint in his eye. "Maybe it was the LGM finally getting their shit together."

She chuckled. "If the Little Green Men are acting up, I don't know what you expect *me* to do about it. But I'll look into it with every resource I can pull together, see what our satellites—and Europe's—have come up with. Collate the data from all the observers who checked in, that sort of thing."

"Good; that's what we need. I have a feeling the Big Guy himself is going to want a report on this thing—and God knows it's the kind of tidbit that has the potential to start a media feeding frenzy. What else do those bastards have to worry about, anyway? For now, Alex, everything else on your desk goes to the back burner. I don't like mysteries, and this is a mystery that's too damned close to the place where Vision disappeared. So get on this thing and make me stop worrying, will you?"

"Right away, boss," she said. She could "get on" it, of course, though she knew she would never make *him* stop worrying.

As she rose and started for the door, Koch spoke to her back. "Just maybe, Al, this thing will get us the funding to advance your timetable by a few years. You might see that mission go off before you're a gramma."

She laughed over her shoulder as she left the director's office. "I have no intention of *ever* being a grandma, Mike!"

Back in her office, she started to pull together all of the information she could find. She started with the papers—both the *New York Times* and the *Washington Post* had the story above the fold on the day's front page. There was no new information in each article, but she did get a sense that this news was intriguing to laymen as well as scientists. Maybe Koch had been onto something when he mentioned her timetable.

The Manned Mission to Mars •(MMM) was the basic goal behind Alexandria DeVane's position at NASA. Although she was employed by the space agency, she worked closely with Bob Wolfe's team at JPL—which operated as a branch of NASA—and she was also charged with keeping the US Air Force up to speed on developments relating to the Red Planet. Strange doings on Mars were going to stir up interest in all these agencies, as well as the public. It was a safe bet that no one was going to suggest they slow down the long timetable toward the manned mission.

Alex spent the morning checking the status and location of the three man-made satellites orbiting Mars. The Mars Global Surveyor and Mars Odyssey were currently on orbits that would not allow for a clear view of the Valles Marineris. The European Union's satellite, Mars Express, regularly passed over the massive canyon, but was currently experiencing communications glitches. Hans Blumenthal, in Berlin, could not give her a confident estimate of when it would be back online.

She was tempted to skip lunch, but her stomach rebelled at the notion, so she wolfed a slice of cafeteria pizza at her desk, still working the phones, madly tapping her keyboard and maneuvering her mouse. She knew that the satellites would not have anything to offer for at least the next few days. By this time she had a series of phone messages, reporters asking her for a statement. (Mike Koch, bless his heart, had referred the whole Public Information staff to her.) She came up with a bland statement that PI could pass on to each outlet, promising that more details would be forthcoming as they became available.

Finally, there didn't seem to be much more that she could do. She had supper out with some of the staffers at a favorite Vietnamese restaurant in Georgetown and, instead of heading back to her apartment, found herself back in the office. Taking the elevator to the top floor of the building, she flashed her ID card at the grim-faced security guard, and entered the Tactical Monitoring Center.

The room was cool and dark, brightened by the green-gray glow of a dozen monitors. A bank of large computers hummed along the inside wall, while several large, exquisitely detailed photographs covered the other sides of the room like rock star posters in a teenager's bedroom.

"Dr. DeVane, hello!"

"Hi, Dirk. So they have you on the graveyard shift now?" Alex said with a laugh, pulling up a chair beside the room's only occupant. Dirk Frederick was a gung ho astronomer out of the University of Minnesota who was rapidly establishing himself as a very astute and hardworking researcher.

He shrugged. "I volunteered. Kinda curious about the Big Red One, you know?"

"Yes. That's why I'm here, too. I need to see some pictures."

Dirk gestured to the monitors. The nearest of them displayed Mars, the image of the planet filling the large screen with a very-high-resolution display. "This one has the live feed from Mount Palomar. We've got pics coming in from Hubble over there. Take either of them, or any of the others, and knock yourself out."

Alex spent some time browsing through photos of the Red Planet, focusing in on various views of the Valles Marineris. She couldn't see any clue to the source of the flash, no mark that showed on the flat, rusty bed of the canyon that was more than ten kilometers deep. She consulted graphs of the satellite trajectories, confirming her earlier fears—no immediate help could come from Surveyor or Odyssey though there was a chance that one or the other might have its orbit adjusted to eventually bring it over the site. Eleven o'clock came and went, and she was still flipping through pictures.

"Doc?" Dirk asked, shaking his head as he looked at a grainy still photo of the flash. "What do *you* make of this thing?"

"I don't know, Dirk. Big mystery, so far. You think?"

He nodded. "It's the strangest occurrence in space that I can recall. Just too *weird*, you know what I mean?"

"Yeah. I guess that's the part that bothers me." She wanted to *know*, dammit! Ever since her days as an undergraduate student at Madison—her dad was still teaching, back then—Mars had seemed like an open book.

Sure, there were mysteries: What happened to all the water? How long ago had the planet been wet? Had any kind of life, however microscopic, ever evolved there? But these were questions that developed in an orderly progression, and the solutions were attainable, though, of course, they would take time. The splendid rovers Spirit and Opportunity had provided so many answers, and Vision had been on track to carry humanity's knowledge even further. Of course, the failure of that recent rover was a setback, but—like any good project management specialist—she was able to manage that failure in the scheme of the larger goal. Now, this flash created a huge question, a gaping anomaly right in the middle of her mental PERT chart.

"Your dad—he wrote a book on Mars, didn't he?" Dirk asked.

"Yes. It was pretty well received, for the time. Of course, lots of it has been overtaken by events, new data from the rovers and so forth."

"But didn't he predict a lot of things that the rovers went on to discover?"

"I suppose he did," she admitted. It was not something she wasted a lot of time thinking about.

"That book had a lot to do with getting me into astronomy. You know, I would have gone to Wisconsin if he had still been teaching. He retired, well, kind of early, didn't he?"

The young scientist wasn't trying to probe at her scabs, she knew, and she tried to give him the benefit of the doubt. "Yes," she replied. "I . . . I guess he likes writing better than teaching. Mainly, he likes to be alone."

Wanting to close the subject, she spoke with a sense of finality. There was still that lingering sense of her own failure, irrational though it was. In any event, she couldn't bring herself to use the term "nervous breakdown." Fortunately, Dirk seemed to sense her mood and went back to perusing his pictures.

"You know, it was almost exactly one day ago, up there" he said, nodding at the clock.

"The flash?" Alex nodded, noting that it was 11:32. "Oh, you mean a Martian day?"

"Yup. Twenty-four Terran hours, thirty-seven minutes and change, if I recall correctly."

"You do," she said. Her eyes went to the live-feed monitor, the huge picture of Mars beamed to them from the observatory in Arizona. The resolution was perfect, the image exactly that being viewed through the powerful telescope, in real time.

And then she blinked, not sure if she had just imagined something.

"Holy shit!" breathed Dirk, his voice hushed with awe. "You saw it?"

"Yes . . ." His own astonishment confirmed her impression. "I saw a brief flash, smack-dab in the middle of the Valles Marineris." She drew a breath, trying to marshal her thoughts as she stared at Dirk.

"It happened again," was all she could think to say.

THREE

I slid the fried eggs, three of them, onto my plate and went to get the sausages out of the pan just as the toaster popped. The perfectly browned English muffin, dabbed with butter—*never* margarine!—went next to the eggs, and the sausages filled in the gaps. A large glass of milk and a small o.j. completed the ensemble. Settling at my snack bar, I touched the remote, opting for the *Today* show this morning, since it was just enough after 7:00 A.M. that I would miss all the bozos screaming and waving signs outside the studio window, yet still in time to catch the news.

The first thing I saw was my daughter's face, and I dropped my fork in surprise. Alexandria looked like she was cornered, trapped against the front of a building—the NASA Administration Building in DC, I recognized when they shifted to a wide shot. She was being interviewed before dawn. The TV lights washed out her complexion, and a few strands of hair had slipped out of her ponytail. She was holding, and squinting at, a piece of paper that fluttered wildly in the wind, and it looked like she hadn't gotten any sleep.

Only after I absorbed all this did I begin to pay attention to what she was saying.

"... appears to have originated in the same spot, exactly, as the flash spotted just before midnight on the twentieth. Furthermore, it occurred exactly one planetary revolution—that is, one Martian day, or 'sol'—after the initial flash."

Several questions exploded from the unseen listeners, the gathered flock of reporters. A dapper fellow in a suit came into view from the side, leaning toward the microphone and offering an oily smile—he was one of the PI flacks, I guessed.

"Dr. DeVane is the agency's leading expert on Mars," he said—a statement that caused me a sudden, and surprising, burst of pride. "Please, allow her to make the statement. Then, if you will give her one question at a time, she will do her best to answer."

Alex raised her eyes from the paper and shrugged. "I'm ready for questions," she said.

"What caused these two flashes on Mars?" asked a male reporter.

"We don't have enough data to say with certainty," she replied, a little more calmly than when I had first seen her. "However, we can rule *out* certain causes. The repeating flash means that we can rule out, for all practical purposes, a random-based anomaly, such as a meteor or asteroid impact, as the basis for the flashes. While not technically impossible, to scientists it is virtually inconceivable that two such impacts would occur at the same place, exactly one day apart."

More questions; I could see that Alex was getting annoyed. She glared at someone in the front row, shook her head curtly, and charged ahead.

"There is no cause for alarm! Whatever this is, we are observing a space-based phenomenon that we have never seen before. However, let me remind you that it is something that is happening tens of millions of miles away. And it was only within the last half century, or less, that we have even had telescopes with the resolution necessary to observe such an event. This might be something that has occurred off and on throughout the history of the planet, and we are only now aware of it."

That made sense—I hadn't thought about it that way, before.

"The two most likely possibilities remain the same as they were yesterday—that is, some sort of volcanic activity, or a highly reflective surface catching a momentary glimpse of sunlight, shooting that light on a visual track toward Earth."

There was another question, and she nodded. "The rotation of the planet isn't fast enough that one would normally expect such a brief reflection. However, if we postulate that the reflective surface is in a deep hole, it is conceivable that the interval when it was exposed to the sun would be relatively brief. And it wouldn't have to be a very large surface, not if it was very, very shiny."

The fact that there had been a second flash was just starting to sink in to my own understanding—this was the first I had heard of it. I found the news disturbing. The study of space, like all science, was a matter of putting things in their proper categories, assigning causes and effects that were explainable, and could be reliably reproduced through testing. Something like this had no explanation. Even worse, it was utterly unpredicted, and as such it seemed to cast serious questions on a lot of our previous hypotheses. We just didn't know what the cause might be, and that was very troubling.

Certainly, I had had no thought of going out the previous night. It had been a cloudy, cool night around here, and there would have been no point in stargazing. Instead, I had gone to bed after the ten o'clock news, out of touch with events until starting breakfast.

But I no longer had much of an appetite.

I felt a sense of relief as the coverage of the interview ended, though I was sure that I had observed only a small amount of Alex's misery. I felt a flash of anger—she was a *scientist*, dammit! Couldn't those PR flacks do a better job of protecting her from this kind of thing? I couldn't help putting myself in her shoes—I would have *hated* those cameras, the lights, the questions. It was remarkable, in a sense, that she had done as well as she had.

I stomped away from the snack bar to turn on my computer. When I came back, the eggs and sausages looked unappetizing. I ate the English muffin, drank the milk and juice, and crammed the rest down the garbage disposal. I ran it for a long time, making sure it smelled clean before turning it off.

When I tried to work I didn't have any more appetite for writing than I did for protein. I had a major article contracted by *Scientific American*, a comparison of the thrust capabilities and relative efficiencies of the Saturn rocket versus the space shuttle. It was due at the editor's within the month, and I wasn't even halfway done, so I couldn't really afford to take any time off.

But all I could think about was Mars. I found myself almost unconsciously going back to the Starboyz site, following the lively debate. There were more posters who were bringing up the unthinkable: Was this proof of some intelligent activity on the planet? The group's mentality was still such that these posts were generally flamed pretty quickly and thoroughly.

Finally, I gave up and went outside. The spring weather of two days ago was but a distant memory. It might as well have been early March, with the gray skies and biting north wind. I took a walk on the trail through my own woods; but as I got closer to Browne's farm, his dogs started to bark, and I turned around in disgust.

Increasing my irritation, the phone was ringing as I came through the patio door. I had to clomp across the kitchen in my muddy boots in order to answer it.

"This is Mark DeVane." I tried not to sound mad; I'm not sure if I was successful.

"Mark? Did you see Alex this morning? She was on all the networks."

It was Karen. On a day like this, of course it had to be my ex-wife.

"Yeah, I saw her. She didn't look too happy."

"Well of *course* she wasn't happy! She hates doing those interviews and stuff like that. She's just like you, that way. Just leave her alone with a bank of computers, or some flowcharts and schedules to organize, and she'll be fine. Did you call her this morning?"

"No. I just saw her on TV a little while ago. I haven't had a chance yet. Did *you* call her?"

"Yes. She's pissed off, but okay. Says they're going to get someone else to the press conferences if . . . well, I don't know."

If there are more flashes. That was the first time I considered that prospect.

"Well, good," I said, rather lamely I suppose. "That's not what they hired her to do."

"Mark?" she asked. I heard a note of concern in her voice.

"What?" I replied cautiously.

"What do you think about them? The flashes, I mean?"

"What do I think about them?" I repeated. Huh. I wasn't sure what to say. "They're strange, that's for sure. I guess we'll know more about them after people like Alex can study the whole phenomenon for a while."

"Right." She didn't sound convinced. "Speaking of Alex, did you remember that Tuesday was her birthday? Did you give her a call?"

"I remembered. Didn't have a chance to call her, though. But I'll take her out for dinner next time I see her."

"Sure, Mark. Of course you will. Good-bye." The line clicked dead before I could say good-bye myself. Was she being sarcastic? I always had a hard time telling with Karen.

Too agitated to work, I went back to the office window, looking out toward the garden. I saw a huge black shape flash past, and I crossed to the living room window, where I saw the marauder stretch upward and pull down a square of suet I had put out just two days earlier.

"I saw that, you bastard!" I shouted, racing into the hall, flinging open the door. "Get out of here!"

Browne's Newfoundland looked at me with a mocking expression and a wave of that huge black tail. Then he was gone, lumbering along the row of pines, the chunk of fatty bird food hanging from his massive jaws. A white shape came into view as his partner in crime, my neighbor's other dog, raced out of the woods, sped past the huge black animal, and streaked away.

By that time I had crossed the patio and stood on the garden walkway, a bed of gravel stones about a quarter's size in diameter. By the time I picked up a few and threw them, the two dogs were well out of range, but the action took a little of the edge off my anger. I went over to the bird feeders to check the damage. The large rack I had erected to hold my array of finch feeders had been knocked askew, no doubt when the huge dog had lumbered past.

The other one was even worse. The white dog was called Galahad. (I didn't know the Newfoundland's name.) Galahad was one of those poodles that looks like evolution must have been up to some sort of practical joke. A big animal in his own right, when he was cleaned up he looked like he belonged on the champion's stand at some fancy dog show. I usually found him running around in the woods. He was white, though at the moment there was no clear visual proof of the fact. His long hair looked like some matted sheep's pelt.

Galahad was the one that seemed to lead the pair on their not-infrequent jaunts across the countryside. I had seen enough from my windows to observe the poodle picking a passage through the fence line, or racing along the side of the road with the clumsy Newfoundland loping along behind. At speed, Galahad's ears trailed like pennants from a knight's lance, while the black dog's banner was his tongue, flopping a half a foot or more out of his mouth, often as not trailing great streamers of gummy drool.

This time, they had gone too far. The destruction of my bird-feeding station compelled me to action. I followed the mutts down my driveway, a winding track through the woods that formed much of my yard. In the ten minutes it took me to reach the road I tried to decide what I was going to say. Another five minutes of walking on the shoulder of my little country lane brought me to Browne's farmhouse, and I stomped up his driveway without hesitation. I passed the two old cars up on blocks, saw the old Jeep—topless, now that summer had arrived—sitting outside of the house. It looked more like a junkyard, I reflected sourly, than any kind of working farm. Certainly my bachelor neighbor kept no livestock. He had a couple of antiquated tractors, but I had never seen him plowing a field.

The two dogs, sitting and panting on the porch, saw me coming and barked, charging forward with ears and jaws flapping. I ignored them as they danced around my legs, though a nudge from the Newfoundland's shoulder staggered me off-balance for a second. By the time I was climbing the porch steps Browne, no doubt attracted by the commotion, had opened the door and stepped outside.

"Hello, Mark," he said. "How you doing?"

"A little steamed, Mr. Browne," I said bluntly.

His face took on a strained expression. He was older than I, gray of hair and thin of frame, but he still projected an almost annoying level of health. His arms were already tanned, lined with wiry muscles under a series of old, faded tattoos. Something about those ancient inkings suggested to me that he had been in the Navy.

"Ah, geez," he said, in what seemed like genuine sympathy. "Did they get into your yard again? I'm sorry about that. It's the spring weather—it warms up, and they get to taking off at the drop of a hat. Galahad runs, and Klondike just sort of trails along for the ride."

Klondike. The name seemed to fit the big oaf. "Well, they seem to take off plenty in the summer, fall, and winter, too!" I pointed out, then decided to focus on the day's events rather than dwell on old grudges.

"They tore down my suet and knocked over my finch feeder!" I explained, working to keep my tone reasonable. "They were barking all over the place. Then it seemed like the white one was going to charge when I went out to chase them away."

"Charge? Oh, gosh. That don't sound like Galahad."

"I thought he was going to bite me!" Well, he *could* have bitten me.

"Bite you? Can't have 'em doing that! *Did* he try to bite? Like snap or anything?"

"Well, no. He turned and ran when I shouted at him. But, Mr. Browne, this is getting to be an aggravating problem."

"Look, Mark. I will try to do better 'bout keeping them in the yard. But I can't chain 'em up—it would just kill 'em. Now, we live here in the country, and I don't know why my own farm ain't big enough to keep these mutts happy. And I'll tell you one thing, if either of these dogs bites you, you have my permission to shoot him."

"Shoot him? I don't want to shoot anything! I don't even own a gun."

"Well, I got several. You're welcome to borrow one if you got a need for it. I have a .12 gauge and .20 gauge in the shotgun department. Nice deer rifle, 30:06. Old, but real steady. And a little .22 if you want something smaller."

"They didn't try to bite. And I'm not going to shoot one of your dogs, or anything else!" This wasn't going the way I'd hoped it would—it never did when I talked to Browne. "Look, just keep them away from my bird feeders, okay?"

"I will do what I can. Let me replace that suet—how much does that stuff go for, these days?" He was reaching in his pocket, taking out his wallet.

"No, it's not the money. I . . . just try to keep them home, could you?"

He was still agreeing with me as I beat my retreat. The dogs cheerfully followed me down the driveway until, just short of the road, Browne called them back.

I felt relieved to be out of there.

May 1

I hadn't been sleeping much for the last week, and the past night was no exception: I was wide-awake even before the alarm, set for 3:30 A.M., buzzed. The first thing I did was look out the window. Though I couldn't see Mars from my bedroom, I saw an array of stars that confirmed the weather forecast for clear skies overnight. Dressing hastily, wearing my hiking boots again and the light leather jacket, I headed for the door. My telescope was all ready to go, sitting in the entryway, where I had propped it up the night before.

Because of cloudy weather and the fact that the blasts had been occurring through the wee hours of the nights, I hadn't been back to Browne's hilltop since the twentieth. Now I made it there easily, in less than fifteen minutes. Unlike my previous visit, I wasted no time in viewing the wonders of the fabulous spring sky. I had one objective, and one objective only. I set up the scope and quickly drew in on Mars, checking my watch as soon as I had the focus tightened.

It was four o'clock exactly. I had five minutes to wait.

With a strange sense of anticipation, I was glad to be out here again. I needed to see the flash for myself once more. For each of the last ten nights the brilliant flare on Mars had been repeated, always at the exact same time on the Martian day; a little more than a half hour later than the previous flash by the Earth clock. Though I hadn't witnessed them in person, the phenomena had been much-talked and -written about in the media. I found the whole thing terribly distracting, so much so that I hadn't been getting any writing done.

Alexandria, thankfully, hadn't been called upon to do any more interviews. I felt certain that she was sequestered in some laboratory, working up theories and explanations about the flashes. I could only hope that she and her peers were coming up with some logical hypothesis. Knowing that she would be very busy, I had put off calling her, though I did plan to do some catching up with my daughter once the current frenzy had passed. I had even started an e-mail, but deleted it before sending. I didn't want to bother her, not now.

In the meantime, each flash was covered by the news. At first they had been priority headlines, but as they continued they had fallen back into the "running story" tangle. Several times I had thought about going out to watch the planet at the regular hour but had fallen asleep. The last couple of nights I had fully intended to go, but cloudy forecasts had made it a waste of time—I hadn't even bothered to set the alarm until that night.

Eleven identical flashes, so far. Would there be a twelfth? And who knew what they all meant?

The official line, issued by NASA and JPL in conjunction with a number of top astronomers, was that the flashes were the result of some hitherto-unknown material, very reflective in nature, located within a fairly deep and steep-sided hole. The orientation matched up—the flash location, or "F-Point" as the media had been calling it—was on the equator of the planet, oriented upon an angle evenly divided by the sun and the Earth each time the phenomenon was observed. The brief duration of the flash was explained by the parameters of the hole—there was only that short interval, every day, when the shaft was lined up with the sun.

Of course, there were no devices capable of looking for such a hole. It was questionable whether even a satellite in orbit around the planet could have seen something potentially so small. That question became moot when the positioning rockets on the Mars Global Surveyor had failed abruptly. That orbiting platform, with its array of photographic and electromagnetic tools, was trapped in an orbit that carried it over both poles of the planet, but only occasionally brought it anywhere near the Valles Marineris—and then, it seemed, there was no chance to get a straight-down look.

Geologists knew of several volcanic rocks capable of naturally forming very smooth, reflective surfaces. As to why the flash hadn't been seen before April 20, the explanations were all hypotheses. Perhaps some subsurface volcanic activity, undetected by satellite, shifted the rock into proper alignment. Or the Martian wind, faint but real, had whisked some layer of dust out of the way.

The second theory, that the flash was the result of volcanic activity, had been laid to rest first of all by the regularity of the flashes—such a precise cadence involving geologic phenomena was virtually inconceivable. Furthermore, infrared analysis revealed no significant heating of the planetary surface at the site of the flashes. The actual emissions, intriguingly, were very hot events.

The blogs, of course, were full of people who had strong opinions about the truth or falsehood of the official theory. Though I had yet to post an opinion, I had made a nightly ritual of scanning the postings about the Martian flashes. It had been about the twenty-fourth or twenty-fifth, on the CosmicCowgirl site, where the first really pragmatic note of alarm was sounded. Of course, the tabloids and the talk shows had been full of kooks since the morning of the twenty-first.

But it was that woman, Luna from Iowa, who articulated it best:

People, what if this is more than we are prepared to believe? What if it is the start of something as yet unimagined? And people, what if that something involves the planet Earth?

We have been bombarding Mars for decades with rovers, probes, and drills. We have satellites orbiting their space. We send rocket after rocket up there.

We know that their world was once very wet, as wet as ours. When the surface dried, perhaps they didn't perish, but instead withdrew underground.

Could it be that, now, they are coming back out?

That one had provoked the usual flames, of course, but also developed into some thoughtful threads. These were some of the first people tentatively to raise the issue of an intelligent cause behind the flashes. Even then, no one seriously postulated a threat to our planet. You could tell that the writers were almost embarrassed about their thoughts, but that didn't hold them back from posting. I wish I had printed some of them out now, so that I could construct the actual words. But I can't. Those messages were lost, like every other piece of digital data, when the computers went down. (If not for my old Smith-Corona typewriter, this account of last year's events would never be written.)

My watch chirped a reminder and I bent my eye to the lens, adjusting slightly for the planetary rotation that had moved the bright red disk toward the edge of my field of view. The Valles Marineris was visible, looking more and more like a leering, laughing mouth across the face of Mars, and of course my attention focused there.

I waited, challenging myself not to blink until absolutely necessary. The minutes ticked past and I continued to stare, not daring to move, unwavering in my absolute attention.

But nothing changed. No flash marred the mocking, serene surface of the distant planet, no burst of light illuminated the depths of the great canyon, or any other place on Mars. I took a brief second to consult my watch—4:13 a.m. and counting—then stared some more. Because of my diligence I felt utterly certain that I hadn't missed a flash in a moment's distraction. But every flash after the first had occurred exactly one Martian day, one sol, after the previous flash; and that time had already slipped past.

For another ten minutes I stared, ignoring eyestrain, the ache developing in my feet, the cramps in my lower back. It seemed that my view of the planet was fading slightly, and I finally leaned back to look around. I was mildly surprised to see that dawn was brightening the east.

There had been no doubt in my mind, heading up to the hilltop, that there would be another flash tonight. After all, for eleven days in a row, they had never varied from the pattern. I—and a great many other humans—had begun to accept that pattern as the new norm, the way Mars would be. But it seemed as though that time was over.

The wave of relief I felt was staggering. Sure, questions remained—we were no closer to understanding what had caused those flashes. But now I could think that the mystery was in the past, a part of history instead of an ongoing phenomenon. And that made it much less threatening.

Mars looked like Mars again, just the Red Planet, not some freakish mystery in space. I even found myself whistling as I disassembled the scope and tripod, and started through the dawn back to my house.

Things were normal again. I could go home, take a nap. And then it would be time for me to get back to work.

FOUR

May 3
Cape Canaveral, Florida

The Vehicle Assembly Building was a square massif, like a man-made mesa, towering over the mangroves, beaches, and tidal pools of the huge base on the east coast of Florida. Pulling her sunglasses down over her eyes, Alexandria couldn't help but stare at the looming structure as she crossed the parking lot. The largest enclosed structure in the world, she knew, so huge that it was capable of generating its own weather within those lofty walls.

It was the only place where a space shuttle could be prepared for a mission, safe from the elements—wind and rain, primarily—that hampered outside operations. Though the next mission was not scheduled until midsummer, the shuttle *Atlantis* was already in the building, undergoing the preparations for a supply run to the International Space Station.

A horn honked, bringing her attention back to Earth. She saw Nathan waiting beside his car, a Porsche Boxster. Alex waved, and the pilot grinned at her. He leaned against the side of the small car, his arms crossed over his chest, his posture resembling a James Dean slouch. He was short, his tanned face showing just enough lines to prove his maturity, while his eyes had that juvenile twinkle indicating he had not entirely left boyhood behind.

"Sorry to have to pull you away early. I hope you were done," he apologized, ambling around the Porsche to open the passenger door.

"No worries—in fact, thank God for the excuse," she said. "If that meeting had gone on any longer, I think I would have screamed. And I appreciate the ride."

"Like I said, Derek's coming in to Orlando this afternoon, so I had a run to the airport planned in any case. And it's always a pleasure to give a beautiful girl a ride on a day like this."

"Well, I don't mind the company either," she said. "And I won't tell Joan what you said."

Nate laughed in that easy way characteristic, in Alex's experience, of confident pilots. And Nathan Hayes had good reason to be confident. At forty-four, he was the senior shuttle pilot among all NASA astronauts, which made him the most experienced space pilot in the world.

They chatted, catching up, as Nate effortlessly guided the small, fast car through the four-lane traffic around Highway 1 and Titusville. His kids were doing well, Tricia finishing her first year of college, Tim getting into the usual troubles associated with thirteen-year-old boys. Pulling away from the city, Nate flicked on the radar detector and opened the throttle as they started across the Beeline Highway.

"So, I couldn't help noticing *everyone* wanted to see you while you were on the base," he remarked. "Fine thing when the only way an old friend can get in some face time is to take you to the airport on your way out of town."

"I swear, Nate, I had fifty meetings in forty-eight hours—and each of the damn things was at least ninety minutes long!"

"Good thing you mastered that pesky time-space continuum thang," he drawled. "What's going on, anyway? Some light colonel had the gall to tell me I'm not cleared to know! It has something to do with Mars, of course."

She looked at him in surprise. "I don't know why you weren't allowed in the loop—not that it's anything that will impact the shuttle, or even the plans for the manned mission."

His eyes narrowed. He seemed to be watching the road, but Alex felt his scrutiny. "Mars . . . so we have these weird flashes in the Valles. No one knows what caused them. Let me guess: We're trying to speed up the timetable for the next probe. Instead of next winter, they want to see if they can send Euclid off, oh, sometime this summer."

Alex laughed. "Security be damned—you're too good a guesser. Except that they want to launch in ten days."

He whistled and looked at her in concern. "That'll pop a few ulcers. Not yours, I hope?"

"No. I'm lucky, I guess. I don't have to do any of the work, just make sure that the people here on the Cape know what JPL is doing, and that some-body is keeping in touch with DC, getting the bills paid and so forth. Remember—after Madison I earned my graduate degrees in project man-agement, while you were off breaking the sound barrier."

"You were working on some exciting stuff at Grumman. How do you like collecting a paycheck from the government?"

"Actually, Nate, it's fascinating. Most of my work is focused on the MMM—talk about a project manager's dream! If I do my work right, we might be sending one of your kids to Mars in twenty or thirty years."

"That would be Tricia," Nate said. "She's a whiz at everything—and Tim is still having trouble in basic algebra. I don't even know if he's going to pass," he added glumly.

"What is he, thirteen?" Alex consoled. "He's got plenty of time to figure out what he wants."

"Yeah, I hope you're right. Teenagers . . ." Nate groaned, at the same time downshifting and accelerating with a burst that knocked her, hard, back into the leather seat.

"Some teenagers never grow up," she joked.

He glanced down at his speedometer, and with a guilty grin backed off a little. "So, you're heading west? California?"

She nodded. "In fact, I'm starting a whole round of new meetings in Pasadena tomorrow morning."

Nate shook his head. "Next time you get down here, try to steal an extra day. Joan would love to have you over for dinner—she's a little jealous that I'm the one who gets to take her former roommate to the airport. Besides, life is too short to race from one meeting to the next."

He downshifted, acceleration once again pressing Alex in her seat as he passed a few RVs, dodging between the right and left lanes to weave through a little congestion. A minute later he was cruising ahead of the pack.

"So, tell me about your brother," she said. "I haven't seen him since he came to visit you in Madison. That must have been, what, twelve or fourteen years ago? We were having a nice time on State Street—then he was gone."

"Yeah. I think that was his first hangover. I guess you could say he's grown up a bit. In the Air Force, you know, flying A10s."

"Nothing like a Warthog," she noted wryly. "I guess you Hayes boys have that pilot's bug up your asses, but good."

"Ah, yeah. He claims he doesn't even mind that he's not flying fighters—but he's *gotta* be lying!"

"Come on—not everyone is as much a throttle jockey as you are!"

Nate nodded, absently; his thoughts were suddenly elsewhere. "How's your dad?" he asked, after a few seconds.

She shrugged. "The same, I guess. Getting out of the classroom seems to have been good for him. It's what he wanted, anyway." Alex looked out the window at the blur of the passing savannah.

By that time Nate was guiding his car along the approach to Orlando International Airport. The engine rumbled impatiently as he slowed to enter the parking lot, then snorted in apparent resentment when he finally came to a halt and turned off the ignition. He looked at her, his expression sly.

"Derek remembers that night in Mad-town, maybe better than you. When he heard you were on the Cape, he moved up his flight by a day, hoping to see you again. So at least you can cross paths in the airport. Eh?"

"You sly dog!" She punched him on the shoulder, pleased in a surprisingly giddy way. Taking her old friend's arm affectionately, she accompanied him through the throngs of tourists, boarding the smooth, speedy tram to the gate where debarking passengers came out of the concourse. Nate checked his watch and one of the arrival monitors.

"Good timing," he said. "Plane's just landed. He should be along any minute."

As if on cue, they heard a shout down the concourse. "Nate! And Alex, hi! You're looking great!"

Nathan Hayes clapped his younger brother in a bear hug, while Alexandria watched, liking what she saw. Derek "Duke" Hayes had been a callow eighteen-year-old, Alex a seasoned graduate student, when they had first met. Then he had seemed to be all skin, wavy hair, and an infectious smile that showed an impressive array of teeth. The smile was the same, but the boy had filled out into a man.

He looked like a less domesticated version of his brother. He had the same buzz cut, the deep tan, the mischievous eyes. His chest was broader and his arms, where they showed beyond the short sleeves of a chaotically colored Hawaiian shirt, had the muscles of a bodybuilder. She gave him a hug as soon as his brother let go, and she could feel the strength in his flesh. He was no taller than she was, and she liked that, and liked that he broke the embrace by giving her a peck on the cheek.

"So, you finally got a haircut?" she teased.

He nodded proudly. "And I learned how to hold my beer." His expression turned serious, those sky-blue eyes narrowing to a tight focus. "It's good to see you again, Alex."

"Al has a plane to catch," Nate said, clapping his brother on the shoulder. "But she rode out here with me to say hi to you."

Suddenly Derek was that youth again, looking crestfallen at the news. Alexandria felt a stab of guilt and a powerful urge to cheer him up. She looked at her watch. "I have an hour to kill before boarding. If you don't mind hanging around the airport, maybe we could go have that beer?"

The young pilot brightened perceptibly, and Alex linked arms with both men as they made their way to the nearest lounge. "Just be warned," she said, giving Derek a tug. "I'm not even sure they brew Schlitz anymore."

May 4
Jet Propulsion Laboratory
Pasadena, California

"I tell you, Alex—it's just ridiculous!" Bob Wolfe was about as agitated as she had ever seen him. His anger was not directed at Alexandria, but—she knew the role she was playing—she was a convenient messenger, and she needed to let him vent.

"I mean, a launch by the end of next week? If they told me late summer, I'd say 'maybe'—and even then it would be a Herculean task. But to get this probe ready for a launch in ten days? Out of the question!"

"Well, we're not going to worry about the drilling apparatus. And the upgraded mini-TES can wait till next time, too. We just want to get some pictures."

Wolfe stabbed a button on his desk and spoke as soon as his secretary buzzed back. "Get Derrick Whitten in here, right away!" he barked.

"I won't be held responsible if something goes wrong!" Wolfe snapped, bouncing to his feet and pacing while they waited for the rover specialist. "You can tell Mike Koch that, personally. Not that I haven't told him myself. I have. Every day since he called me about this last week."

"I know, Bob. It's tough—we've never had to do anything on this kind of timetable before. But the last three rovers have landed flawlessly. Spirit and Opportunity lasted for months, and we only lost Vision when something went wrong on the drilling. We're not drilling, not even scraping off the rocks this time. Just trying to get some pictures of what the heck is going on up there."

"Pictures!" Derrick Whitten stormed into the office without ceremony. "They're using my half-a-billion-dollar rover like it's a hack photographer!"

"I'm afraid so, Professor," Alex said apologetically. "It's the only hack photographer who's got a ticket to Mars."

"We'll have to bring the whole staff back to the lab on an emergency priority," Whitten said glumly. "Vacations canceled . . . spring semester interrupted. I have people from M.I.T. to Stanford and a hundred places in between, and you're telling me we need to get them working on this starting yesterday?"

"And don't forget the security requirements," Alexandria brought up. "None of them can be told *why* we need them, at least not right away. Things might relax once you have your teams in the labs."

"I tell you, it's ridiculous!" Bob Wolfe repeated. "What's the big secret? We've been launching Mars probes for more than forty years, and we never kept it hushed up before."

Alex shrugged. "My guess is that they're worried about starting a panic, shaking up the stock market, and so forth. The administrator said that the president, personally, told him that the public isn't supposed to know about this."

"Yeah, Mike told me the same thing," Wolfe said, finally settling back into his chair. "I just don't see how we can do it."

"All the resources of the agency, plus the Air Force, are at your disposal."

"I don't need the Air Force! And the only thing I want from the agency is for them to keep off my back!"

"Maybe that's where I can help." Alexandria offered the olive branch. "Koch has given me his ear, twenty-four/seven, and wants me to keep an open line to everyone involved. You, Houston, the rocketeers on the Cape. Within the parameters of the assignment, you're to be left alone, and I'll try to help that happen."

"It's the goddamned parameters that have me—ah, never mind," Wolfe said, a last sigh marking his surrender—or, at least, tactical withdrawal. "We'll do what we can to get some kind of picture-taking device onto the planet as soon as possible. Koch did remind the president, I hope, that even after we launch it will still take six months to get the thing to Mars?"

"Yes, I'm sure everyone is aware of that. And it can't be helped."

"All right. Are you going back tonight, or do you need an office? You could always spend a few hours calling technicians, telling them to say good-bye to their loved ones, come to Pasadena—oh, and you can explain that you can't tell them *why* we need them."

"Sorry, Bob. I'm taking a trip out to the Mojave this afternoon, and then it's an eastbound red-eye tomorrow. Besides, if I know your technicians, most of them would only be angry if you *didn't* call them back for a top secret mission!"

"True enough," the JPL director agreed, ruefully. "But don't let on when you get back to DC!"

May 5
Deep Space Network Antenna Complex
Fort Irwin Military Reservation, California

From the first time she saw them, Alexandria had been reminded of giant ears, cocked sideways, straining to hear any tiny sound from the cosmos. The "sounds," of course, were electronic and not audio in nature, but as she got out of the rental car and looked at all five of the massive dishes she still felt that the analogy was apt.

The largest of them was nearly ninety meters across, a diameter almost the length of a football field, supported by a tower that was a substantial building in its own right. The others, massive instruments all, stood around the mighty central dish like mushrooms in the shade of a birdbath. One of the huge antennas was moving as she watched, the barely perceptible hum of power motors shifting the dish gradually until it came to rest, oriented at a different part of the sky.

"Dr. DeVane? Security said you were on your way. I'm Colonel Smead. Come on inside where it's cool." She looked around to see a nattily dressed officer approaching. "A person could roast away to nothing out here in the sun!" the man added.

For the first time since getting out of the car she noticed the baking heat. In May, the Mojave Desert was already warmer than the temperatures she was used to in the sweltering depths of a Washington summer. Yet she had been so awed by the antenna array that she hadn't even paid attention to the climate. She laughed to herself at the old cliché as she followed the colonel toward a low bank of glass-and-adobe office buildings.

"At least it's a dry heat," she said.

"What was that?" Smead looked at her quizzically, standing back to allow her to precede him through the automatic door.

"Nothing," she replied.

Twenty minutes later she was in the briefing room, speaking to a dozen men and women, half of them military officers and the rest civilian scientists and researchers. She outlined the urgency of the new mission, dubbed "Euclid," and told them of the support, and request for coordination, from the president, the NASA administrator, and the Joint Chiefs of Staff.

"We need some pictures of the area, some real data, before we can get a handle on what the heck was going on up there. That's why we're moving up the launch, assigning top priority."

"That's gonna stir up a hornet's nest at JPL," Colonel Smead remarked, raising his eyebrows.

"Believe me, Colonel, it already has," Alex said sincerely. "But they're on the ball. We're going to use the same technology Vision employed—an early satlink through the MGS, until we can get the main antenna boosted for direct signals down to you folks. The main thing is, it all has to come together fast—like, *yesterday* fast."

"Why all the bells and ruffles? Security up to here?" asked the senior researcher, a white-haired Hispanic man of fifty or so. "What do we need with the Pentagon? No offense"—he nodded at Colonel Smead—"but we're a civilian outfit on an Army base."

"I understand it's a precautionary measure," Alex replied. "Your chain of command here, and with the deep space arrays in Spain and Australia, won't change. You'll have to devote a lot of attention to Mars. Not only do we need to keep tabs on the planet, but we're working on a broadcaster that might actually allow us to do some radar imaging. You guys are the receivers, but the Air Force will probably be doing the sending. We're also drawing in the people at LINEAR, the asteroid survey ground down in New Mexico."

An hour later the meeting was over. She was getting good at keeping the damned things moving along, Alexandria reflected as she went back outside. The antenna array loomed over her, looking more ominous in the late afternoon. Despite the heat, she shivered.

On the way back to the city she called her airline and changed her flights around. She decided that she would stop and see her mother.

May 6
Chicago, Illinois

"How are you feeling, Alex? You don't look like you're eating very well."

Karen Barcel—she had returned to her maiden name within a year of the divorce—frowned in concern, took another sip of her latte. The spring sunshine was glorious, Michigan Avenue awash in midmorning brilliance, and the huge picture windows of the Fleur de Lis let in plenty of illumination.

"I'm eating fine, Mom. Just not getting enough sleep, I guess. They've had me on the run for the past few weeks."

"Who has? The Martians?" Karen shook her head in dismissal, then winked. "I won't stand for it! I mean, really! What's up with all this stuff?"

"Well, right now it's still a mystery. First, the rover Vision disappeared. That was really unfortunate—it was functioning so well. We learned more than ever before about how wet Mars used to be. There were rivers flowing through that canyon—lots of water! And not all *that* long ago.

"But before we started to get the really good information, Vision went off-line. It didn't fade away, like Spirit and Opportunity. It just broke down. Then there was the matter of those eleven flashes. I tell you, Mom—it's like we went from feeling like we had Mars pretty well figured out to feeling like we don't know what the hell that godforsaken place is like!"

"With you on the job, honey, we'll get to the bottom of it in no time!" Karen's brow furrowed in concern. "And now that you're working for the government, you're going to stay there, aren't you?"

Alexandria smiled, feeling her fatigue dissipate. "I'm not sure, Mom. You know, Northrup Grumman was paying me pretty well—I took a pay cut to move across the river. But I'll be okay."

"I worry about you, honey," her mother said sincerely.

Alex closed her eyes, listened to the trio of musicians serenading the elegant dining room. They played a jazzy blues number, the sturdy cadence of the stand-up bass laying a subtly powerful foundation for a rambling melody.

"When was it we first came here?" she asked, her eyes still closed.

"Well, wasn't it your thirteenth birthday? Our 'Ladies' Brunch,' we called it."

"Yes. I remember the thrill, coming into the city." Alex looked out the window, watched the strollers and shoppers relish the spring. "Sometimes I wish I was just a kid again. You know, when the biggest stress was whether this boy liked me, or what that girl was saying behind my back."

"Ah, boys. So, are you still seeing that engineer?"

"That was, like, two dates. So, no. He had the weirdest laugh. And he was totally G.U."

"G.U.?"

"Geographically unsuitable. He lived clear up in Kensington—one of us had to fight an hour's traffic just to meet for a drink after work." She chuckled. "I did meet a pilot in Florida—well, actually, saw him again for the first time in ten years. But he was landing, and I was taking off. That's pretty much the way life has been for me, lately."

"A pilot? That's dangerous work," Karen said cautiously. "What's he like?"

"He's Nate Hayes's little brother—remember Nate, Dad's TA back when . . . I mean, during his last year of teaching?" she finished lamely.

"Yes, of course. I hear his name on the news when he goes up in the shuttle. He married your roommate Joanie Stoughton, didn't he?"

"Yep—two kids now, living the Florida life."

"Have you heard from your father?" Karen tried to look casual, watching the musicians, but Alex felt her mother's gaze from the corner of her eye.

"No. We just . . . I guess, we don't seem to have much to say to each other."

"He loves you, you know."

"Well, yeah. And I love him. But he seems to need to be all by himself out there in the woods. So I can live with leaving him there." She looked frankly across the table. "What about you? Do you ever feel abandoned by him, betrayed? Does he make you mad?"

"Ah, honey. He used to—used to make me crazy mad. It seemed that the more I wanted to do, the friends I made, the people I wanted to see . . . he just wanted to stay home. To close the door to his den. He closed me out . . . I guess he's closed the whole world out."

Alexandria sat up straight, ready to change the subject. "How are you and Nick doing, Mom? I mean, really?"

"I'm better than I've been in a long time. Nick's a keeper, honestly, honey. I think he's going to pop the question this summer. He wants to take me up to Mackinac Island for a long weekend in June."

"Sounds nice. When do I get to meet him?"

"When you can come to Chicago for more than twelve hours." Karen looked at her watch. "Your flight leaves in three hours, and with traffic on the Kennedy, I think we'd better pay up and get you on your way."

Three hours and fourteen minutes later, Alexandria felt the acceleration push her back into the A320's narrow seat, the O'Hare runway speeding past the little window.

She no longer felt like a little girl.

May 7
Washington, DC

Alex hit the snooze button on her alarm three times, and as a result she was trapped on I-365 for several miles in the thick of the morning rush. She got off before the Pentagon and took the Lincoln Memorial Bridge across the river, working her way through the mall traffic on her way to the NASA building. She was at her desk by nine, left for her first meeting twelve minutes later, and didn't lay eyes on her office again until nearly six o'clock that evening.

In the interim, she reported to the administrator, rode with Dirk Frederick over to the Pentagon for a briefing with the Joint Chiefs of Staff and the secretary of defense, briefed the NASA department heads on her trip, and somewhere found the time to choke down a vending-machine burrito. At the end of the day it was the burrito that she regretted the most. She popped a couple of Zantacs, sat down to catch up on her e-mail—filtering out the three-quarters of it that was spam, but found herself reflecting instead on the day's events.

Mike Koch had started the morning off with a startling bit of bad news: Overnight, after more than twenty years of faithful service, the Mars Global Surveyor had gone silent. All attempts to communicate with the satellite had failed—there was no chirp, not the slightest hint of a signal indicating that the device still existed. Alex had been charged with discussing the ramifications of this loss with JPL.

After Bob Wolfe's initial—and dismal—prognosis, they had actually concluded that the new rover would be able to function almost normally using only its high-gain antenna, the fat dish that communicated directly with the Deep Space Network on Earth. They would simply bypass the link of the satellite, the rover beaming signals to Earth whenever the two planets were in proper alignment—that is, whenever Earth was in the sky above the rover. When, as would happen half the time, Mars's rotation placed the robot on the far side of the Red Planet, no communications would be possible.

The visit to the Pentagon had been a revelation. First, they had started the procedure to grant her new level of security clearance: Top Secret S/I. The high point of that process had been an hour spent wired to an FBI polygraph machine, answering a battery of mostly inane questions. The full clearance process, she was told, would take months, and would involve numerous interviews with colleagues, acquaintances, and family members. For the moment, she was given a provisional pass for matters pertaining to Mars. The code word for that topic, oddly enough, turned out to be "Jupiter."

All that had been necessary before they even let her through the door of the briefing room. There she had listened in amazement as general officers, primarily Air Force though a couple from the Army, as well as a three-star admiral, spoke, presenting their initial ideas for repelling a hostile power that might approach from space.

Until then, Alex had never seriously imagined any threat to Earth from the Martian flashes. For a time she listened to the briefers in amazement, sometimes stifling the urge to laugh, at other times quelling an almost explosive impatience with this colossal waste of her time. Dammit, she had serious, practical work to do, if the rover was ever going to get off on time! But she was stuck in the middle of a roomful of soldiers.

An officer who had spent his career studying the evolution and applications of radar explained that many instruments were currently trained on space. These included the Deep Space Network at its heart, but also employed polar stations, remnants of the old DEW Line. The dishes were scanning space in the direction of Mars, also seeking any anomalous objects in the space between the two planets. Unprecedented levels of radio power were fueling those signals, from which there had as yet been not even the hint of any anomaly.

Alexandria listened in growing disbelief as she heard about plans to modify some of the nation's ICBMs, rendering them capable of targeting objects in near space. Apparently, it could be done, though aiming the powerful rockets with their multiple nuclear warheads would be a tremendous challenge. Once they had left the atmosphere on a given trajectory, of course, their ballistic nature would mean that they would be unsteerable. Still, it seemed likely that detonation could be triggered by radio signal from Earth, providing some measure of defensive control.

General Darius Williams, chairman of the Joint Chiefs, gave the last of the Pentagon briefings. He had stressed the need for security above all else, underlining the threat of panic if the population became overly concerned about an attack that was, he clearly admitted, "only the faintest of possibilities. We are simply doing our duty, preparing to defend our country against any conceivable threat. Personally, I can't imagine that there's some mysterious danger coming at us from Mars. But I like knowing that we'll be ready for anything if it comes."

Alexandria, on the other hand, didn't like it at all. The whole operation seemed like a waste of resources, personnel, and funding. If they would put half this effort into the MMM, she reflected sourly, they could expect to launch in one decade, instead of two or three!

Back at the NASA offices Alex learned that unprecedented resources were directed toward the new rover mission. Even Bob Wolfe was overwhelmed, though still resentful of the security requirements.

Now she leaned back in her desk chair, the seething burrito surrendering, reluctantly, to the Zantac. She closed her eyes again, wondering. There was no way—*no way*—that she could imagine that the flashes from Mars were in any way connected with some intelligent form of life. The mystery grated at her, however, and she wished that she *knew*.

Her reflections were interrupted by the chirping of her cell phone. She snapped it open, saw Mike Koch's home phone number displayed.

"Yes, boss," she said.

"Don't bother to unpack," he said curtly. "I've got you on a flight to Colorado Springs first thing in the morning. How'd you like a look at the inside of Cheyenne Mountain?"

"Sure, I'll be there," she said flatly. God, she was *so* tired. She was annoyed with herself because she had to stifle a momentary impulse to cry.

FIVE

I made good progress during the first week of May. By the seventh my article "Big Lift: A Comparative Analysis of Shuttle versus Saturn" had reached
some ten thousand precisely documented words. I had another ten thousand to go, but with luck I figured I would be no more than a week or two
late. I needed to let my editor know, but I had been putting off the phone
call until I had a better idea of exactly when I would be done. That was one
reason, anyway.

Then Browne started shooting. He did this periodically, on a skeet
range set up in one of his pastures. The sound of the shotgun blasts
thumped in the near distance, often repeated in rapid succession as he
took a series of shots at a single flying target. Naturally, his dogs were out
there with him, barking the whole time, the sound waxing and waning as
they ran out and back.

I shut down my computer in disgust and seriously considered calling a
complaint to the county sheriff's department. I didn't call because I knew
there wasn't a damned thing the cops were willing to do about my neighbor's noisy habits. A deputy had informed me of this, rather bluntly, several
years ago. As long as he wasn't shooting *at* me, Browne was pretty much
free to blast away during all the hours of daylight.

Pacing from the living room into my office and back again, I tried to focus on my book, but found my mind inevitably wandering. With a twinge

of guilt I remembered that I still hadn't called Alex. But I didn't go to the phone.

Truth is, I wasn't sure what I would say to her. The cause of my earlier concern had passed. Indeed, now that the Martian flashes had ceased, I hadn't given much thought to them. I was like the media, whose collective focus had almost immediately dispersed to the myriad of tragedies, local and global, that provided regular grist for the news mill. Lately there had been steady reports about a scandal involving Army spending on something called an "EMP" weapon, a bomb that set off an electromagnetic pulse that would supposedly neutralize computers and other sensitive electronic devices in the area of effect. I am a bit of a military buff and had been following these reports with some interest.

Conversely, there had been no mention of the Red Planet on the newscasts of the last few evenings, except for a few incidental reports from Jay Manstein on CNN. These had been mainly stories about the fact that there were no new developments, with a mention of rumors that NASA was working up another unmanned mission that might be looking into the anomalies of late April on the surface of Mars. I rather liked the thought that things in the night sky had returned to the status quo of my entire lifetime and the thousand, even million, generations of lifetimes before me.

Unfortunately, the return to normalcy didn't make it any easier for me to work. Opting for an early dinner, I fired up the gas grill and got a couple of hamburgers out to thaw. I was making myself a Bloody Mary when the phone rang. Wincing as I reached for the handset, I hoped it wasn't my editor calling to see how the article was coming.

"This is Mark DeVane."

"Dad?" It was Alexandria, sounding strangely tentative.

"Hi, honey. How are you?"

"I . . . okay, I guess. I just wanted to talk to you—it's been too long. Do you have a few minutes?"

"Sure." I shook a dozen drops of Tabasco into my glass and carried it and the phone out onto the deck. The sunset was a cloud-dappled glory of orange rays and pastel skies. Browne had stopped shooting—for the moment. "I saw you on TV a couple of weeks ago. You did a nice job."

"I was terrible!" she snapped. "They haven't let me anywhere near the cameras, after that."

She was upset, and I winced, feeling a pang of guilt, of shared anxiety. Alexandria has always been calm and capable beyond her years, a rock of stability. I liked that about her; I didn't know what to say to her, but I flailed for words.

"Well, that's what I told your mother. I mean, not that you were terrible. But that you're so good at analysis work, and planning and calculations. You're the most organized scientist I've ever met. They should get someone else, some PR type, to get up there and quack at the media. You have more important things to do!"

"Well, the administrator took care of that. And I have been managing to keep busy. I got back from the West Coast yesterday, and I'm off to Colorado first thing tomorrow."

Alexandria had always loved to travel, but she sounded dejected at the thought.

"Do you have any vacation time saved up?" I asked, trying for a bright tone. "Maybe you could take some time off?"

"That's just it—I *can't* take any time off. It's . . . well, it's complicated. For one thing, they're moving up the launch date for the next rover, and that has me running back and forth from DC to Pasadena about every other day."

The reason for her agitation occurred to me suddenly, a bolt out of the blue. "Are you worried about Mars, still? I thought that was all over a week ago. Just flashes of reflected sunlight, and now the planet has moved out of alignment, so we're not seeing it anymore. Didn't I read that in the paper?"

"I'm sure you did. But, Dad—I just wish that I *knew*. I hate having to make these crazy guesses, coming up with fodder for the press, for the generals. But we really don't know!"

"I take it you don't buy the reflection theory? I thought it made sense, more sense than anything else, at least. If not that, *what* then?" The *generals?* I wondered. What did that mean?

"I don't know. But I'm . . . I guess, I'm concerned."

It hit me, then: she was frightened. The sound of that tremor in my calm, intelligent daughter's voice was the first thing that really scared me. "Is there more to this story? Do you know something that you're not allowed to talk about?"

"Not really." She sounded cool and controlled again, as if she had reined in the emotion that had started to brew. "The Feds have laid on a level of secrecy, sure, but that's just a precaution. No one really knows *what* to think, and that has them all running scared."

"It's tough, not having an explanation," I acknowledged. "But how bad can it be?"

"Dad." Suddenly she was deadly serious. "I don't know. But strange things happened on that planet. The explosions were only the visible proof—but there's more, I'm certain. We have every antenna, every receiver and tool from the Deep Space Network to the astronomy telescopes in a hundred universities scanning space. But Mars is too far away—we just can't know *anything* yet."

"Well, you'll get to the bottom of it sooner or later," I assured her, feeling better. She sounded more like her old self. "And then—well, maybe you could come by for a visit, take some time off?"

"Yes. And remember, I've got a spare bedroom if you ever can get to DC. There's really a lot to see here—I'd love to show you around!"

"I remember. Thanks." I could feel my heart pounding at the thought of an airplane, of all those people. Of being in a city. I hoped my voice wasn't shaking as I answered. "Well, I'll let you get back to work. But thanks for calling, sweetheart."

"I love you, Dad," she said. "Call me when you get a chance, okay?"

"Sure, I will honey. 'Bye." And I loved her, too.

Somehow the words to tell her that didn't form before I heard the click on the other end of the line.

SIX

Alexandria heard the engines before she saw the planes. The initial roar built to a thunder before the four Warthogs came into view, flying slow and low. How could those big, ugly things stay in the air at that speed? Derek "Duke" Hayes flew the lead aircraft, and her eyes went to that plane just as it banked hard. Leading his three wingmen through a sharp turn, Duke flew about a hundred meters high, directly toward the tarmac where Alex stood. The four A10s roared over her head, and she clapped her hands over her ears as she grinned upward.

The Warthogs were aptly named, as ungainly as their name sounded. Twin engines jutted from the fuselage behind the blunt, squared wings. The tail was large and awkwardly square, a vertical fin capping each end of the long, narrow stabilizer. Missiles, guns, and detection gear poked like deformities from beneath the wings, here and there distorting the square and boxy outlines of the body. Though the A10 was a big plane, the pilot seemed almost ludicrously exposed, perched high in a bubble canopy right above the nose.

Of course, Alex had learned that those cockpits were lined with titanium armor, and that the pilots were fiercely devoted to this aircraft, loving it as few warplanes had been loved during the course of military aviation. Duke had told her about pilots in the Gulf Wars bringing their Warthogs in with half a wing shot off, with one engine blasted apart and the other pocked full of shrapnel holes. He spoke of his plane as if it held a very special place in his heart, and Alexandria supposed that it did.

She watched the four A10s land in pairs on the wide runway, wondering again about why she was here. True, she had been flying out of Canaveral on military transport, and Eglin, here in Florida's panhandle, had been a short hop away. And for once in her life, all the stars had aligned: Nathan Hayes had announced that his brother was down here on TDY—temporary duty—detached for six months from his usual base in Nevada. On impulse, she had called him. The delight in Duke's voice when he answered had cinched the decision for her. Mike Koch could get her report tomorrow—she was giving herself a six-hour pass.

Or maybe twelve hours, she thought, as she met the pilot outside the briefing room. He had already changed into khaki trousers, a Hawaiian shirt, and sandals. Grinning, he gave her a kiss on the lips before she could consider whether to turn a cheek or not.

"I am so glad you called!" he declared, holding her a little longer than was strictly necessary. "Can I take you to dinner, someplace nice on the beach?"

"I'd like that," she said, enjoying the languid appraisal of his blue eyes. She was glad she had worn a skirt—he clearly liked the look of her legs.

"You're in Florida, too, huh?" he asked, offering an elbow that she, after a moment's surprise, took in her hands. His arm was strong and his skin smooth, and she sensed that he was pleased by the contact.

"Well, it seems I'm getting to the Cape every month or so, these days. But I spent a week in Colorado not too long ago, and I've been everywhere from DC to California in the meantime. I suspect the administrator would have me running to the moon, if he could get me a flight."

He laughed. "You're seeing some interesting sights, I hope? I love the Colorado Rockies!"

She wanted to tell him that she had spent that week *inside* one of the Rockies—the Air Force nerve center at Cheyenne Mountain, to be precise—but her newfound security paranoia prevented her from elaborating. "Well, the beach sounds like a great idea for tonight," she allowed.

A few minutes later they were in his car, a newish Sebring convertible that was a little more sedate than his older brother's Boxster, heading toward Fort Walton Beach. Soon they had crossed the bridge over the Intracoastal Waterway and followed Gulf Shore Drive along the barrier island. They passed an elegant steak house and Duke looked at Alex. She shrugged, and he nodded, smiling slyly. After another mile he pulled into the parking lot of a ramshackle seafood joint.

"If I guess right about you, this is your kind of shack."

"You read me right—I smell the steamed crabs already."

They were given a table on the Gulf Coast deck, where they enjoyed cold beers and hot crab legs. After a spectacular sunset, they took a walk along the beach, holding hands.

"We've come a ways since Madison, eh?" asked the pilot.

"You were a nice kid, even if you couldn't hold your beer."

"I'm not a kid anymore."

They stopped for a kiss that lasted a long time, and when Duke led her toward the lobby of an oceanfront Holiday Inn, Alex's belly tingled in anticipation.

It had been a long time, too long, since those butterflies had flown.

May 22
Deep Space Network Station
Tidbinbilla, Australia

"Chief, you'd better get in here, right away." The technician kept his eyes on the monitor as he pushed a button and spoke into the intercom. Commander Smythe burst through the door into the cool, dark instrument room just a few seconds later.

"What is it, Sparky?"

"We've got something coming in to the big dish. Here, let me try to tune it a little tighter."

The commander, a forty-year veteran of the Royal Australian Navy, squinted in disbelief. "Are you sure we're not getting some interference? Sunspots or the like? Some kind of network noise?"

"I did a sys-check before I called you, sir. This seems like an accurate readout. We're getting a very faint radar signature, a rather large bogey, anomalous in size and shape, moving through space."

"Look at that blighter's speed! It doesn't seem possible."

"Not for an asteroid, it doesn't," agreed the technician. "I've never seen anything like it. And the strange thing is, it's possible it's coming on a direct bearing toward Earth."

Smythe whistled. "All right. Let's keep an ear on it until we get more specific data on size, speed, and trajectory. I'll open the channel to NASA, but I don't want to send everyone into a tizzy until we have something specific to tell them. Are you tightening the beam?"

"Yes, sir. I've already modified the signal from the punch bowl." Sparky referred to one of the small antennas of the array, the one that had been broadcasting a radio signal into space along a fairly wide spectrum. "In about two minutes we should be able to get a better handle on this thing."

"Fine." Commander Smythe reached for his pipe and clamped his teeth around the stem. No smoking allowed there, of course, but he liked the feel of it. It reminded him of freer days, when he'd been officer of the watch on the bridge of one of Her Majesty's frigates.

"Holy bloody Christ on a crutch!"

Sparky's oath drew Smythe's attention to the screen. "Is that what I think it is?" he asked, feeling a trickle of sweat work its way down between his shoulder blades.

"I'd say so, sir." Sparky drew a deep breath. "We have in space, coming toward Earth at a ridiculous rate of speed, not one but two anomalous objects. The first is twenty-seven million miles away, the second following about two million miles behind. From their trajectory, I would hazard a guess that they originated from the vicinity of Mars."

May 22
CNN Headquarters
Atlanta, Georgia

Jay Manstein encountered Rick Chalmers just outside studio #1. The veteran anchorman was done for the day, though of course the station would continue broadcasting news through the night. Chalmers had already loosened his tie, but he gladly stopped for a few words with the astronomy reporter.

"I'm picking up some buzz—from a source in the Pentagon," Manstein said. "It's too soon to go on the air with it, but I wanted to give you a heads up. It might be big."

"Big?" Chalmers cocked a silver eyebrow. "As in . . . ?"

"As in nine-eleven big. Or more. Think World War III. There's a big stir out of Australia. The Deep Space Network—that's an array of antennas—"

"I know what it is!" snapped the anchorman.

"Anyway, there are preliminary reports that the DSN boys have detected objects in space. Large, like asteroids. On a course for Earth. And it looks like they're coming from Mars."

Chalmers gulped. "How sure are you?'

"Not sure, not yet. But I'm keeping my ear to the ground. And if we break this story, you can bet that the shit is sure going to hit the fan."

May 22
Beachfront Holiday Inn
Fort Walton Beach, Florida

The cell phone chirped in the darkness. Alex barely heard the first ring, then sat up, blinking in confusion, as the device continued to demand her attention. She rolled toward the edge of the bed, then gasped in shock as she came into contact with a warm body—she wasn't alone, wasn't home.

Only then did full memory return. She leaned over Duke, who was only beginning to wake up, and groped for her phone. Her fingers finally closed around it, and her eyes focused on the caller ID.

"Shit!" She groaned, a split second before she flipped it open and answered. "This is Alex, sir. What's up?"

"Listen, Alex. Where are you?"

"Um, Florida. Near Eglin AFB. I'm heading back tomorrow A.M."

"I need you here pronto! We've got a meeting this morning at about the time sensible people will be getting up—just you, me, and about a thousand stars' worth of Pentagon brass," Mike Koch snapped. "I'll be calling the base CO at Eglin, and he will have a jet warmed up for you within the hour. I trust you can make it to the runway in time?"

She looked at Duke. The pilot, wide-awake by now, flicked on the bedside light. His hand came to rest on her knee, and he cocked an eyebrow, looking hopelessly young. She sighed, and shook her head.

"Yes, boss," she said. "I'm on my way."

May 22
Pentagon
Washington, DC

Mike Koch met Alexandria personally at Andrews AFB, ushering her to an official NASA SUV while the turbofans of the small Learjet that had whisked her from Florida were still winding down. Duke's farewell kiss was only a few hours old, and already it seemed like the previous night had occurred in another lifetime.

They both got into the back. Alex was mildly surprised that the administrator had come with a driver—Koch was notorious for wanting to keep his own hands on the wheel. Her initial surprise was overtaken by sheer astonishment when, no sooner had he settled his massive bulk onto the seat, he started to tell her what his call was all about. He had to tell her twice about the findings from the Aussie DSN station—findings that had since been confirmed as the earth's rotation brought the station near Madrid into line with the bogeys.

"They're coming here. From *Mars*?"

She shook her head, staring alternately out the window and back at her boss. "This changes everything," she admitted.

"It sure as hell does. And it's one scary alteration," he admitted. "Who sent these things? More important, what the hell *are* they?"

Alexandria hadn't even begun to wrap her mind around the possible explanations by the time they had pulled up at the Pentagon's main entrance. Quickly they passed through the metal detectors and security check, and were directed toward the briefing auditorium. They joined a stream of high-ranking officers and a few other civilians, patiently making their way through another, much more diligent, security station.

Clearly, the attendees were being very carefully screened. Double ID checks, complete walk through X-ray machines, and a phalanx of grim-faced, and thoroughly armed, Marines drove home the point. Alex extended her wallet and ID to the first guard, stood still for a photo, and passed her paperwork to a second guard, who held it under a UV scanner. He seemed to bore holes in her face as he compared her to the image in the tiny photo. Finally, he nodded, and she almost felt weak with relief as she followed Mike Koch through the doors of what was essentially a large theater.

This morning it would be holding a crowd of more than a thousand. The administrator put his hand on a seat adjacent to one of the aisles, then stood back so that she could step into the row and take the second chair. Glancing sideways as she sat, Alex thought that she had never seen Koch looking so distressed. There was an ashen pallor to his complexion, a sheen of sweat brightening his forehead. That was no less surprising than this 0700 gathering, full of ranking generals and other dignitaries who would normally just be waking up at this hour.

Alex saw a few other people from the space agency, as well as a multitude of civilians she didn't know—a good number of them had the polished, bland look that screamed "FBI"—and a few that she recognized. Among the latter were the secretaries of defense and homeland security, as well as a few senators who chaired important committees relating to defense, space, and intelligence.

She was taking all this in when a murmur rushed almost magically through the crowd. Those in the front stood, and those behind rose to their feet to see what was going on. A side door opened and a general marched in, saluted rigidly, and intoned:

"Ladies and gentlemen, the president of the United States."

Alex had never seen him personally before, but there was no mistaking the prominent brow, the shock of graying hair atop the long, lanky frame. He looked somber as Secret Service agents ushered him to a seat in the lower-right corner of the auditorium. The security detail stood back, and the rest of those in attendance slowly settled into their own cushioned chairs.

Almost immediately General Darius Williams, chairman of the JCS, took the podium. He was tall, his gray crew cut matching the granite color of his penetrating eyes. His jaw jutted belligerently, as if he was ready for a fight. As she looked around the room, Alex thought that never before had she seen such a large group of people be so utterly, collectively silent.

"Mr. President, ladies and gentlemen," the general began. "There is no easy way to begin this briefing except to state the known facts, as unthinkable as they are: Less than ten hours ago the Deep Space Network Antenna complex, near Canberra, Australia, began to form a radar signature—a picture, if you will, of objects in space, well beyond the orbit of our moon. The Aussies were able to identify three of these bogeys before our planetary rotation took them out of range. Now the Deep Space antennas near Madrid are locked on. They have developed a strong suspicion of a fourth. There is every possibility that there are more of these things.

"Three facts are immediately apparent. First, these objects are coming, one after the other, right toward the Earth. Second, they follow a trajectory that makes it seem very likely that they originated from the vicinity of Mars, or of deep space somewhere beyond Mars. Third, the gap between the first and the second of these bodies, calculated against the speed of their travel, would seem to indicate that the trailing object commenced its flight a little over one day after the first."

The chairman paused to clear his throat. He was a big man, ramrod straight. Yet he looked to Alex like a deer caught in the headlights of a speeding car. She began to understand the sickly expression on Administrator Koch's face, and suspected that her own complexion was turning a little green.

"As astonishing as it is to all of you—and believe me, even after one has a few hours to absorb this information, it doesn't get any less surreal—it would appear that the flashes recently observed upon Mars were the launching of these objects. I fully expect that, as they draw closer, and our radar detection becomes more accurate, we will discover that there are eleven of them, one for each of the flashes. They may be solid masses of rock, weapons, or spacecraft. The first one seems to be quite large—bigger than one of our Saturn rockets with all three stages attached, but we need a more detailed fix before we can make an accurate estimate as to its size."

Alex remembered the Saturn rocket on display at the Kennedy Space Center. She had walked underneath it with a sense of awe. It was longer than a football field, packed with engines and fuel compartments, and she had marveled at its size and complexity. And the Martian ships were even *larger?*

General Williams continued, his words as blunt as the blows of a hammer. "What are their intentions? Of course we cannot know. They are coming toward us, and we have to prepare for the possibility that they may be hostile. This may be nothing more complex than a massive artillery bombardment. They may be a series of missionary ships, carrying inhabitants—or invaders—to a new world. They may have a purpose we have not even guessed at yet. We don't have a lot of time to ponder the mystery, however. At their current rate of speed, we expect the first of these space objects to be nearing our planet about thirteen days from now."

This statement provoked the first audible reaction from the audience, a mixed mutter and gasp of dismay. The chairman continued.

"Many of you are aware that preparations for this very eventuality, an eventuality that I myself proclaimed as utterly unthinkable just a few short weeks ago, have already been undertaken at the command of the president. We are not defenseless against this menace. Our arsenal of land-based ICBMs has been undergoing extensive modification. Three batteries in North Dakota have been modified so that they are—theoretically— capable of attacking targets in space. Although they are as yet untested, we have every reason to believe that our nuclear deterrent will be an effective barrier against whatever kind of attack we face. We have adequate warheads and missiles to deliver many devastating attacks, at a range beyond the atmosphere that will shield the world from nuclear fallout.

"In addition, our preparedness will extend through our planet's airspace, and right down to the ground. As of this morning, all military reserve forces and National Guard units will be activated on an immediate basis. The cover story will be that this is a massive drill event, a test of our response to an act of unprecedented terrorism or foreign attack. In addition, we are informing the highest echelons of our allied governments, taking steps to position ourselves for global defense. Our naval assets will put to sea, and our aircraft will be going to full, around-the-clock mission readiness. All of this is commencing, as we speak, by executive order from the White House." The chairman paused again, using his handkerchief to mop at his forehead. He nodded toward the tall man in the front row.

"Mr. President, would you care to elaborate?"

As the chief executive rose from his chair and climbed the steps to the stage, Alex was reminded of Abraham Lincoln—a tall man, stooping slightly from the weight of the nation's troubles. When he began to speak, the accent was Carolina-drawled, not Midwestern-clipped, but she clung to the illusion for her own sake.

"Thank you, General Williams. I can tell you on behalf of the nation that we are grateful to have our military in the capable hands of yourself, the other joint chiefs, and every officer and enlisted soldier, sailor, airman, and Marine. We know that you will rise to meet this unprecedented challenge."

The president paused to let his gaze sweep across the room. Alex felt as though he had personally looked into her own eyes, and she took another small measure of comfort from the fact.

"I firmly believe that the greatest challenge we face in the coming weeks will not be the preparing of a military defense. Rather, it will be the prevention of complete chaos within our society. It is for this reason that I am declaring information regarding the approaching Martian objects to be classified Top Secret S/I. All of you in this room have at least that security clearance—or are in the process of earning it."

Alex thought of the lie detector test the FBI had administered her—just one step on that long clearance process. In light of the strange fate bearing down on the world, thirteen days in the future, such procedures seemed almost ridiculously quaint.

"None of you is to discuss or in any other way disseminate this information to *anyone* who is not cleared for it. I am sure your imaginations can lay out a host of details—effects on the stock market, on food supplies, on the transportation net, right up to mass panic in the streets—that would result from the premature release of the news.

"We will maintain a complete news blackout, with a cover story to be released to explain the massive mobilization—it will be portrayed as the first ever pan-national military preparedness exercise."

The president sighed, looked for the first time at the page of notes in his hand. His jaw tightened, and he looked around the room, his expression a glare of pure command. "News will get out, eventually. Of that there can be no doubt. Sooner or later the people will need to know. But I hope we can gather a lot more information, make substantial preparation, before that time comes. In any event, I am certain that all of you in this room will make certain to do your duties, even as you must keep this stunning piece of information from those you love, as well as your friends, neighbors, and those colleagues who are not cleared to know.

"Good luck, and God Bless America."

SEVEN

May 25
US Interstate 185
North of Columbus, Georgia

Josh Hickam was angry. More than angry: He was goddamned pissed off! He was used to running up against stonewalling, in fact took pride in breaking down a source's will to resist. He could always worry out that one piece of information that made a blockbuster story. But for two days he had been in Columbus, trying to reach any of a number of officers he knew at Fort Benning, the massive Army base. Not only had they been unable to see him, but he had been prevented from even going onto the base! Security at the gate was unprecedented, and included tanks and armored Humvees. Even so, shipments of ordnance and supplies, as well as military units from all over—including apparently every National Guard unit for five states—had been arriving in a steady stream.

Finally, he had given up in disgust, deciding to drive back to Atlanta and work on the story up there. His editor wouldn't be pleased, but what was he supposed to do, scale the goddamned razor wire like some crazed commando? He knew the angles, and he had worked every source, twisted as many arms as he could. Every time he came smack-dab up against a dead end. No one would give him a break. Even more significant, it was clear to him that they were all running scared.

The miles rolled past as he shook his head, grimacing in frustration and disgust. The facts were there for anyone to see: The military was in the throes of a massive call-up, a sudden mobilization of unprecedented proportions. The story of the unannounced but universal drill smelled, to Hickam's experienced nose, like a pile of bullshit. Too many companies were losing their military reserve employees at once, and those corporations were not shy about letting their elected representatives know their displeasure. No, this was not a drill. Something big was going on—big, and very hush-hush.

He pressed down on the accelerator, wondering about the civilian angle. Some of those reservists, the ranking officers, must talk sooner or later. Maybe there would be a chink—a disgruntled husband of a female colonel, for example, or some general's spoiled kids who had a hint as to what was going on. He passed a signpost. Still nearly a hundred miles to Atlanta, dammit. Suddenly he needed to be at his desk, flipping through the back pages of his address book.

The flashing lights in his rearview mirror took him by surprise.

"Ah, shit. Perfect." A glance at the speedometer furthered disgusted him: 88 mph. Even for the country freeways of Georgia, that was probably good for a citation. He drew a deep breath as he pulled over to the right shoulder, forcing himself to be calm, pleasant. Several experiences as a young man had taught him that he couldn't afford to have a chip on his shoulder for the next few minutes.

"Hello, Trooper," he said, as the Georgia State Patrol officer came up to his opened window. He had heard, somewhere, that state patrol cops liked to be called "Trooper." Already he held his license, removed from his wallet, in his left hand. His right rested easily on the steering wheel.

The officer's belly filled the view from the driver's window. This was a big man, with a big automatic pistol holstered to his belt. Looking up, the reporter saw a bulldog face, a pair of dark sunglasses, a straight brim state patrol hat. Two ham-sized fists came to rest on the cop's sturdy waist.

"Mr. Hickam?"

"Yes—here you go." He was already extending his license out the window when the question brought him up short. "Uh, how did you know my name before you looked at my ID?"

"I was looking for you, sir. Would you please step out of the car?"

"What for?" Hickam's heart started to pound, though he struggled to keep his tone reasonable. What the hell was going on here?

"That will all be clear in a minute. Right now, I need you out of this car. Right away. Sir." The big fingers flexed, and the reporter had a momentary, frightening image of himself being hauled by the scruff of the neck through the window.

"Okay, sure. Hold on." He unbuckled his seat belt, his hands shaking. The cop stepped back as he opened the door and got out of the car. Only then did he notice a second state trooper, standing down the shoulder a short distance away. He had a large black gun, the twin of the weapon on the first officer's belt, leveled in both hands, pointed directly at Josh Hickam.

"Holy shit!" the reporter gasped, spinning to face the first officer. "What the hell is going on?"

A car sped past, a blur of black faces looking curiously out at the road-side confrontation. A truck was bearing down, and the first trooper took Hickam by the elbow and guided him around the trunk of the car, where he could see another car parked behind the state patrol cruiser. As if on cue, two doors on that nondescript vehicle opened to disgorge a pair of clean-shaven men in dark suits.

"The fucking FBI is here?" the reporter exclaimed. He was far beyond the point of keeping the chip off of his shoulder. "Now, come on!"

The two men made no comment as they approached on either side of the patrol car. An SUV whipped past, followed by another truck, and Hickam found himself praying that one of them would stop. Acutely conscious of the gun still trained on him, he wondered if they were going to shoot him right there and then.

"Please lean forward and put your hands on the trunk," instructed the first trooper. "I'm going to have to pat you down."

Josh Hickam leaned forward and assumed the position. Amazingly, he felt a little bit relieved.

He didn't think they would be bothering with a search if they were just going to shoot him.

May 27
Magdalena, New Mexico

Betty Caruthers was distraught. At least Eddie had finally fallen asleep. He hadn't made it home from work for three days, and when he got there she had been afraid he wouldn't even be able to get any rest. He was so nervous, jumpy! It seemed like he was afraid even to look her in the eyes. But their twenty-seven years of marriage had taught her a little bit about the man to whom she had pledged her life.

Finally, they had made love with a rare frenzy. It was when they were finished, when he had collapsed atop her and started to cry, that he had revealed the truth. Betty lay beside Eddie and let him talk, making soothing, gentle caresses on his back, until he fell asleep. He was exhausted, drained, frightened. And he had to be back for another three-day shift at the base in twelve hours.

Sliding quietly out of bed, Betty put on a warm cotton robe and slippers, padded to the den. The computer was asleep; but a touch on the mouse brought it back to life with a slight crackle of static electricity. Immediately she went to her e-mail program, clicked her younger sister's address to open up a new message.

She began to type.

Sallie,

Eddie finally came home from the radar base tonight. You were right when you called to say you thought something weird was going on. But you won't BELIEVE how weird it is! He wouldn't tell me and wouldn't tell me. But finally, he did.

Sal, they have spotted Martian spaceships with those big VLA antennas (you know, where he works)! And they are coming toward us! Eddie told me it was really really TOP SECRET!!! But I have to tell you. Eddie thinks there might be a war. He wants me to go to the store and buy all the canned foods I can. Then pack up the camper during his next shift. (3 days, again!) When he gets off duty again we are taking the kids and going up to the San Juans. Eddie thinks the Martians will attack the cities, so we are going far past Albuquerque and Santa Fe, but not to Colorado.

They are tracking these Martian spaceships with the VLA. They think they started with those flashes on Mars that were in the news last month. Nobody knows what is going to happen, but they're really scared. That's why Julie and Chuck got called up for the Guard, too. The government knows all about it, but they're not telling anyone.

So Sallie, if you and the kids want to come to the San Juans with us, you should. It's no farther from Denver than it is from here. Anyway, I love you, and I'm scared, too. But we have to do something!

Love to Troy and Andria, too!

Betty

She tiptoed back to the bedroom door and cocked an ear. Eddie was breathing deeply, sound asleep. Nervously, she went back to the computer, reread her message, and hit *Send.*

The mail box came up and she watched it flash as the message sped outward. Impatiently she waited for it to finish. She wanted to get back to bed, to spend every precious second holding, touching, smelling Eddie. But the screen flashed for a long time, and she started to get worried. She clicked back to the message, hit *Send* again. Too bad if Sallie got it twice—if this wasn't a priority e-mail, she didn't know what was.

Still that light blinked, annoyingly. What was taking so long?

The computer popped loudly, a crack of sound that caused her to let out a small scream. She watched in disbelief as the screen went black, the monitor's brightness shrinking away to a tiny dot in the middle of the screen.

Four minutes later, a man from the FBI was knocking at her front door.

May 28
Minot, North Dakota

Fred Nichols still wore his camouflage jacket and flap-eared cap as he came through the rear door, the employee's entrance, of TV station KHGD. The station was currently broadcasting a string of syndicated *Friends* reruns, so the engineer, Hugh Darkins, and the on-air talent/receptionist, Misty Allen, were playing cribbage in the break room. They looked up but made no move to stop the game as their station manager walked in.

"You won't believe what I saw this evening," he said, still out of breath. His tone was enough to get Hugh and Misty to put down their cards and study him. Fred pulled off his cap and shrugged out of his jacket, dropping them both onto a chair while he remained standing.

"I'll bite," the engineer said, finally. "What is it—you finally caught that twelve-foot sturgeon?"

Fred shook his head. "I never got a hook in the water. Nope, it's the Army. They've got patrols all around up there, and I'm talking *outside* the air base. I would have hit a roadblock if I'd taken the highway, but they didn't have the jeep road blocked. So I tooled out there, happy as a clam and twice as ignorant, ready for a little sunset anglin'.

"Anyway, I get out to where I like to put the boat in, by one of the picnic areas on the big lake. I already got the canoe down off the roof rack. And I hear shots! Well, this was pretty strange. First of all, I know it's not hunting season. And second, these weren't any sporting guns—not a .22 or a shotgun or anything in between."

"You mean, like *machine* guns?" Misty asked.

"Well, not fully automatic. But a burst—pop-pop-pop-pop—in real quick succession. And I hear some guy screamin' and cussin', from right up the riverbank. I can't see, cuz you know how thick the cottonwoods are up there, but I decided to get closer and take a look. You know, that 'nose for news' bullshit, hey?"

"Yep. You sure have that nose, boss," Misty said, admiringly. "Like that time you caught on to them guys bringing all that cheap whiskey in from Canada!"

"I tell you, guys, this is big! Anyway, I sneak through the trees, and there's soldiers—*American* soldiers!— with some poor son of a bitch backed right up against his pickup. The troops have their M16s pointed at the guy and he's hollering at 'em. It turns out that they shot his dog. But they aren't takin' any crap. Quick as you know it, they got this guy handcuffed, tossed in the back of one o' their Humvees. A couple of soldiers drive off with him, while the rest—there was six or eight more—came on into the cottonwoods.

"Well, I hightailed it outta there, you can bet. They might have got a glimpse of my truck as I came up from the river valley, but they sure as hell couldn't catch me. I came straight back to town, until I had to stop for gas on the north side. There I met a couple of pissed off truckers, said that the Army stopped them from taking 83 north! So this is getting stranger, and stranger."

"Maybe the guy with the dog was a druggie?" suggested Hugh, who had no nose for news whatsoever.

"Shit, to get hauled off by an Army patrol? And have them close a major highway, with no explanation?" Fred's eyes narrowed. "You know what's up there, don't you?"

Misty and Hugh exchanged looks. "You mean, besides the big air base?" asked the young woman.

"*On* the base! People, we are talking about nuke-ular weapons! The biggest rockets in our whole Air Force. Each one of 'em topped with ten—count-'em, *ten*—H-bombs, and each of them H-bombs a hundred times more powerful than the Hiroshima atom bomb."

"No shit?" Hugh looked a little green.

"So, I start puttin' two and two together. You know, the big reserve call-up that went out last week? And then the news—more like, the lack of news. Can you ever recall them doing such a major operation and saying so little about it?"

"*I* can't!" Misty declared.

"Anyway, I have to do some checking around. Call some sources down in Bismarck, then touch base with my buddy at the AP. Nothin' real obvious, but I think there's more to this than meets the eye."

His two employees watched, wide-eyed, as he bounced out of the break room and into his office, which was just one cubicle away in the tiny, cinder-block station. He punched buttons into the phone, redialing twice because he kept making mistakes. Finally, he got through to Bismarck, only to find that his good friend and mentor, Davis Charles, was out of the office for two more days.

Deciding to bite the bullet, he pulled a number out of his Rolodex that he reserved for emergencies—the Canadian whiskey smugglers had been the last time he had called it—and dialed carefully enough that he got it right on the first try.

"Jack Rawlings." The familiar gravelly voice came on after the first ring.

"Jack? This is Fred Nichols, out in North Dakota."

"Nichols . . . ? Oh, yeah, Minot, right?"

"Yeah, right. Listen, Jack, I might have a story brewing out here, and it might have a national angle."

"Really?" Jack sounded a little bored. "Hey, look, Fred, I'm late for a dinner date—"

"Just give me two minutes!" Nichols would not be denied. "It's about the Army and Air Force, and nukes. You know we have a ton of them out here, right. Nuclear rockets, used to be aimed at Moscow and the like? Anyway, there are some really strange things going on at the missile base!"

"Hold it!" Jack Rawlings interrupted sharply, no longer bored. "Are you calling me on your office phone?"

"Yeah, of course."

"Shit! Listen, Fred. We can't use anything about rockets, about nukes right now. Understand. And don't call me again!"

The click and following dial tone punctuated the call, but Fred Nichols still held the phone to his ear, dumb with disbelief. A big story, and the AP wasn't interested? What was the journalism world coming to?

Slowly, almost tenderly, he replaced the phone in its cradle. Misty and Hugh, who had certainly caught every word of Fred's side of the conversation, studiously avoided looking at him as he walked slowly past the break room. He sat in the chair at the reception desk, idly watching Chandler and Monica make up some outlandish story so that they could lie to their friends and churn out another half hour of plot.

He didn't even hear the helicopter's engines, not until the Delta Force commandos burst simultaneously through the front and rear doors.

EIGHT

May 29
Delbrook Lake, Wisconsin

I checked the word count as lunchtime approached. Damn. I had written 132 words that morning. I was going to need another couple of week's extension on my deadline, as my progress had fallen to the undetectable range. For all practical purposes, my article had come to a complete standstill.

The ringing of the doorbell was, for once, a welcome, and not unexpected, distraction. I got up from the computer with relief, closed the door to my office, crossed the foyer to the front door, and opened it to see the county deputy who had come out in answer to my call.

"Hello. Mr. DeVane?" he asked. "I'm Deputy Carlson. You called about some gunshots and barking dogs, I understand?"

He was a youngster, probably fairly new to the county sheriff's department. I could only hope he would be able to understand the gravity of my situation.

"Yes. Thanks for coming. It's just that I can't get any work done, and he's shooting out there at all hours! It's intolerable!"

"All hours? You mean he's shooting after dark?"

"Well, no. But mornings and afternoons, sometimes both!"

"Look, Mr. DeVane. I'll be frank." His tone became stern, and suddenly he looked older. "We have a lot of things to worry about these days, and to tell you the truth your situation with this neighbor doesn't even make it onto the department's radar screen. Now, I came out here to tell you this personally. So you can just stop calling, all right?"

I was flabbergasted. He acted as though *I* was wasting *his* time! Very stiffly I closed the door and made my way back toward my office. I veered through the kitchen, toward the picture windows in my sunroom, where I watched the brown-and-white police car pull away from the house and vanish down the winding driveway. It disappeared behind the trees, and I had that sensation again, the feeling that I was utterly, entirely alone.

Normally, that was a good thing, but today I found it strangely agitating. Maybe it was something in the deputy's manner—he had been strangely edgy, now that I thought about it. In fact, I was getting a little edgy myself. That was probably why I had taken the step of calling the cops on Browne again. Perhaps I hadn't expected concrete results, but I had assumed that my complaint would at least be treated with respect. Instead, that wet-behind-the-ears cop had *lectured* me!

My computer hummed in the corner, but there was no solace, no link to the world I knew there. The Spaceboyz site had vanished a couple of days ago, going off-line with no explanation. Space.com hadn't been updated or modified in about four days, and the NASA site was still announcing that the next Mars rover would be launched in a year. Alexandria had mentioned something about it being moved up, but apparently the agency was keeping the fact secret. Finally, just that morning I had discovered that the CosmicCowgirl, too, was nowhere to be found.

I had surfed the sites of a few bloggers who keep up with what's going on in the world, but they were utterly silent about the astronomy sites. If anything, it seemed that traffic was down by a half or more, and several reliable sites showed passage of a day or more since the last posting. Something strange was happening, like the world was pulling away from me, leaving me on my own, with no connection to the rest of mankind. The the deputy's departure seemed to seal my isolation, form the last brick in my wall.

I paced around the house. I had two glasses of wine with my lunch. And I fell asleep for half of the afternoon. When I woke up, I went to the telephone and dialed the only telephone number I knew by heart.

"Alexandria DeVane," she answered, her voice clipped and purposeful, on the second ring.

"Alex? It's . . ."

"Dad? Dad!" The word repeated itself as a gasp. "God, I'm so glad you called!"

"It's good to hear your voice, sweetheart. I'm glad too."

"Listen, are you at home? Of course you are—"

"Yes."

"I've been trying to decide what to do." She was talking unusually fast, even for her. "But there's only *one* thing. I'm so glad you called! I'll be there in six hours. Wait for me, okay?"

"Six hours? You mean, tonight? Well, sure—but what—?"

"I can't explain it now, not like this. But I'm going to be on a plane to Madison in two hours, with a car waiting at the airport. So I will be there as soon as I can."

"Okay, I'll get your room ready. I have some nice prawns in the freezer—we'll have grilled shrimp when you get here." My mind was alive with ideas—I had fresh greens, nice tomatoes and onions from Hernandez's grocery. We could have a salad. And six hours was enough time to make a loaf of bread. . . .

"Dad, dinner sounds wonderful. But I won't be staying overnight. I need to talk to you, face-to-face. And then I'm driving down to Chicago to talk to Mom, but I need to be back in DC before morning."

"Alex, what's wrong?" My elation evaporated, replaced by cold panic. "Are you sick?"

"No, nothing like that. Just—don't worry. I'll see you this evening. I love you."

"Okay, sweetie—be careful!"

She was gone, leaving that fear as a churning ball in my chest, utter and complete confirmation that something was terribly, terribly wrong. What could have shaken my unflappable daughter like this? Why did she have to see me, see her mother, face-to-face—at a time when she was so terribly busy with the accelerated rover project . . . ?

In a flash I remembered the vanished Web sites, the clamping down on information. I saw the truth, the specter of a war between worlds, of invasion by an unimaginable foe, of fear and terror spreading across the Earth. It was coming, probably sooner than anyone could possibly imagine. And of course, those who knew were keeping the truth a great secret—there would be panic, frenzy, chaos if people learned. The Web sites were shut down because people must inevitably have guessed at that truth. Perhaps even the police were tuned in to the knowledge, at least the perception of imminent danger.

I went into kind of a frenzy then, picking up the papers and books I had lying around, vacuuming the whole house, dusting, wiping down the bathroom. I put dough in the machine, starting a loaf of Italian bread. I got the shrimp out to thaw in case Alex had time to eat, put them back in the freezer because I didn't want to pressure her, finally got them out again just so they would be available. I had the news on, but the stories were bland—government waste and contractor bribery on a huge freeway interchange in LA, the remains of a missing Tennessee girl found in north Alabama. The lead story concerned a Hollywood starlet, one of the leading actresses of the day, who had shot her older lover, a venerable star in his own right, and quite possibly paralyzed him. None of that mattered to me.

It was already dark, and the bread was just coming out of the oven when I heard Browne's dogs start to bark. For once I was grateful for the sound, as it might mean that a car was making its way down the lane. I went to the front door and was soon rewarded by the sight of headlights brightening the tree-lined curve of my driveway. From the speed, the bobbing progress of the lights as the car lurched through the potholes, I knew that it was my daughter.

Alexandria pulled up toward the garage, her nondescript rental car skidding to a stop. I was hugging her the moment she got out of the car. "Dad!" she whispered, pulling me tighter than she had since she was a little girl. She shook, slightly, a little tremor suggesting that she was holding back tears.

"Baby, it's so good to see you," I said, choking up myself. "I'm glad you're safe."

"Come inside," she urged, taking my arm as we hurried to the door. "You made bread!" she cried, as we entered. "It smells wonderful, like years and years ago."

I sliced the loaf and drizzled some olive oil and spices onto some dipping plates while Alex poured a couple of glasses of Chardonnay. We sat at the snack bar, the wide windows yawning into the darkness of the woods beyond the yard.

The words exploded from her in a rush—it was clear that she had been waiting, too long, to talk about this. She told me of the latest intelligence briefing. There were eleven objects identified, all of approximately the same size—approximately a kilometer long, and two hundred meters wide. We were prepared to meet them with nuclear warheads exploded just beyond the upper limits of our atmosphere. Utmost secrecy was being maintained, for the reasons I had guessed, but Alex had finally had enough.

"I'm not the only one. I know Mike Koch has told his wife and kids—they're up in a mountain cabin in Vermont. Word is leaking out. You wouldn't believe how many reporters, bloggers, and just ordinary citizens have been locked away, incommunicado. They're not bothering with charges, or anything formal like that. But the news is going to break, and I had to let you and Mom know."

"What should we do? What are *you* going to do?"

"I'm going to keep working, Dad. I'm flying to Cape Canaveral in two days for the shuttle launch. I've been ordered to stay down there for the rest of the week—they're clearing out a lot of the people from Washington, the Pentagon, and so forth. Nate Hayes is captain of the shuttle mission—they're going up for reconnaissance. They're fitting Discovery with extra fuel tanks, and they're going to try and maneuver to get a look at these things before they reach our atmosphere."

"God, that sounds dangerous! What if these are hostile spacecraft?"

She shrugged, trying to look determined, but I saw that her eyes were wet. Nate had been a great assistant for me, back when I could still lecture, and I knew that he had been one of her mentors in college. When he had dated and later wed Alex's best friend and college roommate, it was only natural that he had remained one of her closest friends. The risks were frightening to me, but they must have been appalling to her.

"The whole crew volunteered," she said simply. "As did virtually every astronaut in the program. They had to draw lots; only three are going on the mission."

"And then . . . ?" I didn't know what to say. I wanted to bring her home, to keep her safe beside me, but my sense of reason recognized that for the ludicrous thought it was. Where was it safe? Besides, she was right: She had important work to do.

"I don't know, Dad. Maybe we'll be back to normal again in two weeks. If these things appear dangerous—and everyone is assuming that they are—the president has made it clear that we're going to blast them to pieces before they have a chance to get close. But it's chancy—those guided missiles were not intended for use in space, and there are questions about accuracy. So we'll have to be ready for anything."

"Then what should I do?" I wondered.

"Well, stock up on canned goods and drinking water. Make sure you have gas for the generator—plenty of it! You might consider getting a gun."

"A gun? I don't think that will be much use against Martian invaders!"

"Not for the Martians, Dad. I'm worried about what *people* are going to do."

An hour later she was off, tires spitting gravel as she roared down the driveway. Normal driving time to Chicago was about three hours, but I suspected she might be able to shave an hour off that. At least she'd arrive after midnight, when the city's nineteen-hour traffic rush generally eased back, a little.

I considered going out to the store, buying some canned goods and water, taking care of staples. Yet despite the urgency of Alexandria's pleas, I was possessed by hesitancy that prevented me from moving. I found myself staring out the windows of my dark house, wishing that the clouds would break and allow some glimpse of the night sky. Or perhaps we should be grateful for the clouds. Did they offer some concealment, like a smoke screen, to mask the frenzy of our preparations from the eyes of . . . what?

Speculation on the contents of those eleven great objects, I quickly decided, was fruitless. That very mystery enhanced my fear, and at the same time numbed any sense of urgency. How could I prepare for something I couldn't imagine?

Of course, I reminded myself harshly, I was a scientist, dammit! It was my job, my duty, to imagine things that the rest of mankind found difficult to grasp. But all of my study, my rational analysis of data, the serious debate of varied hypotheses, the testing that grew more sophisticated, more capable, with every passing year—all of that had seemingly done nothing to prepare me for this. Who had sent these things? My mind rebelled at the notion of Little Green Men, sinister aliens cackling and hissing over their nefarious plans.

But I would have to confront that rebellion, actually conquer it. Sitting down, I tried to consider the possibilities. What if these space objects were simply solid rock? There had been many studies done on the potential effects of asteroid impacts upon Earth. At the size Alex had described, any one of the things could wreak horrendous damage, simply by plunging through the atmosphere and smashing into land or sea. If all eleven of them smashed into the world, it would be a catastrophe of biblical proportions—the end of civilization, possibly the extinction of mankind.

If they were merely big, dumb rocks, on the other hand, our nuclear weapons would have a very good chance of destroying them, or altering their courses enough that they would miss the planet. Which led to further theorizing: If they were not solid, then they were hollow. And what did they carry inside?

Restless again, I clicked on the TV. The ten o'clock news was winding down, but even before I heard a sound I was stunned by the expression on the face of the young, square-jawed anchorman.

He looked utterly terrified.

"T-to repeat," he stammered. "CNN is reporting, and the AP, NBC, and Fox News have confirmed, that our planet is being threatened by a fleet of vessels from another world. The danger is imminent, so imminent that the first of these interplanetary objects will be approaching Earth within the next five days.

"It is being reported that the federal government has known about this menace for more than a week but has concealed this knowledge from the journalists and private citizens of the United States, and the world. Reports from Europe and Asia indicate, thus far, that at least some elements of the governments of England, France, Germany, Russia, India, China, and Japan have also been party to this unprecedented cover-up.

"The story has broken only in the last hour, but we already have confirmation from a number of sources. The initial breach came from Josh Hickam, a reporter for the Atlanta *Journal-Constitution*. He had stumbled onto the story while incarcerated at Fort Benning, Georgia; he was able to write a story and smuggle it out of the military brig to CNN headquarters. Almost immediately, there was confirmation from multiple sources. Our own Jay Manstein has confirmed these reports with anonymous sources in the Pentagon. There are stories too numerous to recount of entire families where one member has an attachment to our national security network; the whole family has been quietly rounded up and locked away.

"The news first came over the national airwaves at 10:47 P.M. Eastern. Already the streets in many cities are mobbed. Here in Madison, more than a thousand people have gathered around the capitol, in a silent vigil. Churches have opened their doors, and the faithful are flocking to impromptu services . . ."

The screen showed live shots, the familiar dome of the Wisconsin state capitol—a twin of the Capitol dome in Washington, DC, except about a foot shorter—lit a brilliant white against the black sky. Many people stood around that great building, some holding candles, others holding hands. A few were there with little children. The general mood was calm, though the camera captured many small groups of people engaged in animated conversation.

That scene was followed by shots of churches with the doors thrown open, people filing in for impromptu services. Next we were shown some very crowded bars. Even on State Street the mood was strangely subdued—save for one bearded lunatic standing on a crate in the middle of the pedestrians-only avenue. The camera tightened onto his face.

"Repent! The vengeance of the Lord comes upon us! There is no time to lose!" he cried, his eyes bulging in the TV lights. His expression sent a shiver down my spine, and I was relieved when the scene shifted, cutting to a reporter standing in the parking lot of a grocery store. Cars inched along behind him; even before he started speaking a horn beeped out from the queue.

"We're at the East Town Shopmart, and as you can see the store is already under a state of virtual siege. Within fifteen minutes of the news hitting the airwaves, the lot was full. Now there are cars lined up on both sides of the street—in fact, people have been leaving their cars in the traffic jam and running to the store."

The view shifted, a clip of the line at the front of the store. It was thick and restive, already more than a hundred people simply waiting to get in.

"I'm sorry, but you'll have to wait!" a sweating manager was proclaiming, over and over again. He was a big man, with his shirtsleeves rolled up, a vein bulging in his neck. He could only hold up his hands, palms outward, and address the crowd. "As soon as we clear some customers out of the store, we'll let more of you in. You'll have to be patient."

The crowd pressed in, until the manager was backed against the front door. Behind him the building teemed with people moving frantically. The camera panned around the parking lot, zooming in on the flashing lights of a police car that was nudging through the traffic congested in the lot and onto the surrounding street.

Once more the view went to the studio. The anchorman had recovered some of his composure, spoke with his usual assertive mien. "We are hearing that the president plans to address the nation on these developments, apparently within the next few minutes. We will go to that speech as soon as we learn that it is about to begin. In the meantime, we go once again to—excuse me, we're going to Washington, to the White House."

The screen went black for several seconds, then brightened with the familiar view of the desk in the Oval Office, with the presidential seal on the wall just behind the chair. The president was not there; a few seconds later the shot shifted to a grim-faced Rick Chalmers, seasoned network anchorman.

"We will bring you the president's statement as soon as he is ready to go on the air. In the meantime, these are some live shots of downtown Manhattan. As you can see, traffic is in a state of complete gridlock. The doors of St. Patrick's Cathedral have been opened to all who want to attend; here you see the overflow crowds listening to the impromptu Mass on speakers that have been set up on the outer plaza."

The camera whirled through a series of clips, strings of cars all unmoving in the canyons between the lofty buildings on Broadway. There was a view of a tunnel mouth, police cars parked across the traffic lanes, lights flashing. "Bridges and tunnels leading into the city have been closed—that is, no vehicles are being allowed to enter Manhattan. Similar throngs have been reported in Atlanta, Chicago, San Francisco, and Washington, DC. Incidents of violence are surprisingly rare, as far as we can report so far. We're going now to Maxine Taylor, reporting from Miami—excuse me, no. This is the White House."

The shot of the Oval Office returned, and this time the chair behind the desk was occupied. I leaned forward, my elbows balanced on my knees, unconsciously wanting to give the president every assistance. Like most Americans, I needed reassurance, not just in his words but in his bearing. I wanted to see the leadership that would guide us past an unprecedented peril.

His face was drawn and, in the light of the TV cameras, almost unnaturally flushed. An unfortunate excess of rouge contributed to his surrealistic appearance.

"My fellow Americans. We have all been affected by the news that has come out in the last two hours. First, I must confirm what you have been told by the various media outlets: Our planet is being approached, possibly menaced, by objects traveling through space. These objects are of unknown origin, design, or intention.

"It is true that we have been tracking them for several days. The decision to withhold the information from the public was mine, taken with other heads of state around the world.

"The reasons for the news blackout will be made apparent, but for now you should know that there have been many preparations going on behind the veil of secrecy, planning and preparedness on an unprecedented level. Our military is fully activated, all reserve components either ready to go or will be within a few more days.

"It is important to remain calm. Go to work or school. Continue your daily routines. If and when additional warnings are warranted, your government will waste no time in putting out that word.

"In the meantime, remember: We have brave men and women in our armed forces posted all around the world, and within our own borders. They have the best equipment in the world, and they are at a high state of readiness. If every American, civilian and military, does his or her duty, we will confidently meet and defeat any threat that develops. . . ."

He went on to sketch out some of the things Alexandria had described to me—the ICBM modifications, the upcoming shuttle mission of reconnaissance, the vast array of splendid weaponry and personnel forming the United States Armed Forces. He spoke with conviction, his voice steady, his words direct.

But finally he finished. The network went back to the studio, to Rick Chalmers again. He promised a tour of the nation, cameras peeking in on cities and towns, recording the panic and dismay intermingled with islands of calm and even fatalism, as the news spread across the land. I didn't have the heart, or the stomach, to watch; I punched the Off button almost violently, leaving my house in a stark, sudden silence.

I thought about putting on some music, but there was nothing I owned, no sound in my library, that seemed suited for the mood. Instead I went out onto my deck, and looked up at the sky.

A few stars sparkled through a mist of cirrus cloud. They looked lonely. Isolated. And very far away.

NINE

May 31
Kennedy Space Center
Cape Canaveral, Florida

Alexandria was stuck on the ground at O'Hare for twelve hours in the immediate aftermath of the Disclosure. As the news spread people thronged to the airport, desperate to buy tickets and fly immediately. At the same time, many employees simply abandoned their jobs at the airport and elsewhere. The result was utter paralysis at the ticket counters.

Outside, a general traffic tangle brought all of automotive Chicago to a standstill before dawn, as everyone seemed to take to the roads at once. Phone lines were jammed, and people from taxi drivers to airline flight crews made decisions that did not involve going to work. Gasoline stations and stores were mobbed, most retail centers—operating with skeleton staffs—forced to close their doors against the press of customers.

For many people, the news of the approaching celestial objects and the widely held belief that those objects were filled with hostile Martians rendered every other aspect of life insignificant. Suddenly there were people to see, homes to reach, things that needed to be said and done urgently. Everyone wanted, *needed*, to be somewhere else, and the transportation net in the air and on the ground was taxed, overloaded, and for nearly a full day simply jammed into paralysis.

Alex spent most of her time in the airport watching TV. Network stations were giving the story twenty-four/seven coverage, parading a bewildering—and bewildered—array of scientists, retired generals, high-ranking politicians, and people-on-the-street past the cameras. All of them were limited to speculating as to the nature of this unprecedented phenomenon. In a few short hours she saw appeals for calm from the vice president, the secretaries of defense, homeland security, transportation, and treasury, as well as another appearance by the president himself. When the stations went to local coverage, the governor of Illinois, the mayor of Chicago, and both of the state's senators issued the same pleas. (As far as Alex could see, the requests were for the most part going unheeded.)

She finally got through to Mike Koch on her cell phone—telephonic communications had been nearly as jammed up as the transportation net—and he had ordered her to skip DC and head immediately to the space center. He had even arranged a military transport, as the civilian airlines were forced to cancel more and more flights because of employees abandoning their stations.

The plane, a sleek, small jet that made her feel like a real VIP, made the trip in just under three hours. They came in from the east, over the endless Atlantic beach and its fringe of pearly breakers. Then the runway flashed underneath, and with barely a jolt the plane landed and taxied to within a hundred yards of the terminal. When the enlisted steward opened the door she felt the blast of heat even across the cabin. Squinting, carrying her single small bag, she ducked through the small exit.

"Alex! God, it's good to see you!"

It was Nate Hayes, waiting at the base of the stairs. He was hugging her as she reached the last step. Joan was right behind him, tears in her eyes.

"You, too, pal," she said, holding him close for an extra second. Joan came up, and they hugged each other wordlessly, clinging like they would never let go. Finally, Alex broke free and looked at them. "But don't you both have more important things to do than greet visitors on the tarmac? My God, Nate, you go up in two days, don't you?"

He shrugged, a charming, almost bashful gesture. "They've got techs running all over the shuttle right now. I'd just be in the way. They gave me—and Laura and Jack—today off. Joan and the kids are taking a picnic out to the beach while I swung by to see you land. Do you want to come and join us?"

"I would *love* to!" Alex replied sincerely, thinking what a simple pleasure it would be to walk barefoot on the sand, wade in the Atlantic surf. "But I can't. I need to be in the Op center in the next hour. But I'm so happy to see you!" She looked at Joanie, who was smiling proudly—and tearily—at her husband. God, what a trouper! And what could Alex say in the face of that courage?

Only one thing, really: "Nate—be careful."

"Shoot," he said, with a grin. "I just steer the damn thing. And not too much of that. The computers will do the flying in space. But the modifications to the gas tank have been slick. By sacrificing the cargo hold, we're able to carry about ten times as much fuel aboard as on any previous shuttle mission. We'll make a flyby at pretty good speed, and I'll send you back some snapshots."

He was still smiling, but she sensed the gut-wrenching fear behind his expression—and she knew, for his sake, that she couldn't acknowledge his deeper emotion. Joan took her hands, held them in a crushing grip before releasing her with a wave.

"Well, we got us a real space cowboy to fly that ship," Alex said, giving his arm a squeeze as he led her toward the small arrivals lounge. At the naval air station this was a spare, military blockhouse, nothing like the glass-and-steel elegance of a big civilian airport. But it was blessedly air-conditioned, a fact Alex really appreciated as they stepped inside.

"So—did you stop by and see Duke up at Eglin?" he asked casually as the automatic door whooshed shut behind them.

"He didn't tell you?" she asked.

He grinned again. "Well, yeah. I'm glad," he said. "And just so you know, he's coming down for the launch, day after tomorrow. I hope you'll still be here?"

"I had to come for the meetings," she said. "But you can bet I'm going to stay and catch the main event! Actually, I'm ordered to stay here for the next four days—with an hourly report to the administrator."

"These are the most recent pictures from the Hubble," intoned Major General Lopez, the Air Force intelligence officer running the briefing. Small and wiry, he looked more like a wrestler than a high-ranking staff officer. He was dwarfed even more by the image on the PowerPoint slide, a picture that filled the large screen in the darkened room. Alex was startled at the clarity of the view—the first detailed look that she, or anyone, had gotten of the nearest Martian object.

The cylindrical shape was obvious, even though the camera angle came at it from just off to the side of a full, head-on view. The color seemed to be a murky blur that could have ranged anywhere from rust red through brown to black a bit lighter than the backdrop of the midnight sky. They could discern no details beyond shape and color. General Wattlinger frowned at the screen, as if he viewed the picture as a personal insult.

"This is the first one, of course, the one designated M1. The second is some two million miles behind it, and while we have a visual"—he clicked to the next slide, an image of a faintly luminous spot that might have been a very distant star—"on M2 already, we can't get anything like the kind of detail we have on '1.'"

The image went back to the first object, a slightly different backdrop but similar level of resolution. "We're going to keep Hubble focused in on this one. Naturally, we're using radar, too, both passive and active. Thus far there have been no emissions detected from any one of these bodies. They may well be inert and quite possibly solid."

"I have a question, General." It was Robert Baxter, associate director of the International Space Station project at the Cape. His eyebrows furrowed in curiosity as he studied the image on the screen. "Given the observed trajectories, what will be the fate of the object—that is, if it doesn't start steering, somehow. How close is it going to come to Earth?"

"Good question, Dr. Baxter. And that opens up a bit of mystery. When we first had the trajectory plotted, it looked like the first few of them would go well past our planet, outside even the orbit of the moon. Near misses, of course, but too fast and too far away to get trapped by our planet's gravity. The later missiles were tracking closer, inside the orbit of the moon. Even so, considering their velocity, our best estimates had their momentum carrying them through our gravitational field and on into, eventually, the sun."

"You referred to a mystery, General?" prodded Baxter.

"Oh, yes. Well, it seems that there has been a shift, an anomalous shift, in the precise orientation and speed of the objects—specifically the first three of them. This data has been coming in over just the last ninety minutes."

"*These* data," Bob Baxter whispered, gently nudging Alex in the ribs. "It should be 'these data.'" His eyes were twinkling, and she suppressed her own laugh, settling for a surreptitious nod. The humor was a welcome relief from the tension that had been knotting her stomach.

General Wattlinger looked up again. "Yes. It seems that the first three objects are a little bit closer together than they have been throughout the course of their flight, so far as it can be measured."

"Has there been any observable change in speed?" asked Alexandria.

"Er, let me check." Once more the general pawed through his papers. "The readings suggest that there may be, but that is still being measured. But yes, preliminary indications are that M1 has slowed down very slightly, and that M3 has shown signs of acceleration."

"But no energy emissions have been detected?" Baxter was focused on the problem. "*How* can they change speed?"

"That's just one of the mysteries. It also seems as though their course is veering, bringing them more in line with the orbit of the moon. This change is also just being observed."

"So it's possible that they are still changing course, that they might veer enough to line them up, directly, with the Earth?" Alexandria suddenly saw the objects like a string of guided missiles, hurtling through space until they could curve down into the blue waters, the green landscapes, of her world.

"And changing course without the benefit of observable force," Baxter continued. "Just how are they doing that?"

"Some kind of interior gravitational adjustment?" asked an Air Force general who had been studying the picture with intense concentration.

"You can't adjust gravity internally," replied another scientist, a gray-haired woman named Frieda Maine. "And if there are emissions—well, could we pick that up with the Deep Space Network?"

"Maybe," Alex responded. "If not the DSN, then the Very Large Array in New Mexico should give us some readings."

"In any event, even the slightest change here is significant," Dr. Baxter noted. "I think it means we can rule out, for all intents and purposes, that these things are inert. They are more than just asteroids launched through space."

"The astronauts in the shuttle should be giving us a good look in two more days," General Wattlinger asserted, trying unsuccessfully to sound reassuring. "Even with the ten-thousand-mile limit we have ordered for safety, they'll get some solid data."

All Alex could think of was her good friend, a cherished husband and father, flying the little tin can of a space shuttle toward the most frightening destination anyone could imagine.

Cocoa Beach, Florida

A beautiful strand of beach stretched in both directions from Alex's hotel, only a few feet from the door to her room. But she found herself disdaining the cloudless sky, the pastel sunset, and staying inside as darkness closed in. She sought whatever enlightenment could be gained from CNN and the other televised news organizations.

It was cold comfort: martial law reigned in all the major cities, and the business of government at all levels had come to a complete standstill. Stores shelves were barren, picked clean by a panicked populace, and nobody seemed inclined to deliver food or any other goods. There were increasingly reports of black markets centered around food warehouses, trucks hauling full loads away in the middle of the night for tens of thousands of dollars, in cash. As to normal commerce, no trucker was about to embark on a cross-country trip while the threat of global attack was possible, and even commuters were deciding, in droves, that they had more important things to do than go to work or school.

Alex wanted some diversion, flipped the channel looking for something light. Conan wasn't on—NBC was running all-night news coverage, now mostly rehashing interviews and speculation that had been recorded over the last few days. She found an episode of *Frasier* in syndication, but found that she couldn't concentrate—indeed, she found the flippancy annoying. With a sigh, she went back to CNN.

It was a tribute to journalistic passion that most reporters, and the vast technical support staffs that kept them on the air, continued to work. So, too, did soldiers and policemen, firefighters, and medical personnel. Electricity was being produced at normal levels, and phone service was still available—though the amount of traffic sometimes made connections problematic. According to one news story Alex was watching, certain businesses had thrived. Luxury car dealers were doing a booming business—the news story showed lot after lot, nearly emptied in the buying frenzy.

She thought of her parents, glad that her mother had Nick to look out for her. No one should be alone at such a time, at least no one who didn't want to be alone. Once there was a time when she would have wished that Karen could have gone back home, moved back to the woods with Mark. That was a pipe dream, its smoky nature proven on those few occasions when the three of them had met for a few painful hours. Whether it was Chicago or Delbrook Lake, Alex remembered the stifling sense of suffocation, the strained silences, that inevitably arose when her parents were in a room together.

As to her father . . . she shook her head. He would be fine in his house in the woods, or he wouldn't. Alex reminded herself that there was nothing she could do about it, one way or the other.

Dammit, why was she crying? Annoyed, she got up and went to the bathroom blowing her nose in a tissue, then looking at herself in the mirror. Her ponytail was askew and she pulled out the band, brushing her hair with stern, almost angry, strokes. She looped the crinkly elastic around it and raised her chin, satisfied that she was ready for anything.

As if on cue, the phone rang. She picked it up with a steady hand.

"Alexandria Devane."

"Al—it's Duke. God, I'm glad I caught you."

"Me too." She sat down on the bed and leaned back. "Nate tells me you're coming down for the launch tomorrow."

"No—that is, I'm here now. I have a two-day pass, and I'm already in town."

"Oh?" She found herself standing, pacing around the bed. "Where are you? Are you free tonight?" God, she was gushing like a teenager! She needed somebody . . . no, she needed him! And he had called!

"Actually . . ." She could hear the rasp in his voice, something halfway between a growl and a purr. "I'm in the lobby. I can be there in two minutes."

June 2
Kennedy Space Center
Cape Canaveral, Florida

Conditions were perfect for the launch. The sky was a dome of immaculate blue, cloudless and infinite except for the vapor trails marking some of the jets that circled high above, carrying electronic and human observers. A gentle wind caressed the wetlands and ruffled the flat savannah of the cape.

Alexandria was happy to have the view of the sky, and the companionship of the hundreds of people thronging around the VIP viewing gallery. She could have pulled rank and taken a spot in one of the sheltered bunkers close to the launching pad, but Duke had suggested they watch the launch together from the viewing gallery, the bleachers set up more than a mile away. Officials and agency staff made up much of the crowd, together with families of the astronauts and some media.

Joan and the kids were there as well. They had made their farewells to Nate thirty-six hours before, when the pilot had reported for his preflight quarantine. Alex had embraced her old friend for a long interval, neither woman willing to shed a tear. Now all five of them claimed a section of the bleachers at the very top of one of the viewing stands. Even the normally aloof or reserved teenagers were awestruck by the portent of the moment. Tricia looked wan and frightened, leaning on her mother's shoulder, while Tim glared around belligerently, as if challenging anyone who dared to crowd in on the family's space.

Even at this distance, Discovery and its external rocket boosters dominated the view. The space shuttle was poised above the ground, belly flat against the huge liquid-fueled main rocket, with the two solid-fuel boosters—each of which was longer than the shuttle itself—bracing the huge tank like giant Roman candles.

Which was, in effect, what they were.

Duke's hand found Alex's, fingers intertwining as they looked at the huge launch gantry. That massive structure of girders, elevators, and access platforms had already rolled back, beyond the reach of the incinerating blast due to commence shortly. The gallery around them was full, but there was a strange hush, almost a sense of reverence, among the hundreds of people gathered there. Alex had attended many a shuttle launch, and previously she had always sensed a powerful tension mingled with a definite air of celebration. That day, it felt more like a church service. A very well guarded church service—she looked at the row of armed Humvees parked along the shoulder of the connecting roads. Every intersection on the sprawling space center was guarded by a tank.

Joan Hayes was dry-eyed, but her knuckles were white as she clenched Duke's other hand. Tricia held her mom's left hand, while Tim sat silently beyond her, watching without comment as their father prepared to leave the planet for the sixth time. Only once did he speak—"Kick some Martian ass, Dad!" he whispered, as the gantry and elevator pulled back from the ship.

The loudspeaker droned, warning that the minutes were counting down. The astronauts, three of them, had been sealed into their craft hours ago, and Alex knew that they would be getting anxious, ready and eager for the blast of acceleration that would propel them upward. There was no talking at all as the descending count reached the last sixty seconds, the crackling announcements punctuating the cadence, the same progression that had thrilled Alexandria as a child, when she had first dreamed of space, of going there herself.

"Ten . . . nine . . . eight . . . seven—" White smoke billowed from beneath the craft as the engines fired. ". . . Six . . . five . . . four—"

The smoke was followed later by the roaring sound as the main engines took hold, pouring fire and force from the bottom of the shuttle assembly. "Three . . . two—" And the solid-fuel boosters kicked in, igniting in a blaze of red fire in the midst of the surging cloud.

"One . . ." The space shuttle, strapped to its three massive fuel cylinders, trembled on the pad, surrounded by the shroud of smoke, poised for a terrifying instant as if it wasn't going to move. Then the droning voice took on a note of passion:

"We have liftoff. Discovery has lifted off."

It was almost too slow to see at first, the gradual rising of the whole rocket assembly, the huge structure battling gravity, pulling away from the ground. Faster and faster it surged, blasting skyward, trailing smoke and flame, slicing through the atmosphere with that thunderous roar. The plume of exhaust marked the shuttle's trail, a banner in the sky as the three rockets, flaming together, carried the astronauts and their venerable craft higher and higher, into the stratosphere, angling downrange, climbing at last into the near-perfect vacuum of space.

Always in the past Alexandria had heard cheers, relieved laughter, light chatter from the observers as tension dissipated with a successful launch. Nothing had gone wrong here, today, but there was no sense of relief or celebration in this crowd.

Alex looked at Joan Hayes, and all she could feel was a cold sense of dread.

"Dr. DeVane?" Alex heard her name as she and Duke made their way toward his brother's car, Nate having loaned him the Porsche while he was in Cocoa Beach. The plume of Discovery's launch was nearly gone, a dotted line of pale smoke against the cloudless sky.

She turned, recognizing the Navy pilot who had flown her down from Chicago on the small jet. "Yes, hi."

"I'm sorry—I was supposed to take you up to DC tomorrow, but I've got new orders. It's Norfolk for me, I'm afraid. I leave in a few hours, and I can take you there if you want. Otherwise, I understand there's a KC-135 leaving the Cape tomorrow, going to Dulles. They have room for you, if you want to stay here and leave on schedule."

Duke spoke quietly. "I flew here myself and don't have to go back until tomorrow."

The answer required no more thought than that.

"Thanks, Captain. I'll take a seat on the 135."

"Just let them know in the terminal building sometime today. And sorry about the change in plans."

"No problem at all," she said, as the pilot hurried away. She took Duke's hand in hers. "I'll have to call the administrator. I'm sure he watched the launch on TV, but he'll want an eyewitness. Then . . . maybe we can get out of here for a few hours—it's been too long since I've dipped my feet in the ocean."

June 2
Delbrook Lake, Wisconsin

I ate breakfast in front of the TV, watching live footage of the object that had been designated M1. The images with the best detail still came from the Hubble telescope, but the cameras in the space shuttle were getting better resolution with each passing hour. It had been days since I had even thought of trying to work—the article about Saturn rockets and space shuttles only seemed silly against the new truths shaping the world's immediate future.

Three days ago I had finally stirred myself to drive into town. I was too late—every grocery, each gas station, even the liquor stores were all closed, having sold out their stock within the first forty-eight hours of the Disclosure. I came back home without even getting out of my car.

Taking stock, I was grateful that I had nearly a full tank of gas in that car. I had an assortment of canned goods, I guessed enough to feed myself for a couple of weeks if it came to that. My liquor cabinet was stocked well enough, though I was almost out of beer. Strange to think that I didn't know when I'd be able to buy more.

I had a generator rated at thirty-four hundred watts, capable of powering most of my house with electricity, so long as I didn't go too wild. I heated my water with liquid propane, and the tank behind my house still had more than a hundred gallons.

Alexandria had recommended that I get a gun. Oddly enough, the hardware store in town—which had a whole array of hunting firearms behind a counter—had still been open when I drove through. Still, I never considered going inside, nor did I feel myself to be in any personal danger. The few pedestrians and drivers had seemed normal enough, certainly unthreatening even if there was a little less of the friendly wave, the cheery greeting that usually characterized a small town in Wisconsin.

But I was satisfied to be away from them, out of sight and mind, tucked away in the house behind the wooded hill. I watched the television, saw what was going on in the world, but I was almost able to convince myself that I was not a part of that world. Then they started talking about a man I knew, a man who had been my best teaching assistant.

"Captain Nathan Hayes, the shuttle pilot, is reporting on the progress of the mission. We're going to that feed now, live," declared Rick Chalmers, the anchorman.

The camera cut to that familiar, handsome face. He was tanned and crew-cut, floating in some part of the shuttle's cabin with that expression of weightless glee that seems to transport men, and women, in space.

"Hello, America and the world," Nate said. "We are in expanding orbit, high above the planet. Reaching out with a laurel wreath in one hand, and a sword in the other, to try and expand our knowledge of the universe."

I winced. There was no "sword" on the shuttle, nor any shield. They were as vulnerable out there as toddlers who might have wandered out onto a medieval battlefield. Their only hope was that there would be no war, not so long as they were in space.

The mission commander began to talk, the sound tinny and faint through a myriad of distance and communications technology. He concluded with personal words, delivered with that devilish grin that had been able to capture a lecture hall:

"Joanie, Tricia. I love you. Tim, I love you, too—and do your homework! This is Discovery, out."

His words were for the most part bland reassurance, everything going A-OK. But that familiar voice, the voice of my daughter's friend speaking from far beyond Earth's atmosphere, pulled me back once again into the circle of man.

TEN

June 3
Kennedy Space Center
Cape Canaveral, Florida

Duke dropped Alex off at the small passenger terminal. Still in civilian clothes, he planned to head over to the pilots' locker room and change into a flight suit. Within another couple of hours he would climb into the A10 that was parked with a dozen other small jets in a holding area on the far side of the tarmac.

"Be careful," she urged, between a pair of long good-bye kisses.

"Hey, you're the one who's traveling in a flying gas station!" he declared, shaking his head as he looked at the huge KC-135. Alex knew that it was used primarily to refuel other planes while both aircraft were flying. At heart it was simply a military version of the good old Boeing 707, one of the first of the big passenger jets.

"Look at the bright side. It's probably been flying for forty years. I'm sure they have the bugs worked out by now," she replied. "And the pilot is probably not hungover and worn-out from a wild night in a beachfront hotel, either."

He grinned. "It was worth every aspirin!"

She watched him get back into the Porsche and rumble off toward the military barracks. He waved out the top of the small car until he vanished behind a row of long, low buildings.

The army pilot, Major McNally of the Washington National Guard, met her in the small waiting room as she entered.

"Dr. Devane? We'll be taking off in about an hour—if you could board in the next thirty minutes, I'd appreciate it."

"Sure, Major. Thanks for making room for me."

He waved off her thanks. "I'm glad for the company. Otherwise, it would be just Petey, Sparks, and me. In fact, we have room in the cockpit if you'd like to ride up in front. The view is better—that is, except that you have to look at us pilots."

She laughed. "Thanks. I'd like that. I promise not to get in the way."

Sixty-seven minutes later, she was buckled in to the fourth seat in the cockpit. By turning her head, she could get a good view out the front of the aircraft—which was a rather disconcerting vantage point as the huge refueling tanker roared down the runway with every indication of rolling headlong into the Atlantic Ocean. Finally, Major McNally eased the stick back, gently lifting off just a few seconds before the end of the runway.

Alex took a deep breath and leaned back against the headrest. The aircraft angled sharply upward, and she saw the immaculate sky stretching across her entire field of vision. They climbed higher, and the blue grew deeper until, at the apex, there was just a suggestion of the deep indigo emptiness of space.

Space Shuttle Discovery
75,000 miles from Earth

The approach was a delicate operation. Though they were far beyond the atmosphere, the shuttle still strained against the effects of Earth's gravity, effects that weakened as the small spacecraft flew farther and farther away from the world, although the pull never reached zero. There was plenty of fuel in the tanks, and when the shuttle flew past M1, coming as close as twenty thousand miles, Nate Hayes would turn the shuttle until it was coasting backward, then fire the rockets that would slow the shuttle's progess. Gradually the force of that burn would counteract the craft's momentum, bringing it to a halt—relative to its distance from Earth—then slowly starting it homeward again.

At least, that was the plan. If the rockets misfired, or the directional computers erred, or any other of a thousand things went wrong, momentum would carry them away from the Earth, past the Martian anomaly, past the moon, into the lonely graveyard of space.

Sitting in the captain's chair, Hayes looked out the window. There was no moon in view, it being on the far side of the Earth just then, and because of the orientation of the ship he couldn't see any sign of home. Instead, there was the void of dark space, with one object, visible to the naked eye, much closer than anything else out there.

Even so, the Martian projectile was still no more than a speck of light, a little brighter than a bright star, but not identifiable in terms of shape or color, yet. Ironically, though the Hubble telescope was more than a hundred thousand miles farther away from M1, the astronauts got their best views from images beamed earthward from the giant space telescope, then relayed up to the shuttle from Mission Control in Houston.

"Any change in the data or the image?" Hayes asked.

Laura Daring, the photo specialist, had her eyes glued to a monitor just behind the pilot's chair. "None that I can see," she replied. "It looks that same dark red, maybe a few patches to suggest that the surface is irregular. Still coming on, in stable vertical orientation."

Nate pictured that flight path—M1 flew through space like a spear in steady flight, the long cylinder moving without any suggestion of pitch, yaw, or tumble. He looked at the bright speck, still indistinguishable from a bright star.

"Anybody object if we try to get in a little closer?" he asked. He knew that his two crew mates shared his displeasure at the twenty-thousand-mile barrier. Nate Hayes felt certain that he could guide the shuttle much closer than that, providing them, and by communication relay Houston, with a much better look.

"You're the boss," said Jack Wheeler, copilot and radio operator. "I'll try to run interference with the folks down below if their ulcers start acting up." Wheeler glanced over at the pilot, his expression wary. "Of course, I won't be able to help you much, once we get back onto the ground."

"*If* we get back on the ground, they can lock me up in Leavenworth for the rest of my life. We came up here to do a flyby, and by God I intend to do a flyby!"

"Roger that, Captain," Daring said. "I wouldn't mind a close look at the son of a bitch myself."

Nate was already punching keys, typing new instructions to the computers that steered the ship. They all felt the gentle pulse of the steering rockets, the sideways acceleration. The rockets burned for about thirty seconds, then ceased, and the shuttle's course was changed, angling much closer to the path of the speeding M1.

"Discovery, we are showing a burn," came the tinny voice from Houston, pausing, for a beat. "And a resulting course alteration. Explain."

"We're taking her in for a better look," Hayes replied. "Will maintain safety parameters."

"Negative, Discovery. That is 'negative.' Return to original bearing. You are authorized to make that burn immediately."

The pilot gestured to his earphones, looked at Wheeler, and shrugged.

"We have a fault in the com-link," the copilot declared into his own mic. "Will update at earliest opportunity." He turned off the switch and looked at Hayes calmly. "Well, maybe we can be cellmates at Leavenworth," he suggested.

"Guys, take a look." The urgency of Laura Daring's voice cut through the pilots' chatter. She was no longer looking at her monitor, but at the image outside of the shuttle's front window.

"That sucker has started to tumble," Hayes said, as his throat tightened, anticipation and fear pumping adrenaline through his bloodstream.

It was within their clear view: the long cylinder, no longer straight and level like a spear, but starting a regal spin, coming to the perpendicular, still tumbling until the end that had been the stern became the bow.

Nate shivered—what was happening? He couldn't see, but he sensed the danger on a visceral level. And he knew there was nothing he could do.

The device vanished in an abrupt burst of energy as the whole cylinder became, in the space of a few nanoseconds, a pulse of sheer, unimaginable power. That energy traveled at the speed of light, much faster than human thought, let alone physical reaction. Thus the three astronauts did not have time even to begin mentally processing the incredible brightness that seared their retinas, baked their flesh to ash, dissolved that ash into atoms. Simultaneously it melted the little tin can of a spaceship that surrounded them, dispersing the metal, glass, fuel, plastic, and everything else into cosmic dust. Discovery and her crew were, simply, gone.

Gone.

Nanoseconds later the electromagnetic wave, a pulse of incredible electrical energy following the original burst, reached the place where Discovery had been. But it passed through only the dispersed atoms that had once been three human beings and a splendid example of their species' greatest technology.

Unimpeded by space or atmosphere, the wave of energy swept onward, filling the skies in an eye blink with a brightness that, for an instant, was greater than the sun's. It flashed down, down to the blue-green planet spinning naked and vulnerable below, an electromagnetic pulse of nearly a million volts, flickering across all the facing surface of the world.

Washington National Guard KC-135
Above the Outer Banks, North Carolina

Alexandria was looking out the side window of the large airplane's cockpit, admiring the sparkles on the wave tops, the full extent of the Atlantic sweeping limitlessly to the east. For just an instant the view washed out, a tremendous brightness making her blink. White spots lingered on the inside of her eyelids, like someone had popped a camera strobe right in front of her face.

"Holy shit! Did you see that?" the copilot asked. The plane gave a sudden lurch, and he grabbed for the controls.

"—the fuck?" Major McNally was already wrestling with his own stick. He pulled back, his eyes scanning the bank of instruments. "We've lost stabilizer controls—engine monitors are out—shit, we've lost damn near everything!"

The plane banked more sharply, and Alex jerked against her seat belt. Without that buckled strap she would have fallen headlong into the cockpit wall. Clutching the armrests of her chair, she clenched her teeth and accidentally bit her tongue. The iron taste of blood was a real sensation, and she focused on it, closing her eyes and listening as the pilots grappled with massive system failures. She couldn't stand not seeing for more than a few seconds, so she looked on helplessly, watched the radio operator fumble with his microphone and frequency dials.

"Mayday! Mayday! Flight 43099 inbound to Dulles, emergency on board! Repeat, emergency on board," he declared, firmly but with surprising calm. Then he looked up in astonishment, his eyes meeting Alex's.

"What is it?" she demanded. Already the kernel of the idea had taken root in her mind. Sparks turned a switch, and the radio came over the cockpit speaker. It was only white noise, a wash of crackling static. There was not a radio signal to be heard.

"The flash?" Alex asked.

"Yes," Sparks answered. "It fucked us up good."

Meanwhile, the KC-135 continued to angle downward, dipping into a steeper and steeper dive. McNally and his copilot strained at their sticks, pulling back in a physical test of strength—with all of their lives riding on the results.

And Alex feared that, all over the Western Hemisphere, aircraft were plummeting toward the ground.

Dan Ryan Expressway
Chicago, Illinois

Dennis Black was late for a meeting, and the traffic on the Dan Ryan wasn't doing anything to help his blood pressure. He stepped on the gas, maneuvering his Beemer over to the left lane for a quick spurt, back into the middle after he passed a half dozen cars and a large RV. He flashed past a SPEED LIMIT: 55 MPH sign, running in the stream of traffic at seventy, looking for another opening, a gap where he could pick up a couple hundred yards.

The big camper settled into his rearview mirror as all three lanes closed in. It was a Swan Song, he noted, top of the line for one of his competitors. He sneered at the reflection, remembering the smell of diesel as he had passed the behemoth. The real money was in gasoline-engine RVs, he knew. You'd have to be a goddamned truck driver to want to chug around in one of those Swan Songs.

Black himself dealt only with the Winnebago line. First, and still the best, in the modern RV market, he was fond of saying. It was that prominence, in fact, that had him racing down the freeway toward the Loop, an important conference in the Hancock Building waiting in the balance. Black's dealership was completely out of inventory, and unless he could pry another dozen machines—or, even better, twice that number—from these greedy, gouging distributors, he might as well hang an OUT OF BUSINESS sign on the gateway to his empty lot.

Of course, the last week had been the best week of business in Dennis

Black's long career, a career marked by dramatic peaks and, somewhat less frequently, deep valleys. He was never willing to compromise on his principles, and his principles always involved wringing the last dollar of profit out of every transaction. In times of slow sales, Black suffered, because it wasn't hard for his competitors to beat his prices.

But in times of high demand, Dennis Black had learned that the customers would always beat a path to his door. And never, not once in the history of the recreational vehicle industry, had there been demand like there had been since the Martian space bombs had been spotted. People had cashed in their life savings, mortgaged their houses—those lucky enough to get into the jammed banks—and hocked the family jewels in order to buy something they could drive out of the city. And live in, if it came to that.

Black wasn't worried about Martians. When the time was right, the United States Air Force would knock the bastards out of the skies. But it wouldn't come to that. Dennis Black knew hype when he heard it, and the Martian bullshit was all hype. And he knew how to make hype work for him. Finally, his inventory was gone and, since he regularly made an extra ten thousand or more in profit compared to his competitors, he was sitting squarely on top of the figurative pyramid formed, in Black's mind, by the treacherous, shifting heap of Midwest RV dealers. But he had nothing left to sell!

That thought, as if undetached from the rest of his central nervous system, caused his foot to press harder on the accelerator. At the same time there was a flash of light across the world, in Chicago muted by a gray overcast but nevertheless observed by many of the people sharing the road with Dennis Black. So intent was he on his impending plans, on the arm-twisting negotiations that would net him more products for his sales lot, that he failed to notice the brightness that, in any event, instantaneously faded away.

He did notice the Beemer's engine falter, first the lack of response to the accelerator, then in the sudden silence as the radio failed, the engine quit, and the fast car started to coast. Red taillights flashed on all over the place, and he wrenched the wheel, stomping his own foot on the brakes. Shit! Cars veered from the lanes to either side, everybody struggling for control, skidding and decelerating. A few people bailed onto the shoulders while others braked as hard as they could.

Even those on the Dan Ryan who saw the flash didn't know what it was, didn't understand the electromagnetic pulse of pure energy that washed across Chicago and North America and nearly half of the planet's surface. They didn't understand that the flash of focused power had shorted out, melted down, *burned*, every chip of computer circuitry that it touched. This included the chips that controlled the fuel injection and electronic ignition systems of more than 95 percent of the cars on the freeway, every automobile made in nearly the last two decades.

The engines in those cars all quit, the stream of vehicles traveling at seventy miles an hour suffering nearly universal failure. But not quite: many of the big trucks, their older diesels unaffected, barreled along with full velocity as their drivers reacted with varying quickness to cars abruptly disabled on all sides. A string of crashes began immediately, trucks rolling over the suddenly stopping automobiles cramming three, four, even five lanes of traffic.

The driver of the Swan Song, the diesel-powered RV barreling down on Black's stalled Beemer, was busy eating a sandwich. Not only had he missed the Martian flash, he didn't even see the brake lights.

LAX Control Tower
Los Angeles, California

Moses Ryan took a sip of his coffee—already cold, of course—and looked at the blips on the Big Screen. Scores of planes were in the air in the immediate vicinity of the massive airport, but so far the chaotic choreography of the air transportation system seemed to be holding. A JAL 747 inbound from Tokyo was approaching the main runway, with a British Airways DC10 from Singapore barely a minute behind. An Airbus from Australia queued up just beyond.

Other planes from across North and Central America and the whole Pacific basin were queuing up in the sky, while more than three dozen massive jetliners were lined on the taxiways, waiting for clearance to take off. A United plane destined for Buenos Aires cleared the runway, soaring past Vista Del Mar and into the skies over the blue ocean. Twenty seconds later a Midwest DC9 heading to Denver accelerated along the same swath of asphalt.

The pilots did their parts, the controllers did theirs, and Moses Ryan sat back and watched. The best workdays were those when he didn't have to do anything else. He was rewarding himself with a fresh cup of coffee, his back to the banks of wide windows, so he missed seeing the bright flash of the Pulse. Even so, his eyes registered the instantaneous flicker in the bright, daylit room.

"What the hell?"

"Did you see that?"

The controllers at the windows were blinking, shielding their eyes, and Ryan knew he had not imagined the flash.

"Ouch!" shouted one of the radio operators, pulling his headphones off, shaking his head. Other techs snatched at switches and dials as an explosion of white noise crackled through the lines.

"My monitor's down—shit, they're all out!" Controllers reflexively tapped at keyboards, or stared helplessly out the huge, green-tinted windows.

Moses Ryan was watching the BA-bound 747. Already two miles out from the shore, the big airplane had just commenced its gentle, climbing turn to port, banking slightly and accelerating toward the destination a long continent away. Now the massive jet's climb faltered as the bank grew steeper, more pronounced. Ryan whispered a prayer as he saw the ship level off unsteadily, far short of cruising altitude. With elegant majesty, like a classical actor in a Greek tragedy, the huge plane dipped a wing in a graceful bow and fell from the sky, going sideways into the ocean and vanishing in a plume of spray.

Closer to home, the Midwest DC9 was crippled as it roared toward take-off. Instead of flying, it skidded past the end of the runway and into the flat scrubland. The landing gear collapsed and the aircraft bumped and scraped to a stop, friction being the only thing that prevented it from sliding right into the ocean. Next Ryan felt a shock through the soles of his feet, a thud too sharp and brittle to come from an earthquake. Even before he heard Janice Mueller, the senior controller, sob in dismay, he knew what had happened.

He turned to see a massive fireball surging into the sky, eye level to the control tower and still climbing, marking the place where the British Airways DC10 had gone in. Behind that crash a Qantas Airbus went straight down, as if all semblance of control had been lost. With nearly drained fuel tanks, it landed with a shattered collision, but few flames. Another airliner, a Boeing 767, veered past, the pilot obviously struggling with sluggish controls, desperately trying to bring his aircraft out of the landing pattern.

Somehow he succeeded, the huge aircraft roaring past the control tower a couple of hundred feet off the ground. With a clumsy lurch, the 767 started to gain altitude as it flew back over the ocean it had just traversed.

But the next aircraft was not so lucky, its pilot perhaps not so experienced. Within that ship, as elsewhere, the Pulse had destroyed each link of computer circuitry, every chip and bit and processor. The big jet engines continued to roar, as hungry for fuel as ever, but the myriad controls and monitors, from landing gear warning lights to automatic aileron settings, all failed at once. The new pilot overcorrected for the loss of his flaps, and instead of gaining altitude, the 737 nosed over and smashed into the ground in a full-power dive.

Though every aircraft was affected, most pilots still retained some semblance of control—their flight sticks and pedals were connected to flaps and rudders with actual cables and, even without computer-aided electronic circuitry, the ships responded, albeit sluggishly, to attempts at control. Others, including some of the most modern airliners in the world, were guided via "fly-by-wire" technology, wherein all of the connections between pilot and guidance/steering mechanisms were electronic, not physical. With the shorting out of all the electronic circuitry, those pilots had absolutely no way to influence the performance of their planes. If a fly-by-wire aircraft was airborne at the time of the Pulse, it was doomed.

Around LAX, huge, black columns of smoke rose from three, then five, crashes. Sick to his stomach, Ryan knew that more than a thousand people had just died, right in front of him. No, *lots* more than that—he remembered the 747 that had gone into Santa Monica Bay. He turned, looking back to the west, was almost numb as he took note of two more smoke pillars near the shore.

All the monitors were silent, the radios buzzing with static broken only by a few pops and crackles. The sky was still filled with airplanes, each with a finite supply of fuel, each crippled by multiple systems failures. They would all have to come down within the next few hours, some of them in the next thirty minutes. Some would land, some would crash.

And there was nothing he could do about it.

Boston Memorial Hospital
Boston, Massachusetts

The intensive care unit was shielded in the middle of the building, no windows to reveal the sudden flash. High walls, even brick or steel, were no barriers to the Pulse, however. The failure of all digital and computerized equipment was instantaneous, and complete.

The first to die was a patient undergoing a heart transplant. Even as the emergency lights came on and backup power systems took over, the computerized motherboard in the heart/lung machine, the sophisticated device that had been pumping his blood during the procedure, failed. The perfusionist cried out in frustration, frantically punching buttons, turning switches, as the patient's circulation failed. Even the best efforts of a tremendously skilled surgical team could not start a heart in a chest where no heart currently resided.

Breathers, medication applicators, dialysis machines, a vast array of monitors and automation and essential, life-giving care, everything that relied upon computer circuitry or even moderately complicated electronics, was brought to a standstill. Automatic medication dispensers ceased to function, X-ray and CAT scan machines went dark, arthroscopic scalpels lost their cameras in the midst of crucial procedures.

As his respirator failed, an old man slowly suffocated. A woman, hooked to a kidney dialysis machine, didn't even know that the blood coming back into her body was the same poisoned plasma that had flowed out a few minutes before. Nurses ran from station to station, increasingly frightened and despairing, while doctors sewed and stitched, administered CPR, tried to restore heartbeats and respiration.

And patients continued to die.

Kennedy Space Center
Cape Canaveral, Florida

Duke Hayes was strapped into his Warthog. The steady roar of the twin General Electric turbofan engines vibrated through the fuselage, gave him confidence that his A10 was ready to vault into the skies. His helmet was on, his goggles secure over his eyes, and he touched base with the small control tower on the Cape.

"A10 Alpha Beta, you will be cleared in another few minutes. We have a couple of thirsty Tomcats coming ashore."

"Roger, Cape Tower. I'll take in the view."

Hayes leaned back in his seat. Perched above the nose of the big airplane, he had a good vantage. He saw the F14s flying side by side, noses pitched in the air, landing gear fixed and ready. They were coming in low and steady from the ocean—he wondered if they had catapulted off of a carrier that morning.

The Pulse was everywhere for that instant, then gone. To the pilot it was something that he felt all the way to his gut. It was light, of course, but it was also sound—a *crack* sparked loudly in his earphones and left a wash of white noise. His airplane reacted in ways that he didn't immediately understand—his targeting and weapons systems failed, all the lights blinking off. Gauges went to zero, readings went blank, and his gyroscope, GPS, and a host of other useful, computerized components went kaput.

But the flash had barely faded from Duke's retinas before his eyes were on the Tomcats, his hand clenched unconsciously around his own stick. The Navy fighters shuddered in the wake of the Pulse, both noses dropping sharply. The first one landed, bounced high, and landed again, finally steadying to race down the runway.

The second F14 was not so fortunate. It came in with a little yaw—"Pull up!" Hayes shouted into his own sealed cockpit—and landed only on the port gear. Overcorrecting, the pilot lost control and the fighter bounced and tumbled, cartwheeling by the time it next came down. The A10 pilot was still shouting advice, pounding his fist against his knee, as the Tomcat came apart. The wings and fuselage crumpled and broke, while the armored cockpit broke free to roll like a deformed bowling ball chasing the wingman down the long, flat runway.

Only when it stopped rolling did Duke notice that his own engines, those steady and reliable GE 'fans, had fallen utterly silent.

CNN Headquarters
Atlanta, Georgia

Rick Chalmers straightened his tie, but had his hands flat on the news desk as the camera light blinked red. He stared into the lens, reaching out to tens of millions of viewers. This projection of himself was a trick he had always possessed, since his first teenage video clips, but never before had it felt so perfect, so sublime.

It was the Martians, he realized. They had brought the people of Earth closer together, united mankind in a sense of mission as nothing in history ever had before. He wished, now, that he had something new to share with those people, the citizens of a nation and world who were desperate for each new tidbit of news. Unfortunately, it was only a recap of the last twelve hours' status quo. He read the words on the TelePrompTer and brought them every ounce of immediacy he could.

"The space object known as M1 continues to close upon our world this evening. The space shuttle Discovery is now some seventy-five thousand miles away from Earth, aligned to pass M1 in a little more than four hours. We're going to go to Jay Manstein in Houston. Jay? Anything new to add?"

The balding reporter's face, unusually serious, filled the screen. Behind him was the steel-and-glass tower of a NASA control building. "Rick, they're pretty tight-lipped around here. The M-objects continue to close with our world on a steady bearing, with no alterations in speed. As you stated, the shuttle Discovery is closing fast on its unprecedented mission. Everyone from the Pentagon to NASA to the JPL is pretty much holding their breath, waiting to see what kind of data those brave astronauts in that little ship can send home."

"Thanks, Jay." Chalmers was back on-screen. Looking grave—it required no effort that day—he turned his attention back to the Tele-PrompTer.

"Thus far—"

He faltered as the graphic text image blanked out, then remembered the story from thirty minutes earlier. "—there has been no reaction, no sign of energy emission or any other activity . . ."

He trailed off. It wasn't just the TelePrompTer—his picture had vanished from the nearest monitor. The emergency lights in the studio flashed on, but Chalmers could see several monitors, each a screen of gray snow. One by one those images faded to dead, still blackness.

"We've lost the satellite," announced one of the producers. "Something has just knocked us off the air. All our computer systems have crashed."

"Well, go for the magnetic tapes then!" snapped the anchorman. "Dig them out and get this place up and running the old-fashioned way!"

The producer, fresh out of college and some three decades younger than Chalmers, looked at him blankly, so the anchorman amplified. "The old man has them stored in a safe—he calls it the Armageddon Vault. Supposedly he's had them there for years, in case the end of the world comes along and we need to stay on the air. I guess this is as close as we're likely to get—so hop to it! We should be able to do *something* with the old technology!"

"Right, Rick—people, let's get on it! Samantha—get up to the archives. Joe, Stu—pull out those cables and hook up to the old reel-to-reel!"

It was the show's director, taking control. She was ashen, sweat shining on her forehead, but her voice barked in tones of steady command.

"Let's see if we can't get this dog and pony show back on the air!"

Washington National Guard KC-135
Approaching Dulles International Airport, Washington, DC

"Okay, if you have any pull with God, now is the time to call in your debts," Major McNally said.

"I've said every prayer that I know. That wasn't many, so I did a few extra off the cuff," Alex told him.

She could see the airport by then, a crisscrossing net of runways scarring the wooded countryside of Virginia. A dozen or more columns of dark smoke marked the environs, and she didn't have to ask to know that each marked a place where an aircraft had gone down.

McNally had proven himself a master at operating the big KC-135. After the initial systems failures caused by the Pulse, he had leveled them off and flown, slowly and steadily, toward Dulles. With no instruments or radio, only a limited command of the most rudimentary controls, they followed the familiar coastline toward Chesapeake Bay and up the Potomac River. By the time they were over Virgina, Sparks had replaced a burned-out circuit board in the radio, but had yet to establish contact with any kind of signal, much less the control tower of the big airport. Either the radio still didn't work, or nobody was broadcasting on any channel.

They had more fuel than a lot of airliners flying at the time of the Pulse, so they circled for two hours, waiting for a gap in the crowd of ungainly, barely controlled airliners. All of them had to land, and none of them could communicate with the ground controllers, or with the other aircraft, so it was a dangerous dance. Every minute or so another pilot would guide his plane in to claim the landing approach. McNally was content to yield under the assumption that fuel was running low in many of the civilian planes.

Holding a reasonably steady circle now, the pilot looked over his shoulder at Alex and raised his eyebrows. "Dr. DeVane—you're a NASA scientist, right? So tell me, what the hell do you think is going on? This is the Martians fucking with us, isn't it?"

In between her prayers, she had been giving a lot of thought to that question. She had checked her cell phone, found that the screen was utterly blank, learned that the radio operator's phone had suffered the same fate. And she had begun to form a hypothesis.

"Have you noticed the highways down there?" she asked. They were passing over an eight-lane freeway where the impact of the Pulse was obvious: The roadway was crowded with cars and trucks, none of them moving. Numerous vehicles had slid down the shoulders, parked haphazardly, or been pushed sideways by minor wrecks. Some of the wrecks were not so minor. In several places lingering smudges of smoke indicated the aftermath of automobile fires.

"I think they hit us with an energy weapon, an electromagnetic pulse. It's not that radical a concept. We have EMP weapons ourselves, the big ones capable of knocking out all the electronics in an area several city blocks across. The one the Martians set off, of course, must be many orders of magnitude more powerful. I'm afraid it might have wiped out computers, radios, automobiles, God only knows what else, across a very large area."

"How can something *do* that?"

"You might compare it to a lightning strike nearby when your computer is online. It can do a lot of damage." She was about to explain that she didn't know the specifics, just that it was an extreme power surge that would be picked up by antennas, wires, cables, and other metallic conductors. But she saw McNally's attention suddenly rivet to his flying, and she suspected—correctly—that he had seen an opportunity to land.

They closed in on the airport rapidly, descending. Alex noticed an unusual sight: lots of airplanes parked around the green space beyond the runways. The tiny dots trailing away from many of them, she realized, were long files of passengers who had debarked and were making the long trek toward the terminal building. As they came in she tried not to look at the smoking wrecks, one of which was right at the end of a runway. Strangely, there were only a few fire trucks, and no ambulances, at the scene.

She got a glimmering of this new truth as they passed over the airport access road.

Then the runway was beneath them. The 135 touched down hard, jolted upward, and very slowly rolled to a stop. The people walking beside the runway didn't even look up as the big airplane rolled past. Looking around for just a few seconds, Alex counted dozens of planes, estimated thousands of passengers, embarked on this bizarre odyssey.

"Doc, I guess you were a good luck charm," said the major, turning around to shake her hand. "Thanks."

"Major—thank you," she replied. "It's not an exaggeration to say that you saved my, saved all of our, lives."

"So what do you think happens now?" asked the pilot.

She drew a breath and shook her head. "I'm not sure. But I think all of the rules have changed."

Space
Approximately 5,000,000 miles from Earth

The first cylinder had been reduced to a speckled array of microscopic atoms, essentially vaporized by the burst of energy that blasted across nearly half of the planet's surface. Those atoms zipped through space, unconnected and dispersing, and would play no further part in this story.

The second and third cylinders, each identical in structure and purpose to the first, continued on, their missions as yet unfulfilled. At a rate of more than a hundred thousand miles per hour, they sped toward the Earth, awaiting only the right moments for activation and self-destruction.

It was the fourth cylinder, no longer tracked by the neutralized electronic systems on the target planet, that first began to display signs of a more subtle eventual purpose. Differing from the flat caps at both ends of the first three cylinders, it and the later vessels were marked by great, convex bulges on the fore and aft sections of the metallic device. Now, these curved surfaces began to open, layer upon layer peeling away to reveal a dark, cavernous interior.

When the two end caps had curled away, the long side of the cylinder began to open as well, the movements gradual and deliberate in the soundless vacuum of space. As they came apart, smaller objects became visible, silver canisters that had been borne in the belly of the great mother ship.

They lay there like peas in a pod, or—more ominously—cartridges in the magazine of a very powerful weapon. Glinting with silver metal, each of them was a cylinder in its own right. Clustered together, for the time being, they continued to speed toward the blue-green planet that was still spinning sublimely in its orbit around the sun.

BOOK II
INVASION

ONE

June
Delbrook Lake, Wisconsin

My television popped loudly, and the picture vanished, the image replaced by snow, the sound limited to an irritating crackle. Slowly even that fizzled away until the screen was dark, the speakers silent. Only as I was snatching up the remote, belatedly hitting *mute*, did my brain process another fleeting perception, more of a question than a certainty:

Had something happened outside?

Clouds of steel gray formed a low ceiling, and the afternoon light was unusually dim. No storm lingered in that overcast, yet it contained an unmistakable threat of rain—or worse. And it had grown brighter for just a second, I could swear. It happened at the same instant the TV had failed.

I made the connection at once, viscerally and intellectually: This was an attack by the Martians. Strangely enough, I didn't feel any significant agitation or alarm. If anything, it was a relief to know that this was going to be war. I put my hand to my wrist, counted my heartbeats—fast, but steady—and exhaled slowly. The first volley had been exchanged, and I was unscathed.

Then I started to ponder the nature of the attack, and fear grew inside me. *How* had the Martians broken my television? What else had they destroyed in that nanosecond of flash? I hurried to my computer, turned it on. The fan hummed when I pushed the power switch, but there was nothing else, not even a flicker on the screen. I picked up my cordless phone, heard nothing, no sound even when I punched the *on* button several times. Remembering the old model in my bedroom, a phone where the handset was connected to the base by a cord, I hurried to try and and was comforted by the sound of a dial tone as soon as I lifted it to my ear. Checking my cell phone, I saw that it, like the computer, was utterly dead—I couldn't even get the welcome screen when I turned it on.

Alexandria! Where was she? What was she doing? I lunged for the bedside phone, punched a call to the only number I had memorized, my daughter's cell phone . . . and even as I finished dialing I knew that her phone, like mine, would be dead. I finished dialing, relishing each chirping tone as I pressed the keys. I waited, but nothing happened. There was no error tone, busy signal, no indication that some piece of equipment out there knew that I was trying to make a phone call.

The electricity was still on, I noticed with some surprise. I checked in the kitchen: my microwave was out, the display dark, as was the digital timer on the oven. The heating element still worked, as did the electric stove. Conversely, I couldn't get the programmable coffeemaker to turn on. I took out the cheap pocket calculator I used when paying my bills, pushed the *on* button. Nothing happened. Feeling a little more frantic I returned to the living room. No computer, no TV—how could I find out what was happening?

I thought of the radio and went to my sound system, which I wasn't surprised to find nonfunctional. Another radio? I went and looked at the digital clock radio beside my bed: it was dark. Spurred by a sudden memory, I ran down into the basement, found the old, dusty boom box that I hadn't listened to in years. Karen used to use it outside when she worked on the gardens. The antenna had broken off and I had bought a replacement, but never attached it. The power cord was wrapped around the hooks at the back, but not plugged into the machine or the wall.

I attached the cord and turned the power switch, and felt almost weak with relief when I heard the crackling hiss from the speakers. It worked, at least! Digging through my drawers of parts, I found a small screw and took it, the radio, and the replacement antenna back upstairs. My hands were shaking as I screwed the antenna on and plugged it in again.

Now, was there anybody broadcasting? I tried not to think about that terrifying question as I balanced the boom box on the snack bar, extending the telescoping whip of the antenna. Sitting on one of the stools, I slowly started to adjust the tuning dial, leaning close to the sputtering speaker, straining for some distinguishable sounds. Turning the dial steadily, I moved up and down the FM spectrum. Nowhere was there anything that caused that steady hiss of white noise to waver. Fighting off my growing apprehension I switched to AM, and started the same procedure all over again.

There was nobody out there—at least, nobody who was sending out a radio signal in the normal bands.

It shouldn't have been a surprise, but when the lights went out and the radio faded away I just stood still, stunned and disbelieving. Of course my electricity had failed; in a sense, it was surprising that it had lasted as long as it had. I paced to the window, watching the glowering clouds. It was much darker than it normally would be at six o'clock on a June evening.

The phone in my bedroom rang, a jarring intrusion into the silence. Like a maniac I raced through the house, stumbling over one of the bar stools in the kitchen, staying on my feet to race into the bedroom by the third ring. Gingerly I lifted the phone from its cradle.

"Hello?"

"Hi, Mark? Mr. DeVane? This is Dan Browne, your neighbor. Sorry to bother you, but did your power just go out?"

"Power?" I almost laughed. "The power is the least of it—didn't you see?"

"See what?" He sounded curious, not alarmed. "I was in my basement workshop, sawing some lumber for my new garage. I had the table saw and the router on when everything shut down. I was afraid I blew out the power to my whole house."

"No, it wasn't you, Mr. Browne. It was the Martians."

"What do you mean? What the hell did the Martians do?"

"I'm not sure, but I think it was an electromagnetic pulse," I explained, trying to clarify it in my own mind. "I've heard about it, an effect of a nuclear explosion or some other kind of weapon. There was a bright flash, and everything that I own that has a computer chip failed. All the radio stations are off the air. Cell phones, calculators—toast."

I pictured him wrestling with his skepticism. Would he have to try and turn on his own computer before he believed me?

"You're—you're *not* kidding, are you?"

"No, Mr. Browne. I'm not kidding."

"Come to think of it, I was using my newfangled level, you know, one o' them digital ones? Couldn't get the damned thing to work a few minutes ago, and thought I had a bad battery in there."

"Computer chips—fried," I guessed.

"Why does the phone work?" he challenged.

"I assume you're calling from a phone with a cord, right?"

"Yes."

"Well, my cordless phone isn't working, but the one connected to the phone lines by a wire is. You know how, even when there was a power failure, the phones would still work?"

"Yeah, sure. I get it. But . . . well, what about airplanes? Cars? Have you tried to start your car?"

"No, I haven't," I admitted.

"Try it," he said. "I will, too. I'll call you back in a few minutes."

The phone went dead in my hand, though that dial tone was still reassuring. I shrugged off my initial resentment at his order—trying our cars was a good idea. I went out to the garage and pressed the automatic opener before I remembered that it wouldn't work without electricity. I got into my late-model sedan—a very boring old man's car, Alexandria had teased—and put the key in the ignition. Taking a breath, I turned it, heard the whirr of the starter motor turning the engine over.

But there was no ignition. I cranked it as long as I dared, before I shut it off. I didn't want to run the battery down completely—somewhere in the back of my mind was the thought that, someday not too long away, the electricity stored in the car battery might be something I needed. Besides, it had always started in the first second or two, so I didn't need further proof to convince myself that it was disabled.

Back in the house, I stared at the phone, willing it to ring, Browne confirming for me that his car was also dead. But it sat there, silently, for several more minutes. I was on the point of reaching for my phone book, looking up my neighbor's number, when I heard the basso rumble of a vehicle engine, poorly muffled, outside. Looking out the kitchen window, I saw Browne's Jeep coming up my driveway. It was a silly-looking contraption, with rust holes in the body, no top, and tires that were almost ludicrously too big for the little body. But it was moving.

I was out the door and down the steps by the time he pulled up before my house.

"It runs!" I exclaimed, almost giddy with the knowledge.

"Yours doesn't?" Browne asked, shutting it off and climbing out through the low door. Because of the big tires, he had to step down a ways just to reach the ground.

I shook my head in reply. "No."

"Neither did my Chevy. It would crank, but not fire. Only two years old, too. Still under warranty."

"How come your Jeep still runs?"

"This EMP thing. You said it would fry all the computer chips?"

"That's my understanding," I replied cautiously. "Of course, I was hearing about man-made weapons, something capable of taking out the electronics in a few city blocks. This Martian attack might be as different in nature as it is in scope."

"I don't think so." He clapped the hood, pocked with rust and painted—if you could call it "paint"—with a different color of brown than the rest of the vehicle. "This ol' bitch is so damned old that she doesn't have a computer chip anywhere in there. It's got a coil to make the spark, and a carburetor to feed the gas into the engine. Your car, and my Chevy, get better mileage, start faster, and run cleaner, 'cuz they have electronic ignitions and fuel injectors. Most every car made in the last fifteen years uses electronic ignition. Carburetors are a thing of the past. Wonderful thing, fuel injection. Except—"

"It needs a computer to control it?" I guessed, strangely eager to show him that I wasn't a complete ignoramus.

"Exactly!"

"So all the modern cars out there on the road, they're all disabled by the EMP?"

He squinted at me. "You're the one who told me about that," Browne said. "And if it's really what you say it is, that's probably right."

I looked at him, scrutinized him in a way I never had before. He was a little older than I, though probably not quite sixty yet. Lines that looked like they owed more to laughter than tribulation creased his face around his eyes and his mouth. A brushy gray mustache bristled, too unkempt, on his upper lip, and his shaggy gray hair covered his ears and spilled over the collar of his denim shirt. His humanity was a comfort. I dwelled on that image, allowing him to project strength, calm, competence.

"What do you suggest we do about this whole thing?" he asked, facing the woods but looking at me out of the corner of his eyes.

The question took me by surprise. "Well, I've got to get in touch with my daughter," I said. "And then I . . . I don't know. Wait and see what happens, I guess."

He nodded at my house. It was beginning to look ominous and dark as the sunset progressed into twilight. "You got food? Water? Candles?"

"Yes. I even have a generator. I bought it a couple of years ago, when the spring floods kept taking out our power lines." In a flash of panic I wondered if the generator, too, had some computerized circuitry. To the best of my knowledge, it didn't: it was simply a gasoline engine rigged up to some sort of electricity-making device. I pulled the cord, the engine ran, and if I plugged it in to my home circuit it gave me enough juice to run a few appliances like my refrigerator, water pump, lights, and computer. Of course, I wouldn't need power for the computer . . . the thought made me feel a little dizzy.

"Well, I'll be okay, too, for the time being. Don't have a daughter to call. Or anyone, really." He looked at me, frankly. "What about a gun? You got one?"

Mutely I shook my head, still thinking about Alexandria. She had wanted me to get a gun. How in the world was I going to reach her?

"Why don't you come over to my place, and I'll loan you one—say the .20 gauge. That's easy to handle, not too much kick."

"No!" I said reflexively, but then I started to think. "That is, why would you do that?"

He shrugged, apparently embarrassed. "Well, looks like it's you and me, alone out here on this country road. Let's just say I like the thought that someone with a gun might be guarding my back."

Browne stuck out his hand and I shook it, comforted by the strength, the workman's callus on his rough palm. "And I'll do the same for you," he promised.

"All right. Thanks. Yes, I'll borrow your shotgun, if you don't mind."

"Well, it's too dark now to show you anything about shooting. Why don't you come over first thing in the morning, and I'll give you the compact course."

"Sure, yes. I'll come over." I was glad for that invitation, for at least one meaningful task that I could keep in front of me.

I was surprised at the loneliness I felt as I watched him drive away. I went inside, decided to start up the generator. It fired on the second pull and the little Briggs & Stratton engine chugged away reassuringly. With my refrigerator and freezer once again chilling, I felt a little better. I allowed myself a couple of lights in the kitchen, living room, and bedroom, then went back to the radio. Turning it on and spinning the volume up all the way, I rotated the dial with my thumb, quickly moving through the AM and FM frequencies.

But there was only that static, the cosmic snow. I sat down and began to change the frequencies much more slowly, as slowly as I could move the clumsy tuner. Again, the FM dial was silent. It was somewhere about 1100 Khz on the AM span that I heard the first sign of life, a break in the static. Hunching over, I touched the dial almost imperceptibly, seeking any clarity I could find. I wiggled the antenna, shifted the boom box on the counter. Slowly the hiss faded, and I began to make out a tinny voice.

". . . out there. I don't even know if anyone can hear me. I am in Dubuque, Iowa, KGHL broadcasting from the bluffs over the river. All our network feeds are off the air. Our main antenna went out, but Kim and me found some replacement parts in the storeroom. The dials say we're on the air, but don't have much of a signal. We're running on emergency power.

"No one can get their car started. The westbound side of the bridge over the Mississippi is blocked by a chain-reaction accident and a big fire. We think a gasoline truck exploded there, right after the flash."

He coughed slightly. I realized that he sounded very young, wondered if he was some intern working at the station, just watching the syndicated playlist. Whoever he was, he had had enough wherewithal to work some significant repairs. God, I was glad that he was on the air.

"The power is off in Dubuque. This station is broadcasting on a generator right now. Down on the river, there are a couple barges lining up at the one lock I can see from here. It hasn't opened in . . . well, since the flash. That was observed at 4:32 P.M. Central Time. Um. Two hours and thirty-two minutes ago," he clarified.

"Look," he said. He sounded like a teenager asking for an extension of his curfew. "I might have to go for a while. Check on my family and stuff. My car won't start so I have to go home. Kim already left, but when she gets back she'll get on the air. In the meantime I am going to play something so people who are looking will know we have a signal. Sorry about the quality—I have a little cassette player that I'm going to start up, next to this microphone. It has a one-hour tape of some old Smashing Pumpkins tunes. I hope Kim will be back before it runs out.

"Um, I will talk to you later. Good luck, everybody."

Sounds exploded loudly from the boom box, and I quickly turned down the volume. The music was not my cup of tea, but I left it on anyway. Somehow, a band named Smashing Pumpkins seemed fairly appropriate, under the circumstances.

June 4

I was eating breakfast cooked on my stove, with the generator providing power, when I heard the rumble of Browne's Jeep in my driveway. I shoveled in the last forkful of eggs and ran outside as he pulled right up to my front step.

"Hop in," he invited.

Somewhat awkwardly I climbed up into the Jeep's passenger seat. Fortunately, there was a handy bar to hold on to right in front of me, and I took it with both hands as Browne started his vehicle down my driveway.

"That's the 'Oh shit' bar," he said, nodding at my white knuckles. "If you hear me say 'Oh shit!,' then grab it and hang on tight." He tapped the accelerator, and the little vehicle surged through the kettle and up toward the lane. With another burst we sped along the road and quickly turned into his driveway. There he slowed as Galahad and Klondike came racing down from the porch, barking. The two dogs stationed themselves in front of the Jeep, bristling and barking and slowly backing up as my neighbor inched forward until he was able to park in front of his house.

"They mean well," he said apologetically. "I just hope they don't try to stop someone who's willing to run them over. I don't think they understand about cars."

Or property lines, I thought to myself, though I held my tongue as I dismounted and followed him inside. I was willing to call a truce with the dogs.

Browne's house was surprisingly well decorated, considering my impression of him as a rough-and-ready outdoorsman. His living room was tastefully decorated, with a rustic touch—hardwood floor and paneled walls—and leather furniture. His gun cabinet was shiny, dark wood. I was a little surprised when, right in front of me, he reached behind the big cabinet and pulled out a small key. Opening it, he selected the smaller of the two shotguns.

He held it sideways, extending it toward me. "Let's go out into the field. I'll show you how to load and shoot it."

"Okay," I agreed, taking the weapon. I was acutely conscious of the only gun safety rule I could remember: I shouldn't point the barrel at anything I didn't want to shoot. That was hard to do inside his house, so I settled for pointing it at the floor as he led me through the immaculate kitchen and onto his back porch. He pulled several boxes of shells off an upper shelf and handed me one. I was surprised at its leaden weight, though when I thought about it the heft made perfect sense.

We went out into his backyard. The dogs had apparently sensed our progress through the house, since they were waiting for us there. When they caught sight of the gun, Klondike started that deep "woof" of a bark I knew so well, while the poodle raced away from us, then streaked back, adding his own higher bark to the chorus. They both scrambled and bounced around underfoot, almost tripping me; but I forged ahead and found that they did get out of my way.

We went past his barn so that we faced only open pasture, a sweep of grassy ground rolling toward that hill where I had gone to observe Mars during what now seemed like a previous life. He showed me how to check the chamber, making sure the gun was unloaded, how to set the safety to on or off, and how to feed shells into the magazine until, with five rounds loaded, it was full. I cocked it once, loading a shell into the chamber, and he inserted one more into the magazine for a total of six.

"We won't worry about skeet—too hard to hit, and you can't learn much by missing a moving target with your first shots." I noticed that he was carrying a couple of beer cans. He took them forward, only about twenty paces or so, and set them on top of a pair of wooden fence posts.

"Try to knock them off," he said simply when he had returned to my side.

I raised the shotgun, sighted along the top of the barrel, and steadied myself. Drawing a deep breath, I pulled the trigger as I mentally braced for the discharge. Nothing happened; the trigger barely moved. Sheepishly, I remembered the safety, and pushed it over with my thumb. Once more I aimed, choosing the can to the right as my target, and tried to shoot.

There was a sharp explosion, and the gun leaped in my hands, bumping my shoulder with less kick than I had expected. The beer can, however, didn't move at all.

"Try again," Browne encouraged.

I popped off another shot and when that one also missed I fired again. The beer can vanished from the fencepost, and I felt an inordinate amount of pride. Without waiting for instructions I shifted targets and, with the second of two more shots, knocked the other can off the post.

"Not bad, for starters," Browne said. "We can pick up here some other time if you want to keep practicing. For now, I'll give you my boxes of .20-

gauge shells—I have a couple dozen of them. And you'll have a means of defending yourself."

"Okay. Thanks." I worked the pump a couple of times until I ejected the remaining shell from the magazine. We went back to the house so he could load a large box with shot and slug ammunition for the gun. He carried the heavy box to the Jeep while I took the gun. I was surprised by the feeling of security I got simply by holding the gun across my lap—with the barrel pointed out the side of the Jeep, of course.

Back in front of my house, we shook hands again, and I felt that sense of isolation again when he drove away. Slowly I entered the house, putting the gun and the ammunition down on the table in the front hall. It was only midmorning, and there was only one thing I could do: I went to the radio, hoping to find KGHL back on the air.

TWO

June 3
Dulles International Airport
Washington, DC

"I'm heading to the passenger terminal—my car is in the parking garage over there," Alexandria told Major McNally. "I don't suppose it will run, but I have to get a few things out of the trunk." She stood with the three National Guard officers on the tarmac under the massive KC-135.

"Good luck—we'll check in with the Air Force at the military terminal," the pilot replied.

"Good luck to you, too. We're all going to need it." She didn't even try to plan what she would do after she got to the Firebird—those long roadways filled with disabled cars painted a grim picture. Still, her plan was to try the ignition, steeling herself for failure. After that, she would decide what to do next.

She walked for nearly a mile across the neatly mowed grass alternating with wide strips of pavement where taxiways and alternate runways crossed. Occasionally a plane landed, only about one every five minutes, and she stayed well away from the main runway. Other airliners were parked all over, dotted here and there on the fringes of the airport, and many people were filing away from them, making their way toward the dark terminal. It was a strange and ghostly procession, people apparently too stunned and disoriented to be visibly agitated.

Alex avoided thinking about Duke. All she could do was worry—she knew that he had planned to take off sometime after she did, but had he been in the air during the Pulse? There was no way she could find out.

As if to fan her fears, the dozen or so huge fires around the airport continued to burn, each plume of smoke rising so high that it merged into the sky, a dark and ominous cloud. Alex tried not to look at them. But it was impossible not to look at the people filing miserably along, trickling from the airliners parked all around the airport. More and more of them converged along the edge of the runway, following the same route Alex was taking. They shuffled, often trailing carry-on bags, carrying personal computers and PDAs and cell phones that had been turned into so much plastic junk by the Pulse.

The passengers made their way toward the terminal like refugees, together in family units but isolated from each other. There was no talking to strangers, though Alex looked into the eyes of people and saw expressions that spoke volumes. A young flight attendant trailed behind her older colleagues, looking like she was on the verge of tears. A little boy asked incessant questions about the big fires, and his father patiently provided him with innocuous answers.

There were many doors to the terminal down on the ground level, doors that usually allowed access and egress to passengers boarding small commuter jets. Now they all stood open. Alexandria picked one, and went inside, starting up the stairs to the concourse. Emergency lighting cast the hall in weird orange shadows, an effect that continued into the concourse. She was mildly disturbed to see that, even at the door leading into the concourse, there was no one checking IDs.

As she walked out of the gate area and approached the main concourse, she saw the uneven shadow and glare of the emergency lights, battery-powered beacons set high on the walls and shining like automobile headlights on the mass of silent, frightened humanity. Alex advanced into a place unlike any she had ever known. All the seats in the gate areas were occupied, and lots of other people were sitting on the floor. They lined both sides of the concourse, sitting and staring, talking in low tones. Many of them scrutinized the new arrivals, but there was very little movement. Mothers had opened their carry-on suitcases, laid out clothes as crude bedding for small children, families clustered like nesting animals amid the luggage piled up against the walls.

She thought of film she'd seen of Londoners during the WWII Blitz, huddled in the wide subway tunnels, and felt an empathy she had never known. Towing her suitcase down the middle of the concourse, Alex was one of a small stream of people making their way toward the main terminal, toward the baggage claim area and the way out. She passed a bar, strangely dark but full of people drinking, talking quietly. A bartender worked without lights or a cash register, drawing tap beers from the pre-pressurized kegs. The magazine shop was closed; a snack stand had been picked utterly clean and sat abandoned by customers and proprietor alike.

"Did you come from Atlanta?"

Alexandria whirled in surprise as an old woman grabbed her elbow and pressed home her question. "Today?"

"No, not Atlanta," Alex replied.

"Anybody else? A plane from Atlanta?" the woman hobbled away, peering into the faces of the people trudging down the concourse. Alex hoped that she would find someone, soon, who could tell her something about the flight from Atlanta.

The moving sidewalk was disabled, of course, and as she walked along beside it she began to get a cramp in her leg. She was limping from a pain in her right knee by the time she passed through the tomblike baggage area and out to the busy curb where arriving passengers were picked up.

The doors there stood open, and as she approached she noticed the mob, rumbling voices and seething activity as people pressed around a bus. The big motor was running, belching diesel exhaust, and a throng of pushing, shoving individuals fought to board. Finally, someone inside the bus gave a push, knocking a fat woman back into the crowd. The door hissed shut, and the bus rumbled very slowly away. It was jammed full of people, she saw when it passed. Most of the passengers tried not to look at the waiting crowd. A few did stare, eyes searching the sea of faces for . . . what?

The whole roadway, all five lanes of it, was full of stalled cars. Another bus approached, weaving between the autos like a dancing whale, and a new mob quickly converged on it. The bus nudged a Volvo out of the way, the car bumping into an old man and knocking him down. The crowd swept right past.

Alex's small, wheeled suitcase had become a leaden weight at the end of her arm by the time she crossed the street, weaving among abandoned sports cars, SUVs, minivans, and sedans. It was getting dark, and the parking garage looked huge and ominous, like a block of mountain against the sunset. She was the only person on her side of the road as she approached the parking garage. A lone person, a young black man, was coming toward her. His hands were in the pockets of his jacket, and a huge knit beret covered his head. He looked at Alexandria as she approached.

For the first time in her life, she wished that she had a gun.

"Goin' to yo' car?" he asked.

Alex stopped. "Why do you want to know?"

He shrugged. "Dey all dead. Tha's all." He stepped past her and continued toward the terminal.

Shaking her head and gritting her teeth, Alex entered the parking garage. Enough of the fading daylight, barely, seeped through the open edges of the structure to illuminate her path. She decided to walk up the autoway instead of taking the stairs. There were several empty spaces, suggesting that perhaps a few vehicles had been able to drive away.

By the time she reached the Firebird it was almost fully dark outside, and the interior of the garage was thick with shadow. She threw her bag in the trunk, went around and unlocked the driver's door. She tried to breathe slowly as she got in and buckled her seat belt and, by habit, locked the door. Her hand shook with apprehension, but she finally slid the key into the familiar ignition slot. Turning it, she heard the motor crank, then roar to life. Closing her eyes in relief, she leaned back against the headrest and congratulated herself for driving a classic car.

She thought about all those disabled cars, knew that there were highways full of them, and garages and parking lots and everywhere else cars might be found at the late-afternoon hour when the Pulse had occurred. They were disabled, utterly broken down, and they would be for quite some time. She understood beyond any doubt about the electromagnetic pulse. It was their complex circuitry that had failed. Her old Firebird, though restored to its prime and well maintained, operated with parts from the 1960s. There was not a computer chip in the whole car.

She popped it into reverse and started to back out. A sharp blow suddenly smashed the vehicle, rocking the Firebird on its springs.

"Get out, bitch!" It was a man in a business suit looming just outside her door. He was out of breath and his eyes were wild as he cocked back his fist, aiming a punch at the driver's window. "I need this car!"

"No!" She released the clutch and the tires squealed, jerking the Firebird backward. The man was sobbing, beating at the hood as it slid past him. She spun the wheel, shifted to first, and the vehicle jolted forward. With a desperate dive the man came at her again, but by then the car was squealing into motion. The front fender knocked him in the hip, sent him sprawling.

Alexandria sped away, down the spiraling ramp as fast as she dared to go, tires howling a protest around each sharp turn. The headlights bobbed and weaved through the shadows and she saw another man to her right, a pair of them to the left, poised and crouching. Apparently her speed was too intimidating, for she avoided further attacks until she got to the bottom of the garage. There was no one in the exit booth and that gate, which was set in the down position, had already been broken off.

With steady pressure on the accelerator she roared through the exit, sent the plank of the broken gate bouncing. She burst over the merging ramp and onto the street, where she immediately hit the brakes to avoid a series of stalled cars blocking the end of the ramp. Edging around them, she moved onto the airport departure road, weaving her way gingerly between the many disabled vehicles. She saw a group of young businessmen, suit-coats draped over their shoulders, trudging along the roadside. They turned to look at her as she drove past; she forced herself not to look back. There were others who looked at her longingly from the roadside. How far were they planning to walk, she wondered?

Of course, she should help—she had a working car, and could take more than herself back to the city. But the incident in the garage had left her un-nerved, hesitant. Dodging around a string of cars that had come to a stop in a chain of fender benders she came upon a woman pushing a stroller, a couple of young soldiers walking with her. The three of them simply looked at her as she stopped the car; a toddler craned her neck in the stroller, eyes wide at the sight of the fire-engine red car. The soldiers, nei-ther of whom could be twenty years old, stepped forward protectively.

"Do you want a ride into DC?" Alex asked.

"*All* of us?" asked the woman. She was perspiring heavily in her nice traveling suit. She wore sneakers instead of dress shoes, which was un-doubtedly the only reason she had made it so far. "That is, yes—thanks."

"Hop in." They tossed the stroller in the trunk and the woman took her infant on her lap in the backseat. One soldier sat in the back, the other in the front. The latter's hard-eyed stare, as well as his at-the-ready M16, helped Alex's sense of security considerably as she started out again.

"I'm Mandy Smith, from Arlington. This is Private Parker and Specialist Watts; they were kind enough to keep me company on the walk. And this is Stacy."

Stacy, a cute little blond, smiled shyly. "Hi," she said.

Alex introduced herself as she started out again. "So where were you headed, Mandy?"

"Arlington. We live there. We were going to meet my husband, at the airport—he was coming on a flight from Chicago." There was a catch in her voice, but she spoke cheerily for her daughter's sake. "He probably landed somewhere else, so we'll see him when he gets home."

"Go home!" Stacy declared, proudly holding up two fingers.

Alex smiled at the girl in the rearview mirror,

"How come this car works and none of the other do?" asked Private Parker from the backseat. He was a black youth with flat Midwestern accent.

She explained her theory about the EMP and its effects upon electronic ignition and the old coil-and-distributor system in old cars.

"Makes sense," Specialist Watts said. "That's why the buses and some of the trucks are still running. Maybe my Harley will fire up. It's about twelve years old."

"There's a good chance," Alex agreed.

"Of course, it's down at Fort Bragg now," he said glumly. "Don't know how we're going to get back there."

"What are you doing in DC?" Alex asked.

"We're attached to the 101st," the specialist explained, in a drawl that placed his origins well south of the Mason-Dixon line. "Our battalion was sent up here, TDY, when the news about the Martians broke. We been doin' shifts at the airport, were just driving up today when this—what did you call it, again?"

"EMP. I guess 'Pulse' is as good a name as any for it," Alex repeated.

"Yeah, we saw the flash and our Humvee broke down. We stayed with it for a few hours, broke up a couple of fights right away. But when everybody had wandered off, we didn't know if we should make for the airport or back to Fort Belvoir. We were still wavering when Miz Smith came along here. She was being followed by a couple of guys didn't look too right, so we decided to keep her company."

"I—I don't know what I would have done if they hadn't stepped up," Mandy Smith said, a tremor in her voice. "Those men were like wolves, a hunting pack. It's awful—how quick civilization falls away from people."

"I ran into a wolf myself," Alex said.

The Firebird passed around a pile of cars that looked as though they had been bulldozed. Just beyond, she saw the reason: a lane had been cleared for the buses that were occasionally coming out of the terminal. She was able to accelerate onto the highway and for several miles they rolled down the open road. Many of the cars to the right and left were scraped and dented, and before long she learned how. She came up behind a large highway maintenance truck fitted with a snowplow. It was rumbling along, tapping and scraping the scuffed vehicles to widen the open lane.

She was able to pass the truck before they reached the Beltway, then ended up following a large city bus the rest of the way into the city. She turned onto the Lee Highway to go into Arlington, and slowed down immediately—no truck had plowed through the disabled cars there, and she went back to weaving between all the lanes and the shoulder in order to make progress. Eventually she approached a stretch of congestion where all of the travel lanes were blocked, and braked almost to a stop.

Shifting into first, she pulled far down on the shoulder and passed a long string of cars. After a hundred yards she had to pull off even farther on the grassy slope to get around a big SUV straddling the shoulder. The car leaned dizzily and the tires skidded as she pressed the gas until the car grudgingly inched its way back to the pavement.

A mile later she was totally blocked by a tangle of cars on a bridge. The two soldiers got out and manhandled a little Fiesta out of the way and, though it cost her a scrape down each side of her Firebird, Alexandria was able to squeeze through the gap. A few minutes later she let Mandy and Stacy out in front of a small, tasteful town house on a street just off Military Road. She turned to the soldiers.

"I have to report to NASA, so I can't run you two down to the fort."

"That's fine, ma'am," said the specialist. "Can you just drop us at the Pentagon? Somebody *there* should know what we should be doing."

"Sure," Alex agreed. Deep in her heart she resisted the thought, the truth, that nobody on Earth really knew what they should be doing right now.

Two hours later and her passengers discharged, she made her way toward NASA headquarters. She had considered stopping at her apartment first, but there was nothing she needed there. More to the point, she wouldn't be able to learn anything there. And at that moment, more than anything else, Alexandria craved information.

The city streets had been cleared, somewhat, with many disabled cars simply pushed unceremoniously to the curbs, seemingly bulldozed onto sidewalks or nestled against privacy hedges, stoplights, and fire hydrants. There were a few buses moving around. She saw a couple of large Army trucks and several old cars and pickup trucks rumbling down the dark streets, but the city was for the most part empty of traffic.

So were the sidewalks. There were very few people about. Those she saw were usually in small groups, moving purposefully. The darkened storefronts and shuttered shops added a forlorn element to the scene. Most striking to her was an intersection with four normally bustling gas station/convenience stores. She regularly passed it between her apartment and work, and it was a scene of activity no matter what the hour.

But all four stores were dark and silent. Stalled cars were scattered haphazardly in the driveways and parking lots. Several sat at the pumps, disabled by the Pulse even as their owners had blithely refueled. In one quadrant of the corner a dozen young black men slouched on the hoods of a Lexus and a Cadillac. Their eyes followed the Firebird as she rolled through the intersection, unhindered by traffic lights. She couldn't help but punch the gas a bit as she rolled through the turn onto Three-hundredth Street.

She passed between federal office buildings, and at least the Army was visible. There were pairs of soldiers outside every door, and some large, multibarreled guns—Alex guessed they were antiaircraft—protected by sandbag abutments at a few commanding intersections. She saw several of those large trucks, and a couple of Army buses, olive drab versions of the yellow school buses she had ridden twenty-five years ago. But she couldn't find a Humvee or anything resembling a tank.

Coming up to NASA headquarters, she hesitated only a moment before she pulled into the director's parking space. Since Mike Koch's Expedition wasn't parked there, she knew it wouldn't be needing the slot for a long, long time.

Two young soldiers, barely more than a boy and a girl, watched her warily as she locked the car and approached. The male held his M16 ready as the female GI extended her hand for Alex's ID card.

"Dr. DeVane?" she said, immediately recognizing the name, but then consulting a handwritten list on her clipboard. "You're one they'll be really glad to see. Can you go right to the Watts auditorium?"

"Not up to the director's office?" she asked in surprise.

"Actually, the offices are pretty much abandoned," the young soldier, a sergeant with two stripes, explained. "With the computers and electronic phones out, those who are at work have moved into the cafeteria and auditorium. Also the motor garage."

"How many are here?" Alex wondered aloud, taking her ID card back.

"Well, Doctor, not too many. The Pulse happened when most of the staff was on its way home from work. With all the cell phones out, it's hard to find out where people are." She looked sympathetically at Alexandria. "Why don't you look up Mr. Frederick? He was pretty worried about you, was afraid you were on a plane that had gone down."

Alex found Dirk Frederick at an old-fashioned drafting table that had been set up on the stage of what had once been the auditorium. Now the room was harshly lit by an array of freestanding floodlamps. Many of the theater seats were occupied by people reading through sheets of paper. The doors at the front and the back frequently slammed open to reveal hurrying messengers, many of them out of breath, bringing in more of these individual pieces of paper.

Dirk looked up as Alex touched his shoulder, then wrapped her up in a startlingly intense hug. "God, girl, I thought we lost you. I knew you were en route during the Pulse. . . ."

"I had a good pilot. There were lots of good pilots out there," she said. "I did see about a dozen crashes in the neighborhood of Dulles."

Strangely, he brightened at this news. "There were twenty or more that went down at National," he said. She noted that, even then, the resolutely liberal Frederick refused to call the airport "Reagan National."

"You mean, you didn't have news from Dulles until I got here—by car?" she was incredulous at first, then frightened as she absorbed the implications. "God, we're really paralyzed, aren't we?"

"That's about the size of it. All satellite and cellular communication is kaput. Phones, the local lines are jammed, and it's impossible to get anywhere outside of town. To even place a call you have to have a phone with a cord attached. You wouldn't believe how rare they've become. We've got some trucks, buses, and diesel trains running, but as far as planes and automobiles, forget it."

"And the Martians . . . ?"

"Nobody knows. But, hey. You're more likely to find out than the rest of us."

"What do you mean?"

"If—I mean, *when*—you come in, you're supposed to go to the garage. They've got an Army truck waiting to take you somewhere. They need you."

"Where?" Alex was a little taken aback.

"I don't know, but I gather it has something to do with the president."

The truck didn't go toward the White House, and Alexandria knew better than to ask questions of the grim-faced Marine captain charged with taking her to their mysterious destination. The two of them rode in the big cab with an enlisted driver, Alex perched carefully in the middle. They went south through the city, and she guessed their goal, correctly, a few blocks before they pulled up to the main gate of the Anacostia Naval Station.

A concrete-reinforced barrier blocked their paths, and the Marines on guard had their weapons—including a wheeled recoilless rifle—aimed directly at the truck while the captain climbed out and presented a folder of documents for inspection. The chief of the guard detail was a full colonel, and he scrutinized each page, then asked a question.

The captain opened the door. "Dr. DeVane? He needs to see your ID."

She passed it over, and it was a minute later before the concrete barricade started rumbling sideways, opening the way. They drove right past the administration buildings, through blocks of immense, drab warehouses, until finally the truck braked to a stop near the edge of a concrete quay. Several Navy boats, like sleek and modern versions of World War II PT boats, were lashed here. But the captain escorted Alex toward a civilian fishing boat, a large craft with two outboard motors. The words *Lunker*, and *Annapolis, Maryland* were stenciled onto the transom.

This security check was conducted by men in dark suits, and Alex didn't have to guess to be certain they were Secret Service. The captain left her there, and one of the suits led her through the cockpit and into a salon, where four other people looked up as she entered. He indicated a seat at a low table, and left.

Two of the other passengers were in uniforms, an Army and an Air Force general, respectively. Another was a civilian, an older black man with a tonsure of gray hair around the fringe of his scalp. She remembered seeing his picture, thought that maybe he was the secretary of health and human services. The fourth person was almost certainly Secret Service: young and clean-cut, wearing that telltale suit, he seemed to look at no one and nothing while his eyes took everything in.

No introductions or any other words were proffered. It seemed to Alex as though they sat there interminably, but it was really no more than fifteen minutes before they felt the boat rock slightly as more people came aboard.

Seconds later the cabin door opened, and the president, stooping under the low bulkhead, came in. "Please, stay seated," he said immediately, as they all started to rise. "We can dispense with the formalities." He turned to the Air Force general. "Mac, thanks for the boat."

"My pleasure, Mr. President. I'm just glad I held on to those two old Evinrudes out there—they started up, right as rain."

"Good." The president sat at the head of the table, looked at the others. "Among other things, modern marine engines seem to have been neutralized by this Pulse. Fortunately for us, General McCanders likes his antiques."

Those twin Evinrudes were already rumbling into life. Moments later Alex felt the boat begin to move. She wondered what she was doing aboard.

"General Midders," the president greeted the Army officer. "And Secretary Rutherford. It's good to see you here. Sorry for the abrupt notice. And Dr. DeVane." He nodded his dignified head, and she felt honored. "We haven't had the pleasure. But thank you for coming also."

"Of course, Mr. President," she replied.

"We're going to Norfolk," explained the chief executive. "There, we'll board a submarine, the *Seawolf*. We established radio contact with her an hour ago—she was running nearly a thousand feet under the surface during the Pulse, and suffered very little damage. So we're going to treat her like a submersible Air Force One."

He leaned forward, putting his elbows on the table, and swept his eyes around the little salon. Alexandria was impressed by his demeanor—she could detect no sign of fear in his eyes, or his posture. He clenched his teeth and winced, the expression one of frustrated anger; and then he spoke.

"General Midders. What kind of hit did the Army take?"

"A bad one, Mr. President. As far as I've been able to learn, every AFV— that's armored fighting vehicle, of course, including all our tanks and the Bradley infantry carrier—is disabled. They can't even get the engines going. Not to mention targeting systems down, all of our detection apparatus knocked out. We can shoot the guns, but God only knows how we'll find the targets."

The president nodded. "General McCanders?"

The Air Force officer couldn't brighten the mood. "All our planes are grounded, sir, at least for the time being. The more sophisticated aircraft, the F15s and the like, are so much expensive junk right now. Until we rebuild our entire computer-manufacturing infrastructure, they're grounded. Other types, less dependent upon electronics for basic flight operations, might be repairable, given enough time and spare parts. Even if we get some aircraft up, our smart bombs are now dumb as toast. And our nukes—shit, we can't even launch the rockets, much less set off the bombs."

"Dammit!" The president flushed, and his voice rose for one explosive word. When he continued, he spoke through clenched teeth. "I've followed the budgets, the technology! We've spent billions, tens of billions, to shield our systems against EMP! And you're telling me that none of that shielding did a goddamn lick of good?"

"Well, the MU-metal shielding proved somewhat effective, especially on self-contained units such as rockets. But wherever there was a cable attached to something—even a power cord—or an antenna, the metal in that cable or antenna served to capture and focus the effects of the Pulse."

"So it's all shot? What about repairs?"

"The jury is still out on that, sir. But it is clear that such hardware as was directly exposed—planes in the air and the like—were utterly disabled. Much of the computer circuitry in our missile silos did survive, but those systems have sustained such damage as to make any attempt at a launch hazardous to the point of recklessness."

"How did this happen?"

"There was simply no way to anticipate the size of the burst, Mr. President. I have heard estimates of strength ranging up to a million volts. Our shielding anticipated, at the most, a pulse of no more than twenty percent of that. No power on Earth was capable of generating such an assault!"

The chief executive next looked to Alex. He drew a breath before he spoke, bracing himself for more bad news. "Dr. DeVane, your director has told me that you are one of the top brains in NASA, especially when it comes to matters Martian. I know you have been traveling extensively in the last month. What can you tell me about the vulnerabilities of our top research centers, like JPL? And the sensing facilities such as the Deep Space Array, and the VLA?"

"Nothing good, Mr. President. I am sure that the Pulse would have utterly fried any sensitive listening or radar station. At the voltage levels described by General McCanders it would have been a signal of unprecedented power—I wouldn't be surprised if people wearing headphones, listening to the VLA, might have ruptured ear drums. As to JPL, I am afraid they—like every university, every lab—hell, every college kid's dorm room—will have lost every bit of digital equipment they possess. That means records are gone, or at the very least inaccessible. I don't know if CDs have been damaged, but there will be no working device that can play a CD anywhere under the effects of the Pulse. That, right now, I am assuming is our hemisphere. So the DSAs in Spain and Australia should still be operable. At least, the Martians couldn't take out all three of them with one—" She stopped in surprise, then continued urgently.

"Sir! What if this was the first of at least two, possibly three EMP attacks? It doesn't make sense that they would target only half of our planet! So we know that M1 was an EMP weapon, probably nuclear—certainly of unprecedented power. It is a very sophisticated attack, only making sense if they have an appreciation of our mastery of electricity. What if M2 and M3 are also Pulse weapons? The first one targeted the Americas. What if the second one takes out Eurasia? Then the third could go off over the South or North Pole, wherever they felt they needed the extra coverage."

"God damn it." The president looked pale. "Of course! How much time do we have?"

General McCanders looked at his watch, an old-fashioned windup. "We're almost nine hours post-Pulse right now."

"What options do we have? Any way to shield against the next one?"

The two generals looked at each other. McCanders glanced at Alex, raising his eyebrows in mute question.

"The *Seawolf*'s experience gives some hope," she said. "At least, for subs that can get to deep water. As to subterranean shelters—have you heard any results from Cheyenne Mountain?" she asked the Air Force general.

"At the Pentagon they got a shortwave antenna up and were broadcasting within the first two hours. They did that at Cheyenne Mountain, too, so we got a report." He shook his head grimly. "Most of the equipment fried. They saved a few PCs in the deepest bunkers, and even they suffered some damage."

"What about moving things out of the presumed target zone? Like jets?" Alexandria proposed. "Planes that are in Europe now could be sent back to the States, hopefully get here before the next Pulse. Our planet itself is the most effective, really the *only* shield we have."

"Good idea," said the president. "Can we get an order out yet, Mac?"

"Yes, Mr. President. We have radio contact with Norfolk from the *Lunker*. Most military stations have at least established UHF radio contact. We can relay word to Europe and the fleet. Just off the top of my head I can think of units based in Europe, Southwest Asia, Guam, and Okinawa—even a detachment on Diego Garcia, down in the Indian Ocean. Do you want me to call them all home?"

"Dr. DeVane, what's your best guess as to when the next pulse will occur?"

Alexandria suddenly felt very much alone. She tried to think. "Well, each M is about 24.7 hours behind the previous. But that won't work for staged EMP pulses—if each of the objects is in relatively the same quadrant of space as the others, they will strike the same target, except for that extra .7 hour of rotation. So they will have to travel a little farther, Pulse closer to the Earth in order to affect a different part of the world."

She had a chilling thought. "Or," she added grimly, "they could be set up from farther out in space than M1. Perhaps the first one came in closer than it had to, so that the others could be detonated farther out. This would compress the time frame for three attacks instead of drawing it out. We really don't know how powerful their weapons are."

"So, if M2 affects a different part of the Earth, and is capable of doing damage from farther out in space, it could ignite at, well, just about any time, couldn't it?"

"I'm afraid so, Mr. President. Though I would be willing to bet that it will have to get significantly closer than it is right now, which is still more than a million miles away."

"Would you be willing to bet the lives of all the aircrews that will be in the air, if we call our overseas aircraft home?" demanded General McCanders, his jaw jutting pugnaciously.

"General, that is not the kind of decision I expect my scientists to make," the president interceded. "I need as much information as Dr. DeVane can provide, then *I* will decide whether we're going to make the gamble. In the meantime, put out the word over the radio—I want those planes gassed up and ready to go at a moment's notice."

"Yes sir, Mr. President!" The Air Force general left the salon from a second bulkhead, a hatch leading deeper into the boat, toward the bridge and radio Alex assumed. She didn't have any time to answer, since the president was addressing her with another question.

"So, M1 through perhaps M3 are EMP devices, as best as we can guess.

Bombs designed to soften us up. What do you make of Ms 4 through 11, then?"

"I can't be sure, sir. But it only makes sense that they would be the invasion transports."

THREE

The generator thumped away, powering an array of floodlights that had been set up in the hangar. Duke Hayes watched nervously as a team of aircraft mechanics, men and women he had never seen before, swarmed around his beloved Warthog. These included a few Air Force technicians, but were mostly naval mechanics stationed at the Cape Canaveral Naval Air Station.

In the wake of the Pulse, with communications out across the state and the country, the base commander had ordered that disabled combat aircraft be prioritized—which were most likely to be repairable in a short period of time? There were several Navy F14s and F18s at the base as well as Duke's group of four A10s. The mechanics had been unanimous in electing the sturdy and relatively basic Warthogs as the focus of their efforts. Privately, one crew chief had whispered to Duke that he doubted that any of the Tomcats, fighters that depended upon computer circuitry for fundamental characteristics such as the shape of the wings, would fly before the year was out.

"If ever," he had concluded grimly, before climbing up a stepladder to get to work on the A10.

Nearly eight hours later, Duke had caught a short nap on a cot in the corner of the hangar while the mechanics had worked through the night.

After confirming that the techs would need some more time, he made his way over to the air station's control tower to see if he could pick up any news. Dawn was a rosy blush on the eastern horizon, slowly reaching out from the ocean, as he moved away from the bright lights in the hangar and across the tarmac.

He was startled to see aircraft lights in the eastern sky, several of them. Closest were the bright white landing lights of several small aircraft. Duke's heart was in his throat as he stood still and watched four F15 Eagles, flying in pairs, come in for perfect landings. Two F117s—commonly called "Stealth" fighters—came in next, touching down smoothly, rolling toward the hangar area, and finally stopping not far away.

There were still more airplanes coming in. Duke watched with resurgent hope as three massive B-52s came down one by one, followed by, finally, a KC-135 tanker very much like the one that had carried Alexandria away on the day of the Pulse. At the memory, his heart gave a lurch—he didn't know what had happened to her. He kept trying to convince himself that her plane had landed, intact, somewhere.

He met the pilots of the F117s as they climbed down to the runway, shaking off the weariness and cramps of a long flight.

"Nice to see that the bastards didn't get all of our birds," Duke offered. "They sure as hell fucked up my Warthog. Where did you fellows come from?"

"Diego Garcia," one of the pilots said. "We came over the South Pole, sucking that tanker's teat all the way. I guess we got out of there just before the second Pulse hit."

"There was a second one?" Hayes asked, surprised and dismayed.

"Yeah. Seems like it toasted Europe and Asia, from south of the equator up to and over the North Pole. Santa ain't gonna be taking off anytime soon."

"Well, welcome to Florida," Duke said, shaking hands with each of them. "We can use all the help we can get—let me show you to the locker room."

Within the control tower he found barely controlled chaos. Disabled equipment, including computer monitors, keyboards, and hard drives had been dumped unceremoniously into a corner of the lobby. Communications specialists were busy at work, testing and replacing radio components. Old-fashioned UHF radio was the order of the day. He asked about seeing the base commander, a Navy captain, and was told to wait for a few minutes.

"Any luck with the radios?" he asked one weary-looking specialist, a woman sitting in the waiting room holding a cup of coffee in her hands, taking a break after a long night of work. He poured her a refill and sat down beside her.

"A little," she said, shaking her head in discouragement before looking at him. "Every component that was attached to an antenna during the Pulse is pretty much toast. But we have a small warehouse full of spare parts, and a lot of those—especially solid-state components—survived pretty well. Can't say the same for computer components, though. Just about everything that had a chip in it, whether it was hooked up to a hundred miles of copper wire or was just sitting in a box on a shelf, is shot."

"Yeah, they slammed us pretty good with the first Pulse."

"Major, it's even worse than that," the specialist said, looking at him intensely. "It's not just that they wiped out all computers, so we have to start making new ones. They even wiped out the machines that make computers, and the vaults full of information about how to do that. It's like they've knocked us back thirty years in time before the shooting starts."

"The shooting has already started—my brother was the captain of the space shuttle," Duke said quietly. He hadn't been willing to think about it before, but the truth was inescapable: Nate Hayes and his two crew mates would not be coming home.

"I'm sorry, sir." The soldier shook her head. "My sister's a flight attendant with United. She would have been in the air when it hit. I don't know what happened to her."

"We'll get the bastards," Duke said, with more conviction than he felt. "Just let 'em try and come down here."

"Major Hayes?" It was the captain's aide, summoning him toward an office. The pilot rose and followed the young lieutenant, stepping inside a spartan cubicle. The only thing to recommend the place were the two windows, looking east and south from the corner of the building. Dawn had spread across most of the sky, Hayes noticed.

"Captain Kenseth? Sorry to bother you, sir—I was wondering if you have been able to establish any contact with Eglin."

"Yes, Major." The base CO looked up from his desk. He had a bulldog face and looked like he wanted to bite down on a fat cigar. He settled instead for the end of a mangled pencil. "We have a hardwired telephone net back up in the state, and we're working our way up the East Coast. Your CO authorizes your detachment to stay here, even if we can get your ships airborne. In the absence of higher orders, we both felt that the Cape is an area we want to be able to defend. He concurred with the opinion of my own tech staff—the A10s are as likely as the best, and better than most, to get flyable again. What's the word from the hangar?"

"Your men—and women—are miracle workers, Captain. That crew chief, Walker, really knows his stuff. He thinks he can get me airborne before noon today, with my three wingmen coming online maybe one every twelve hours afterward."

"Good," Kenseth said. "If Chief Walker says it, it's the truth. When you're both satisfied that the ship is as ready as it can be, under the circumstances, let me know, and I'll authorize a test flight."

"Will do, Captain."

"Thanks, and good luck."

The captain went back to his pencil-chewing and Hayes departed, crossing the tarmac on an already steamy morning. Back in the hangar he saw Chief Walker looking up with a cat-that-ate-the-canary grin.

"Found out we could bypass that avionics box. You should be able to run all the controls through full range of motion. It might take a little extra effort, like steering a car after the power steering fails."

"I can handle that," Hayes promised. "What about the engines?"

"The engines. Shoot, there's no problem getting a jet engine to run without a computer," the chief said breezily. "We just need to dump fuel into that big fan and find a cigarette lighter that sparks in a 1,000-mph wind!"

"That's all?"

"Hell, yes. We can start these babies up anytime, and they'll shoot you out of here like a Roman candle. Of course," he added, scratching his chin and frowning thoughtfully. "I'm not quite so sure we can get them to stop, again."

"I don't care!" Duke replied, elated at the thought of taking to the air. "I don't plan on landing until I run out of fuel!"

June 6
Solar System
Trans Martian/Terran Belt

All eight of the remaining containers continued in their stately progress from the red, dry planet toward the verdant world that was their destination. The first three had fully opened, each exposing silver contents—nearly a hundred smaller cylinders—to the rays of the sun. The others would remain closed until they drew closer to the target.

Soundlessly they soared in a great cosmic train, millions of miles separating each from the other, but all following the same course, metal gleaming brightly in the reflection of the distant sun. They drew closer to that sun with every passing second.

But the sun was not their destination. Courses adjusted, bringing the containers, and their silent, waiting cargoes, in line with the planet Earth. They progressed inevitably toward that much nearer target, a planet awash in water and air, a bright speck of verdant vitality amid the blackness of the solar system . . . a planet that, for the moment, still teemed with life.

Fort Bragg, North Carolina

The old Sikorsky helicopter rattled and smoked its way from Norfolk to Fort Bragg through a muddy dawn and into the surprisingly cool daylight of a gray day. Alex clutched her handlebar through the entire flight, clenching her teeth against the airsickness that lurked just behind her veneer of self-control. Halfway through the flight a red warning light on the instrument panel illuminated. The pilots tried a couple of adjustments, with no results, and the light stayed on for the rest of the flight.

The aircraft had been borrowed from the Coast Guard. It had become essential because, in the words of the pilot, "It was too damned old to know that it was obsolete." Now, with newer helicopters grounded because of a multitude of electronic and computer failures, it was state of the art.

When they finally landed, Alexandria stepped carefully down the steps. Her knees didn't shake, but she feared she would collapse at any second as she ducked and moved beyond the circle of the sweeping rotor. Fortunately, a lieutenant with an old, but carefully maintained, military jeep was waiting for her just beyond the landing pad.

"Dr. DeVane? I'm Lieutenant Stewart—glad to see that you had a safe trip. I'm here to take you to the HQ."

Leaning back in the stiff seat, Alex fastened herself in as the young officer accelerated away. He nodded over his shoulder, back at the Sikorsky. "That's the first aircraft we've had in here, since it happened."

"What about military vehicles? Any word on the prospects for repair?"

Stewart shrugged. "The damage varies. I'm sure the general will fill you in on the latest details. Though I heard the sergeant major in charge of repairs predict that he'll get a few Abrams rolling in the next couple of days. That oughtta count for something."

"Yes, it should," Alexandria agreed. She knew her military equipment well enough to know the lieutenant was talking about the M1A2 tank. Huge and fast, with its whisper-quiet turbine engine, flat turret, and deadly 120 mm cannon, it was the premiere battlefield weapon in the Army arsenal.

The "general" turned out to be Major General Paul Davis, whose perpetual frown and piercing brown eyes struck Alexandria as the perfect accessories for a high-ranking commander. "Dr. DeVane?" he said curtly, after shaking hands and gesturing her to a chair in his office. He remained standing, pacing slowly behind his desk as he talked. "Before we begin, I am to convey you some news on the personal orders of the president." He cleared his throat and fixed those penetrating eyes upon her.

"There has been a third Pulse, more or less over the South Pole. The entire surface of the planet has now been exposed to that energy blast. The president asked me to tell you that more than a hundred aircraft have been retrieved from zones two and three, returned to bases in North America. And he wanted me to thank you for him."

Alexandria tried to think. A hundred planes? There were a lot more than that overseas, she knew. Had the others tried to return, and failed? The general was staring at her, she realized. "Thank you, General. I don't know why he asked you to tell me that, but thank you."

"Hell, thank you from me, too, if you helped to get a hundred of our aircraft back home intact. God knows that's a lot more machines than I can put in the field, as of now, at any rate." General Davis looked up, his frown deepening into a scowl. "Now, let's clarify your mission here. Do you bring orders from the White House?"

"No, General. I left the president at Norfolk. Obviously, he is trying to prepare for any contingency. The largest striking force of US arms in the eastern half of the country is here, with the 101st Airborne and First Brigade of Third Armored Division. If it comes down to a shooting war, I am to be available to you as a resource, to help you understand these Martians, their tactics and technology, any way I can."

"So tell me, Doctor, just how likely is it that we're facing a shooting war? What do you think is going to happen next?"

"General, the first three of the eleven Martian devices have proven to be

EMP weapons. They demonstrate several things, including the obvious: Those who sent them against us have hostile intentions. And these 'Martians' possess an amazingly high level of technology. The explosions themselves were acts of incredibly complicated science and manufacturing. In both power and focus of effect, they were far beyond what our best scientists and industry could achieve on Earth.

"And they displayed some knowledge of our own planet. The first EMP Pulse was directly over the center of North America. Possibly a coincidence, but I suggest that it shows the Martians knew that their most formidable resistance would come from the military in this part of the world. Eurasia was next, and the South Pole blast mopped up anyplace that might have been sheltered from the first two by the curvature of the Earth's surface."

The general waited, more or less patiently, for Alexandria to continue. She took a breath and forged ahead. "I find it highly unlikely that the remaining eight devices will also be EMP weapons. I can only think of two other explanations, both of which are grim:

"A—these are weapons of mass destruction that will strike the planet and wreak terrible havoc, up to and including ending all civilization and, conceivably, all human life on the planet. Or

"B—that M4 through M11 are some type of invasion fleet, intending to deliver attackers to our planet."

"Nice," the general snapped, in a tone that wasn't nice at all. "An invasion, huh? Well, what kind of an attack do you expect it will be?"

She squirmed for a moment, but grasped that she had to meet him head-on. "It's impossible to say with any precision at all," she said. "We have no idea what kind of organisms will be aboard those ships. If any—this might be an army of robots, advanced and deadly versions of the rovers that we've sent to their world."

"I need more than that to go on, Doctor. There are eight ships left. Do you think they'll spread out all over the world? Or land in one place, and move out from there? Is concentration of force an interplanetary concept?"

"I'm sure it is. But I wouldn't assume they will be attacking in eight ships. Our best information is that each of those is over a kilometer in length, fully a hundred meters across. I don't see them riding those down to the planet. My guess is that they will disgorge smaller carriers—landing craft, if you will. Since they will be launched from orbit, it's possible that there could be hundreds of different landing sites."

"All right. That makes sense. Will they parachute in? Set down with rockets, or perhaps glide?"

"Again, impossible to say for certain. But I would tend to rule out their using anything that depended upon the air, such as a parachute or, like the space shuttle, an airfoil. Whatever their environment is—and I have to believe that the whole civilization has long been based underground—they would not have an atmosphere capable of supporting flight, such as we know it.

"On the other hand, they have technology that we haven't developed ourselves—the power of their EMP bombs being a case in point. Also, they traveled through space faster than any craft or satellite that we have been able to launch. So they could very well have some advanced means of wielding energy that might allow them to set down as gently as they want."

"What about the oceans? Will they likely start there, or do you think they'll go for land?" General Davis rattled off his questions like a machine gun.

"My guess is the land," Alex said without hesitation. "I have to believe that their objectives, whatever those may be, will be found outside of the oceans. Certainly their EMP pattern suggests some study of Earth; no doubt they know that our population centers are all on land."

The general was about to shoot off another query when she had a sudden thought. "If they do deploy an army, I don't think they'll depend much on air forces. I doubt there's an analogous theater on Mars—certainly, there isn't above the surface."

"A ground army, eh?" Davis was still glaring at her, but she had realized that this was not a signal of displeasure—at least, not displeasure directed at Alex. "Well, we'll meet the bastards then. I have a division and a half here, and we're getting more tanks, more guns, more of our transport back with every hour. We'll give 'em the fight of their lives, I promise you that."

"I know you will," she replied. "What's the status of your own air arm?"

"Unsatisfactory!" he snapped. "Our helicopters are mostly disabled for the foreseeable future, except for a handful of Vietnam-era Hueys. All the high-altitude fighters are down, too. There's one bright spot. I've heard that there are three squadrons of A10s this side of the mountains that will be ready to fly. Those Warthogs are tough sonsabitches, if you don't mind me saying so."

"That's wonderful!" Alex exclaimed, thrilled.

The general narrowed his eyes and allowed the ghost of a smile to whisk across his lips. "I take it your interest is more than technical?" he asked.

She nodded. "Duke Hayes—he's the younger brother of the shuttle pilot. He's with the Thirty-second Bombardment Squadron out of Eglin AFB in Florida. He was possibly airborne at the time of the Pulse—I haven't heard from him, but that's good news. It gives me hope."

"The boy's probably fine, and mad as hell. Well, good for the lucky fellow," Davis said. "And I have a hunch we'll need him—those A10s are the best damned tank-busters that ever took to the skies."

"I hear you, General!" she replied.

The rap at the door was just a little too loud to be polite. "Intercom's out," the general explained to Alex. "Come!" he barked.

A female lieutenant colonel came in bearing a sheet of paper, typewritten, Alex noted with surprise. "A message rated Urgent just came over the UHF receiver," she said, extending it to Davis.

"Read it," he said. "Dr. DeVane is cleared Top Secret SI, isn't that correct?"

"Yes, it is," she said, startled by his knowledge, and willing to assume the as-yet-unofficial classification.

"Very well, sir." She raised the paper near to her face and stood at ease. "It's from SecDef at the Pentagon, to all commands. Visual contact with object M4 has been established via telescope. That is to say, we can see what's left of it. As of 0120 EST, 8 June, the object appears to be a number of smaller devices. Count confirms more than twenty (20) such positively identified. There may be many more. Subobjects have accomplished minor course alteration, bringing them directly in line with Earth.

"It is believed that the smaller devices may be the vanguard of an invasion force. At current course and speed, they will arrive in Earth atmosphere at approximately 2300 hours, today."

"Shit," the general said, looking at his watch. "The bastards aren't giving us much time, are they?"

FOUR

June 7
Delbrook Lake, Wisconsin

The ringing of the phone jarred me awake. I fumbled for it, instinctively frantic to seize the instrument, my sole link to the world beyond my house. "Hello?" I croaked.

"Mark?"

I recognized Browne's voice with a mixture of relief and alarm.

"Yes—what is it?" I could see only darkness through the partial shades on my bedroom windows.

"You'd better get outside and take a look—hurry."

I didn't even reach for clothes, taking the time only to grab my glasses before stumbling out onto the bedroom deck wearing my boxer shorts and a T-shirt. From here I had a good view to the north and west, and saw immediately why Browne had called.

My first thought was that all of Madison was burning. A red glow blossomed in the western sky, almost bright at the horizon and fading only gradually as my eyes swept higher in the night sky. I had to turn my head to encompass the full scope of it from side to side, and I held out my hand, half-expecting to feel reflected heat. It was flaring, incandescent, like a cosmic event viewed up close and personal.

Against my skin there was only the cool night air, but that fantastic glow was a distortion of my whole world. Something had come from space, I knew—something Martian.

Barely had I reached this conclusion when the sky seemed to explode in fire. It was another one, bright and speeding, crackling like some insanely fiery meteor as it burned up in our atmosphere. But this thing wasn't burning away. Instead it was plunging downward with sickening power, an unknown but terribly potent menace. I watched as it got brighter, flaring like a vicious, alien sun until I had to shield my eyes. I saw stark shadows outlined from the trees in my yard, and the sky turned a sickly shade of gray, more like daylight than night.

Then the light vanished as the blazing object passed below my horizon to the southwest. Because of the corner of my house, I couldn't see exactly where it came down. A few seconds later, however, I *felt* it through the soles of my feet, the rippling force of a massive impact against the planet—my planet—somewhere not terribly distant. Leaning on the porch railing I looked around my house, in the direction of Janesville. Slowly, a crimson illumination blossomed there, a dome of brightness smaller than the brightness from the direction of Madison. Probably that was because it was farther away than the impact of the first object.

I felt sick to my stomach. Retreating back to the imaginary shelter beneath the overhanging eave of my roof, I stared at that silent, menacing glow. There was a strange racket underneath the visual sensation, though it took me a long time to sense it. Then I heard them, coyotes singing their eerie music, frantic yips and yodels echoing through the night, apparently coming from everywhere. Browne's dogs chimed in, and I almost felt relieved at the sound, like the noise was some anchoring point, a connection to society against the cosmic uncertainty of that unimaginable fire.

I backed into the house, closed the door, and—ludicrously—pulled down the blind. The fabric shade glowed an eerie orange from the backdrop of the inferno. I sat on my bed, trembling, feeling sweat soak my T-shirt, growing chilled from the wetness. I wanted to climb back under the covers, to pull them over my head, to hide. But I couldn't even muster the energy to do that.

It seemed like a long time that I sat there, though perhaps it was only a few minutes. My inertia broke with a sudden shock, and I was propelled to my feet. I looked around wildly, toward the windows, the bed, the door. I ran out of the room then, racing downstairs, pacing in agitation between the kitchen and the living room. The generator was off, and I went out the back door, half-thinking I would start it. But I stayed on the porch, unwilling to go out under that hideous sky. Finally, I left the generator alone, went back in, and lit one of my oil lamps. With that dim yellow illumination I got the shotgun out of my closet, took one box of shells off the refrigerator, and carefully loaded the weapon. Making sure that there was no shot in the chamber, I set the safety, then rested the weapon on my dining room table.

But I couldn't just wait there, in the darkness. I needed to learn more, to see what was going on. Going to the phone in my bedroom, I tapped a call to my neighbor.

"Yeah?" he answered brusquely.

"Um, this is Mark," I said. "I want to get a better look—I'd like to climb that hill in your back pasture and see what I can from there."

"Good idea. I'll meet you there in a few."

I pulled on my jeans and boots, grabbed a flashlight, and was out the door. Just as I reached the trail into the woods I remembered the gun, but decided not to go back for it. The beam of the flashlight bobbed and danced in front of me, but when I raised my eyes I could still see that fiery radiance brightening the night sky. Coming into the pasture at last, I all but jogged up the steep, grassy slope. I got to the top to see the headlights of Browne's Jeep coming from his house. The vehicle splashed through the creek on the farm track and turned straight onto the slope of the hill. With a grinding of gears the Jeep lurched, then started slowly up, growling steadily along. Spotting me in the glow from the headlamps, Browne switched his lights off, drove up beside me, and parked.

His two dogs were in the back of the Jeep. The poodle leaped out as soon as the little vehicle stopped, while the big Newfoundland waited until Browne came around and opened the tailgate. Both dogs came over, gave me a few sniffs, then paced around the hilltop, marking every bush with a few squirts of urine. They were nervous and agitated, pacing to and fro with their hackles raised.

In the darkness that wasn't dark, we stood side by side and stared to the west. We couldn't see far enough to spot the point of impact, but there was a clear spectrum of light and, by inference, we could locate the epicenter of the fire. The hellish vortex was an area on the horizon as wide as my hand when I extended my arm and spread my fingers apart. There the color was brightest, such a pale yellow that it was almost white, like a concentrated blast of daylight somehow creeping around the curvature of the earth. That illumination was fully incandescent along the horizon, quickly fading to orange above and to either side. A wider band of dull red light, not so different from a cloud-diffused sunset, arced around the orange. Beyond that, a pale brightness extended across the great sweep of sky, so light that very few stars were visible. One of those, ironically enough, was Mars, peering redly through the curtain of chaos falling over the world.

"It's closer than Madison, a little north of there," I guessed.

Browne nodded, then glanced to the southwest, where the second blazing object had fallen to earth. "That's farther, maybe down to Milton or Janesville way."

"Jesus God," I said, shaking my head. "What did they bring down here?"

"Do you think it's a bomb? Something that's just going to burn up the world?" he asked.

I hadn't thought of that. "I think anything they came down in would be likely to make a crater. Unless the fire keeps getting bigger, I would assume this is the effect of a celestial impact, not a bomb."

"Comforting. I guess," Browne said dryly.

For a time we watched in silence. The coyotes were still singing, but his dogs sat attentively beside us, panting a little bit but making no other noise. The fire didn't seem to get any larger, and in fact when I extended my hand a half hour later the strip of brightest light was a little smaller than my finger span.

"Do you hear that?" asked my neighbor.

The unmistakable rumble of diesel engines, of large trucks rolling, sounded from the south. I realized that the noise had been there for some time; it was a normal enough sound that I had to process the notion, remember that there had been very few vehicles driving around since the Pulse.

"They're on the county highway!" I said with certainty, looking to the south. Wooded, rolling hills blocked our view of the wide, well-graded road, which was only a couple of miles away.

"Let's go have a look," Browne said. "Get in!" he barked peremptorily. I was momentarily taken aback until I saw he had spoken to his dogs, both of which hopped into the bed of the little Jeep. Black and white, they seemed almost to overflow the space, dancing and squirming around in excitement and agitation. Klondike's tongue was a slick, lurid pink in the surreal illumination.

I hopped in as well, and soon we were crawling down the hill, both of my hands clamped gratefully around the oh shit bar. Browne gunned it as we got to his farm track, and we bounced and jolted through the stream, across his pasture, between the barn and the house, and out onto our lane.

I glanced back, saw that each dog had his head hanging over the side, tongue dangling and ears trailing in the breeze. Galahad stretched his neck far out, over Browne's shoulder, while Klondike, on my side, was content to let his drooling lips rest on the shoulder of my flannel shirt.

The lane is a hilly road, and I had never taken it quite so fast, but I shared my neighbor's curiosity and, more importantly, sense of hope. We came over the last hill and rolled down toward the stop sign, the brakes squeaking as we lurched to a halt.

For a moment the headlights captured a fascinating view of the highway and the traffic passing by: a bright orange county snowplow rumbled past, towing a boxy trailer. Next came a large pickup, many years old with a body pocked from years of road-salt-induced rust. But the frame was solid, the dual rear tires large, and it strained to haul a load after the dump truck. In the second before Browne snapped his lights off, we saw that it was pulling a large cannon painted olive drab.

Soldiers were already approaching, drawn by our approach. We were quickly surrounded by men in camouflage uniforms, most of them carrying M16s, wearing Kevlar helmets and full combat gear.

"The highway is closed, gentlemen," said one of the soldiers. "You'll have to turn back."

"Okay, no problem. But hell, it's good to see you guys," Browne declared affably. "Going to kick some Martian ass, I hope?"

"You got it, sir!" the speaker replied.

Another soldier, an older man with captain's bars on his collar, approached, and the men respectfully made way for him.

"I'm Captain Mueller," he said. "Are you gentlemen from around here?"

"Yes, just up the road," replied Browne.

"Did either of you observe the landings?"

"We both did, Captain," I explained. "We think the nearest one is this side of Madison, just a little north of there. The other one is farther away."

"Yep. That first one blasted the shit out of downtown Sun Prairie," the captain said, his eyes hard. "The other one landed right around Newville, put a crater next to the Rock River."

"Where is your outfit from?" I asked, surprised that they were here this quickly after the landings.

"First Battalion, 126th Field Artillery, Wisconsin National Guard. We're out of Kenosha, but have depots in Burlington and Whitewater. We're the advance contingent. The rest of the unit should be along before dawn."

"Do you think those guns will do the trick?" I asked, as another large piece of field artillery, this one towed by a very old-looking military truck, rolled past.

The captain gave me a reassuring nod. "They knocked out a lot of our communications and transport, sir—that's why all the mix of old trucks, snowplows, and so forth. As well as a few Hummers our mechanics have returned to operational status." His voice took on an unmistakable note of pride as he pointed at one of the passing artillery pieces. "But these are 155 mm howitzers. The biggest, and most powerful guns in the US Army arsenal. And there isn't a damned piece of essential electronics on the whole thing. So, to answer your question, sir: The bastards won't have a chance."

"What do you expect to find up there?" I had to ask.

The captain scratched his neck. "Word is, they have big ships that landed hard, made these craters all over the place. If we can get our guns zeroed in on those ships while they're just sitting there, we might be able to destroy them right away. If not, the bastards will be fragged as soon as they try to open their hatches and come out."

"Good luck, Captain," I offered, sincerely.

"Give 'em hell!" Browne added.

"Luck won't hurt," Mueller acknowledged. "But it's training and equipment that will carry the day. Besides—we're fighting for *our* homes, too."

With that he returned to his Humvee, which I noticed, for the first time, parked on the shoulder of the road. With a rumble he was off, merging into the convoy, heading west and north to prepare for the first interplanetary battle in the history of the world.

FIVE

"Dr. DeVane? Sorry, ma'am, but the general said to wake you up right away and get you outside. Quickly, ma'am!"

Alex was sitting up on the Army bunk before she was even awake. She saw a female sergeant extending a hand, then she was standing, steadied by the NCO's strong grip. "This way, ma'am—there's a balcony where you can see the sky."

"The Martians—?" Alex hurried along, and the sergeant broke into a trot beside her.

"Yes, ma'am. It looks like they're landing." Pushing open a door under a lit EXIT sign, they emerged onto a second-floor landing atop a stairwell leading down to the small parking lot.

Alex saw them immediately, four—no, five—blazing trails of light descending like the dying remnants of a fireworks display. Long columns of smoke and fading sparks extended upward toward the heavens. The base of each plume was a sparking, blazing fireball. Two of them were already out of sight below the western horizon, and within a few seconds the other three vanished, one by one, from her view, marking a distant line to the north.

"Where do you think they're coming down?" asked the sergeant, her tone shaky.

"More than a hundred miles from here, I'd guess," Alex said, "Probably on this side of the Appalachians, though. But it's hard to be certain—can you take me to the general?"

"Yes, ma'am. He's in the Op Center—I'm to bring you there as soon as you're ready."

"Give me ninety seconds." Alex ran back to her room, jumped into a pair of khaki slacks and a shirt. She thought about her hair for a second. "Screw it," she decided, pulling on a baseball cap and rushing out the door.

"Impressive!" the sergeant said, looking up from her watch. "Eighty-two seconds."

The officer's dorm where Alex had been given a room was less than a half mile from the headquarters building. The two women crossed the parade ground at a jog, climbed the steps to the HQ. An MP on guard held open the door as he saw them coming, and it surprised Alex considerably when she wasn't asked for an ID or any kind of pass. Instead, the sergeant ushered her down a hall and into a large, well-lit room. Officers and enlisted personnel bustled about, marking maps, consulting rosters. New dispatches came in all the time, carried by breathless messengers who dropped off their sheets of paper and turned to hurry back to the radio room.

General Davis was neither louder, nor taller, than anyone else in the room, but his commanding presence drew her attention instantly. He was talking to a young colonel when he saw Alex. He waved her over, a command disguised as an invitation.

"Doctor! Looks like the waiting game is over. Take a look at where the bastards have come down, so far."

He gestured to the map on the table before him. It was a good-sized display, perhaps eight feet wide, of the United States. There were a number of red pins stuck in the map, and Alexandria's eyes were immediately drawn to the Midwest. She saw two of them in Wisconsin, one very close to Madison and one south of there. Several more were spread out in an arc across the Illinois plains, four of them ranging from west of Rockford through the middle of the state until the last was near the Indiana River, closer to the Ohio River than it was to Chicago.

There were lots of pins in the East, beginning with five of them forming a belt across central Georgia. A string of them advanced northward, staying just to the east of the Appalachian Mountains, slicing through Virginia, Maryland, and Pennsylvania, continuing on through New York until the line of pins met the sea just north of Boston. There were no pins west of the Mississippi, not yet anyway.

General Davis's jaw was clenched, and a strange light glowed in his eyes. He was ready to do battle, she sensed, and grateful that, at last, they faced an enemy that was no longer utterly remote and out of reach.

"So many of them?" Alex remarked in surprise.

"Yeah. Thirty or more in the USA alone. It looks like each of those big cylinders must have opened up to disgorge a dozen or more of these smaller bastards—the actual landing craft."

"Lots of them along the East Coast, I see," muttered the NASA specialist. "And they seem to have Atlanta pretty well surrounded."

"What do you make of the way they came down?" he asked.

"It looks like they've clearly tried to surround the main East Coast population corridor. They've studied us, that's for sure. They've made a cordon from Richmond to Boston, with—what?—some fifty million people backed up against the coast? And then here, in Georgia—that looks like a ring getting ready to snap around Atlanta. And up there, in the Midwest—"

They practically landed on my father's house! She wanted to scream, but she kept her tone level, scientific.

"Up there it looks like they've cupped a string of them around Chicago and Indianapolis. They're surrounding population centers."

"Well, that's my take on it, too. They know where we live, but they don't seem to have focused in on the military. And I swear to God, I'm going to make the slimy sons of bitches regret it!"

He looked at the young colonel he had been talking to. That officer was dressed in a sharp battle dress uniform, and he stared at the map intently until, once, he glanced at Alexandria. She sensed hostility in that brief look, and wondered what was going on.

General Davis stabbed at the map, his finger coming to rest just west of Fayetteville, North Carolina. He traced a line north by northeast into Virginia.

"We have received orders from the Pentagon via UHF," he said. "I am to send out a reconnaissance in force against the south of this position near Richmond. Colonel Lee here"—he indicated the glowering officer—"is going to lead that reconnaissance, which will consist of an understrength armored battalion—all the goddamned M1A2s we can get rolling, from the Third Infantry Division. Also some light armor, from the Third Battalion, Seventy-third Armor, together with whatever support can get motors running. It's not the punch I want to throw, but it'll do for starters. Right, Colonel?"

"Yessir, General!" Colonel Lee stood ramrod straight. "I expect to have thirty Abrams, and almost as many Sheridans, ready to roll within the hour."

"And Dr. Devane?" The general was looking at Alex, now.

"Yes, General?"

"I can't give you an order, of course. But I'd like you to go along on this little junket and see what there is to see. Can you do that?"

"I'd be honored, General."

"Colonel, you have a place for a science observer in your unit?"

"We'll make room, General." His voice was flat, his expression still unhappy. He would follow his orders, but the CO hadn't ordered him to *like* it.

The general ignored Lee's tone, turned back to Alex. "Good. Here's a little token of luck, perhaps you'd carry for me?" Davis unpinned something from his uniform blouse—at first she thought it was a small watch, but when she took it she saw that it was a tiny compass, like something a kid might take camping. "It showed me the way out of Cambodia, in '69," the general said. "Maybe it will help keep you out of harm's way."

"Thank you sir—I appreciate it, very much. And Colonel, I promise not to get in the way."

"Very well," said Lee. His eyes were hard, suspicious. "We're departing at 0400. Can you be ready by then?"

"Colonel, I'm ready right now," she replied.

Eglin Air Force Base, Florida

There were fourteen pilots in the briefing room, even though it was common knowledge on the base that only ten of the wing's Warthogs had been rendered operational. The CO, Colonel Willard, entered the room at 0325 and immediately had the full attention of his fliers, as he offered an explanation.

"This will be a volunteer mission," he said. "We have five target zones scattered across Georgia, and we are sending a pair of aircraft at each. You will be armed with a full complement—that is, sixteen thousand pounds—of bombs, in the Mark 84 configuration. So each plane will have eight of those big suckers. Make them count.

"You will also be charged with learning whatever you can about these objects. It is quite possible that you will be the first human beings on the planet to get a look at the bastards. And it is also quite possible that they will be shooting at you with weapons we cannot even begin to imagine. Anyone who wishes to decline this mission is hereby invited to leave the room—with no repercussions for making what anyone would agree is a very intelligent decision."

Naturally, no one so much as shuffled a foot, much less moved to get up from his or her desk.

"Good. You don't surprise me." Willard's face betrayed a flicker of pride, then immediately grew grim. "But even before we try to take the unknowns into account, you have to know that this will not be an easy mission.

"Our ground crews have put in heroic efforts on these old Warthogs. They've bypassed most of the upgrades, so you'll be flying the planes pretty much as they were flown during the eighties. You'll have full control over engines, flight controls, and landing gear. You also will have use of the Gatling gun, and will carry a full load of ammunition.

"As to bombardment, you'll be about as high-tech in your Thunderbolt IIs as your grandpappies were in their P-47 Thunderbolts over Normandy in '44. The entire LATSE system is disabled, so you'll be attacking without low-altitude safety and targeting enchancement. Basically, when you pull the switch, the plane releases the bomb, and the rest is up to gravity—and your own seat-of-the-pants aiming skill.

"You'll have to wait for first light before taking off, since the NVIS is also useless—but we want you all in the air by 0500. You'll have no CDU, so you'll have to check your instrument panel the old-fashioned way, and you'll have to find your targets without GPS. Fortunately, we have plenty of Georgia state highway maps to hand out; your targets will be clearly marked on them. I recommend you follow the road net until you get close enough for visual."

He said the last without a trace of irony. Duke Hayes glanced over at his wingman, Kathy Stiles—known as "Stylin' "—and raised his eyebrows. She shrugged her shoulders, and he could almost hear her Texas drawl saying "What else are we gonna do?"

"Furthermore," Colonel Willard went on, "your EAC and GCAS are inoperable—you'll have to maintain altitude with a steady hand on the stick, and it will be up to your own eyes to tell how far you are away from a ground collision. Hopefully, you haven't gotten so dependent on the electronics that you've forgotten the basics.

"As to approach, you should come in from the east. Clear skies are forecast, so at least you'll have the sun behind you. Regarding altitude of your bomb runs, the general wants you to stagger those. In each pair of attackers, one of you goes in high, the other low. This order is aimed to increase pilot survivability odds, and also enhance the accuracy of the bomb run.

"Each aircraft has been fitted with a UHF radio. You are to observe strict radio silence on the way to the target—we have no way of knowing if they'll be listening, possibly even homing in our signals. Once you've dropped your ordnance, chatter needs to be held to a minimum to avoid crowding the channel. Good recon information and urgent BDA should be broadcast in the clear, and immediately—if you get a look at these bastards, or their equipment, or the effects of their equipment, we want to know right away. Target damage assessment reports can wait until you get back on the ground. If you are hit and going down, broadcast coordinates and bail out—your ejection seats and parachutes should work normally."

The pilots remained silent, staring at the CO. "I appreciate all you men—and woman—being willing to take this mission on. You will go in order of seniority. That means that Smitty, Ace, Beagle, and Chuckie, you fellows will sit this one out. Stand by in case we need you—the crews are working on two more ships right now, and they might be airworthy by 1200. The rest of you, good luck, and God bless you. You will be flying in pairs—Sergant Simmons will hand out ten sets of orders, including our best data on target locations."

That respected NCO, a stern-faced woman of nearly forty, square in face and physique, was already passing out the packets. The colonel waited as the pilots opened the envelopes. Duke found, as promised, an official Georgia state highway map. A series of large red dots, five of them, were emblazoned on the map across the middle of the state. The one in the middle, perhaps twenty miles west-northwest of Macon, was circled on his and Stylin's maps.

When all the pilots had confirmed their targets, the colonel spoke once more.

"I want you all to go out there and let them know that humankind isn't going to take this crap lying down. Good luck, and good hunting."

There was little talking as the pilots rose from their desks and headed for the flight line. The four who would stay behind quietly offered their wishes of good luck to the other ten, then watched as the fliers, wearing flight suits and carrying helmets, started outside. Dawn was just a pale strip along the eastern horizon. It was 0421.

Duke and Stylin' found their A10s already fueled and armed, eight two-thousand-pound bombs slung beneath each jet. She had been flying on his wing for the last year, and the two of them didn't need words to offer their good luck and best wishes. A firm handshake was enough, before they climbed into the narrow cockpits, the glass canopies sliding tightly shut as they strapped themselves in.

By then daylight was spreading across the sky, and there was enough illumination to see the other aircraft arrayed, in pairs, outside the hangars where they had been hastily repaired. The turbofan engines rumbled and whirled, slowly building up rpms until each was blazing and roaring. Waves of yellow heat emerged from each jet, shimmering the air across the tarmac in the growing light of day.

Duke looked over to Stylin', and she gave him the thumbs-up signal. He responded in kind, released his brake, and throttled the engines enough to start rolling his Warthog out from the flight line. The A10 moved smoothly, trembling from the force of the roaring engines, straining against the brakes as he turned onto the runway, bearing almost due west into the slight breeze. Stylin' was there to his right. For just a second he had a jarring thought as he looked at the eight huge bombs slung underneath her aircraft, knowing that he had the same load on his own ship. How were these things ever going to get off the ground?

But he shoved that thought aside when the light down the runway—a low-tech replacement for their usually reliable communications—flashed to green. Duke released the brakes and opened the throttle wide, pouring fuel into the jet engines, adding another dose of it behind the fiery combustion, firing the afterburners that gave the turbofans their maximum kick. Despite its massive weight the Warthog all but leaped forward, accelerating until it was racing down the runway, bumping and rattling over the little bumps in the concrete surface.

And then those bumps were gone. He eased back on the stick gradually, took the plane through a climbing turn to starboard, and leveled off at five thousand feet. Stylin' was with him, a couple of hundred yards behind his starboard wing. Duke looked at the road map on his display board, seeking the landmarks that would carry them toward their target. He spotted I-10 immediately, and they cruised north of the freeway, the twin stripes of white pavement clearly visible amid the gently rolling verdancy of the Florida woodlands. Soon he spotted the serpentine-shored waters of Lake

Seminole. Banking gently, he led his wingmate toward the northeast, passing over the lake and generally following the meandering track of the Flint River.

For a half hour they cruised on this bearing, altering course only slightly to avoid flying directly over the city of Albany. By the time they reached Lake Blackshear, I-75 was visible to the right, and Duke knew that would take them all the way to Macon. He kept that wide freeway, six lanes, just barely in view, and began to pay close attention to the northern horizon.

Soon he could discern a murk there, like a dark and low-lying bank of cloud. They flew closer, and he knew that the smoke was generated by a massive fire. Duke was surprised by the raw anger he felt, the sense of personal affront provoked by this proof of vast devastation. They skirted Macon, and he swiveled his head around, made eye contact with Stylin' as she held perfect formation. He pointed at her, followed by an upward gesture; then to himself, and down. She nodded, pulled back on her stick, and began to climb toward ten thousand feet. Backing off on the throttle a little bit, he began to weave slowly, taking the time to look at the ground, and at the same time let her make the first bombing run.

The first thing he noticed were the people fleeing the impact zone along every road, highway, track, and lane that he could see. Most of them were on foot, though he saw bicycles, a number of old pickup trucks, and more than one farm tractor towing a wagonful of humanity. Many of them looked up as he flew over, and some waved encouragement. Before he knew it he was over a blackened swath of landscape, once-green Georgia hills scoured overnight by a furious blaze that had mostly burned itself out. He flew lower and lower, losing sight of Stylin' in the clouds overhead. Banking a little toward the east, he skirted the edge of the fire zone.

There were no people, nothing living, below him now. Passing by a low ridge, he caught his first glimpse of the crater, and his anger surged anew. It was an obscenity, a vulgar wound in the surface of the world. At least a mile across, surrounded by a belt of reddish earth thrown out by the impact. This ring of evictus was several miles wide, devoid of buildings, trees, roads—or any sign that those things had even existed there. Clearly, the impact of the space object had devastated a wide swath of countryside.

The crater itself was deep, filled with swirling smoke. Duke's fingers clutched the control stick tightly as he kept his eyes on the gaping hole, knowing that Stylin' should be near to the point of dropping her bombs. Even so, the explosions took him by surprise, eight crumping blasts so close together that he was unable to count the individual blasts. Fire blossomed in the crater, huge pillars of orange flame roiling into the air, churning into black columns of smoke.

Duke watched, anxious, for any sign of return fire at his wingmate's plane. There was no reaction beyond the billowing fire and smoke. He circled over the wasteland, waiting as the explosions settled and the freshening wind slowly swept some of the murk from the crater. When the target was clear he closed in, flying only five hundred feet above the ruined landscape. The edge of the crater was a low ridge, but he maintained his level flight and still passed several hundred feet above the crest.

The inside of the crater was like a bowl of thick soup, black murk that swirled along the ground, obscuring much of the landscape. What he did see was utterly barren ground, dirt and sand with no suggestion of plant life. A gust eddied the smoke at the bottom of the crater, and he caught a glimpse of something huge and shiny: it was a sheet of metallic material that looked remarkably like stainless steel, badly stained with soot and smoke. It gave him an aiming point, and he made a small adjustment to the stick, bringing him directly toward that artificial surface.

He flipped the switches four at a time, feeling the aircraft bounce as the heavy, ground-penetrating bombs fell away. Immediately he shoved the throttles forward, acceleration pressing him tightly against the back of his seat. Never before had he dropped bombs so low, and he braced himself for the shock.

The blast was much more powerful than he expected. It felt as though a giant fist smashed into the belly of his plane, kicking him hundreds of feet upward. He struggled to control the Warthog, careening wildly as he raced away from the damage zone. His engines were still running fine as he raced away from the crater, and he had enough fuel to allow him another look. Taking a long, leisurely turn, he waited for the smoke and fire from his own bombardment to drift away.

Ten minutes later he made another pass, low over the impact crater. Again he saw that surface of metal, got a good enough look that he could make a report as he flew past and started climbing toward a safer altitude.

"Hog flight Delta," he reported, pressing his microphone switch for the first time on the mission. "All bombs away; up to sixteen direct hits. I got a look at the target after the run. Metallic, circular—possibly the end of a cylinder sticking out of the ground." He took a breath, biting back the fury that almost choked off his words.

"Lots of direct hits. But it looks like we didn't make a fucking dent."

SIX

Alexandria had lost her first argument with Colonel Lee, which was why she was now riding in the windowless troop compartment of a Bradley M2 Infantry Fighting Vehicle instead of the front seat of a Humvee or truck, where she would have been able to see what was going on.

"You'll see plenty once we get there," the colonel had snapped. "Until then, I'm going to do what I can to keep you alive!"

She was wearing jeans and a field jacket, with a pair of military boots on her feet. But she had drawn the line at the Kevlar helmet and vest that had been offered. For the last eight hours she had shared the back of the Bradley with six soldiers of B company, Third Infantry. The vehicle commander, Lieutenant Hickman, and a gunner were up in the small turret, and the driver had his own compartment up front, accessed through a small passage the men called the "Hell Hole."

"It's not a Lexus," admitted the friendly specialist—his tag said JONES—who had slid over to make room for Alex in the back of the rumbling armored vehicle. "But at least we don't have to pay for gas!"

Like the other soldiers back there, he looked amazingly young. As a group these GIs were curious and, so far as she could tell, unafraid. They had cheerfully accepted her into the already crowded crew compartment, and after the inevitable invitations to sit on one or another lap they had shifted around to make room for her on one of the seats. Thus they rolled northward toward a confrontation with something they could not begin to imagine, and each of the soldiers seemed lost within his thoughts. They wore full battle armor and had their M16s in their hands.

Alex knew they were stopping only when the steady, rumbling progress of the Bradley slowed. With a creak of brakes and a final lurch, the IFV halted, and the soldiers stirred.

"Hey, L.T." Jones shouted up into the turret. "What's up?"

"The colonel's on his way back," replied the young officer. "Pop the hatch—dismount, everybody."

Alex felt a startling wave of relief when the rear door of the M2, a hatch that folded down to form a short ramp to the ground, gave way. The outside air smelled like smoke and ash, but it was a welcome break from the claustrophobic confines. The GIs had obviously drilled the dismount—they shot out of the vehicle in a couple of seconds. Alex came a little more slowly, working the kinks out of her muscles as she stood up straight and stepped down to the ground.

The column was stopped on northbound I-85. The first thing Alex noticed was the great crowd of civilians, an uncountable number of them, filing past on the southbound lanes of the interstate highway. Most of them were on foot, though a stream of bicyclists passed on the inside shoulder. The latter were not, generally, the helmeted and gaudily tunicked cyclists that had been so common on trails and country roads. These were regular people pedaling along on a wide variety of two-wheeled conveyances, some of them with suitcases, backpacks, and bundles strapped haphazardly to handlebars and fenders. Here and there an old truck or antique car poked its way along the other side of the stream of refugees. The people formed a steady column, moving away from Richmond toward North Carolina. Many were watching the military columns with a mixture of hope and apathy.

"Give those bastards hell!" someone shouted, and there were a few ragged cheers. Most of the people just kept walking.

Alex saw more Bradleys behind them, at least a dozen parked in the right lane of the northbound freeway. Stepping around her own vehicle, she saw that they were at the crest of a low ridge. In the valley before them she saw another dozen M2s, and then a number of huge, flat tanks that she recognized as the Abrams, the Army's main battle tank. A few smaller tanks had rolled down the embankment and were parked off to the side; she assumed that these were the Sheridans. Many Humvees were interspersed among the armored vehicles, and one of them was rumbling against the flow of traffic in the left lane. It braked as it drew closer, and Alex saw Colonel Lee sitting high on the passenger side, his head and shoulders visible above the windshield.

"Dr. DeVane?" he barked.

"Yes, Colonel!" she replied crisply, fighting the urge to offer a mocking salute.

"We're approaching the impact zone. If you are willing, I would like you to ride with me, to assist in our preliminary analysis."

"Of course, Colonel," she said, deciding not to wonder about his change of heart. She turned to Jones and his squadmates. "Thanks for the lift, guys. Good luck."

"You too, Doc!" offered the young specialist, as she climbed into the back of the colonel's Humvee.

Before she had fastened her belt the little vehicle curled through a U-turn and started rolling forward beside the parked column. Though she didn't have a great view, Alex found it a relief to be able to see anything, after the long ride in the buttoned-up Bradley. Leaning over slightly, she could see past the colonel's shoulder, the view through the windshield grim and daunting. Massive clouds towered like black thunderheads into the sky, smoke still rising from a vast area of utter destruction. It was taller, darker, more ominous than any storm cloud she had ever seen—indeed, in the shadowy recesses between the roiling, churning tendrils it seemed to be a perfect black, if there could be such a thing.

They rolled over a gentle crest, and the view opened up to a horizon several miles away. There were only a few people on the other side of the road and about half of them were sitting listlessly or even lying motionless, as if they had collapsed. It seemed wrong to Alex that this great military column was just rolling past, not stopping to offer assistance, but a cold and rational internal voice reminded her that important work awaited the soldiers. If they failed, they would suffer an even harsher fate than the wretched refugees scattered wearily along the southbound road.

"Have you gotten any reports from the flyovers yet?" Alex asked the colonel.

He turned around, scowling. His jaw was clenched, and he studied her through narrowed eyes.

"I have Top Secret S/I clearance," she snapped. "And I presume I was sent along to help evaluate the situation. It would help if you shared a little of your recon data with me."

Lee looked as if he wanted to argue, but apparently decided that her words made sense. With a shrug, he shifted around in his seat, resting his left arm on the back so that he could meet her eyes. "We've had aerial recon on several of the landing sites, also a few bombing runs. Pictures have been taken, but we don't have the facilities to get them out here, not after the EMP. So we're going on descriptions that have been passed on verbally.

"These things appear to be metal, cylindrical in shape. Hard to tell how long they are, since a good portion of each is buried in the ground; they seem to be about twelve meters, nearly forty feet, in diameter. The impacts formed craters about a mile across—some bigger, some smaller, depending more on the type of ground they landed in than anything else. That is, each cylinder we've observed has had the same dimensions. In places our pilots have seen surfaces that look pretty shiny, like stainless steel. Most of the metal surface is charred black."

"You mentioned bombing runs. Do you have any BDA results?"

Lee shook his head grimly. "Nothing useful. A number of pilots reported direct hits, but when they flew past after the smoke had cleared they couldn't see any holes, not even dents, in these cylinders."

Alex nodded. "Whatever that metal is, it has to be damned strong to survive entry into our atmosphere. I don't think anything short of a nuke would penetrate."

"And every goddamn nuclear weapon in our arsenal was fried by the EMP," growled the colonel. "At least, the triggering mechanisms were toasted. God only knows when we'll be able to get a few of them patched together."

"And even if we do, we're looking at nuking half the East Coast if we use the bombs." Alex felt sick to her stomach. "Even if we kill the Martians, we'd have to be evacuate a lot of important real estate for the next fifty years or more."

"So we'll meet the bastards the old-fashioned way," Lee replied. "With tanks and cannons and machine guns. And goddamn bayonets, if we have to!"

"Colonel?" said the driver, calling Lee's attention to the road. "We're approaching the impact zone.

"All right. Stop here. Sergeant, get out the flags—give the order to deploy the first three platoons in line of battle. The rest of the battalion waits in reserve."

"Yes, sir." The fourth passenger in the Humvee, Alex realized, was a signalman. He slid out of the vehicle as soon as it stopped, unrolling several segmented staffs and quickly attaching colorful flags.

"Each of my company captains has a working radio," Lee explained to his passenger. "But we haven't had time to repair the radios in all the vehicles. So we're using signal flags to communicate. And we don't know if these SOBs are listening in to our electronic communications, either."

In short order the sergeant reentered the backseat, and the Humvee started to roll again. Looking to the side, Alex saw several of the huge, flat-bodied Abrams tanks rolling to the right and left, smashing through the chain-link fence lining the freeway, starting through fields of tobacco and corn. A half dozen Bradleys came behind, and Humvees equipped with machine guns and a couple with larger weapons, probably recoilless rifles, sped off to guard the flanks. The colonel's Humvee, with a tank and two Bradleys as escorts, continued along the two-lane freeway. High on the road's embankment, Alex suddenly felt very visible, and very vulnerable.

The sturdy vehicle lurched as the driver guided them across a large crack in the pavement. Soon they were bobbing and bouncing over slabs of concrete that had broken, shifted, and heaved under the force of the cylinder's impact. The Humvee canted crazily to the left then lurched to the right as the sergeant at the wheel made his way across an increasingly broken roadway. The four-wheel drive became essential, the front wheels pulling the vehicle up sharp slabs of stone while the rear pushed, sometimes skidding or scattering gravel.

A hillside rose to the left, covered with a dense blanket of trees that had been denuded of leaves. Blackened and gaunt, the once-lush vegetation had been ravaged by fire. A freeway bridge over a crossing road had collapsed, and the little convoy made its way down the grassy embankment, around the rubble of the broken span, and back up to the continuation of the interstate.

The landscape looked alien to Alex, like some vista on another planet. There was no sign of the greenery that had blanketed the ground so thoroughly a few days before. In places she saw remnants of buildings, splintered detritus of roofs and walls that had been smashed by a cascade of dirt ejected from the crater by the impact. The broad outlines of the twin spans of interstate highway were visible as more or less symmetrical ridges, but the actual roadways were covered with so much dirt, mud, and debris that only a few small patches of pavement showed through.

As they crept slowly forward even those bits of concrete vanished. Everywhere the land was bare, churned dirt, layered thickly enough to obscure even tall trees and houses. How quickly all of clues of humankind's presence could be wiped out! The featureless ground rose before them, a wide, low hill leading toward a flat horizon. The ridge of that horizon extended to either side, a smooth summit of dirt curving gradually away to the right and left, and Alex guessed it to be the rim of the impact crater.

The Humvee churned and lurched up the increasingly steep slope, the driver working the wheel methodically, engine whining. Alex held on, feeling the tires slip in the soft earth. Amazingly, one of the huge tanks climbed the same incline a hundred yards to the right, bobbing on its tracks and springs, negotiating the ascent far more easily than the smaller-wheeled vehicle. The Humvee's engine roared as the driver pressed the gas, but the forward momentum slowed, dirt shooting in a rooster tail behind one rear tire.

"Sorry, Colonel—this is as far as we're gonna get," reported the driver.

"We'll take it on foot, then," Lee replied, pushing his door open and climbing out. Alex followed, noticing that the tank had also halted. They were a few dozen meters short of the ridge.

Another Humvee stopped behind theirs, disgorging a couple of soldiers with M16s and a lieutenant carrying what looked like a small cassette player with an attached microphone. As he approached, she saw that the device was held together by a crisscrossing web of electrical tape. Seeing her look, the young officer explained. "It's a jury-rigged Geiger counter. We put it together out of spare parts, in the electronics shop."

"Good idea," she acknowledged, impressed. The base was a cassette player, she realized, hearing the ticks caused by charged ions as they popped from the speaker. The rate was low, about what she would have expected from normal background radiation. One small bit of good news.

Helicopters chattered in the distance, and she saw several of them approaching, rattling close to the ground, coming fast. They were Hueys, in Army olive drab: a total of four aircraft, and they split into pairs, two going to either side of the command group. They hovered about a kilometer away, low enough to remain below the rim of the crater as Alex followed Colonel Lee up to that crest. She was glad she had the Army boots on, as each step sank ankle deep into the loosely piled earth. She leaned forward, pulling her foot free, and instinctively crouched as the small party approached the top of the earthen hill.

Finally, they lay prone on the surprising cool dirt. Alex crept forward until she could see past the horizon, down the rounded slopes of the deep crater. Indeed, they had to crawl forward, a little past the rim, before they could get a look all the way down to the bottom.

Smoke or steam swirled in that pit, but she could immediately make out the shape of the Martian cylinder. The butt end of it was a perfect circle, blackened and charred in appearance, with several smoldering patches on its surface. It was huge, larger in diameter than the Saturn rockets she had seen at the Cape. Jutting from the ground at an angle, only a small portion of the cylinder was actually visible, but she pictured it as a missile, a cosmic javelin that had buried most of its length in the body of the planet.

It was that image of a stabbing attack, more than the EMP, the destruction, the columns of refugees, that truly made Alexandria feel violated. That violation brought rage, and she clenched her hands into fists, sensing that the same emotion was seizing the soldiers to either side of her. Colonel Lee raised his hands and gestured to Alex and the others to fall back. Quickly they scooted back over the crest of the crater rim, clots of dirt clinging to their uniforms as they lay low on the earth.

"Radio," Lee barked, and a sergeant came forward with a handheld set. The Colonel took the mike as he squinted at the low-flying Hueys. "Greenbird flight—hit the bastards with everything you've got. Simultaneous volley, then stand clear."

The helicopters accelerated with startling speed, engines whining and rotors chopping as they raced over the rim of the crater. Alex kept her eyes on the pair to the right, advancing with the colonel until they had a line of sight to the cylinder again.

For the first time she noticed that each chopper was armed with an array of rockets, lethal-looking missiles slung to the right and left of the fuselage. Those rockets flared into life and shot forward, trailing straight columns of smoke. She followed their progress as they arced into the crater, converging on the base of the massive cylinder. They were straight-flying, nonguided missiles, but the pilots had aimed well. One after another they impacted, a series of explosions so close together that it roared like a single convulsive blast, massive destructive power blasting squarely against that alien material. Alex clapped her hands over her ears, but she couldn't tear her eyes away from the glorious, compelling violence.

Flame and smoke billowed around the object, obscuring every detail from view. For a few seconds she thought that the Martian craft was blazing, but she soon realized that the fires were the result of the rocket warheads. Sparks trailed down to the ground, and she smelled the stink of acrid vapors. The helicopters retreated as a wind curled past, clearing away the thickest of the smoke. When she looked again, Alex could see several gleams of silvery metal on the base of the cylinder, and she realized the sole effect of the rocket attack.

"They just knocked some of the tarnish off," she said, unable to hold back the bitterness of her disappointment. What kind of metal was that?

Any further speculation was interrupted by a crackle of radio static. The signalman quickly called the colonel over, and as soon as Lee was down below the rim of the crater he took the handset.

"This is Rebel Leader," he barked.

Alex couldn't hear the voice emerging from the earpiece, but from the grim set of Colonel Lee's jaw she gathered it was not good news. "But, sir!" he protested after perhaps twenty seconds of listening. "We are on-site now, with direct visual contact established. Don't pull us back!" There was more squawking, and the field commander shut his eyes—as if to block out the vexing words. "Yes, sir," he said eventually. "Rebel Leader out."

Handing the radio back to the sergeant, he glared at Alex as if she herself had infuriated him. Or maybe it just seemed like that; she vaguely perceived that he was encompassing the entire scouting party in his glare.

"We've been ordered back," he snapped. "To a three-mile radius of impact. General Davis got personal word from the JCS, right from the president. They're worried that these things are bombs, and they won't risk men—personnel—in the potential blast zone. So let's mount up and move out."

"That's ridiculous!" Alex replied sharply. "That cylinder in there is no more a bomb than it is a goddamned peace overture. It makes no sense to pull back and give them freedom to do whatever they want in the crater!"

"Dr. DeVane, I don't recall asking for your opinion. And I know for damned sure that the general, and the president, didn't ask for it. Now, we're bugging out, and that's an order."

She drew a breath but bit her tongue, remembering her father's insisting upon some ludicrous restriction when she was in high school. She had never managed to change his mind by open defiance, but had learned that there were subtle ways of influencing a stubborn man's opinion.

"I meant no disrespect, Colonel," she replied. "But there is a point worth making: The president *did* ask for my opinion! That's exactly why he sent me to Fort Bragg and why General Davis sent me along with your task force." Alex shook her head, a gesture of regret, of weariness, and she sensed that the officer was not unsympathetic.

"Think of the logic—from an attacker's point of view. If these were bombs, they must be intended for massive explosions. Surely they would have been detonated in the atmosphere, not after they are mostly buried in the earth. Also, you remember the map in the general's office, the fall pattern of the cylinders in the eastern US?"

"Yes," Lee allowed cautiously. She held for a beat, sensing that he was drawing the same conclusion that she herself had.

"Get me General Davis," barked Lee, and the sergeant handed over the radio headset as he dialed in a frequency.

"Rebel Ears, calling Braggart," the signalman called. In a few seconds he extended the handset to the colonel.

"Sir, I have to report that this thing does not, repeat—*not*—appear to be an explosive device. Dr. DeVane has reached the same conclusion, and wants the opportunity to make this case to high command. Yes, sir, as high as necessary."

Alex was impressed by the force of Lee's voice—and she was a little nervous when he motioned her over, and extending the receiver to her.

"DeVane?" Davis's rasping voice was unmistakable. "Do you want me to take this argument to the president of the United States?"

"Sir, I am more convinced than ever that we are looking at a landing craft, not a bomb. I suspect that it's going to open up, and I think it's imperative that you have your troops in position to open fire as soon as they can. It's analogous to our own amphibious operations during World War II—the troops are never more vulnerable than when they're aboard the little boats taking them in to shore. Once they seize a beachhead, the task becomes more difficult by an order of magnitude."

"Just how did you make that decision, Doctor?"

"Think about the fall pattern that we saw on the map in your office." She remembered the image clearly, with the red push pins forming that long line up the coast, just inland from the major population centers. "Did that look to you like they were setting up a blast zone, or a line of battle preparatory to moving against our largest cities?"

"Shit." She pictured the general grimacing, looking again at the map, realizing that she was right.

"One more thing, sir," she prodded, after several seconds had passed.

"What is it?" Davis didn't sound happy.

"If this is a bomb, then it's far bigger than any bomb package ever manufactured by the human race. There is no way of knowing how powerful the effect—blast, radiation, heat, whatever it is—might be. Two miles back or ten, retreating from the craters is no guarantee of safety, even if I'm wrong. And if I'm right, and you order your men back, you're doing the equivalent of handing over the beaches to the invading army."

"That's enough. Give me the colonel."

She handed the radio back to Lee, who was kneeling in the dirt a few feet away. The colonel took the handset and listened for a short time. "Yes, sir!" he said, enthusiastically. "And I'll be sure to tell her, General. Rebel Leader out."

Lee was half-smiling as he handed the instrument back to his signalman. "The general said he'd take your arguments on up the chain of command. Until then, he authorized us to hold pat. And he told me to tell you that, if you're wrong, whatever these Martians do to you will be a picnic compared to the wrath of the CO."

"I can live with that," she said, realizing that "die with that" might be a more apt acknowledgment. Even so, she felt no wavering of her confidence as Lee started ordering his tanks forward and called for artillery spotters to get the range for his big guns.

SEVEN

"Wake up, Doc."

It was a captain on Colonel Lee's staff, poking her in the shoulder. Alex grunted and shifted awkwardly in the front seat of the Humvee. The sky was still dark, though the rim of the crater glowed in the reflected brightness of dozens of mast-mounted spotlights, all directed at the Martian cylinder within. She climbed awkwardly out of the vehicle and saw that the captain was offering her a helmet. Rather gratefully she took the Kevlar and strapped it on to her head, then followed the officer up the slope to the rim. Kneeling, she saw that the inside of the crater was lit up like Camden Yards for a night game.

At the focal point lay the cylinder, still smoking, though not so much as before. In the harsh illumination it looked sinister and terribly unnatural, like some metallic mole working its way out of the earth for malevolent purpose. Blinking to clear the sleep from her eyes, she saw that her impression of movement was not mistaken: The end of the cylinder was slowly rotating, while the great body of metal remained motionless and buried in the earth.

"It looks like it's almost showtime," Colonel Lee declared, with what Alex thought was remarkable aplomb. It was as if he was relieved that the waiting was over, happy that—at last—he'd be able to take some concrete action.

"How long has it been turning?" she asked.

"Just started. I marked that slash there, where one of the rockets scraped the metal clean. Looks like it's finished one full rotation."

"Just like they're unscrewing a cap," she said, amazed at the primitive simplicity of the device.

"I sure hope we're right about it not being a bomb," Lee added, with a cocksure grin.

In contrast to the soldier's eagerness, Alexandria felt sick to her stomach. She saw soldiers down in the pit, was awed by the courage that made it possible for them to move up so close to this incredible, alien presence. They were wearing full NBC suits, she realized, plastic garments with individual air supplies that couldn't help but restrict movement and dexterity. Even so, the soldiers were armed with rifles and, in several cases, heavier weapons. There were dozens of them down there, deployed in a ring above the base of the crate, sighting their weapons down upon the slowly rotating cap at the terminus of the cylinder.

Looking around the rim of the crater, Alex raised her hand to shield her eyes from the blinding lights. She saw tanks nearby, in either direction, and as her vision adjusted she saw that the ring of armor extended around the entire depression. Obviously, some digging and bulldozing had been going one while she had been resting. Now, the big Abrams were situated right at the rim of the incline, their low, flat bodies hopefully concealed from the Martian device. The sinister, long-barreled 120 mm cannons poked over the crests, depressed enough to draw a bead on the cylinder. She could hear a whisper of sound from the nearest tank, knew that the turbine engines were running, ready to move the sixty-ton chariots with startling speed, if necessary. The Sheridans, taller and lighter, perched on the rim itself, their smaller guns also depressed to bear on the alien target.

She found her eyes drawn, almost hypnotically, to that slowly rotating base. It seemed to keep turning forever. By following the same mark Colonel Lee had indicated, she watched it go through six more full circles, each lasting less than a minute. Then, abruptly, it stopped moving. Surprised to find that she was holding her breath, Alex forced herself to exhale. She lay flat on the ground, staring, unwilling even to blink.

It was as if the whole combat team felt the same way. The air was palpable with menace, violence, possibility. . . .

Slowly, the massive circular tail of the cylinder began to bend away, gradually revealing a vast, cavernously dark—and apparently empty—

space. The soldiers in the pit raised their weapons, crouching, kneeling, or lying in firing positions depending on their situations.

"Send in a flare," ordered Colonel Lee.

A nearby soldier launched a projectile that hissed and sparked like a Fourth of July firework, a rocket that streaked unerringly toward that great, black hole. Just above the bottom of the pit the flare burst into magnesium-fueled brilliance, like a falling star—but instead of the heavens, this was a star that revealed the dawning image of Hell itself.

"Holy Christ on a crutch," gasped Lee.

"What the *fuck*?" added one of the staff officers.

Alexandria just stared. She knew that she was looking at a creature from another planet—from Mars!—but she could not fully wrap her mind around the fact. She wasn't even sure if it was one creature, or several.

Her first impression was that they were staring into a nest of snakes that had somehow catapulted itself through the cosmos. They were black and shiny, slithering this way and that in clear agitation. Only after a few seconds' scrutiny did she discern that the snakes were connected to a body, like a slick blob of tarry oil at the center of the flailing vipers. It had elements of squid or octopus to it, but was more alien, more fundamentally *wrong-looking* than any Terran creature could possibly be.

Barely had she begun to absorb, to process, the hideous image than the creature vanished, replaced by a dome of silvery metal that gleamed brilliantly in the fierce light of the flare. The surface was larger than the creature and seemed to cover it entirely, suggesting to Alex that it was some sort of shield or armor.

The same thought apparently came to Colonel Lee. "Open fire!" he barked.

The men in the crater, in their bulky NBC suits, were the first to react. Automatic weapons erupted in a buzz-saw chatter, more than a hundred M16s and machine guns firing at once. Several men launched rocket-propelled grenades, small missiles that sputtered directly toward the silver dome. They exploded against the shiny surface, each leaving a black smudge across the smooth metal.

But they didn't do any visible damage. Instead, the dome began to rise, climbing smoothly toward the huge round gap at the base of the cylinder. Alex couldn't see any means of propulsion, but her vantage point limited her to a top-down look at the thing. It came to the very edge of its container, and a pair of appendages—like tentacles, only segmented and silver metal—uncoiled through small vents in either side of the dome. Each of those tendrils brandished a shiny box at the end, reminding Alex of the mini-TES, the drill, and other tools that had been wielded by the Martian rovers.

She felt sickeningly certain that these tools were much more lethal in nature. Once again, the colonel made the same realization at the same time.

"Hit that bastard with everything!" he was ordering, even as the tanks opened up with their main guns. In contrast to the whispering turbofan engines, the nearby Abrams' main armament went off with an earsplitting crack. Almost simultaneously a large explosion flashed against the front of the silver dome. All around the rim, the rest of the M1A2s let rip a shattering volley, a mixture of high explosive and armor-piercing rounds that struck the Martian device with the force of a tornado.

Finally, the sinister dome recoiled, withdrawing into the cylinder, vanishing in the churning veil of smoke and lingering flame. The fire, both small-arms and tank, continued unabated, the soldiers reacting with the same sense of revulsion and horror that Alexandria felt. Rather surprisingly, she wished that she had a weapon of her own, something with which to rain death down upon the obscene invader.

The first return attack emerged from the swirling smoke in a staccato series of flashes. They stabbed outward as spears of light, like beams from the laser show at some sporting event, stuttering across the base of the crater. Alex watched as that beam swept past a platoon of soldiers. At its touch they twisted and writhed, silently falling away, lying in grotesque postures as soon as the bizarre flash passed them by. Each of the bodies was smoking, she realized, and saw that several of them had been burned practically in half.

The silver roundel was coming forward again, emerging from the smoke—and still apparently undamaged. One of the steel tentacles was held high, and it was the box at the end of that one that was emitting the light. Still watching in horror, Alex saw that lethal ray dart this way and that through the crater. The soldiers in their NBC suits were falling back, but they couldn't outrun this flashing beam. Within seconds, every man she could see was down, the bodies motionless and invariably smoldering.

She crawled over to Lee, who was saying nothing, but clenched his microphone in a white-knuckled fist.

"They have some kind of laser weapon," she shouted over the din of the pounding 120 mm guns. "We have to report that!"

Nodding, he gestured to a radioman, one of several waiting nearby. Following some shouted instructions that Alex couldn't hear over the din, the man crawled up and passed her the hand mike and earphones, then crouched and awaited instructions.

"Patch me back to General Davis," she barked.

He adjusted a few dials, made a test call. "He's waiting," the young soldier said calmly, apparently oblivious to the crashing steel monster a few dozen yards over his shoulder.

"General?"

"What the hell's going on up there?"

"We saw one of the Martians, General. More important, I think, we're getting a look at weaponry. The Martian has a metal shield protecting its body, with what looks like two attached weapons. One of these appears to be a laser, much more lethal than anything we have on Earth. The dome is mobile, seems to move pretty fast."

"What about the other weapon?"

She crawled forward, the radioman wriggling beside her, until she could look into the crater. The dome had advanced, even in the face of renewed cannonade, until it was poised at the lip of the cylinder's aperture. Dozens of charred bodies were visible, scattered across the bare dirt. Now she could discern light underneath the dome as it slipped out of the container and appeared to hover about a person's height above the ground. Alexandria counted three wide beams of ghostly blue light shooting directly downward from the thing, and to all appearances this light seemed to wield enough energy to hold the Martian machine above the ground.

"Don't know yet, General," she continued. "But they seem to have some kind of frictionless mobility—shit!"

She couldn't hold back the profanity as more shapes moved out of the murk. "We've got more of the bad guys." Alex reported as she watched: There were three of the silver domes in sight, all of them emerging from the cylinder, advancing across the floor of the crater just as if their light-beam "legs" were walking along. Each of the machines was equipped with those twin, silvery cables; for the moment, they brandished only one of the two, raising the devices that stabbed forth that searing, lethal laser.

The tanks redoubled their firing, the big cannons backed up by all manner of heavy machine guns, grenade launchers, and portable rockets. Zooming missiles crackled through the air overhead, and when that sound was immediately followed by thunderous explosions within the crater, Alex realized that the heavy artillery was coming into play.

She heard a cheer from some of the men along the rim, saw that one of the machines was staggering sluggishly after the volley of 155 mm shells. Slowly, that silvery device lowered itself to the ground, the tripod of lights fading away.

"One of them appears to have taken damage, from the artillery barrage," Alex reported. "Not destroyed, but maybe immobilized."

The other two machines took up stations to either side of the damaged dome, which looked strangely harmless sitting flat on the ground. The two lasers came up, and they sought targets along the rim of the crater. Alex squirmed backward in sudden fear—it look like the son of a bitch was aiming straight for her—then cried out in shock as the nearby tank exploded into a Roman candle of pyrotechnics.

The radioman screamed and toppled over; she saw that a piece of shrapnel had ripped away half of his head. Gagging, she turned away, knowing that she needed to keep talking. She clapped a hand over the earphone, straining to hear, but only when she saw that the coiled cable had been neatly severed did she realize that her reporting was finished.

The colonel was on his hands and knees, shaking his head groggily, and a nearby soldier ran down the hill, flames enveloping him, consuming his uniform, his hair, even his skin. She could only watch in horror as he toppled forward and stiffened. He was dead, but still burning, as his corpse tumbled down the steep incline on the outside of the crater. Just beyond the colonel another soldier crawled back to the rim, rose onto his knees, and fired a burst from his M16. Almost immediately he toppled back, his body from the shoulders up literally burned away.

Another tank blew up, and another, each with an explosion that showered flaming gasoline and exploding shells all around. It seemed that the laser had to no more than fix its deadly spot on the front armor or the turret of one of the armored behemoths to transfer enough heat to blow the Abrams into pieces.

More artillery shells howled overhead, with a sound like a train passing very nearby, and Alex felt the impact through the ground even before she heard the massive explosions. She lay flat, pressing her face to the ground, her arms over her head, as more and more high-explosive rounds slammed home. She felt a flash of heat to her left, turned enough to see that yet another tank had been incinerated.

Jesus! Shaking her head, trying to clear away the shock, trying to *think*, she found herself crawling back to the rim of the crater. Grateful for the

Kevlar helmet, she raised her head just enough to see—and immediately had a childish wish to cover her eyes and run away. She saw Lee nearby, the colonel's face locked in an expression of pure anguish as he knelt at the crest, glaring in impotent rage at the ruthless invaders.

Within the vast, circular depression, chaos reigned. Most of the bright lights had been extinguished, but every detail was clearly outlined in the hellish glow of the fires. Tanks were burning all around the rim of the crater, at least two dozen of them spewing fire and smoke into the night sky. Others had backed away, rumbling down the slope. One Abrams still fired, bravely and futilely, shells ricocheting off of the top of the nearest attacker. Alex moaned in despair as two of the tripods swept their lasers toward it, instantly incinerating the AFV and its courageous crew. The first thing she saw was that all three of the Martian machines were on the move again, striding up the steep slope on their light-beam tripod legs. They had diverged, and one of them was coming almost directly at Alex and the colonel.

"DeVane—come on! We're bugging out!"

It was the captain from Lee's staff, tugging at her shoulder. She pulled herself away from the almost hypnotic view of the approaching tripod—she couldn't believe how fast it moved, climbing the steep, loose dirt on the inside of the crater—and followed the officer, almost tumbling down the slope.

Three Humvees, including the one where she had taken her brief nap, were idling, pointing downhill. "Get in!" cried the captain, diving into the nearest, with Alex falling practically on top of him. She lifted her head, saw Lee jumping into another vehicle even as the thing was starting to move. A spot of red light flashed against the back of that Humvee, blowing it into a crackling ball of fire, and, with a sickening realization, she knew that the Martian tripod had crested the crater, was firing down at them.

Then everything turned white. She felt heat on her face, her hands, all of her exposed skin, and she guessed that she was screaming even though she couldn't hear any sound.

EIGHT

June 9
Delbrook Lake, Wisconsin

"I'm thinkin' about packin' up the Jeep," Browne told me. "Maybe take the dogs and head up north. 'Least, as far as a tank of gas will get me."

It felt like a summer evening, but not like any summer I could remember. There was a taste of ash in the air, a scent of smoke and . . . something far worse than smoke. Maybe it was death. (Later, I would learn that the Martians had that famously distinctive scent all their own, but on that day they had yet to emerge from their cylinders.) Browne had driven over a little while ago, and now we stood on my porch, looking at the gray skies to the west. That slate color was not the result of clouds, I knew. It was the lingering smudge of the fires that had pretty much burned themselves out over the last twenty-four hours.

"So," Browne continued, somewhat awkwardly, "I got room in my passenger seat if you want to come along."

I blinked, surprised. I hadn't really considered evacuating, leaving my house . . . leaving everything. Nodding thoughtfully, I tried to consider his invitation, knowing immediately that I wouldn't be going.

"You catch anything on your radio today?" I asked. "Do you think it will be any safer up north?"

"I got a few snippets here and there. Word is, that Sun Prairie cylinder is the farthest north in the area. Seems like they made a ring around Chicago, and down south of Indy. My guess is that they're going to come out of those things and start closing in on the cities."

That conclusion was not uncommon. I had picked up some newcasts on my own radio the previous day, and overnight. All the news was local in origin, but it seemed that some operators were monitoring other stations, so information was being spread in this kind of electronic Pony Express from one coast to the other. It seemed that, on the East Coast, Martians had already come out of their cylinders, and were moving on New York and Washington, DC. I had heard something about another ring around Atlanta, though details were sketchier there. Still, when we learned that a line of the objects had landed in an arc starting at Madison and extending into southern Indiana, the invaders' plan seemed obvious enough.

But . . . to leave? I wasn't ready to make that decision. Finally, I shook my head.

"Thanks, but I plan to stay. Who knows, I might even get a look at one of these things. Field research, for my next article, call it." I laughed awkwardly, surprisingly touched by his offer. "Really, I appreciate it. I'll . . . well, I'll do what I can to keep an eye on your place."

Browne was scratching his chin, looking at me appraisingly.

"Um, if you want your shotgun back, you can—"

"Nah, keep it," he said. "Maybe you've got the right idea, anyway. I might just stick around myself and see what happens."

His words made me almost weak with relief. It was amazing to grasp how lonely I had felt at the prospect of his leaving. Naturally, I did my best to conceal my feelings from him, not wanting to embarrass either of us.

"Well, we can stick it out together, then," I said simply. Spontaneously, I held out my hand, and he shook it. His grip was firm, dry, solid. We held that clasp for several seconds.

A ripple of sound reached us, a rolling crackle suggestive of a distant storm, but not precisely right. "That's not thunder, is it?" I wondered aloud.

He shook his head with a dismaying air of certainty. "That would be those 155s we saw rolling past the other night. Takes me back to the Delta, '67. They sound just the same now."

"You were in Vietnam?" I asked, realizing that it was a stupid question even as the words left my mouth. "I mean, I don't know why I should be surprised. I . . . I just didn't know."

"Yep, I'm an old wardog," he said "Third Marine Regiment, as a matter of fact. Worst year of my life. So, did you get called up?"

I shook my head. "My eyes were too bad, even for the US Army."

"Count your blessings."

"You want to stay and have something to eat?" I asked, trying not to sound desperate. Browne's presence was solid and comforting. Knowing that he had been a Marine added, irrationally perhaps, another level of reassurance. "I still have some steaks in the freezer."

"You talked me into it," he said.

We talked for a while as I grilled on the back deck. Night closed around us, and the steady thunder of the artillery barrage provided a backdrop that was at once sinister and comforting. Every so often the sound would die away entirely. Then, after a pause of ten or fifteen minutes, the barrage would resume with a furious and intense rattle.

"They're really pasting the bastards," Browne said approvingly, as the firing rose to a constant, rattling pitch of intensity.

Just after sunset the coyotes started up, howling and singing and wailing in their frenetic style, as if their own cries were a challenge to the invaders, a plaintive plea to send them away. We ate our steaks and shared my last couple of beers, well chilled by the generator-powered fridge, while we listened to the mournful chorus.

"You know, I always pictured coyotes as desert animals. Never knew we had them around here, not till I moved out to the country," I remarked.

"Funny thing about that. When I was a kid, there weren't many around here. When my dad was a kid, he *never* saw a coyote in Wisconsin. You always hear about us humans wiping out ecosystems, destroying habitat, ruining it for all the creatures of the woods. But there's a lot of animals that have adapted pretty good to us, and our houses and roads and farms . . . even our cities. Coyotes, why, their range has expanded like gangbusters. Same with raccoons. And whitetail deer, they never had it so good as when they can fatten up around a nice cornfield. Those things actually thrive in and around civilization—they do better now than they did than when this whole continent was wilderness."

"But lots of others animals are extinct, or endangered," I countered. "How many species have we wiped out altogether? Too many to keep track of!"

"Sure," he said, with a shrug. "It's all about adaptability. We humans are the masters of earth, and those critters that can adapt to us have managed to do okay. Those who can't, well, it's not so good for them. . . ."

His words trailed off against the backdrop of more artillery fire. There was no mistaking two facts: first, the shots were more sporadic than before, and second, they were originating much closer to us than they had been before.

"Sounds like the army is falling back," he said laconically. "I better get on home and see to those two hounds of mine."

I could hear Klondike and Galahad barking—I realized they'd been doing it for some time, though I hadn't noticed. There was a pitch of savage courage to that frantic baying, a challenge to the unknown that, for the first time, brought a glimmer of affection to my heart.

"Yes, well, nice to talk," I said. "Good luck."

"Let's watch each other's backs. Let me know if you see trouble coming," he replied.

"I will—and you, too."

"Will do," Browne said, before hurrying out to his Jeep.

I watched him go, even as the sounds of the big guns swelled to another crescendo. I heard the impact of shells pounding home, a crump of sound that was a visceral experience, a churning in my guts as much as a vibration in my ears. Looking to the west, I saw the glow of flames over the tree-lined ridge, and suddenly a sense of fear overwhelmed all the curious detachment, the calm rationality, that I felt had been guiding my decision.

Running back into the house, I found the shotgun on the kitchen table where I had left it a day and a half before. It was still loaded, with no shell in the chamber. I pocketed some spare shells and went to the back of the house—no, I needed a backpack. Setting the gun down again, I raced into the basement, pulled an old nylon pack from my pile of dusty camping equipment. Grabbing a sleeping bag, densely compact in its rip-stop stuff sack, I ran back upstairs, trying to think.

Let's see . . . flashlight! I found one in the kitchen, tossed it in. Spare blanket, poncho . . . bug repellent. Those vanished into the musty sack. Food? Cans were too heavy . . . refrigerated food would spoil. I tossed some bags of rice, a package of tortillas, some freeze-dried beans into one of the pack's compartments. Water! I found a two-quart plastic bottle, filled it from the tap. Spare clothes? There was no time.

The whole house shook from the impact of a high explosive, somewhere not far away. I ran out onto the deck again, looking to the north. Flames were flickering along the western ridge, trees—even though they were green, lush, and damp with dew—burning like incendiary flares. In that garish light I could see movement along the township road about a mile to the north. It looked like a number of people, on foot, running to the east.

A truck, headlights glowing, came rumbling along, and in the illumination I could see that these running people were soldiers, helmeted and wearing battle dress camouflage. The men dove off the road, making way for the speeding vehicle. Something flashed red along that pavement and in the same instant the truck exploded, a fireball of burning gasoline sloshing across the narrow roadway, incinerating humans on both sides. The big vehicle, a blazing wreck, lurched to the left, and tumbled onto its side, burning furiously.

Another vehicle, a military Humvee, was racing across the fields, bouncing through a ditch. It turned into Browne's pasture and the driver hit the gas, accelerating toward the big hill from which I had observed the Martian's first launch. Again that stab of red came out of the western darkness, and the Hummer vanished in a blossom of fire, a fierce conflagration that almost immediately consumed the vehicle and its human contents.

It was then that I saw the first of the Martian machines. It was a silver platform, domed at the top, with the now-famous tripod of blue light-energy legs extending underneath. It "walked" in that rolling gait, the front leg extending forward, then the two rear legs swinging up to either side. That pair of rear limbs took a momentary stance, balancing the machine while the lone foreleg again swept forward. It looked like an awkward pace, but the platform of the machine moved smoothly along, without any lurching or up-and-down bobbing.

One supple limb waved above the thing, and the silver box attached to that tentacle-like extension blinked again and again. Each time, a visible spear of light stabbed out, and, wherever those lethal missiles struck, fire immediately erupted. I saw individual soldiers in the field incinerated, one after another, every time that deadly laser struck home. One man, scrambling past the burning hulk of the Humvee, was cut in two by that searing, yet strangely benign-looking, beam.

In a shockingly short time, the machine had run out of targets. There were no more men running in the fields, no vehicles making their way down the township road—though by then I could see six or eight flaming wrecks on that short strand of pavement, as well as a few other burning -wheel-drive pickups and Humvees that had tried to make an escape s the countryside.

ore flames erupted as the Martian turned its laser against a farm at the intersection of my lane and the road. The house, the barn, the sheds all erupted. The three tall silos, shiny dark blue—climate-controlled and ultramodern—melted away, one after another, from the mere touch of that blazing beam. A second, then a third machine came into view behind the first. All of them fired their lasers, striking the houses of a small subdivision north of the road, turning the luxurious houses—the small ones had cost a half million dollars to build—into blazing pyres.

Only then did I see that one of the machines had started down the lane and was approaching Browne's farm, with my house waiting in the woods just behind. My hands were shaking as I ran inside and snatched up the shotgun. Grabbing my pathetic backpack, I ran out the back door, slid down the hill, ignoring the thorns that tore at my face and arms, and came to rest behind an ancient stone wall at the bottom of the hill. Peering over this dubious protection, I stared across the field, toward Browne's house atop its low rise.

The silver machine on its tripod legs strode closer, that red laser flashing this way and that. It struck the barn behind Browne's house, and immediately the old wooden structure—a classic red barn, like so many in the Wisconsin countryside—was enveloped by fire. Flames shot from the upper hatches, where hay had once been stored, and in a matter of seconds the roof was collapsing in on the seething-hot interior.

I heard a series of booming blasts in short succession, and I knew Browne was firing his shotgun at the tripod. I heard the dogs barking in frenzy, my neighbor's voice shouting something—later I would realize that he was calling "Galahad!" There was a yelp, then Browne fell silent. His house was burning, a line of fire starting in the middle as if an invisible knife of energy had chopped down from the sky, neatly bisecting the old wooden structure.

Once it passed Browne's house, the Martian tripod turned into the field, striding right along the stone wall where I crouched. The shotgun, the backpack, everything was forgotten as I stared in horror at the approaching menace. I could see the "belly" of the domelike body. There were three holes in the otherwise smooth metal. Each of these was the source of one of the blue-green light beams that served as the device's legs. The light glowed steadily, forming ghostly images of three straight limbs, pivoting smoothly where they emerged from the machine to carry it along.

I crouched down among the trees and underbrush. The tentacle held its laser device aloft, spitting deadly rays here and there, incinerating trees, haystacks, even a luckless deer that stood, transfixed, at the edge of Browne's small pond. As it passed me, only a dozen meters away, I caught my first whiff of that awful carrion smell, like the stench of long-spoiled meat, that was characteristic of the Martian within that metallic dome. I watched as the translucent legs came to rest in the long, wet grass; each time, the limb pressed the foliage to the ground, stomping a circular imprint into the soft earth. The scientific quarter of my brain processed this data instinctively, wondering with a sense of detachment how the light beam could actually bring weight to bear against the ground.

The practical part of my mind made sure that I stayed hidden, unmoving. My eyes followed the thing as it marched past the burning Humvee without so much as pausing to inspect its handiwork. Continuing on, it moved up and over the rounded hilltop, finally vanishing on the far side of the elevation.

Only then did I dare to look around. Trees to either side of me were burning, but the fires were already failing. Despite the intense heat, the natural wetness of the verdant woods was too much to be overcome by individual blazes. Instead of yielding to the conflagration of a forest fire, the woods themselves were gradually dousing those flames that had managed to take hold.

Still, it was growing hot. I moved out into the field, looking around, but could see no sign of the machine that had passed so close to me. One of the tripods was still visible up near the road. It was immobile, poised like a sentry, and I ducked as I moved, trying to stay out of sight.

Up on the rise, Browne's house was an inferno. There was no sign of life up there, but with that tripod still watching I couldn't bring myself to cross a half mile of open ground to go see. Instead, I plunged back into the woods, swatting at sparks that fell from the lingering flames in the treetops, and forced my way up the hill to my house.

It stood there as I had left it, no doubt spared discovery by the long curtain of trees. Carrying the shotgun and the backpack, I went through the front door, closed and locked it behind me. Taking only the gun, I went downstairs into the basement, closing the door at the top of the stairs—a ridiculous gesture, since the louvered barrier would have yielded to a stout kick—and descended into the damp, chilly cellar.

I didn't dare to turn on a light. Instead, I sat there in the darkness, shivering, wondering, afraid.

NINE

June 10
Eglin Air Force Base, Florida

"We have some eyewitness reports of the Martians coming out of one of their cylinders—this tape was the last signal received from a NASA scientist attached to an army unit out of Fort Bragg. The scene was a crater just south of Richmond."

Colonel Willard had an old-fashioned reel-to-reel tape recorder at the front of the briefing room. Duke and the other pilots were occupying the desks, waiting for details about their next mission. The pilot straightened up at the mention of a NASA scientist—and he felt a chill of fear as he recognized Alexandria DeVane's voice on the scratchy tape.

". . . getting a look at weaponry. The Martian has a metal shield protecting its body, with attached weapons. One of these appears to be a laser, much more lethal than anything we have on Earth. The dome is mobile, seems to move pretty fast."

She sounded remarkably composed, if a little breathless. Duke realized that his hands were clenching the laminated edge of the small desk attached to his chair; he forced himself to react as Alex answered a question posed by some unknown questioner, who was obviously not on the scene with her.

". . . they seem to have some kind of frictionless mobility—shit!"

He jumped as she swore, wished he could have been there with her, agonized over the fear she was so obviously feeling. He continued to listen, fascinated and horrified, as she described the light-limbed tripods. The pilots could hear the blasting of artillery and also Alex's assessment of damage: "Not destroyed, maybe immobilized."

There followed more shooting, a female scream—then only the hiss of static as blank tape rolled by.

"That's all we've got," the colonel said, snapping off the machine. "But it's clear that the big cylinders, like we bombed three days ago, are disgorging these machines. The little ones are some kind of hovertanks, I'm guessing."

"Colonel?" Duke interjected. "That unit at Richmond . . . what happened to it, sir? Did they make it out?"

"That's the last anyone heard of 'em, Duke," Willard replied. "Com was wiped out, but we don't know if any of them got away." His eyes narrowed. "Why?"

"Just want to know, sir," the pilot said quietly. His voice was flat, but his heart, his guts, his mind were churning with fury, with a primordial hate. Alex had been there when the bastards came out of their ships! She had faced them down and—he had no doubt—she had died to get this information out. He fought against his grief, knowing he would have to make time for that later. For the time being, he would do everything in his power to make sure that she hadn't died in vain. That meant dropping his bombs right on top of one of these "frictionless" mobile domes.

Somehow he kept his composure as the colonel finished the briefing. Once again, the Warthogs would go out with two-thousand-pound bombs. This time, they were to attack the machines that had reportedly emerged from several of the crates and were advancing northward, toward Atlanta. Two more A10s had been added to the operational force, so they would attack three targets, with four planes assigned to each mission.

Once again Stylin' had Duke's wing. He was in tactical command of the other pair of flyers, Two-fer and Ziggy, as well. After a thorough preflight check, the twin-engine jets roared down the runway and climbed into the warm, humid skies over southern Georgia. Relying on the UHF radios for communication, the Warthogs broke into their three groups, two pairs apiece, and followed the highway net toward Atlanta. Reports had the Martians advancing along several vectors, with a group of three of the bizarre machines having emerged from each of the cylinders.

In the absence of their sophisticated electronic targeting equipment, coupled with the fact that they would be aiming for small, mobile targets, they had decided to go in low. Duke led his three comrades past Macon, across I-75, angling northeast until he spotted a serpentine body of water known as Jackson Lake. Here they banked to the northwest, and dropped down to five thousand feet.

The trail of the Martians was clearly visible, swaths of black carved brutally through the verdant, hilly countryside. The latest reports, crackling from the UHF receiver, had the enemy about ten miles ahead of them, so Duke used a hand signal to order the group even lower. No sense in giving the bastards a lot of warning, he told himself.

Soon they were cruising at only a few hundred feet of altitude. They climbed slightly to come over a ridge of low hills, and their targets came into view immediately, plainly visible no more than two miles away. Three of the tripod-propelled domes were advancing northward, dispersed perhaps a mile apart. Burning buildings marked their path, and Duke immediately observed the red flashes of the energy weapons that Alex had described. They flickered across a wide range of targets, generally stabbing at objects within about a quarter mile of the tripods. Duke watched as, in short order, a farm tractor, several houses, and a gas station burst into flames. The latter went up with a massive fireball, spewing a churning cloud of orange flame and black smoke into the sky.

The jets were coming up fast, behind the Martians. Duke glanced to port, caught Stylin's eye, and pointed her toward the left-most of the tripods. Ziggy and Two-fer, off his starboard wing, he sent toward the machine on the far right, while he lined up his bombsight on the one in the middle. After they dropped their bombs, the plan called for them to make a second pass and strafe with their chin-mounted Gatling guns.

They came on fast and low, the A10s cruising easily, diverging in course as they closed on their targets. The Martians were only a mile away, still striding northward, as Duke locked his hands around his bomb-release switch, knowing the other pilots were doing the same. With a minute adjustment of his rudder pedals, he lined up the gleaming metallic shape with his bull's-eye.

He heard the first explosion to his right, couldn't help glancing to the side as one, then a second Warthog disintegrated in midair as their bomb loads—sixteen thousand pounds of TNT on each plane—exploded prematurely, ignited by the touch of that laser. He spat a curse as he turned back to his own target, pulled the switch to release his bombs.

A spot of red light glowed atop the Martian machine, as the energy weapon came to bear. A bolt of brilliance shot toward him and the A10 lurched violently—it was only the release of the heavy bomb load, which bounced the jet upward, that spared him. Even so, he saw that a long section of his starboard wingtip had been sheared neatly off by the searing laser.

He pulled on the stick, banking to port and diving, instinctively aware that he had to get out of the line of sight of that deadly ray. A fireball lingered in the air before him and he knew that Stylin's Thunderbolt had been destroyed with bombs still aboard; the aircraft was gone, though he saw the pilot above, careening upward from the force of her ejection seat. Even before her parachute deployed another deadly beam of light slashed into the tumbling, helpless shape, incinerating her in the instant that Duke flashed past.

"God damn it to hell!" he cursed, as his Warthog plunged toward the ground. He waited until the last minute to pull back the stick, vaguely aware that his bombs were exploding behind him. He swept along the contour of the ground, climbing slightly, brushing the treetops with the armored belly of his A10.

Moments later the forested crest of the hill flashed past and he dove lower, placing the ridgeline between himself and the Martians. A cloud of smoke spewed upward, churning black, rising from the impact of his bombs. Only when he was several miles away did he climb slightly, guessing that he might be out of range of that deadly laser. He had no thought of returning for a strafing run—his powerful 30 mm Gatling gun, capable of firing thousands of rounds per minute, seemed like a pathetic popgun when compared to the speed-of-light lethality of the Martian ray.

But he did gain enough altitude to look back and make an assessment of the effect of his bombs. He saw all the proof he needed in the sight of all three Martian machines, gleaming silver in the afternoon sun, gliding smoothly over another ridge. Beyond, not terribly far away, the skyscrapers of Atlanta rose boldly into the sky.

June 10
South Richmond Crater, Virginia

Alexandria DeVane was aware of the cool dirt pressing against her face. It felt comforting, healing, and for a very long time she welcomed its soothing pressure. She was *part* of this earth, and it felt vaguely right that she should return to it. There was a moist, fertile smell that filled her nostrils, overcoming even the lingering background of char and soot.

Gradually, however, pain began to intrude upon her senses, and with that pain came, very slowly, the return of consciousness, and memory. She became aware of an obscure gray illumination that, when she forced her eyelids open, became the flat metallic wash of full daylight under a gray and glowering sky. Lying on her belly, with her cheek pressed against the ground, she was looking uphill, past the bare dirt ridgeline of the crater.

Shifting slightly, she felt the crackling of her skin, and a deep, throbbing ache in her muscles and her joints. The gaunt shape of a burned-out Abrams tank came into view, the massive armored vehicle flipped upside down like a discarded child's toy. Smoke still wisped from the charred undercarriage. One of the treads had broken and trailed downhill like a grotesque piece of intestine.

Memories came flooding back—she remembered the captain, the Humvee, the start of the mad dash down the slope. Grimacing against the pain, she slowly turned herself around, mildly surprised to find that none of her bones seemed to be broken. The formerly olive-camouflaged vehicle, now charred black, was fifty yards away down the slope, lying upside down. The rear end was shattered, and she knew that the gas tank had exploded. Alex guessed that she must have been blown out of the Humvee with the start of that explosion—she didn't need to look closely at the charred black figures in the wrecked scout car in order to know that she was the only one who had survived the blast.

Next, she knew that she would have to stand, and she almost sobbed at the thought of such painful exertion. A part of her suggested that it would be easiest just to lie back down on the cool, welcoming earth, to meld herself to that ground again, permanently. Angrily, she shook her head, rejecting the notion. She thought of the Martian machines, climbing out of the pit, ignoring the explosives plastering them from tank guns and field artillery, and that thought opened up a well of hatred, a grim desire for vengeance, a refusal to submit.

Those dark emotions gave her the strength to move. First rising to her hands and knees, she took a few deep breaths to establish her equilibrium, then staggered to her feet. She almost fell on the steeply sloping ground, but by leaning forward, bracing her hands on her knees, she was able to remain standing. As an additional advantage, her posture allowed her to focus just on a small patch of bare ground—she was not yet ready to behold the full scope of the defeat inflicted by the Martians upon Colonel Lee's armored reconnaissance team.

But she could only delay for so long. Finally, she straightened and climbed to the very rim of the crater so that she could see the disaster in all its grisly extent. The flat skies deadened the daylight, eliminated shadows, a fitting illumination to the vast swath of lifelessness. Smoke still wisped from many of the wrecks, and the stenches of melted plastic, charred rubber, and worse all mingled in her nostrils. She took out a handkerchief, pressed it across her mouth and nose, and turned through a circle. The last direction she faced was the interior of the crater.

The charred cylinder still occupied its place in the center of the steep-sided depression. The exit portal at the end lay on the ground, hinged flat, with the black hole of the container's interior yawning beyond. The menace in that image was palpable—if there was a Hell, surely its gate would have looked something like this. Alex's breathing grew ragged, a nearly insurmountable desire to flee welling within her. She needed to run, to hide!

But another interior voice spoke against her emotions. Reason told her that this was an unparalleled scientific opportunity, that she could learn about these aliens if she went inside that ship. She stood at the crest for what seemed like a very long time and, inevitably, reason won out over emotion. That dark aperture yawned, beckoning, and she would go to it.

Alex crossed to a Bradley that lay on its side, smoke still wafting from the crew compartment. A Martian laser had scored the armored surface like a knife carving flesh. Without looking inside the vehicle, she went to an exterior equipment crate that had broken free when the IFV crashed. The lid was smashed, and she poked around the mess of tools and rope until she found a large handheld flashlight. A click of the switch projected a powerful beam. Remembering the steepness of the cylinder's sides, she took the coil of heavy rope and slung it across her shoulder.

Carrying the light, she crossed the ridge of the crater and started down the steep slope, her feet sliding in the loose earth. She stumbled but regained her balance before she fell, and continued cautiously. When she approached the first line held by the infantrymen, she passed between two charred bodies, taking care not to look to either side. Finally, she halted at the cylinder.

A look at the loose ground confirmed some initial impressions. There were no tracks, nothing to mark where those illuminated legs had touched the ground. If they served as supports, as had seemed obvious, they did so by exerting force in a way that she couldn't immediately comprehend.

She made her way up the steep slope of the ramp that had been formed by the cylinder's end cap. There was no visible hinge at the place where the ramp met the ship's body. Instead, it was as if the metal had bent smoothly, with no sign of stress or cracking. The interior of the ship was very dark, and a smell like rotten food made her gag. She considered precautions, wondering if the environment might be toxic, or booby-trapped. But there was nothing to do about that except be careful.

Daylight filtered down into the metal shaft, illuminating a series of compartments around the interior wall. Pipes and fittings, as well as numerous brackets, studded the walls. Kneeling, she tied the rope around a nearby valve stem and let the rest of the line tumble down into the dark cylinder. The interior descended at more than forty-five degrees, but with the rope she figured she'd be able to climb back out.

The stench was overpowering, a putrid stink that reminded her of nothing so much as terribly rotten meat, or carrion. After her first gagging reaction, she took out a handkerchief and tied it around her mouth and nose. It served at least to muffle the vile odor. With one hand she wrapped the rope around her waist, while the other held the flashlight. Playing out the line, Alex stepped from one foothold to another, the pipes and rungs allowing her to brace herself pretty well on the incline. She probed the beam of light through the shadows that grew increasingly thick the farther she moved from the entry.

The metallic shell of the ship, and the Martian machine technology, might have been more advanced than anything known to humans, but the interior of the ship reminded Alex of nothing so much as the bowels of an old steamship, with soot and grime and bare, functional metal to all sides. The first compartments she came to contained black powder that seemed like nothing so much as finely ground coal. In other locations she found what appeared to be clean sand. She passed something that seemed like a hangar/workshop, with three separate bays, and guessed that the chamber was where the tripods had been stored for transportation.

She continued down until she reached the end of the rope. From there she played the light still farther, probing the very depths of the cylinder. She saw irregular shapes, nonmetallic, like a big stack of canvas or plastic sheets was piled there, but it was too far away to discern any detail.

Sitting on a metal stanchion, she caught her breath and looked around, playing the beam to both sides and over her head. Nearby she spotted what appeared to be a ladder, with rungs some two feet apart, continuing all the way to the terminus of the cylinder. Swinging slightly on the rope, she crossed to that ladder and secured her line to a rung over her head. Then, still holding the flashlight, she started to make her way carefully down the metal rungs. The bars were too big for her hands, but she braced a foot before each step and was able to draw closer and closer to the tumbled mess.

Her handkerchief shifted, and she coughed, fighting back bile that rose in her throat. She couldn't breathe this air for long, she knew, but she had to reach the bottom. On the lowest rung of the ladder, she straddled the bar and leaned down, close enough to touch the stuff. In the light of the bright flash she saw that the tumbled sheets of material were rubbery membranes that were apparently organic. There were three of them, and they looked like suits that might have contained the tentacled bodies she had first observed when the cylinder opened. She wondered if they might have been outer skins, possibly shed by the Martians like a snake molting on earth.

With clinical detachment she took out her Swiss Army knife and cut away a section of the membrane, which felt pliable and a little sticky in her hand. With nothing else to do with it, she stuffed it into her pocket—and almost immediately felt a compelling urge to get out of there. She nearly dropped her flashlight as she scrambled back up the ladder, reached the end of the rope, and continued to claw her way toward the precious daylight above. When she was close enough to see her surroundings she did drop the light, using both hands to pull herself up to the mouth of the cylinder and out into the comparatively clean air in the scorched crater.

She vomited as soon as she stumbled off the entry ramp, dropping to her hands and knees and pulling the handkerchief away just in time. Her guts heaving, she quivered and puked uncontrollably, until she had nothing left in her stomach. On shaking legs she stood and started up the crater's interior slope.

Almost immediately, she realized that her nose was running. By the time she was halfway to the rim she was hacking and coughing, as if she was wracked by a furiously rapid cold or sinus infection. Her eyes were blurry, and her head started to hurt. Without conscious thought she continued upward, mindlessly plodding one foot ahead of the other. When she fell to her knees she crawled, and her hands were raw and bleeding by the time she reached the crest and tumbled over the rim, leaving the hateful cylinder behind.

She still had the piece of Martian membrane in her pocket, but she wanted to get it away from her, avoid any further contact with it. She thought of the military ambulance she had seen overturned at the bottom of the outside slope of the crater. Making her way down there, still coughing and sniffling, she poked through the wreckage until she found a plastic sample container, with an airtight lid. She put the sample of the membrane inside, and closed it with some relief.

However, she continued to feel sick, and felt a cold stab of terror at the thought that she might have been fatally infected by something in the alien environment of the ship. Frantically she pawed through the ambulance's medical supplies until she found a large jar labeled PENICILLIN. She gulped several of the pills, and sat, sweating and coughing, beside the wrecked Humvee.

Sometime later she heard a crackle of sound, immediately recognized the static hiss of a radio. She leaped up and pulled open the door, saw a red light blinking on the dashboard of the ambulance. There was a microphone attached to a coiled cord nearby, and she quickly snatched it up, pressed the speak button.

"Hello! Can anyone here me? This is Alexandria DeVane, at the Richmond Crater!"

There was a moment's silence, then a sound, faintly, came through the speaker. "Hold on . . . we read you. Hold."

She waited expectantly, hopefully, and a moment later she heard a strong voice, blunt and forceful and vaguely reassuring.

"Dr. DeVane? This is General Davis. What is your situation?"

"It sucks, General," she replied, then curtly informed him of the battle, or massacre, of Colonel Lee's detachment. "But I have removed a sample from the cylinder—something that needs analysis. Should I return it to Fort Bragg?"

"That's a negative, Doctor," said the general, and for the first time she heard a faltering in his bluster, his solid confidence. "We expect to be under attack within a matter of hours. Our situation . . . you might say that it sucks, too."

"What do you want me to do?" she asked. "Where should I take it?"

"There is a strong defensive position posted south of DC," the base CO replied. "Suggest you make your way north, using any available transport, and try to link up with friendly forces. You'll have the best chance of getting it to POTUS or his agents in that direction. And good luck, Alex."

"Thank you, General. Good luck to you, also. This is DeVane, out."

She set the microphone down slowly and leaned back against the wrecked ambulance. Feeling her forehead, she was relieved to discover that her fever seemed to have abated. Also, she was no longer congested, nor did she have the urge to cough.

Looking at the bottle of penicillin, she shook her head in amazement, then took another capsule. Finally, she tucked the bottle into her pocket and took the sample container in her hand.

It was time to look for a ride.

June 10
Eglin Air Force Base, Florida

"I'm the only one who came back?" Duke Hayes asked, numbly. The question was purely rhetorical—the grief etched into Colonel Willard's ashen face was enough confirmation, as if the somber mood of the ground crew and the absence of aircraft on the broad runway hadn't been enough.

"Like they flew into the Bermuda Triangle," Willard said, shaking his head. "We didn't even get word on what happened to the other flights."

"Those fucking lasers," the pilot said with a groan, slumping into the chair across from his CO's desk. "How can we avoid a weapon that shoots at the speed of light?" He looked at Willard, his own anguish rising to the surface.

"The bastards got Stylin' before she could drop her load—same with Ziggy and Two-fer. Shit, Colonel, it seemed like we had the drop on 'em, came in low from behind, closing . . . had the range down to less than a mile. Then—*zap*—they swiveled those weapons around. We never had a chance."

"Looks like you lost a good chunk of wing," the colonel noted. "We're lucky to have you back."

"Yeah, but for what?" Duke asked angrily. Even his trust in the normally rock-solid Warthogs, the rock of his faith in his own abilities as a warrior, was shaken. "Hell, I dumped sixteen thousand pounds right on *top* of the son of a bitch, and he just came walking out the other side of the blast! What the hell can we do to them?"

"Well, there might be something," Willard allowed. "I heard from the armaments boys down in the bomb shack. They've managed to bypass all the fried circuitry on one of the Mark 72s. . . . They think it will be operational, with a manual trigger, by tomorrow."

"One of the tactical nukes?" Duke said. The weapon, an unthinkable nightmare in the back of the ordnance closet throughout his career, suddenly gleamed in his mind like a very wicked beacon of hope. "*That* might give them something to think about."

"Yeah, I expect it will. The crew is going to work on your wingtip—that's the only plane we have left, now."

"One is enough." Duke leaned forward, his eyes boring into the CO's face. "All I ask, Colonel, is that you let me fly that mission."

TEN

June 11
South Richmond Crater, Virginia

From the mouth of the cylinder Alexandria took in the blackened corpses in the crater, the wrecked equipment and dead soldiers all around the rim, scattered down the outer slopes. Nowhere did she see any sign of life, of movement. The vast swath of dirt ejected from the cylinder's impact masked any natural formations, and she couldn't get her bearings, couldn't even see any sign of the great interstate highway that had run so close to this place. Turning her attention to the sky, she tried to guess the location of the sun, but it was fully masked by the overcast. Her watch had stopped in any event, so she didn't know if it was morning or afternoon.

Only then did she remember the simple compass that General Davis had given her. It was pinned to the flap of her shirt pocket, and when she looked at it, the needle centered unerringly on a direction that she felt certain was north. That way lay across the crater; to the south lay Fort Bragg and the illusory security of the army base where even now the enemy was closing in.

But some of the Martians, she felt certain, had gone north from there. The pattern of the landings, encircling as they did the major population centers, suggested compellingly that the invaders would move from their landing sites to close in on those great cities—from there that meant Richmond, just a few miles away, and Washington, DC, a hundred miles beyond.

Alex knew what she had to do. Holding the compass in her hand, she started along the rim of the crater, making her way around the great hole in the ground, heading resolutely toward the north.

She came upon a Humvee parked behind a massive boulder, a slab of limestone that had been hurled out of the ground by the impact of the cylinder. The vehicle was intact—apparently the rock had concealed it from the Martian tripods when they had moved past the area on their way to the north. The soldiers who had parked the thing there, she could only assume, had never made it off the battlefield alive.

But they had left the keys in the ignition! She climbed in, started the engine, felt a thrill of accomplishment when the V8 diesel rumbled to life. Next she checked the radio, but the device installed in the vehicle was dead—no doubt it had not been replaced following the EMP. If the crew had brought another radio with them, they had taken it when they parked the vehicle.

The lack of communications did nothing to temper her resolve. Adjusting the seat, she shifted the automatic transmission into drive and started to negotiate the scout car down the rough, sloping dirt of the barren landscape. She pinned her compass to her knee, but noticed immediately that the magnetic field generated by the Humvee's engine caused the needle to spin crazily. In any event, the mound surrounding the vast crater was enough of a landmark—as long as she kept that in her rearview mirror, she knew that she was traveling generally northward.

Within a few miles, she began to discern traces of the old landscape, as the debris ejected from the cylinder's impact began to thin. She drove past several shattered buildings that had presumably been nice hotels at one time. The windows were gone, shattered by the cylinder's impact no doubt, and the facades were charred and blackened by fire. The hulks of smaller buildings were smashed, virtually unrecognizable as structures, around them—she saw a shattered Texaco sign lying on the ground, and nearby made out another remnant—yellow letters on a broken piece of green plastic, reading only PER—no doubt the mark of what had once been a Perkins restaurant.

The shattered spans of a twin bridge loomed before her, and she knew that she had found the interstate again; she was approaching it from the southwest. Picking her way past the tangle of a traffic jam, cars half-buried in debris, she found herself blocked by the collapsed bridge, unable to reach the northbound lanes. Only then did it occur to her that such restrictions were utterly quaint in this new world. She drove up the shoulder of the southbound exit ramp and proceeded on the wrong side of the freeway, heading north.

Like most of the roadways in the US, this one was littered with vehicles that had been disabled by the Pulse. Still, she was able to make good time, generally following the inside shoulder. Within a few minutes she had driven past the last of the debris tossed by the cylinder's impact, but that only brought the devastation into sharper focus. At Petersburg she picked up I-95, still going north. Passing through the outskirts of Richmond, she knew that she was following along the track of at least one of the Martian machines. No matter what type of building she passed—warehouses, hotels, apartments, factories, whole subdivisions—the fiery laser had done its damage. She was reminded of pictures she had seen of Hiroshima, Berlin, or Manila taken after World War II, whole cities rendered into charred rubble by violence.

In that whole vast metropolis she didn't see a single living person. Instead, she smelled death all around her, the stink of rot, of decaying flesh. Once she saw something moving out of the corner of her eye, slowed the Humvee to look, hopefully, down the steep shoulder and into the city street below.

The movement was repeated—rats, hundreds of them, scuttling out of sight. Flies buzzed thickly around shapeless objects on the sidewalk, in the weeds, and she didn't look closely. Instead, she turned her eyes front and started again toward Washington.

She couldn't even begin to imagine what she would find there.

June 12
Alexandria, Virginia

Alex drove into the city that, she had claimed since her father had taught her about the early battles of the American Civil War, "was named after me." The trip from Richmond to the DC area required, in the past, something around two hours, depending on the traffic. Now, in the wake of the Martian invasion, she had needed the better part of a day. Wrecked bridges, and numerous blockages of battle debris—or the chaotic scatter of disabled vehicles left from the Pulse—had forced her through countless detours.

At Fredericksburg she had encountered evidence of a major battle, a litter of tanks and bodies—and thousands of cawing crows—spread across the ground on the north side of the river, opposite the bluffs where Hooker had launched his infamous and bloody attacks against Robert E. Lee in 1862. Apparently the Army had attempted to make a stand on the north bank of the Rapidan, with no more success than the brave but outgunned reconnaissance force at the crater.

Low on fuel, she had stopped at an abandoned farm about twenty miles back, a palatial estate in the rolling Virginia countryside with several large pole barns, including a motor shed. Although she had been prepared to siphon diesel fuel from a tractor or combine, she discovered a raised drum that the farmer kept for his equipment. The discovery of that reserve had spared her the need to siphon, and she had topped off the Humvee's tank. She found a pantry with some chips and several tins of nacho cheese, and made from them a humble meal, chased by a warm Coke.

From there she had driven on, taking local, two-lane roads in lieu of the expressway, since the country highways tended to have fewer disabled vehicles obstructing the way. Also, she felt a little less conspicuous making her way along tree-lined roads than she had on the broad, open expanse of the increasingly wide interstate. Since departing the crater she had seen no sign of any of the Martian tripods, but there had been proof of their passage along every mile. Many buildings still smoldered from the searing effects of those deadly lasers, and all of the people—and even livestock—had either been driven off or killed. All the way she watched warily, seeking signs of living people or Martian machines.

Alex saw proof of a second brutal battle as she drew near the Beltway. She lost count of the number of burned-out tanks, Bradleys, and other military equipment that she passed. Here and there the ground had been utterly torn up, cratered by intense aerial bombardment, artillery fire, or some combination. But she saw no sign of any Martian machines—as far as her own experience had indicated, they were utterly impervious to human armament.

The city of Alexandria, like Richmond and Fredericksburg and every other urban center she had passed through on her journey north, had been abandoned by living humans, and many of its structures had been utterly burned. Gaping black facades loomed to either side like death's-head skulls, grinning and mocking with their vacant windows and shattered doorways. In other places the surroundings were pristine, trees green, gardens lush and verdant, buildings undamaged, unscarred—except for a loosely swinging doorway, or a dropped suitcase or broken storage box left on the grass with a pathetic array of belongings strewn around.

Bodies, marked by the ubiquitous flocks of crows and ravens, were common. The flesh of the dead was burned and torn, charred and seared on the battlefields. Even more disturbing were the dead sprawled on the sidewalks of the undamaged neighborhoods, sometimes a score or more corpses scattered on a street. These showed no signs of wounding, no burns on skin or clothing, but the faces that she saw—she didn't look too closely—were agog with terror. Tongues protruded from blackened lips and eyes—those that had not yet been pecked by the crows—stared in mute, sightless horror.

But surely not *everyone* had been killed! She rejected the notion that the whole population could have been destroyed. But whether the bulk of the survivors had managed to flee inland, or were trapped against the coast, she couldn't even guess. So she didn't try, instead focusing on the need to bring her precious sample to someone who could commence some analysis.

The atmosphere had been smoky, the air acrid, during the entire course of her journey, but in Alexandria she came to burning buildings, saw the orange flames lunging from the rooftops, consuming wooden frames and walls. Driving down a street with active fires to either side, she knew she was following directly along the path of one of the tripods. She had the sense that she was catching up to the Martian invaders, because of the number of blazes still advancing. A whole block of upscale apartment buildings spewed smoke and flame as she drove past, and the tall steeple of a colonial church collapsed nearby just as she maneuvered her Humvee off the increasingly congested streets through the old city's neighborhoods. Nobody moved—if there was anyone alive, they were doing a very effective job of hiding out. Many cars were stalled on the streets, but a path wide enough for her to roll along relatively unimpeded had been plowed down the middle.

She passed through the neighborhood where she had lived—her own apartment building was a burned-out shell—and continued north, toward the river, avoiding Mount Vernon Avenue and taking side streets. It was in a poorer section of the city, brownstone apartments lining both sides of the street, where she began to encounter survivors. She spotted a few young men in sweatshirts and caps, watching her warily as she rumbled past in the Humvee. Their dark faces were hostile and suspicious as they leaned against a pair of dented SUVs that had been unceremoniously plowed out of the street.

A week ago she might have stepped on the gas and hurried past. Now, for some reason she couldn't fully explain, she stopped the vehicle. Two men, a skinny teenager with his hands in his pockets and a large man with a rolling gait and small, angry eyes, approached her. For the first time, she wondered if she should have picked up a gun. Still, she didn't accelerate away, but instead rolled down the window.

"You wit' d' Army?" asked the younger one, squinting skeptically. "Fight's over. You lost."

She shook her head. "I'm . . ." What should she say? That she was with NASA? She almost laughed at the thought.

"I'm a scientist," she declared, finally. "Trying to find out what happened."

"Hap'n?" sneered the big man. "Mu'fuckers came through wit' lasers 'n' shit. Nasty killer gas, too. Wipe out Arlington and south DC."

"Gas?" Alexandria pressed. "Poison gas?"

The youth rolled his eyes, and she felt stupid, helpless in the face of his experience. "Shit, yeah. Black stuff—flowed 'long the streets, down the creek. My boys 'n' me climbed on the roof. Watching that killer shit jus' wipe out the block."

"Oh, God . . . I'm sorry," Alex said, feeling lame and helpless. "How did they make it—where did the black gas come from?"

"Silver boxes on them snakes. One be shootin' laser, the other one spit out gas. Big clouds of th' shit—fill up a street like *that*." He snapped his fingers, a sharp crack of sound.

"Where did the Martians go? Which direction?"

"She-it! Where they *ain't*?" demanded the youth. But he pointed generally toward the north and west. "Mu'fuckers took off that way—after nobody left alive in town."

"You all that's left here?" she asked.

"We got peeps, back off the street. Lots of pieces, too. Them mu'fuckers come back, they be in the shit." His bravado was more than bluster, she sensed. If the Martians came back here, she believed this young man would try to stop them—and probably die in the attempt.

"Good luck," was all she could offer.

Alex drove off through the ghostly neighborhood. The smell of death was everywhere, and when she turned onto one main arterial road she saw that the pavement was a mass of crows, the black birds pecking vigorously at grotesque shapes all over the ground. The smell of death was everywhere—she could only imagine a whole crowd of people killed by the lethal black gas. Those bodies were obscured by the birds, and the swarms of flies buzzing audibly in the still air. Alex hit the brake, hard, then backed away from the intersection so quickly that she slammed into the bumper of a small car canted sideways at the curb. Frantically turning the wheel, she maneuvered the Humvee around until she was driving away from the scene of death.

She tried to think, rationally, about the lethal gas. Clearly it was heavier than air, since those men had survived it by climbing to the roof of their building—while it had killed everyone on the street below. That explained the second of the two weapons that each Martian tripod seemed to be equipped with. The first, the pinpoint deadly laser, was a battle weapon, while the second, the gas that could fill a whole block with one spuming blast, was simply to exterminate all life in a given area. Clearly it didn't linger long—the birds certainly seemed unaffected, nor did she smell, or feel, anything that suggested a remaining toxic presence.

It was not unlike the way we humans would wipe out a nest of annoying insects, she thought with a sickening shiver. That's what we are to these invaders: pests, bugs, vermin. The thought filled her with rage that quickly turned to despair, quashed by a helpless sense of humanity's impotence.

By then she was skirting Arlington National Cemetery, so she crossed the river on the Arlington Memorial Bridge and drove right up to the vast, colonnaded facade of the Lincoln Memorial. There she parked in the front, the area that had been closed to all vehicular traffic since 9-11, of 2001. Only when she tried to open her door did she realize that tension had virtually fused her fingers around the steering wheel. With considerable effort, she flexed her digits, pulled the door latch, and got out.

Alex paused for a moment to take in the craggy features of that magnificent president. She had visited here many times—to her, it was the temple to the secular American religion—but never had the sorrow in that chiseled visage seemed so poignant, so acute. She sought some comfort there, some glimmer of the wisdom that had guided the nation through its worst crisis, but she saw only a vast, encompassing sadness.

Finally, nearing tears, she turned to stare wearily up the length of the National Mall, blinking her eyes and determinedly clearing her vision. The entire lawn was deserted, though—unlike the city's southern environs—there was little sign of overt damage here. The Capitol, the Washington

Monument, the buildings of the Smithsonian were still intact. The streets were clogged with wrecks, most of which had been there since the Pulse, though a single traffic lane had been plowed through the congestion all around.

But there were no vehicles moving. And all the people were gone.

Crows and ravens flocked along the edge of the Tidal Basin, and she didn't stare too closely at whatever it was that attracted them. Suddenly she had a powerful urge to get away from there. But there was one more place she had to see. Taking Independence Avenue along the mall, she turned on seventh, going down to E Street, where she turned left. She was two blocks away from the NASA Administration Building, but she saw at once that she could get no closer—nor was there any real destination to reach, even if she could go there.

The south face of the massive Department of Transportation Building had been blasted to pieces by powerful explosions. She saw the shattered bulk of an Abrams tank, nearly buried by the cascade of debris. To the right a pair of Bradleys lay on their sides, charred and wrecked. She saw the bodies of soldiers scattered among the rubble. Farther away, Saint Dominic's Church was a broken shell, and the NASA building was, simply, gone. There was nothing left for her there.

Except, maybe, for one thing. She saw the body of a dead officer, his Kevlar helmet still strapped to his head, a wound—crusty with dried blood—making a horrible hole in the BDU camouflage of his shirt. His hands were splayed out before him and, a few feet beyond his reach, a heavy .45 service pistol lay on the pavement. Alex crept forward and, almost apologetically, picked up the heavy automatic. She checked the magazine, saw that it was full, and determined how to set and remove the safety. Carrying the weapon in her hand, she hurried back to her vehicle.

Placing it on the passenger seat where she could snatch it up in a second, she maneuvered the Humvee through a cramped Y-turn. Knowing that she had to get away from here, she decided that she would go west, out of the center of the once-great city. She needed to find out where the people had gone. Some must have survived! And she needed to know where the Martians were, too, even though she was growing increasingly pessimistic about humankind's chances of ever defeating such a plainly superior foe.

Driving past the Mall, she made her way up to Route 29 and followed the K Street Canyon. The square office buildings were stark and vacant, the lawyers having fled the city with everyone else. Turkey vultures soared lazily over Washington Circle, and she unconsciously sped up as she drove onto the Whitehurst Freeway, an elevated road through Georgetown. As she went by the vacant windows of once vibrant apartments and offices, she tried to avoid thinking of what had been. Exiting onto Canal Road at the *Exorcist* stairs, she made her way to the Clara Baron Parkway, continuing toward Bethesda. The road followed the river valley, tree-lined and pastoral, insulating her from views of abandoned civilization.

There, at last, she began to encounter refugees, people moving out of the city. Some rode bicycles, others pulled wagons or pushed wheelbarrows and buggies, conveyances piled high with all manner of indispensable treasures. There were a hundred or more of them in the first group she reached—people of all ages and both genders, white, black, Asian commingled in no apparent pattern. Most of them ignored her, but one old man stopped and glared angrily as she approached. On impulse, she pulled over to the shoulder, stopped the Humvee, and opened her door.

"What do you want?" demanded the fellow. His face was a mass of lines and bristling white whiskers. He wore workman's clothes and stood protectively before a young couple, each of whom carried a child.

"I . . . I want to know what happened," she said, starting to get out. Only then did she sense the menace, the almost palpable hunger in his look as he eyed the battered military vehicle.

She pulled the door shut as the old man suddenly lunged across the road. The pistol was in her hand, the big barrel pointed out the window, and he stopped, suddenly weary and utterly dejected. Without another word she stepped on the gas, quickly drove past the file of people.

But there were still more of them, all proceeding wearily along the road. They seemed to congregate in groups, at least twenty or thirty together, and so many of them had that desperate hunger in their eyes—not for food, but for something more intangible. Safety? A way back into the past?

A loud rumbling came from the road behind, and a look in the rearview mirror revealed a string of leather-clad motorcyclists rolling along the parkway, coming up behind. She pulled over and allowed the group to pass, not surprised to see that the big old Harley-Davidsons had withstood the disabling effects of the Pulse—or, at least, had been repairable afterward. After the bikers had passed she continued on, seeing more and more pedestrian refugees.

She knew that she had to help, and decided to stop when she came upon a group of five children, four youngsters and a girl of about fourteen. The older girl glared at Alex suspiciously when the woman stopped, but quickly decided that the group should accept the offer of a ride.

"I'm Pam Lucas," she said, after getting the small, wide-eyed children settled in the vehicle's backseat. "I came to DC with a school group, but we got trapped here by the Pulse. Our teacher went out to look for a bus, but we never saw her again. Some of the kids decided to walk home, but I stayed here in the city."

"Where's home?" Alex wondered.

"Harrisburg, Pennsylvania. It was gonna be a long walk," Pam allowed. "But then the Martians came, and I was trapped with everyone else. They attacked from the north, south, and west, trapped lots of people in the city. I climbed up the Washington Monument with some soldiers—we saw the whole Mall get covered by the black gas."

Alex shivered at the image, but she had to learn more. "How long did it last? The cloud of gas?"

Pam shrugged. "Not long. Maybe an hour, probably less. It seemed to flow away, and by the time we came down you couldn't even smell anything. And the Martians were gone, too."

Alex looked in the rearview mirror. The four children, who looked to be only five or six years old, were listening raptly. "Were they with your school group, too?" she asked.

"Nope. I found them down in Georgetown. After the gas came through. I think they were at a day-care center for a while, maybe in an upper story of a building. Anyway, that seemed to save some people. But they were just out walking in the street when they met me."

"Lucky thing you came along," Alex said sincerely.

"I guess," Pam allowed. "Don't know how much luck there is for anyone, anymore."

That expression of hopelessness, so similar to Alex's own emotion, seemed to drive home the fact of defeat too plainly to bear. She blinked back tears as she continued on, weaving the Humvee around stalled cars, driving slowly past the shuffling pedestrians, the whole file of humanity moving up the river valley. The trees were dense on either side of the road, though occasionally they could catch glimpses of the river off to the left. Having reached the end of the parkway, they continued northwestward along a surprisingly rural two-lane road, passing a few side streets climbing the steep hill to the right, or bridging the channel of the Chesapeake and Ohio Canal to the left.

The first sign of danger was a pair of young men coming into view ahead of them, running down the road against the stream of refugees. They were shouting as they ran and, as they passed other pedestrians, those people, too, turned and starting running back toward the city, until there was a mob stampeding toward the Humvee.

"The black gas!" cried one man. "It's coming! The Martians are ahead of us!"

"Oh God!" Pam cried, a sound of pure terror. In the back, one of the children started to cry, and in seconds all four were sobbing.

"We'll get away!" Alex declared, stomping the brake. "Get to high ground!" she cried out the window to the approaching crowd. "Get away from the river!"

Remembering an intersection just a few hundred yards back, she wheeled the Humvee through a screeching U-turn that skidded them into the dirt of the left shoulder before she had reversed direction. Alex stepped on the gas, and the vehicle roared ahead, as more people on foot dropped their possessions and turned around, starting to run.

"High ground!" Pam shouted, as Alexandria drove as fast as she could. "Climb the hill!" The teenager swung around in her seat, spoke calmly to the four terrified children in the back. "We're going to be okay—she's taking us up the hill, and the Martians can't get us up there."

To Alex it seemed like slim assurance, but the kids' crying faded to a few sniffles. Many of the people on the roadway were taking that same advice, or figured it out on their own, leaving the road to enter the woods or to cross the manicured lawns of the occasional yard, moving away from the river. Others seemed not to hear, or to care—they simply ran as fast as they could down the blacktop pavement of the river valley road.

Reaching the crossroad, Alex squealed through a sharp left turn and started up the narrow side street, climbing steeply away from the river. Her foot pressed the gas pedal to the floor, and she careened wildly around the few stalled cars that almost blocked the road. She knocked the fender of a disabled pickup with a jarring crash, but kept going, climbing. The kids hung on with wide eyes and white knuckles, while Pam shouted at her to go faster.

Finally, they reached the crest of the low ridge that framed the valley of the Potomac River. The Humvee bounced from the hilltop onto level ground, and Alex steered into the small parking lot of a strip mall. From there they could look back across the low ground, the strip of glimmering water behind them.

It seemed as though the whole valley was filling with a shroud of midnight black, an ominous, gaseous glacier rolling along the course of the river, roiling over the banks, streaming along the channel of the C&O Canal. The black gas was thicker than any natural cloud. It clung to the low places, seeping along the land, filling the whole space over the river, churning like a sinister tide toward the city. People were running along the roadway down there, but they couldn't go faster than the hungry, lethal vapor; it quickly swept up and over the pedestrians. The darkness obscured their fates for the time being, but Alex's imagination created vivid pictures of the scope of suffering and dying.

Some people—many, actually—tried to reach high ground. Several came running up the same road that Alex had used, with the tendrils of dark smoke trailing at their heels. Others scrambled through the woods and the yards and parking lots to either side, gasping for breath, eyes wide. One man staggered into view through the murk, stumbling weakly, trying to climb the hill as the gas wrapped sinister tendrils around him. They could still see him as he toppled forward, thrashed a few times, then lay still.

And the killing gas swept on.

ELEVEN

For the whole night and most of the next day after the Martian attack I stayed in my basement. For hours I simply stared at the walls, the stairs . . . I wasn't thinking, seemed like I was barely alive. I doubt if I would have been capable of a physical reaction even if a Martian machine had barged right into my house.

Near dawn, I shook off my near-catatonic paralysis, lifting my head to look around, drinking a little water. I kept the shotgun nearby in case of . . . what? It seemed like a ludicrous weapon to think about using against the silver tripod with its inexplicable antigravity propulsion, its instantly lethal laser weapon. I imagined a bug under assault by some toxic pesticide, and could relate to the sense of utter helpless, yielding to an incomprehensibly superior enemy.

Remembering the sharp bang-bang-bang reports of Browne's gun in the face of that looming machine, I could only shudder at the hopelessness of his actions. I admired his bravery, even as I understood its utter futility. As for me, there was no choice of such a valiant gesture—I understood that when I had crouched, quaking and nauseous, as the tripod strode past me in the field. I could only hide. Nor did I restart my generator—I didn't want the noise of that little gasoline engine to attract any attention to my house, hidden as it was by the surrounding curtain of woods. I didn't even dare to turn on an electric light.

Instead, I lit a small oil lamp in a windowless room of my basement and wound up an old spring-driven alarm clock to keep track of the time. Using battery power, I twirled the dial of the radio, heard a few sketchy reports of attacks in Rockford, and south of Chicago. There were maybe five or six stations broadcasting that first night. Two were from Milwaukee, the rest from Illinois. Tellingly, none of the many Madison stations I usually listened to were on the air.

When I scanned the dial the next morning, both Milwaukee stations were gone. I could only come upon a couple of signals, both from Chicago. As usual, every reporter was pretty much limited to what he or she could see with their own eyes or could hear on radio reports from other, more distant stations.

Still, there was some news, all of it grim. The whole country was under attack, it seemed. I heard reports of terrible clouds of poison gas, of huge battles fought between our armed forces and the invader. Southern Indiana was the scene of a two-division attack by the US Army, and though the stories didn't offer a lot of detail, it seemed clear that the human soldiers had suffered a devastating defeat. Much of Indianapolis was reportedly in flames. Other reports, relayed from distant broadcasts, suggested that both Toronto and Mexico City were besieged by the invaders. There was no news at all from overseas, but I saw little cause for hope in that absence.

I huddled in the basement until the little alarm clock told me that it was after eight in the evening. Finally, restlessness compelled me to move. I came slowly, quietly upstairs and peered through the gaps between my window blinds. Afternoon shadows had started to stretch into twilight. Around my house I could see that dark green circle of woods, the trees looking frightening and more sinister than they ever had before. Still, there were finches and grosbeaks at my bird feeder, and the sky—though slate gray and sunless—looked more or less natural.

But I didn't dare open the door. Instead, I slept on the couch in my living room, with the gun and the radio close at hand. For a time I listened to a broadcast from downtown Chicago, a station that had formerly been an all-sports broadcast with a strong signal. The announcer was talking about a solid stream of people leaving the city, mostly on foot, heading north along the lakeshore toward Waukegan and, eventually, Wisconsin. I fell asleep after a while, and when I woke up in the middle of the night my batteries had died. I replaced them with a fresh set, only to find that the station was off the air.

At first light, I got up and made a circuit around the inside of my house, looking out from one window after another. Mist swirled among the trunks of the trees, clinging stubbornly to the shadows as the early-morning sun brightened the world. I was checking out the back when a solid thump sounded against my front door, a sound that almost caused my heart to stop beating. Sweat beaded on my forehead, and my hands were trembling as I snatched up the shotgun from my living room coffee table. The sound was repeated—something large was moving around on my porch! Falling back to the kitchen, I clutched the gun, half-aiming it as I stared at the door, expecting something horrible to come bursting through. Sounds, subtle but definite, continued to indicate the presence of something moving around out there.

After a few seconds of this, I realized the foolishness of my retreat. How long would the mysterious trespasser delay before attacking? I needed information! So I crept through the house, holding the shotgun at the ready. The scuffing noises, the creaking of the deck boards, continued. A loud, sudden crash froze me for several seconds, but I somehow forced myself to continue forward. Confronted with the need to manipulate the doorknob, I managed to hold the gun in my right hand as, with the left, I opened the door.

Browne's big Newfoundland, Klondike, looked at me in surprise. He had been snuffling around my flower pots and knocked over a small garbage can, which was probably the source of the crash I had heard. After a moment, his massive brush of a tail started to sway slowly back and forth, knocking solidly against a one of the support pillars. Somewhat sheepishly, I recognized that sound as the thump that had originally drawn my attention to the trespasser on my porch.

"You?" I grunted, not sure if I should be irritated or relieved, quickly settling on relief. I lowered the gun guiltily, looking down so that I could carefully reset the safety. It was then that I realized I had failed to release it in the first place. If something horrible *had* come through my door, I would have aimed and pulled the trigger to absolutely no effect. Quickly, I set the gun down in the front hall.

"Where's your master?" I asked. Stepping out onto the front porch, I looked down the driveway hopefully. There was no sign of Browne, though I saw the poodle, Galahad, watching me warily from thirty or forty meters away. Klondike nudged a massive black shoulder against me, knocking me a step to the side, but there was nothing hostile in his gesture. Rather, it was an almost pathetic attempt to get my attention.

I scratched the big animal behind his ears, and his tail thumped noisily against the side of my house.

"Come here," I called to the white dog. "Galahad, come!"

Instead he backed away, down the driveway, still watching me. I came down the steps, Klondike bounding beside me, and the poodle turned and started to trot away, frequently looking over his shoulder at me. When I stopped at the edge of my yard, Galahad stopped and, with almost visible impatience, sat down and stared at me.

I had seen enough *Lassie* episodes to figure out the dog sign language: He wanted me to come with him. I took the time to go back to the house and get the shotgun, the Newfoundland bounding at my heels the whole way. Then I followed Galahad down the driveway and along the lane toward Browne's house. The mist had continued to dissipate, but my shoes were wet with dew. On a morning like this, the woods should have smelled of moist honeysuckle, but instead I almost gagged on the pervasive stench of char, smoke, and worse.

As soon as I came out of the woods, I saw that there wasn't much of my neighbor's place remaining—the fire that had started two nights ago had consumed all the buildings, including the barn, house, and sheds, leaving only a blackened swath of wreckage and a little tin outbuilding standing. Smoke still rose from the skeletal timbers of the charred house. I felt a sense of dread, a fear of what I would find there, that almost drove me back home.

But the white dog ran ahead, then stopped beside something in the yard, staring urgently back at me. Only as I approached did I think of the Martians, looking around wildly, feeling terribly exposed now that the fog had almost totally burned away. None of the silvery machines were in sight, though I could see the wrecked Humvee out in the pasture. There were black clumps in several places, and I felt sick as I realized these were turkey vultures, huddled thickly around the places where soldiers had died.

Then, reluctantly, I looked closer at the yard, knowing that I didn't want to see. Approaching, I saw that Browne hadn't even made it into his house when the Martian came. My neighbor's body was charred and stiff, lying grotesquely on the ground, with one leg bent at the knee so that the foot was up in the air. He had been burned almost in half, cut down five or six yards from his front door. One of his guns, a larger version of the shotgun he had given to me, was bent and twisted beside him, the wooden stock charred black, the barrel melted and misshapen by alien heat.

"Ah, geez. Oh, shit," I said numbly. Galahad lay down, resting that white head on his paws next to Browne's body. He stared up at me, his expression as mournful as any grieving human's.

My knees were shaking, and I felt sick to my stomach. I couldn't just leave him there, but . . . what? I had to do something! Relieved, at least slightly, by the decision to act, I went to the small toolshed—the only building that hadn't been burned by the Martians—and found a shovel and an old canvas tarpaulin. Bringing them over to the corpse, I knelt and gingerly tried to wrap the remains in the tarp. I had to push and fold Browne's brittle limbs, but at last I covered him, wrapped him entirely. There were some ropes attached to grommets at the corners of the tarp, and I felt a little better as I wound them around and tied the whole bundle shut.

I had to bury him, and I wondered where to dig. My eyes swept around the burned buildings, the fringe of woods where my property began. That ground was too low—it flooded every spring. There were a few tall trees in his yard, but they had been savagely burned by the lasers, would probably die before autumn. I looked across the pastures, to that tall, grassy hill. There was only one place that seemed appropriate.

I spotted his Jeep beside the ruin of the house. The keys were in it, and I figured that I could remember, more or less, how to operate a stick shift. I flooded the engine on my first attempt, but finally got the old vehicle started. Slowly, with many lurches, I drove it over to park beside Browne's body and got out.

Grimacing, I hoisted the shifting, too-solid weight of that blackened corpse. Normally it would have been too heavy for me to lift, but somehow I loaded it into the back of the vehicle. I set the shovel carefully beside the body and, after a second, put the broken shotgun there as well. My own gun I put in the front seat, near to my hand as, once again, I climbed behind the wheel.

This time I started it proficiently. The dogs loped along behind as I slowly drove out to the hill in his pasture. I had to downshift, levering the transfer case into low range, in order to climb the steep slope, but eventually I was able to grind up the hill. I came to a stop to park on the summit, right at the spot where I had set my telescope nearly two months—and a whole lifetime—before. Getting out I remembered, too, that this was the place where Browne and I had come out to witness the falling cylinders.

The ground was rich black dirt, soft and free of rocks, but it still took me most of the afternoon to dig a reasonable hole. Soon I had blisters on both hands, and the muscles in my legs and shoulders all but cried out in protest against the unfamiliar labor. But I kept at it until, finally, I had a proper grave excavated.

Carefully I eased the body out of the Jeep, crying out in frustration as I lost my grip on the tarp and the corpse thumped heavily into the earthen gap. I adjusted the awkward bundle as much as possible, wanting to leave him in some reasonably comfortable position. Though I recognized that notion as illogical, insofar as it applied to insensate flesh, it seemed terribly important. Finally, I got him arranged on his back and put the charred remnant of his big shotgun in there with him.

The dogs watched solemnly as I filled in the grave. With each shovelful of dirt I found myself pausing, shaking my head in regret. Should I pray for him? The idea seemed absurd—I certainly didn't believe in any God, and nothing in my conversations with Browne had led me to believe that he did, either. How arrogant was it, in this context, to think that humanity was somehow favored by the Creator of the universe?

"You were a good man," I said, finally. "I'll miss you. I'm sorry I couldn't do more."

I didn't even notice that I had been crying, not until I wiped my face with a dirty hand, and it came away muddy from tears.

I opened the tailgate of the Jeep and gestured to the dogs, who both hopped in. They sat there, looking out the back at the hilltop, as I drove through the pasture and toward his house. I didn't even slow down at the smoldering wreckage, but continued out to the lane, down to my driveway, and up to my house. When I got out, the dogs did, too, and followed me expectantly up to the front door.

There wasn't even a point in thinking about stopping them there. I was surprised to realize that I *wanted* their company. They followed me inside and immediately started sniffing around the hall and the living room. Klondike headed into the kitchen, put his big snout into the wastebasket, and knocked it over. I picked the trash can up and set it on the counter.

"You must be hungry, eh?" I said. The sound of my own voice, even if it was only talking to dogs, was somewhat comforting. "I don't have any dog food—but let me see what I can do."

Remembering the generator that hadn't been running, I knew that I had some once-frozen meat that would have started to thaw by then. The two dogs waited at the top of my basement stairs as I went down to rummage. The meat was still cold, but had indeed started to thaw. I pulled several large beef roasts from my chest freezer, and their ears perked up enthusiastically as I came back up. I gave each dog a prime rib roast, after cutting off a generous steak for myself. I cooked mine, while they worried and gnawed at the red meat and white bone.

After we all ate, I got out my radio. The batteries were fresh, and I turned the dial, slowly and patiently, for a long time. Finally, I got that sports station from Chicago, heard the announcer speaking in a surprisingly calm voice.

"They're coming from the northwest and the west, now . . . I can see them out the window, from sixty stories up in the Hancock Building. There's a tripod on the Dan Ryan, another on the Eisenhower. They're heading for the Loop, and I don't see anyone out there trying to stop them.

"Wait! There's an explosion! Looks like artillery, somebody's getting off a few shots. They're coming from behind me, off the other side of the building—Dan, can you see where they're coming from?"

There was a pause, a few seconds that seemed interminable. "They got damn near a direct hit. But the thing is still coming on, didn't seem fazed by it. Not at all. Here's Dan."

Another voice came on. "There's a Navy ship offshore, a mile or two out. Looks like a frigate or something. She's popping off with her deck gun— those are the blasts we can see from here. Now—shit!—there's another one, coming up from the southeast along the Skyway. The Navy has shifted to that one, and it's shooting back. But it seems like the laser can't reach it—too far away!"

"Any sign of damage to the tripod?" asked the original speaker.

"No—not a thing. Damn, I don't believe it. The fucker is walking on the water, moving right out across the lake! The ship is turning around, oh Christ, not fast enough. Now that laser is hitting, starting fires. Jesus, the whole thing is going up in flames!"

There was a choking sound, static filling the airwaves. Frantically, I turned the dial, got the signal back, weaker, with a background of white noise.

"The ship is gone, just blasted out of the water . . . they're all gone. . . ."

And he was right: The airwaves went dead, and nobody was there.

BOOK III
ANNIHILATION

ONE

June 12
CNN Headquarters
Atlanta, Georgia

Rick Chalmers knew that his makeup was running, and there wasn't a damned thing he could do about it. A part of him—a *large* part—yearned to be in his Mercedes right then, racing up I-75 toward Chattanooga. But instead he was there, in the studio, broadcasting to the nation as the fucking Martians closed in.

He looked at the camera, saw the red light, knew that the network was back up, that he was on the air.

So, by God, he would tough it out. It had not been easy to make it this far, to the first post-Pulse broadcast of a television signal. The EMP had knocked every station off the air. The Armageddon Vault had been little help—the station had been prepared for Christ to come down to Earth and proclaim the Rapture, but no one had predicted the utter shutdown of all electronics. For the last days it had been galling in the extreme to the television journalist: The biggest stories of his or any other lifetime were unfolding practically in the backyard, and he had had no means of telling the country, or even his own city, about what was going on.

But dedicated technicians had been working around the clock, repairing burned-out components, bypassing whole systems that were once believed to be crucial. They had no computers, and a lot of cobbled-together circuitry in the cameras and broadcasting equipment. The signal was going out over the airwaves from a large antenna on top of the building. Nor was there any chance of a satellite relay, of course—it would be decades, probably, before mankind again was able to use space-based devices. And even that was assuming that we figured out a way to win the war, Chalmers thought. Thus far, there was little basis for making such a rosy prediction.

Chalmers didn't even know how many people had working TVs—not many, certainly. But for those who had repaired their sets and lived in range of the Atlanta signal tower, he was determined to give them information about the world that was crumbling around them. Here at the network they were recording this historic broadcast on tape and film, preserving the record for an unknown future. How long they would broadcast was an open question, but he was ready to get this program under way.

Clearing his throat, he took a glance at the director, her fingers splayed as she counted down the seconds until the station was back on the air . . . four . . . three . . . two . . . one.

Chalmers glared into that unblinking lens, put all the gravitas of his thirty-nine-year career into his voice.

"Good evening, America—or, as much of you as can hear me, now. I am broadcasting to you from our home studios—and also, from the lines of battle in a new kind of war. We are back on the air, though for how long I cannot say. But for as far as our signal will reach, and as long as we can keep broadcasting, we will bring you the news.

"That news is not good. Right now, the Martians are closing in on Atlanta from three sides. They have overwhelmed all attempts at resistance, including the heroic efforts of our armed forces, as well as local police forces, and such militias as have mustered in the face of this unprecedented onslaught. These include countless hundreds or thousands of civilians who have taken to the trenches armed with their deer rifles, shotguns, and even target pistols."

He drew a breath as the monitors switched to the live feed, pictures coming from two hastily refurbished cameras operated by crews in the backs of old pickup trucks. The image from Camera One was chilling: Two Martian tripods were stalking past the Georgia Dome, blazing away with those deceptively innocent-looking flashes of red light. The camera panned to the façade of the once-beautiful building, caught the images as piece after piece was seared away by the infernally hot lasers. In the background, huge columns of smoke rose into the air, the pyres marking the fuel tanks at Hartsfield-Jackson Atlanta International Airport, set ablaze when the tripods passed across that vast installation a few hours before.

The reporter was Jay Manstein, who had reached Atlanta from Houston only hours earlier. His odyssey across the south had used an assortment of rudimentary transport, and enlisted the help of countless citizens. Chalmers didn't know how Manstein had been able to do it, and Jay had promised to write a book about it "when this is over." Now he came on the air in a voice-over, sounding remarkably calm under the circumstances. Chalmers pictured the veteran reporter, balanced in his truck, staring at the awe-inspiring onslaught and struggling to project an aura of calm professionalism.

"The Martians have left a swath of destruction on their approach to this great city. These tripods you are seeing now have generally followed the I-75 corridor up from Macon, varying by as much as a few miles from that path. Everywhere they went, they incinerated houses and other buildings, and killed any men and women they encountered—even those who were simply trying to get away.

"I have personally witnessed the sacrifice of many heroic individuals, men burned to death even as they fired simple guns at these nightmarish invaders. A tank company from the Georgia National Guard, backed up by a battery of regular Army artillery, stood its ground near Stockbridge, and died to the last man." Manstein's voice broke, momentarily, but he quickly recovered his composure—though a strong pulse of anger underlay his words. "As far as I could see, their guns didn't even put a dent in the Martian machines. I witnessed numerous direct hits, fiery blasts right on these domed tripods that seemed to have no discernible effect on the invaders' advance."

The remote feed continued to roll, the whole grim view taken in by the camera lens. The photojournalist panned across the face of the huge stadium, then zoomed out, making it clear that the shot was being taken from some distance away from the scene. If anything, the wide shot looked even worse, as it revealed that the top of the roofed stadium had vanished, presumably caved in, and that the Martians were advancing on both sides of it. No fewer than three tripods were visible.

"My crew and I will move north," the reporter declared. "Trying to stay ahead of these monstrosities. They appear to be advancing on the downtown area. Back to you, Rick."

"And indeed, we see them, still moving north toward the downtown area," Chalmers reported, ad-libbing as his face came back on the screen. "Our best reports indicate that these are tripods from the Macon and Thomaston cylinders—they have been advancing from the south for several days. The tripods that came out of the Eatonton, Buckhead, and Athens craters are still reported to be advancing from the east. We had a crew in Pendley Hills, hoping to get some footage of that approach. Unfortunately, we lost that unit shortly after they broadcast their first test signals."

Chalmers took a deep breath. The director of that crew had been Marion Smithers—he had mentored her when she was a young college grad twenty years before. He was certain—though he wouldn't broadcast the news—that she was dead. He glared at the camera. "Can we go back to the live feed?" he asked curtly.

Immediately, the director shifted to the picture from the camera in the field. Chalmers's eyes went back to the monitor. The camera was in motion, rolling jerkily. "Our crew is moving northward, now, pulling away. They are shooting from the back of a pickup truck, risking their lives to bring the world these images. Oh . . . oh God . . ."

The broadcaster's voice trailed off as he, like every viewer, was transfixed by the view on the screen. The truck carrying the camera was driving recklessly along a street lined with stores, strip malls, fast-food restaurants, and gas stations. The image veered crazily as the vehicle dodged and darted around the disabled wrecks littering the street.

And one of the Martians was in view, clearly pursuing the pickup. Those three red legs swiveled along with deceptive ease, carrying that shiny dome very, very fast. There was a wink of red light, just a momentary flash, and the picture went white.

Now the image came back to the studio, to Rick Chalmers's clenched jaw and stern glare. "I am afraid we have lost that . . . camera," he said. "We will do what we can to get them back on the air. In the meantime, we have reports, picked up by shortwave and UHF radio, from other points on the East Coast."

He drew a breath. "Washington, DC, this nation's capital, has reportedly been abandoned. The Martians have moved through the city, driving the population before it, killing those who remained behind. There are some reports, as yet unconfirmed, of lethal gas being spread by the tripods. New York City has suffered heavy damage, with much of the area from Central Park south to the Battery in flames . . ."

His voice remained calm, level, strong, even as each piece of information brought to his mind vivid pictures of good friends, favorite restaurants, treasured landmarks destroyed.

"We will continue to broadcast here, for as long as we can," he said. There were no external pictures any longer, nothing but the litany of destruction gathered from across the country. "The West Coast is reportedly under similar attack, with population centers including San Diego, Los Angeles, San Francisco, Portland, and Seattle, all facing attack from the inland direction. Denver has been surrounded. There has been no word out of Chicago for nearly forty-eight hours. . . ."

An hour later, CNN was again off the air.

June 13
Kremlin
Moscow, Russia

General Dmitri "Karla" Konievsky was a veteran of many campaigns, had directed battles in venues ranging from Afghanistan to Chechnya. For much of his career he had led divisions, corps, and ultimately an elite Guards Tank Army that had been poised to roll through the Fulda Gap— up until Gorbachev's betrayal of the Soviet dream, in 1989. Before the Martian invasion, that had been the most bitter defeat of his career, extra galling in that it had been inflicted upon him by his own commander in chief.

Over the course of that career he had fought many implacable foes, had seen suffering on scales both massive and intimate. He had inflicted death upon others and seen it inflicted upon his men. He had viewed killing with dispassion on some occasions, and grieved for the wasted lives upon others. Through it all, he had learned to hate—and been hated in turn—as a result of war.

But never had he known such hatred as possessed him at that moment. His eyes flooded with unchecked tears as he watched the greatest tanks in the Russian arsenal get tossed about like playthings. The vaunted T82s had once been intended to plow through the NATO lines, leading the way toward the inevitable victory of world communism. Now, they were being sacrificed in a last-ditch effort to defend this grand old fortress that had, for so long, stood at the heart of the Russian state.

Red Square was ablaze across the whole vast plaza, a litter of wrecked equipment and dead men. In the end, Karla had ordered massive rockets fired upon the Martians in the center of his beloved city, had seen his own weaponry inflict massive destruction across Moscow. If the nation's nuclear arsenal had been available, he would not have hesitated to use it, but the EMP had rendered all those expensive rockets into so much junk. Now, there was nothing for it but to have the survivors of his army prepare for their final stand.

"Fire!" cried the general, giving the order with a wave of his hand to the batteries of artillery arrayed before the lofty walls. The guns ripped forth again and again, high-explosive shells raining down upon the seemingly invulnerable tripods. The machines came through the hail of fire, spewing their own flashes of deadly light, but the Russian artillerists—as their forefathers had done in battles from Borodino to Stalingrad—stuck to their guns, continued to blast away.

Clouds of black gas rolled in, spreading like a tangible nightmare from the silver boxes mounted upon the Martian machines. The Russians were prepared for this threat—each soldier donned his mask with smooth precision, barely slowing the pace of the shooting. The gas churned up and over the guns, and the artillerists fired blindly, hoping for point-blank targets as the apparently invincible tripods loomed through the roiling murk.

But then the beams of the lasers darted through the clouds, finding the ammunition trucks. One by one, they exploded, and these blasts, at last, brought the great walls tumbling down.

June 14
Neumayer Research Station, Antarctica

As director of the first German research station on the seventh continent, Friedrich Schultz—called "Fritz" by the other nine residents of the station—felt a powerful responsibility toward his homeland, and toward the world. It had been an honor to be stationed here, and a higher honor to be given the directorship of this small, dedicated staff and this remote but valuable installation.

For several years he had stayed there even through the long polar winter, recording data on the landscape and the sky, sending that data back to his support staff in Germany, the rest of the EU, and the world. They had documented the depletion of the "ozone hole" over the South Pole, had studied the changes in the continent's climate, even done astronomical observations of the southern sky.

In the end, however, they were bystanders to the truly important event of their lives, and the station was a trap. It galled him to be there when so much was befalling his fatherland. They had heard scattered and confused reports of the EMP strike against North America as European centers—unaffected by that first attack—had broadcast a number of speculative stories in the first hours, until the second Pulse had knocked all of them off the air. The third EMP had occurred directly over the South Pole, momentarily brightening the polar night into a brilliance exceeding a sunny day. At that time the station had lost all of its communication and computer equipment.

Never had Fritz Schultz felt so helpless, and so alone. The night seemed darker, colder, than it ever had before. The ten scientists and researchers had huddled together, first making sure that power-generating, heating, and cooking equipment remained operational. But there had been no word, nothing, from the outside world.

Finally, Carl Meyer, the electronics specialist, had managed to assemble a working shortwave radio from an amazing array of spare parts. For long hours through the unbreaking night the scientists and technicians had followed the fragmentary radio reports coming from around the world.

They had heard of the objects falling from the skies across the other continents of the world. Though they had observed nothing at the Neumayer Station, they had picked up one brief report of such a device falling on the other side of Antarctica. Then had come the shattering news from across the European Union: Paris, Brussels, Hamburg burned. People fleeing north across the Baltic Sea, seeking shelter in Scandinavia. Berlin—Fritz Schultz's beloved Berlin, the city that had suffered so much for so long, and yet still survived—was now ravaged by a new invader, the great buildings, parks, vast miles of houses and apartments, reportedly burned to the ground. It was, according to the last reports, simply *gone*.

People were said to be fleeing toward the Alps. Scandinavia had proven to be elusive shelter, as they learned that Oslo and Stockholm were burning. Gradually, one by one, the stations that had been broadcasting the news went off the air.

"Fritz?" It was the electronics specialist, waking up the director during his restless period of sleep.

"*Ja*, Carl?" He was up, already shrugging into his parka, stepping into his boots.

"You'd better have a look at this."

He joined the other members of the team, stepping out of the domed residential shelter, looking across the flat expanse of the starlit Antarctic ice cap. Something was moving out there, taking shape in the starlit night. The red legs were visible first as ghostly, sinister appendages. As it came closer, the Martian tripod was revealed. In long strides it moved across the frozen surface.

It was coming right at them.

June 15
Pyongyang, North Korea

"Launch Missile Number One—now!"

In the absence of the Supreme Ruler, who had not emerged outside since the Pulse, General Choe Sun Yung gave the order. From his command post high in the Ministry of Defense Building, he could see three tripods close in on the capital. Two were coming over the tops of a pair of rugged mountain ridges, while one followed the river valley between them.

His nation's entire nuclear arsenal was concentrated in the warheads of the three truck-mounted rockets arrayed in the gray, empty plaza below. Technicians swarmed around those awful weapons—bombs that had once been intended to incinerate Seoul or Tokyo—making the last-minute checks of the crude guidance systems.

In a sense, it was that very crudeness that allowed the nuclear weapons to be used. There had been little computer-controlled circuitry, and such as there was had been bypassed. Now the rockets were not much more sophisticated than the V2s that Wernher von Braun's Nazis had launched toward England. But an atomic bomb, Choe knew, was not a weapon that required pinpoint accuracy.

He watched with an emotion of mingled pride and fear as white smoke and red fire flashed from the rear of the first rocket. It streaked skyward like a terribly lethal spear, trailing smoke as it arced upward and away. Higher and faster it flew, shrinking in apparent size until it was a tiny dot in the viewing image of his binoculars. Nearing its apogee, the rocket's fire faded, and the warhead flew on, propelled only by the ballistic force of that brief burn. Still, it trailed enough smoke that the general could follow its arc through the sky. It tumbled downward, toward that narrow pass—right on target.

Dropping his binoculars, Choe pulled dark goggles over his eyes. Through their filters he saw the flash of white light signaling the nuclear explosion. Immediately the valley vanished, replaced by a hellish frenzy of smoke and flame and dust. The cloud billowed upward, horribly powerful and monstrous, gradually assuming the ominous mushroom shape that Choe had pictured but never personally observed.

Nothing could survive in that inferno, he knew. The Martians coming through the pass were annihilated. He grinned, fiercely triumphant. Now they would incinerate the tripod coming over the northern mountain ridge.

"Launch Missile Number Two," he ordered.

This rocket also flared with a surge of fiery power, streaking up from the truck, trailing a plume of smoke as it rose into the sky. Almost immediately, Choe sensed that something was wrong: it did not follow the smooth trajectory of the first rocket, but instead wriggled and corkscrewed chaotically, climbing more or less straight up.

"Destroy it!" he shouted, watching in horror as the nearby technician frantically pressed the self-destruct button, to no effect. The rocket's engine burned out, and the warhead—set to detonate five hundred feet above the ground—tumbled toward the heart of the city, toward the Ministry of Defense. The technician pressed the button several more times, then screamed and covered his ears.

General Choe, confirmed atheist and dedicated communist, prayed fervently that the warhead on the malfunctioning rocket was a dud.

It wasn't.

June 16
Tokyo, Japan

Tadaki Yamashita felt like he was living through some grotesque parody of the movies he had watched as a child, and had been making during his adult career. He had generated scenes like this, in special effects, on many occasions. But this was no SFX wonder—as he watched, his city was burning before him.

He aimed, focused, and continued to roll the hand-cranked 16 mm film camera. Nearby, his wife—ever his most able assistant—sat at the wheel of an old Toyota pickup. In the back were a dozen reels of exposed film, carefully wrapped and secured. He was using his second-to-last roll now; he was saving the last one for the end.

Tadaki's camera image zoomed in as the Martian tripods set fire to the Imperial Palace, and strode through the wreckage of that hallowed institution. The lowlands of the city—the same place the Americans had scorched with their devastating firebombs in March of 1945—was now a sea of black gas. Nothing could live in that seething mass, and the vapors continued to expand, flowing along the low ground, seeping toward the coast.

The camera clicked, and the large reel spun free as he reached the end of the roll of film. The gas was coming closer, but the veteran filmmaker calmly knelt, removed the reel from his camera, and stowed it in a waterproof, lightproof, bag. He put it in the back of the truck, locking the case containing all the rest of the film he had shot, documenting Tokyo's last day.

"Go!" he said, slamming his hand against the side of the truck. "Up into the mountains. You know the cave where we went, so many years ago? Hide there!"

"Get in!" urged his wife, tears streaming from her eyes, "Come with me."

"No," he replied, removing his final roll of film from its protective wrap. Quickly, smoothly, he mounted it on the camera. The wave of black gas was coming closer, surging less than a mile away. "You must go—preserve these pictures!"

He turned his back, heard her crying as she stomped on the gas, driving the little truck away. Tadaki lifted the camera, took focus, and started to shoot.

TWO

June 16
Delbrook Lake, Wisconsin

My last set of batteries was fading away in the old boom box, but I could still get a crackle out of the speakers. I turned up the volume, and slowly turned the dial through the full span of AM stations. Nothing . . . not a solitary voice, nor the hint of a radio signal, broke that crackling wasteland. Still, I kept turning, searching, until the last of the battery power faded. As the last whispers of sound emerged from the machine I had to resist the urge to punch it, to shake the radio as if I could coax some kind of report, some words from a fellow human being, out of the black plastic box.

It was a bright, sunny day, but the solar illumination could not dispel the murk of gloom that had settled around me. Galahad barked outside the back door, startling me. Even then I was reluctant to leave the radio, but I forced myself to get up, let him in. Klondike was still drinking from the bucket of water I had been keeping on the porch. He looked up at me, wagging his tail, then went back to his slurping gulps. Finally, he finished and, trailing drool, ambled through the door I was holding open.

Both dogs had been prowling around outside since I got up that morning, and I had found that their patrols added considerably to my sense of security. Ironically enough, they never seemed to go far from my house. Now, as usual, their company brightened my mood a bit, though even they seemed a bit melancholy, as they paced around the rooms of my house before collapsing in their places beside the couch in my living room. Both of them eyed me as I walked across the room.

I busied myself chopping up a rolled sirloin roast, raw, into what I imagined were bite-sized pieces for such big dogs. I put the food in a couple of large bowls and set the dishes down on opposite sides of the kitchen. The animals dug in quickly, gulping so fast that it didn't seem as if they were even taking time to chew. In a few seconds, each had cleaned his bowl.

"That was the last of the beef roasts," I said, a bit apologetically. Of course, they had probably never eaten as well in their lives as they had during the last few days as I had, one by one, removed the steaks and roasts that I had been saving for some future date—in a future that was never going to happen.

My fear of the Martians had overcome my desire for electricity, and so I had resisted the urge to restart my generator. As a result, the food in my freezer had gradually thawed and, by then, was approaching the point of spoilage. I had plenty of canned food and packages of dried rice, beans, and pasta, but I didn't imagine any of that would appeal much to the dogs. I looked at the deceptively gentle weather outside, thought about the unknown world that lay beyond the fringe of woods surrounding my house, and made a decision. I didn't even feel strange as I announced it, aloud, for the benefit of the two dogs.

"I need batteries, and you need food. Let's go for a ride."

They seemed to recognize the phrase, as they both got to their feet and bounced excitedly to the front door. Carrying my shotgun, I led them outside, opening the tailgate so they could hop into the back of the Jeep. I climbed in, put the shotgun in the passenger seat, and started it up.

The engine growled to life without flooding, and I gave myself a mental pat on the back. Not sure what I was looking for, I examined the gauges and quickly noticed the needle indicating I had less than a quarter tank of gas. "Hold on a sec," I said, leaving the dogs staring after me as I went into the garage. I found a five-gallon gas tank, and a length of narrow hose suitable for siphoning. Putting the gear beside the shotgun, I shifted into gear, and made my way down the driveway and onto the rural lane.

I avoided looking much at the charred wreckage of Browne's house and barn, except to note that the fires had, at last, gone out. I drove slowly, watching the sides of the roads, looking at the other houses I passed, seeking some sign of life. The country road was empty, and I rolled unimpeded right into town.

Coyotes scattered out of the main street as I drove through Delbrook Lake. The Martians had come right through there, and I was reminded of pictures I had seen of the capricious nature of tornado damage. One side of the street was burned and blackened, a few brick walls and chimneys being all that remained of a whole slew of small businesses. The post office was a shell, and the bank building had been razed practically to the ground, leaving only a squat steel vault standing on its stone foundation. The drugstore, a couple of mom-and-pop type restaurants, and a little Mexican grocery store were all gone, as obliterated as if that tornado had picked them up and whisked them away.

On the other side of the street, however, the old Ambrose Department Store stood proudly, next to an antique shop, a gourmet coffee shop, barbershop, and martial arts school. None of these buildings showed much damage at all, though the glass doors of the department store and coffee shop had been smashed.

Many vehicles were parked haphazardly through the town, most of them still resting where they had been disabled by the Pulse. I stopped next to a tall pickup truck with a large external gas tank. Unscrewing the cap, I fed my hose down into the fuel, then knelt on the roadway next to my portable gas can. I sucked on the hose—unfortunately, and inevitably, gagging on the first taste of gasoline—then let the siphon run until my can was full. I poured the contents into the Jeep's tank, then repeated the process once more, giving me enough fuel to top off the tank.

My mouth was sour with the taste of oil and gas. Spotting a Coke machine on the sidewalk outside the barbershop, I felt my pockets, chagrined that I didn't have any change. The front of the machine was glass, but I couldn't bring myself to smash it. Instead, I hunted through the Jeep until I found a few quarters in the ashtray. These worked, and I rinsed my mouth out with a warm, still-well-carbonated, Coca-Cola.

I drove on through town, crossed the railroad tracks, and stopped at the feed mill on the outskirts. This, like everthing else, was abandoned, the front door of the office smashed in. Going inside, I found a dozen raccoons swarming over the mound of dog-food bags. Many of them scattered as I approached, but several large, fat coons sat atop the pile and growled like pit bulls. I shouted at them, and they just growled more loudly.

"Dammit," I grunted, shaking my head. How quickly the trappings, and the protections, of civilization fall away. Going back out to the Jeep, I opened the tailgate and let the dogs out. "If you want food, you're going to have to chase the varmints off it!" I informed them sternly.

They followed me into the door of the feedmill, and immediately charged the raccoons—who quickly scampered off the food bags and disappeared into the back of the mill. Galahad barked frantically, while I pulled two reasonably intact sacks of the bland-looking pellets out of the mess of dog-food bags. Carrying my prizes back to the Jeep, I set them on the floor of the passenger seat, next to the shotgun.

Next I drove to the hardware store, which was in a small strip mall with a grocery store, bank, and beauty salon just outside of downtown. The buildings hadn't been ravaged by the Martians, but it looked like people had done a pretty good job of plundering even before the invaders made it onto the scene. I found the shelves of both the hardware and grocery pretty much picked clean. There was some moldy produce and rancid meat behind the counters, but all the nonperishable food, as well as useful items such as candles, bug repellent, matches, and so forth, had been removed. The same proved true in the hardware store—there remained some tools, lots of paint, and all kinds of plumbing equipment, but things such as batteries, propane fuel, flashlights, and the like had all been taken. I did find a bin of leather work gloves and impulsively snatched up a pair of those.

Frustrated, but not discouraged, I got back into the Jeep and drove out toward the lake. I had yet to see a living person, and I suspected that, if I was vigorous in my search, I would be able to scrounge up the things I needed—most notably, fresh batteries for my radio. I came to a housing development, fifty or sixty small, single-family houses on half-acre lots. The desolation was eerie—I saw abandoned swing sets and tricycles, a clothesline with several garments still hanging, lots of houses with the front doors and garages just standing open.

But there were no people. A pair of coyotes emerged from the first house I came to; Galahad started barking as I rolled past, and the wild canines streaked across the yards, heading for the woodlot at the edge of the development. I parked at the end of a cul-de-sac, with five houses facing the turnaround at the end of the street. The dogs hopped out even before I could open the tailgate, and I was comforted by their presence as I pulled on the new pair of work gloves and walked up to the first house.

Feeling strange and intrusive, I knocked hesitantly at the door, which was closed and locked. When nobody answered, I punched through the windowpane, the heavy glove protecting my hand from the broken glass. Unlocking the door, I stepped inside the home.

It was small, comfortable. I saw a picture on the wall, a handsome young couple with the wife pregnant, and a smiling baby sitting on the husband's lap. Guiltily, I moved past, into the kitchen. Opening the doors of a small pantry, I found many canned goods and some packs of dried food. I gathered up a couple of plastic grocery bags full of these provisions, then looked through the kitchen drawers, hoping to find batteries. I was not successful, so I moved on, repeating the process at the next, and a third home. In that one I found several fresh packs of C- and D-sized batteries. With the groceries piled high in the passenger seat, and the batteries tucked next to the door, I started the Jeep again, and drove on.

I followed the scenic road along the lakeshore, where many expensive homes stood abandoned. Signs of looting were more common there—lots of windows were broken, and odds and ends such as beds, chairs, and tables had even been dragged out onto the lawns. Continuing past without stopping, I came around a curve and saw several people wearing backpacks, trudging toward me—two men and two women, looking to be around thirty years old. I felt a momentary panic, but when one of the men waved at me I pulled up to them and stopped the Jeep.

"Are you from around here?" he asked.

"Yes—I live outside the other side of town. Where are you coming from?" I replied.

"We've hiked all the way from Lake Geneva," he said. "I guess we're about the only ones who survived. They filled the whole lake valley with that black gas."

"Gas? I heard something about that on one of the radio reports . . ." It was hard to imagine a weapon more lethal than the deadly lasers.

"It killed everyone who got even a small breath of it," said the man. "Sinks into the low spaces, so the whole valley around the lake was a death trap."

"We were lucky," said the other man. "We lived on a hillside, near the cemetery. When the gas came through, we climbed to the top of the hill. It was like an island, in the middle of a sea. If the gas had climbed another dozen feet, it would have gotten us, too."

"Everyone dead?" I asked, horrified.

"Except for those who got away before the Martians came. They moved in so fast, no one else had time."

I saw him looking, longingly, at my pile of grocery bags. "Can I offer you some food?" I said. "I found a lot this morning—more than I'll need."

"Thanks, yes," said one woman, a wan-looking blonde who, under other circumstances, might have been gorgeous. Now she had dark rings under her eyes, and her hair was a matted tangle. She stepped forward eagerly, and I let her and her companions help themselves to a couple of bagsful of food.

"What are your plans?" I asked them.

"We're going north," said the man who had spoken first. "We hear the Martians haven't hit up there yet."

"Where did they go from Lake Geneva?" I asked.

"South and east. Like they're closing in on Chicago," he replied.

Wishing them luck, I drove off, suddenly determined to see for myself. Still sticking to the back roads, I made it to Lake Geneva in about forty-five minutes, and paused at the top of the hilly highway that was starting a steep descent into the city.

I remembered this as a tourist-attracting community on the shore of a vast, beautiful lake—one of the largest, deepest, and cleanest bodies of water in Wisconsin. I had learned, long ago, to avoid it at all costs during the summer, as the creeping traffic would line the main street so much that it might take a half hour or forty-five minutes just to drive through. Those were the kinds of crowds that would make my skin scrawl, my throat tighten with anxiety.

From above, I could see that the lake still dazzled, tiny waves reflecting like diamonds in the light breeze. On the surface the city looked much the same—there was green foliage everywhere, such that I could see more trees than houses even when I looked down into the neighborhoods. But the sounds were all wrong—instead of motorboats, and cars, and loud music, I heard the cawing of what sounded like a million crows. I shuddered at the thought of what they were eating, and when the wind shifted I nearly gagged on the stench of death. Even the dogs were solemn, staring at me as if they were worried that I was going to take them into that charnel valley.

Instead, I turned around, and drove away as fast as I could, wheeling off the highway as soon as I found a good crossroad. Skidding recklessly on the narrow pavement, I careened back into the countryside, though even ten miles away I seemed to taste that foul perfume with every breath.

Surprised, I noticed that it was starting to get dark, and I turned on my headlights—more out of reflex than practicality, since there was still plenty of light to see. Driving more slowly, I made my way back to Delbrook Lake, avoiding the city, taking the township road out toward my own house.

The shadows were growing thick, and I needed the headlights to penetrate the gloom as I followed the narrow road through an almost enclosed tunnel of overhanging trees. Only a couple of miles from the entrance to my lane, I was startled by the sight of a man's face glaring at me from the culvert next to the road. He gestured with a peculiar urgency, and once again I stopped.

Though he was haggard and unshaven, he looked vaguely familiar. It wasn't until I saw the remnant of a camouflaged military uniform and the captain's bar dangling loosely from his collar, that I remembered.

"You were with that Kenosha Guard unit, weren't you?" I asked. "The artillery?"

"Yes," he whispered, looking around. "Pull that Jeep off the road—there's a little drive up ahead. I need to talk to you!"

His manner was furtive, but—perhaps because of the dogs and my shotgun—I didn't feel threatened. Instead, I did as he asked, pulling between the trees and shutting off the engine. He came out to me, put his hands on the edge of the Jeep, and looked at me almost desperately.

"We've got to get away from here!" he said insistently.

I felt a glimmer of panic. "The Martians? Are they coming back?" I asked.

"It's only a matter of time!" he said. "But we'll be ready. I know how we can prepare—how we can survive!"

"How? What's your plan?" I remembered him from our first meeting: calm, commanding, cool. He had been a man in charge, confident in the power of his big guns, certain that the Martians were in for a thumping defeat. It was hard to reconcile that memory with this furtive, desperate-looking fellow.

"We've got to go underground!" he said, his eyes wild. "The Cave of the Mounds—take me there! We can hide out, for years if we have to. We can't beat these Martians, but we can still survive. We'll gather others like us—women, too, for breeding. They'll never find us there, and we *will* survive! We'll adapt, become subterranean. Stock up on food. Even raise children there, in the cave. There's lots of room, and we can stay there for as long as it takes. The human race will go on! And that's the important thing."

"You mean, just hide from them? Give away the whole world?" I countered, appalled. The thought of living in a cave seemed more like condemnation to a slow death.

"We can't fight them! They're invincible!" the captain insisted. "We have to get away! I'll lead us, lead us to a new future. One where we're maybe not masters of the world but, dammit, we won't be extinct, either! We'll have children, and they will grow up underground with us. The more women we can bring in, the more children . . . don't you see? It's the only way!"

My reaction was immediate, instinctive, even visceral—I had to get away! I started up the Jeep then, shifted into reverse. He was still clutching the edge of my door as I started to move, but I didn't care—I needed to move..

"The *only* way!" he cried, shaking his fist at me as I tore off down the road.

He was wrong, wasn't he? There had to be another way, a path that offered hope, some prospect of a future for the human race that didn't involve our becoming vermin, breeding simply for the sake of survival, dwelling in a world where we had turned our back upon the sun? We were humans, dammit! We had purpose, destiny . . . this was *our* world, and I wasn't willing to give it up.

It was almost fully dark as, at last, I rolled up the hill of my driveway and parked the Jeep outside my house. Despite the warmth of the night, I was shivering as I hurried to unload the food and supplies and carry everything inside. The dogs raced beside me as I left the bags on the kitchen counters—something I never would have done a few weeks ago. Still disdaining the use of the generator, I lit a candle and an oil lamp, then replaced the batteries in my radio.

I craved only the broadcast signal from another person, the sound of a human voice, someone who could offer me a kernel of hope, some words of encouragement. Huddling over the boom box, I turned the dial, slowly, carefully, seeking a signal on any band, any part of the spectrum. There was only that empty crackle, and in the echoes of the nothingness I thought of the artilleryman's mad scheme, knew that he was wrong—he *had* to be wrong! His was not the only way. I renounced the path of defeat, of despair.

But if there was another path, I had yet to discover where it lay.

THREE

"Alex—stop! There's a man down there, by the water!"

Alexandria quickly pulled the Humvee over to the left side of the road and looked down through the branches, toward the waters of the Potomac River, which glimmered through the trees. "Are you sure it's not just another body?" she asked.

"No! I saw him move—he raised a hand, like he was trying to wave to us."

"All right. I'll go see—you stay here with the kids."

Pushing the door open, Alex started through the underbrush below the highway's shoulder, trying to see the man. Bushes snapped beside her, and she looked in surprise to see Pam following her. Before the woman could speak the girl waved away her objections. "I told the kids to stay put—they'll wait for us. The guy was just down here, next to that tree trunk."

They made their way around the branches of a big oak that had toppled over some time in the past, and finally Alex saw the fellow. He sat against the tree, wearing a wet suit, with a face mask and SCUBA tank lying on the ground beside him. As the two approached he raised a hand in a feeble wave of greeting.

"Thank God you spotted me," he said. "I've been here for two days, figured I'd starve to death before anyone knew I was here."

"What happened? Are you hurt?" Alex asked, kneeling beside him.

"Broken leg," he said, wincing. Somehow he managed a smile. "But things are looking up, now that you two angels have come down from Heaven."

Alex grimaced. "To say we're on our way out of Hell would be a little more accurate," she retorted. "I'm Alex DeVane, and this is Pam Lucas."

"Donald Earnest," said the man. "Late of the Underwater Rescue Team, Maryland State Patrol." He gestured to his right leg, which was twisted at a ghastly angle. "Guess I'm sort of on leave of absence for now."

"How did you get here?" Pam asked. "Were you skin diving?"

"We call it SCUBA," Earnest said, "but yeah. There were six of us, some miles upriver from here. We were trying to get people out of the river valley before the Martians came through, but there was a whole crowd trapped in the valley with tripods coming from both directions. Some tried for high ground. Me and my five buddies, we went into the water."

"To avoid the gas?" Alex guessed.

The diver nodded. "I watched the gas go right over us. We went deep, hoping to ride the thing out and it looked like we were going to make it, too. I was down at the river bottom, resting against a bridge abutment so that the current wouldn't carry me away. Every once in a while I'd swim to the surface, but I could see that gas just hanging there, a cloud. I had plenty of air—we all did—so I went back below to try and wait it out. It almost worked."

"Then what happened?" Pam pressed.

"There was a blast in the water, a real ball-buster of an explosion. 'Scuse the expression. I was slammed against the piling, and that's how my leg got busted. I floated down the river until I was able to get to shore. Crawled out here, must have been two days ago. And you two angels know the rest."

"What kind of explosion? You mean the Martians are using bombs, too?" asked Alex, dismayed.

"Didn't see any sign of that. I think it was probably one of them lasers hitting the tank of one of my buddies—superheated the thing so much that it exploded." For the first time he looked distressed, his eyes filling with pain as he looked from one to the other of them. "My buddies . . . I guess I was the only one who made it out."

"I'm sorry." Alex placed a hand on his arm. "We'll try to get you . . . God only knows where we can find help."

"I have a suggestion," Earnest said. "There's an emergency hospital and refugee center in the hills just south of Hagerstown. We were trying to get the folks to head there when the Martians came through. Looks like you have transport, right?"

"Yeah. We can squeeze you in," Alex assured him.

"What about you two? What's your story?"

Alex gave him a quick accounting of their experiences in DC and Bethesda. "What we really need is a radio. I've got some important information for . . . well, for the president. I need to get the word out."

"That camp I told you about. One of the local whiz kids was working on a ham set. He had it running two mornings ago, before I headed down to the river. Maybe we can get you together with him." He smiled, wryly. "The president, huh? You know him?"

"We've met," Alex said. "I guess I kind of work for him." For the first time in several days she thought about the container and the sample she had taken from the Martian cylinder. "I need to get in touch with him."

"Well, if you two angels will help me up the hill, I'll see if I can't get you to a radio."

"Okay." Alex and Pam each took one of his arms. "We'll do our best, but I'm afraid this is going to hurt a little."

She was wrong. It hurt a lot, but an hour later Don Earnest was laid into the passenger seat of the Humvee, with Pam and all four small children wedged in the back. Alex put the military car in drive and started up the valley, relieved beyond all expectation to finally have a destination in front of her instead of merely relentless terror behind.

June 18
Eglin AFB, Florida

Colonel Willard seemed to have aged ten years in the past two weeks.

To Duke Hayes, the CO looked like an old man: stoop-shouldered, a relief map of lines crossing his face, his crew-cut hair gone almost snowy white. Where he had once stood tall and confident at the front of a briefing room, presiding over an elite squadron of highly trained pilots, he now sat at his side and spoke only to Duke, his voice so quiet that the flier had to strain to hear.

"It took longer than the armaments people thought it would, but your nuke is ready. A Mark 72, tritium-enriched, fusion bomb—stripped down, no computer chips. Your mission will be about as complicated as the one when the *Enola Gay* dropped Little Boy on Hiroshima. Though your bomb packs about fifteen times the punch of that little firecracker. You'll release at twenty-five thousand feet, and it will detonate at seven hundred. I don't need to tell you that you want to haul ass outta there before it cooks off."

"Right, Colonel. I can do that." Duke's pulse was racing. His earlier nervousness was gone—now, he relished the chance to really hit back at these Martian sons of bitches. "What about the target?"

"We have orders directly from POTUS," he told Duke, leaning his elbows on his desk as if he needed it to support his frail frame. The pilot remained tautly alert. The fact that this mission was ordered by the president himself only added to his resolve.

"There are two other bombs ready to go, and the CIC has ordered a combined strike. So you'll be flying to Maryland. You'll be joined over DC by two other A10s, one out of New York and the other out of Carolina. The three of you are to take out the Martian front that, at latest reports, runs north from the Potomac River, through Frederick, Maryland, and up almost to Gettysburg, in Pennsylvania. You'll be on the left wing of the formation—you'll need to keep the Potomac River in sight, but stay north of it as you make your run. Radio silence until bombs away, for all three of you cowboys. After that, use an open channel to report as much info as you can."

"All right, Chief. When do I fly? And what about refueling? I don't suppose we have any tankers ready to go?"

Willard shook his head and looked at his watch. "You'll need to be airborne in two hours. You'll carry reserve tanks, enough to get you to the target, with a few hundred miles to spare. But you won't be able to make it back here."

"Yeah, I was doing the math. I guess you have some idea where I should land," Duke suggested, going for a laconic drawl to cover up his sudden attack of nerves. This was starting to sound like a one-way mission. Even so, he wouldn't have given up his claim to it for any incentive in the world.

"Looks like Pittsburgh International is going to be your best bet. There's a strong Army presence there, as well as Air Force maintenance crews. And the Martians haven't gotten into western Pennsylvania yet."

"Where exactly *are* they? I mean, besides camped out all along the East Coast?"

"Last reports have tripods moving south and east from Indianapolis. Louisville and Cincinnati are under attack, and Cleveland is expecting the bastards any day. If they keep moving east, obviously Pittsburgh is going to become too hot for you to stick around. But I expect they'll find something for you and your Warthog to do."

"No doubt. Uh, Colonel . . . ?"

"What is it, Duke?"

"Has there been any more word from that Richmond team? You know, the doctor who was reporting from the crater when the cylinder opened up?"

"No." Willard's voice was flat, unemotional, but his eyes seemed to reflect a deep well of grief. "Fort Bragg is gone—that's where they were based—so there hasn't been any detailed confirmation. Now that the bastards have torched Atlanta, they're across the South. Matter of fact, we're pulling out of here, just a few hours after you take off."

"Jesus." Duke hadn't imagined this powerful airbase could be vulnerable, but it only seemed to make sense. "Where are you going?"

"Truck convoy, down the peninsula. Best guess is we'll end up at Homestead AFB, make our last stand there—if we have to. But you need to worry about your own mission, Duke. I don't need to tell you how much this means to us all."

"You don't, Chief. But good luck to you and the rest of the unit."

"Thanks—and you, too. We're all going to be pulling for you. Don't forget to take your kit along—you might be living out of a suitcase for a few days, until this thing settles down."

If it settles down, the pilot thought, with a powerful sense of melancholy. Like most Air Force bomber pilots, he had trained for nuclear missions, but it had always seemed like an abstract fantasy. These weapons hadn't been used since the two bombs dropped on Japan in 1945, and he had always imagined they would never be used again. Now, not only was he embarking on a nuclear attack, but he was dropping his lethal payload on American real estate.

The new world, he realized, was a strange, frightening, and increasingly lonesome place.

Three hours later, Duke was guiding his Warthog around the flaming wreckage of Atlanta, keeping his airplane and its precious cargo well away from the danger zone. He saw the scars of war, the smoky pyres of wreckage, extending northward from the once-great city, and knew the tripods were advancing toward Chattanooga and the rest of Tennessee. Flying the A10 over the rural countryside, passing above the deceptively pastoral crests of the Appalachians, he was moderately surprised to see signs of human activity below.

Some of the winding mountain roads were crowded with traffic, including lots of old trucks and cars, farm tractors and wagons, all moving farther into the mountains. In several hollows he saw that huge, sprawling tent cities had sprung up, people crowded together for all the world like the refugees of war in some third-world country.

We're *all* third-world countries, he reflected bitterly, in light of the Martians' superiority in everything that seemed to matter. It was heartening to know that so many people survived, but depressing to speculate on what the future held. Would the enemy crisscross the nation in an increasingly tight grid, driving the population into smaller and smaller quadrants until mankind faced inevitable annihilation?

The landmarks passed below, checked off visually: Knoxville in its verdant valley, still apparently untouched by the war. He followed the crests of the Smokies and the Alleghenies, picking out the Shenandoah Valley to his right. There he turned to the east, flying high above a Virginia countryside that had been utterly ravaged. In large areas he couldn't even see the ground through the thick smoke, and in other places he saw only great swaths of charred landscape.

Finally, he caught sight of the bright Potomac, the estuary south of Washington where it expanded into a broad, placid bay. He followed the water north until the sprawling cityscape of DC itself came into sight—first the towers of the Virginia suburbs, then the hallowed ground of Arlington National Cemetary. So much of the city looked untouched—he saw the Pentagon, the Capitol, and the major monuments still intact, though he knew that the population had been annihilated or driven out by the clouds of lethal gas.

As ordered by his briefing, he went into a holding pattern in a wide circle over the Tidal Basin and the Mall, using the Washington Monument as the center. Scanning the skies over the city, he quickly picked out another Warthog with the markings of the New York National Guard on its tail. He could see the deceptively slim package, the Mark 72 hydrogen bomb that was identical to his own weapon, slung beneath the other aircraft's fuselage.

Soon they were joined by the third A10, this one bearing the insignia of the USAF, and also armed with a nuke. He made eye contact with the other two pilots but they all maintained radio silence. Each, like Duke, must be feeling the burden of the vast destructive power they carried and the knowledge that they would finally slam the Martians hard.

With an exchange of "thumbs-ups," the three warplanes started north-westward, climbing to their bombing altitude of twenty-five thousand feet. They dispersed, Duke staying on the left flank, just keeping the Air Force bomber in view, ten or twelve miles to his right. Instead of his so-phisticated targeting system, he had a pair of good old-fashioned binocu-lars, and used them frequently to scan the ground ahead of him and maintain his position in respect to the center plane. The Guard pilot, he trusted, was doing the same thing on the far right flank of their dispersed formation.

Again Duke found himself thinking of history, of his role in the events that would shape the future of the world. He felt unworthy, small, even pa-thetic, as he guided his powerful jet—with its infinitely more powerful payload—toward a destiny with the alien invaders. He found himself, for the first time since he was a boy, murmuring a sincere prayer, hoping that his words were being heard by some kind of Supreme Being.

Then, just like that, the time for reflection was over. Frederick came into view, a flaming hell of burning gas stations, buildings, lumberyards, and an apparently inexhaustible supply of fuel. He clapped the binoculars to his eyes, and quickly spotted two of the tripods. They were a half mile or so apart, advancing westward out of the flaming debris of the city.

Duke had his targets. The three jets were too far apart for visual coor-dination of the bomb run, so he could only hope that the other pilots, too, had located something to bomb. He consulted the calibrated dial of the manual bombsight, quickly set the rating to his airspeed of just over two hundred miles per hour. When he released the bomb, it would con-tinue to move along his west-by-northwest bearing at that speed, but it would also be falling rapidly toward the ground. When it reached the det-onation point of seven hundred feet above the Earth, it would explode, and nearly everything within a mile or more of that point would be im-mediately incinerated. He hoped to hell that would include at least two tripods.

It was time. He pulled the lever, felt the plane lurch slightly as the bomb dropped away. It was a curiously tame reaction, nothing like the sense of lightness he felt when he dropped the full eight tons of a maximum load. But his heart was in his throat as he vividly imagined the lethal power of that deceptively simple-looking device.

He banked to port, hard, and put the jet into a power dive, flipping the switch that would dump raw fuel into the fiery exhaust of his turbofan engines. The afterburners kicked in with a powerful jolt, the A10 screaming away from the target, quickly accelerating to its maximum speed of over four hundred miles per hour. The ship vibrated underneath him, shaking and roaring with barely contained power. Duke kept his eyes on the horizon, his hands on the stick, and prayed for enough speed to get him away from the lethal blast.

It took a curiously long time for the bomb to fall, so much so that he had begun to wonder if it was a dud. Even so, he seemed to be moving terribly slowly. The ground rolled past at a leisurely clip, the waters of the river glinting before him in a deceptively pastoral display.

The flash came from behind him, a shockingly bright flicker of light, even more intense than the EMP of the initial Martian attack. He knew what was coming, but still held his hands on the controls, kept his concentration forward. Wind caused by his extreme speed rattled the cockpit, and he felt as though the plane was about to shake itself apart. Still, he didn't dare slow down.

The blast wave, when it came, was a physical thing, hurling the A10 hundreds of feet through the air, slamming Duke into his seat. Frantically, he struggled for control, got the ship leveled, and saw the Potomac flash by underneath. Finally, he eased back on the stick, switched off the afterburners, and resumed a more normal flight, banking to starboard, coming around to a westerly bearing.

He circled back over the Virginia countryside, saw the churning murk, the ominous pillar of smoke swelling into the vast mushroom cloud, rising from his blast and, more than a dozen miles away, from another place to the north. There was no sign of the third bomb, or aircraft. Streaks of fire shot through those clouds, each of which seemed to be the size of a whole city. The twin pillars churned upward, boiling and angry, furiously swelling into the sky. More flames burst from the blackness, and in those eruptions Duke could imagine all the fires of Hell.

It was time to break radio silence.

June 18
Hagerstown, Maryland

"Alex—get up here! I hear something! Hurry, dammit!"

Pam Lucas was shouting down from the tower platform, her near-hysterical urgency compelling Alexandria into a reckless sprint as she raced from the makeshift first-aid tent of their little encampment. She was panting for breath by the time she made it to the upper platform, where she found Pam jumping up and down in excitement, clutching her binoculars, pointing off to the east, toward Frederick. They were atop a forest service fire lookout tower, the place that had been the observation post of the small band of survivors gathered here in the forested Maryland countryside just outside Hagerstown. Below them, in a hollow behind the hilltop, was the refugee encampment where Don Earnest had led them, and where the trooper now slept peacefully in a makeshift medical tent.

"Listen!" Pam was saying. "It's an airplane—a jet! The first one I've seen all week! And it's coming this way!"

"Give me the binocs!" Alex demanded, and the girl quickly complied.

"Look! Can you see it?" Pam asked frantically.

The woman was scanning the skies, hearing that distant thrumming, cursing the intermittent clouds. Then she picked it out, a tiny speck, tens of thousands of feet above the ground. It was a military jet, she perceived, smaller than an airliner, and a little lower than a typical commercial flight would fly. She would have been willing to bet, she thought with a strange little leap of familiarity, that this was an A10 Warthog. Even across the vast distance the squared wings and tail, the boxy engines, suggested nothing else.

"Maybe they're going to bomb those shithead Martians!" Pam cried.

Alex winced, though—days earlier—she had given up trying to correct the teenager's remarkably profane vocabulary. Indeed, she had come to rely on Pam more and more as a very useful companion. Together they had carried four frightened children to safety—they were now being cared for by a group of nurses and teachers who had organized a youth shelter just a mile away—and had joined forces with this group of survivors, ranging from state troopers to veterans to housewives.

In addition to the medical facilities and relief station here, the group had been able to provide Alex with access to a radio, and she had been able to raise Norfolk Naval Base and convey her observations to military authorities. They had broadcast from a truck, moving through the hills. The whole group was prepared to move at a moment's notice, but for several days the Martians had shown no sign of coming closer.

Instead, from this camp they had aided other survivors with first aid, had helped direct them toward West Virginia or the mountains to the west of the Shenandoah, and kept an eye on the continuing devastation of Frederick. The group included others who had studied the Martians, always at the risk of their lives. Their reports, broadcast intermittently and always from locations remote from their mountaintop headquarters, had, Alex hoped, been relayed to the president aboard the *Seawolf*.

Now all these thoughts fell into the background as she watched the jet. She was surprised to see it dive, changing course suddenly, picking up speed as it curled around and raced away from its previous bearing. For a moment she wondered what was the reason for this strange maneuver—and then, in a horrifying instant of understanding, she knew.

"Get down!" she screamed, pushing Pam toward the steps leading down to the ground. "Run for your life!"

The girl, for once, made no effort to argue, but took off like a shot. Alex raced at her heels, around and around the spiraling steps of this old forest fire lookout tower. The flash brightened the world before they reached the ground, but they kept running.

"Everybody get down!" Alex shouted, as some of the group, drawn by the commotion, streamed out of the first-aid tent. "Hit the deck! Cover your ears!"

She and Pam stumbled off the bottom steps of the ladder, and sprawled onto the ground. Alex threw her arms over her head as the blast wave swept over them, a rocking gale of wind and noise tearing at the trees, shaking the tower on its solid foundation. But they were far enough away to avoid the truly devastating effects, and in a few seconds, the rush of wind and force was past. Together, they stood hesitantly, looking to the east.

The churning column of smoke and flame was rising into the sky, already visible between the trees, swelling ever higher.

"My God!" Pam said with a strangled gasp. "Is that what I think . . . ?"

"A nuclear bomb," Alex confirmed, feeling a mingled sense of dread and wonder. "They've wiped out what was left of Frederick—but maybe they took a couple of Martians with them."

The radio in the tent crackled into life. A pilot started talking, giving a calm, dispassionate damage assessment.

"... cloud now surpassing forty thousand feet and still climbing. Ground zero approximately five-point-five miles north of the Potomac, in the area of intersection Highways one-five and three-four-zero. Two tripods visually tracked within blast zone. No direct observation possible at this time ..."

Perhaps it was the numbness, or the shock of the blast, but Alex wasn't even that surprised when she recognized Duke's voice.

FOUR

June 19
Delbrook Lake, Wisconsin

It was becoming a galling habit, this slow turning of my radio dial. I had lost count of the days since I had last heard a signal, but knew it had to be nearly a week. Still, since scouring the houses of the abandoned subdivision, I had a plentiful supply of batteries, and nothing better to do with my time. I had already gone through two packs of the D-cells, but wasn't worried about that. I would just go out and scavenge some more when I needed them. Until then, I would search and listen, begrudging every second spent away from this set, which had begun to seem like my only tangible link to the rest of the human race.

This afternoon, just after 1:00 P.M., I was rewarded by a crackling break in the static. Tuning carefully, I focused in on a man's voice. He was speaking in a calm tone, almost whispering—like an old rock 'n' roll jock on some really hip FM station in the seventies. This was an AM signal, but it was strong, and I latched on to it like a drowning man clutching at a lifeline.

". . . broadcasting across the street from where the Cubbies played. I'm in the mobile unit, as usual. The van looks like it's still ready to haul hippies to Woodstock, 'cept for the psychedelic paint. I've learned a few things that, so far, have helped to keep me alive and, at least sporadically, on the air. For one thing, these alien bastards will home in on a radio signal, so I can only talk to y'all for about fifteen minutes. Then it'll be time to shut down, and move. But I got a lot of city to roam, and I'll be back on the air at the starting time of a night game, if you want to check in. Same spot on your radio dial—and no annoying sponsors."

A night game? Cubbies? Baseball—he must be talking about baseball! Immediately I saw the efficacy of his code: Even if the Martians were capable of translating our speech, they would certainly lack the sense of cultural awareness to decipher his meaning. The man continued, relaxed and laconic, as if he didn't have a care in the world. Still, his words belied his tone.

"Listen, Chicago is pretty well cleaned out. Most everybody has gone, either killed by the gas, or moved out. Lots of people left on boats, and it seemed like they got away—the tripods can move onto water for short stretches, but they don't seem inclined to go too far from shore. Those folks who went south, well, it wasn't good. Tripods came up through Gary and Champagne, all the way around to points west of O'Hare, thick as fleas on a mangy dog. Most everyone who went that way got gassed.

"There were some more gaps toward the north side. The fool Martians didn't come down the lakeshore until south of Waukegan, so lots of folks made it up to the Land of Cheese—still heading north, from what I hear.

"We got some tripods in the Windy City, still, roamin' around. Most of 'em moved out though, looks like they're headin' for Saint Looie. I picked up another scrap of radio earlier today—the land of the Twinkies still ain't been hit. Guess it's just a matter of time, though. That big ol' river sure ain't deep enough to keep them out.

"And speaking of time, mine is up for now. Gotta take down the antenna and move. But I'll be back, folks—remember, just in time for the first pitch. Maybe I'll broadcast from the deck of an old Nazi submarine, if you want to look me up. This is the Wrigley Guerrilla, signing off."

The signal vanished, but left me with a tingling sense of energy, an idea of hope that I had all but abandoned in the week since the Martians had come through Delbrook Lake. I got up and paced around, trying to recall what he had said? Why hadn't I thought to tape him? No matter—I could recall enough to keep me thinking. And maybe I could dig up my old cassette recorder and get it ready in time for his next broadcast.

Parts of his code were immediately apparent to me. There was only one Nazi submarine in North America, so far as I knew. The U505 was one of the premier exhibits at the Museum of Science and Industry, in downtown Chicago. If I was in the city, I would have gone there to meet him, feeling fairly certain that was the place where his next broadcast would originate. But as to the rest—what was the land of the Twinkies? Was he talking about some sugary packaged dessert product? That didn't make sense to me. And when, exactly, was he next going on the air? The starting time of a night baseball game, of course, but I wanted a specific time, dammit!

I moved around with growing urgency. The dogs took note of my sudden animation, lifting up their heads, watching me in wonder as I raced into the kitchen, dug through the pile of old newspapers that had I regularly stockpiled up to the time of the Pulse.

I wasn't a baseball fan, though I thought I understood in an anthropological sense the place that the game occupied—or *had* occupied—in the national psyche. The "Cubbies" clearly were the Chicago Cubs. They played at Wrigley Field, I remembered. So his broadcast had originated from there, this morning. That triggered another thought, about the "Twinkies." Was that another baseball reference? It seemed vaguely familiar. And what time did a night game start? Six? Seven-thirty? Eight? Desperately, I wished that I had payed closer attention to the national pastime.

Finally, I pulled out an old copy of the *Milwaukee Journal-Sentinel*, a paper from early May. I paused in wonder at the ludicrous headlines. It was like an icon from an ancient past: stories about taxes, about traffic congestion and highway construction, about the *weather*! Never mind, I told myself, as I pawed through to the sports section.

Night games . . . Let's see, it was a Tuesday paper, and the game time for the Milwaukee team, the Brewers, was there, under the standings: 7:05. Just to be certain, I checked some other games—the Cubs had played in the afternoon on that day, but the Cardinals and Twins, both in the Central Time Zone, also had starting times of 7:05. Twins—Twinkies! There it was; the Wrigley Guerrilla was referring to Minneapolis and Saint Paul, Minnesota. There was some comfort in knowing that the large state to the west of the Mississippi had not yet been struck by the invaders.

The rest of the day passed at a crawl. Knowing that I could expect a broadcast at a certain time, I forced myself to leave my radio. I took the dogs—and the shotgun—and went for a walk around the surrounding countryside. I didn't see any people, but scattered a pack of coyotes that was gathered around an abandoned dairy farm up the road. Still, I couldn't stay away for long, and soon found myself back home, staring at the clock, waiting for that broadcast, my one link to the rest of the human race.

Marveling at the man's courage, I thought about what he had said: that the Martians could home in on radio broadcasts. It made perfect sense, of course. But he moved around, apparently in an old van. "Guerrilla," I reflected, was an apt sobriquet.

To help pass the time, I got out a *National Geographic* map of the United States, laid it out across my kitchen table. I started to mark, in red pencil, the places I knew the Martians had struck, and drew arrows indicating their presumed routes of advance. Starting with Madison and Janesville, I made estimates, remembering what I had heard about the landings in central Illinois, estimating the path as they reportedly moved from Chicago toward Saint Louis. As the afternoon passed into evening, I watched the clock carefully and turned my radio on well before seven.

At precisely 7:05 he came back on the air.

"Hello, humankind—if there are any of you livin', and listenin', around our little corner of Lake Michigan. This is the Wrigley Guerrilla, broadcasting all by his lonesome from the beautiful, magnificent, and utterly abandoned Musuem of Science and Industry in Chicago. Gotta pick up the pace a bit—there was a tripod closing in on the scene of my earlier broadcast today, and I was only on the air for twelve minutes. Still, I don't know if y'all understand how it is with us radio jocks: We just gotta keep talking.

"First, the news. I've been monitoring the air, shortwave style, and picked up a few tidbits from around the country. Not much to cheer about, I'm afraid. That arch in Saint Louis? They burned it down just this morning, tripods came walkin' right across the Mississipp. People are leavin', heading west. Nearest Martians out that way seem to be in the Denver area, though I got that secondhand.

"There's some technical information, coming from the Army around the East Coast. These lasers seem to have a range of about a half mile, at their usual settings. They can blast off pretty constantly, like a machine gun. But if they save up their power for a bit—they said ten seconds was one estimate—the laser can shoot a lot farther, like three or four miles, and still burn the hell out of whatever it hits.

"Also, don't know if you folks have figured this out or not, but those tripods are not the actual Martians. They're machines, and each one seems to have one Martian inside. The actual aliens sound pretty hideous—we have one or two eyewitness reports, also from the East Coast. One scientist saw one comin' out of a cylinder near Richmond, Virginia. Said it looked like some kind of awful octopus, three big legs, lots of wiggly little tentacles, and a big, bloated body. Disgusting, huh? She also said that they seem to eat coal—at least, that was what they brought in their ship.

"We know that the bastards stink to high heaven, like rotten meat. And they seem to like the stink of dead bodies. Several people have reported seeing them dragging old corpses together, piling them up, and then sitting around in their tripods, just taking in the aroma. I know, sickening. Sorry I had to tell you about that.

"But people, we are survivors—you know that, if you're alive right now. And we are goin' to ride this thing out, and figure out a way to beat these bastards. We gotta stick together and, most important, we gotta communicate."

He said the word like it was a complete sentence in itself: comm you nih cate!

"I gotta fly, for now. But I'll be back. I'm in the mood for a Matisse, if you want to look me up. Think I'll go on the air at starting time—that's starting time, like Dolly Parton sang about in that rockin' piece of music about that poor working gal. Until then, people, keep the faith, and keep on fightin'.

"This is the Wrigley Guerrilla, signing off."

He was gone, though I let the radio hiss away for a few minutes, just in case. But that was all he said. After a while, I turned off the radio and sat in the dark, thinking.

Again he had given his clues in terms of human culture. The reference to Matisse struck an immediate chord—I suspected that his next broadcast would originate around the Art Institute of Chicago. Although I knew who Dolly Parton was, I wasn't really familiar with her work, and couldn't think of a single song she had sung. But even that was okay. I had enough batteries that I would simply keep the radio on. From the context of his message—"starting time"—I guessed he would be back on the air in the morning, at seven or eight . . . or nine.

Suddenly the song was there, thumping through my mind:

"Working nine to five, what a way to make a livin'"

I actually leaped to my feet at the realization, bringing both dogs to full attention. They bristled and growled; Galahad even barked a few times, but I didn't care. Instead, I found myself humming that catchy tune. I didn't know any more of the words, but I was certain that I had figured out the starting time of the next Wrigley Guerrilla broadcast. Making myself busy, I fed the dogs, checked the windows, and watched it grow dark outside. Somewhere in the back of my mind I clicked on the thought that tomorrow would be June 20, just two months after I had seen that first flash on the surface of Mars.

It didn't seem possible that so much could vanish, in so little time.

The coyotes were howling in a frenzy, causing the dogs to pace around the house in agitation. Galahad glared at the curtained windows, and Klondike snuffled noisily as he clomped through the kitchen. Still the coyotes kept up their eerie song.

It seemed like they were right outside my door.

FIVE

Alexandria parked the Humvee on the shoulder of the smooth, white interstate. She had found the flattest stretch of road for miles in either direction, and it just happened to be the long bridge over the Potomac River. Their impromptu crew of state troopers and other helpers had used pickup trucks and a small bulldozer to clean the span of stalled vehicles, working through the night.

"He's gonna take you to see the *president?*" Pam demanded somewhat crossly, as the woman and girl got out of the durable military vehicle. The teenager glared at her companion as if she still suspected some sort of trick.

"That's what it sounds like to me," Alex said, with a shrug that did little to conceal the tumult of emotions she was feeling. "I guess we'll find out more when he lands. Like what kind of airplane he's coming in—I don't think there's room for more than one person in the ship he usually flies."

"Huh," Pam grunted. "Well, what if he's radioactive or something? You know, cuz of the bomb?"

"I think he was as safe as we were," replied the scientist, somewhat lamely, realizing she didn't know nearly enough about nuclear fallout to feel reassured herself, much less speak soothingly to anyone else.

Still, she and Duke had pieced together a pretty decent plan in a short radio conversation the previous night. After she had identified herself to the pilot while he was still in the air, he had told her to expect a message. Duke's tone had seemed flat and professional—or was that merely the effect of the poor transmission quality? Her own heart had been in a turmoil since then, and she sat by the receiver through the long afternoon and into the evening, only taking a few moments outside to watch the gradually dissipating mushroom cloud over Frederick. That day's wind had been blowing eastward, which was lucky for them, though it boded ill for the DC and Baltimore areas—she knew that the sinister cloud was laden with radioactive fallout. She was not a nuclear scientist, but she understood the physics enough to view the attack with very mixed emotions.

Finally, the radio had crackled to life. Duke was in Pittsburgh, calling from an Air Force command post. Again he sounded calm and unemotional, even detached. Alex had bitten back her own joy and responded in kind. He told her to find a place for him to land, declared that he had orders—from the "highest of the high"—to pick her up and get her to a meeting, of all things. Hence, the selection of this freeway bridge as a landing strip. A brief midnight transmission had communicated the location and set up the details of the rendezvous, leading to this impatient, fidgeting wait on the shoulder of the wide roadway.

"Who is this Duke guy, anyway?" the girl pressed. "You looked like you were ready to cry when you talked to him on the radio."

"A friend—a good friend, from before the invasion."

"He's your boyfriend, isn't he?" Pam accused.

"Well, you could say that. But he's an old friend, too. His brother . . . his brother was flying the space shuttle, was one of the first people to die when the Martians attacked."

"Oh." That seemed to set her back, for a few seconds anyway. "And Duke is the pilot who dropped that atom bomb on the Martians yesterday?"

"Yes . . . it was. I . . . guess I thought he was dead," Alex admitted.

"Well, he's not. So don't get all silly over him. And I hope he can drop a few more nukes on the goddamn Martians!"

Shivering, Alexandria remembered that towering, sinister cloud. Throughout her life that mushroom black image had personified horror, death, and doom. Even if it had destroyed two or three tripods, it was hard to imagine that it was a beneficial effect. She found herself fervently hoping that there weren't any more nukes available.

"Hey—I hear it!" Pam cried, suddenly excited.

Alex strained, detecting no unusual sound, but she had learned to trust the girl's keen hearing. Sure enough, in another minute she could make out the distant drone of a piston-engine airplane—definitely not the Warthog. A short time later a little civilian aircraft, high wing with fixed tricycle landing gear, sputtered into view, banking down the valley of the Potomac, following the course of the river between Maryland and Virginia.

Getting out her flare pistol, Alex stood at the edge of the cleared landing zone and fired a red, blazing torch into the sky.

Duke waggled his wings and banked up to the south, turning to fly into the wind that, just then, was northerly. He came in low, banked ever more gradually as he lined himself up with the bridge. Alexandria was amazed to see how slow the little plane could fly; it seemed almost to hover over the freeway span before touching gently down on the twin rear landing gear. A second later the nosewheel came gently down, and the plane was taxiing down the highway bridge. The engine brayed, snarling in complaint as the pilot applied the brakes. Alex ran forward as the stubby aircraft came to a stop a hundred meters short of her initial position.

The side door popped open and Duke climbed out. God—he looked so much like Nate! It was not that he had changed, physically, but there was a veteran wariness to his look, a sense of maturity and, simply, age, that had not been there two weeks before.

They held each other for a minute or more, not speaking, not kissing, simply relishing the strength of each other's clasp. Alex breathed the smell of his dirty flight suit, a mixture of male sweat, fuel vapors, and other unidentifiable odors—and it was the sweetest perfume she had ever inhaled. She sensed his own emotion in their wordless embrace and, for the first time since Richmond, allowed herself to believe that there might be a future for humankind, for her.

"Ahem," Pam said finally, from about two steps behind Alexandria.

The woman smiled and broke the embrace. "Duke Hayes, I'd like you to meet another survivor—Pam Lucas."

The pilot grinned, that boyish look returning instantly. "Pleased to meet you," he said.

The girl reached forward to shake his hand solemnly. "I saw you drop the bomb, yesterday," she announced. "Way to take those fuckers out."

His eyes widened slightly, and Alex had to laugh. "She sounds older than she is," she explained. "But she's very brave—she brought four little kids out of DC by herself, saw them safely off into the mountains with a refugee group. Pam had the chance to go, too, but she decided to stay here—she's helped to save a lot of lives at our makeshift hospital here in Hagerstown."

"We gotta do *something*," Pam declared, sounding cross but clearly pleased by the praise.

"Nice work," Duke said. He turned back to Alex. "And God, it's nice to see you," he said.

"Are you going to take her to the president?" Pam asked.

"Yes—that's POTUS, to us insiders," the pilot replied seriously. "And he wanted me to get her there as soon as I could." He turned to look at Alexandria. "They'll have a boat waiting for us at Norfolk, to take us to the sub. They were going to send a chopper for you when I radioed your position, but I persuaded them that I could get you there faster, and safer. Had to leave the Warthog, though—it's not set up for a passenger. But . . ." Holding her by the shoulders, he looked directly into her eyes. She was startled by the haunting sense of fear she could see in that anxious gaze. "I'm never letting you out of my sight again!"

"I can't believe you're alive," she said, finally kissing him. "When the Pulse happened, I was afraid you were in the air . . ."

"A couple of minutes from taking off. And then I thought I heard you die," he said shakily. He told her of the tape-recorded message his colonel had played, and of the ill-fated bombing mission that had followed.

"You did a lot more damage yesterday," she said. "From what we could see from the lookout tower, nothing survived in the blast area. The Martians haven't tried to move west out of there, not yet, anyway."

"I got maybe two or three of them," he said, bitterly. "By the time we turn the whole East Coast to glass, we'll have put a real dent into the bastards."

"There's more . . . there *is* hope," Alex said. "That's why I have to get to the president." She told him about the sample, still in the container back in the Humvee. Pam ran to get it.

"You'll have to trust my flying," he said with a wink. For a moment he was the old Duke, boyish, flirting, sexy as hell. "But I promise to behave myself."

Two hours later they touched down on the landing strip at Norfolk Naval Base. A petty officer was there with a truck, the engine already idling, and Alex and Duke piled unceremoniously into the back for a racing drive across the base, Alexandria clutching her sample case. Soon the smell of salt water overcame even the taint of diesel fumes, and they climbed out onto the dock.

The boat waiting for them at the Norfolk quay was the redoubtable *Lunker*, the fishing vessel of the Air Force's General McCanders that had carried the president—and Alex—away from Washington, DC, the day after the Pulse. "Welcome aboard, Dr. DeVane, Major," said the young lieutenant who greeted them at the stern. "Make yourselves at home—and hold on. We're to get under way the very moment you two come aboard."

"Thanks for the lift, Lieutenant," replied Duke. "Where will we be out of the way?"

"The view's best from the bridge up there," the officer said, ducking to go into the low cabin. "I'll be piloting from inside."

The twin Evinrudes chugged away resolutely as Duke and Alex climbed to the higher vantage. In a few seconds the engines burst into a throaty roar, and the boat lurched away from the dock, planing slowly as it gained speed. Duke held an arm around Alex, and though she didn't need his support, she was glad for his touch.

The two of them stood side by side, and hand in hand, on the small bridge as the lieutenant guided them at full speed through Hampton Roads, and out into the swell of the open ocean. Cold spray flew up and wet their faces, and the gray skies glowered over a sea of the same colorless shade. Even as the waves jarred the small hull, Alex found herself unwilling to go below, to leave the vista, or the man.

Two hours later they were long out of sight of land, but the officer piloting the ship seemed confident as to his course and bearing. Alex was looking across the water when she saw a stretch of ocean about a mile away start to churn. A black conning tower shot up from the depths, quickly followed by the rounded top of a sleek, dark hull as the *Seawolf* came to the surface. The top of that metal tube barely cleared the waves and, in fact, an enthusiastic swell would not infrequently wash right over the metallic shell.

"This is as far as I go," said the lieutenant, slowing the *Lunker* to an idle, about a hundred feet off to starboard of the submarine.

"Are you ready to swim?" Duke asked.

Alex was pretty sure he was kidding. Already they could see sailors busily working outside a hatch on the foredeck, inflating a rubber dinghy, affixing an outboard motor with the smooth efficiency of a NASCAR pit crew. One sailor hopped in the boat, started the motor, and quickly raced over to the fishing vessel, bobbing and weaving through the uneven swell. In the meantime, Alex got a small backpack from one of the sailors, carefully placed the sample container inside, and strapped it to her back. She and Duke donned life jackets.

The submarine was rolling very gently in the easy swell, but Alex found the transfer from the *Lunker* to the *Seawolf* to be rather a daunting prospect. Still, she wasn't going to let her nerves show, not in front of these men—this particular man. She and Duke dropped over the transom into the rocking, too-flimsy craft. She held on for dear life as the sailor wasted no time in bouncing them across a hundred feet of ocean, to the submarine's curved hull. A sailor tossed down a rope ladder.

"You first," Alex said. Duke took hold of the rungs and quickly scampered onto the hull. She followed, managing to avoid embarrassing herself.

They were quickly ushered down a hatch into the claustrophobic confines of the submersible craft. With her last glance of the air and sea, Alex saw that the outboard had already been pulled from the dinghy. She had no doubt that, within a minute or two, the boat would be deflated and aboard, and the submarine diving for the safety of the ocean depths.

Inside the sub, in a narrow passage, a sailor ushered them along to an open door and showed them into a small wardroom with a table and a few metal benches on either side. Asking them to "please wait here," the seaman withdrew and closed the hatch behind them.

"Alone at last," Duke said, taking her arms and looking directly into her eyes. "Should I light a few candles to set the mood?"

Before she could reply—she was tempted to say "yes"—the door opened, and the president, stooping to pass underneath the arched bulkhead, stepped inside.

"Alexandria!" he said. "Welcome aboard."

"Thank you, Mr. President," she replied, still a little awed by his presence.

"Mr. President, hell—God, it's good to see you!" he said, embracing her like they were old classmates. "We thought we had lost you at Richmond."

He released her, and extended a hand to the pilot. "You must be Duke Hayes."

"Yes, sir. It's an honor to meet you."

"I'm sorry about your brother. He was a very brave man, one of our very best."

"Yes, sir. I couldn't agree with you more."

"You struck back at the bastards yesterday. Nice piece of work, at Frederick. What's your assessment of the damage?"

"Well, Mr. President. There was a helluva lot—of damage, I mean—and I don't know how much of it was to the Martians. Best guess is that three tripods were taken out with each bomb. But so was a whole stretch of Maryland, between the river and the Pennsylvania border. It's a little like swatting mosquitoes with hand grenades."

The chief executive's expression was grim. "Yes, that's—unfortunately—about what we expected. We'll see if our nukes give the Martians pause. But I don't think we can go tossing them around willy-nilly."

"I will do it again, sir, if you give the order," the pilot offered.

The president looked truly touched. He reached out a big hand, clapped Duke on the shoulder. "I know you will, son. And I respect that. We need men like you—and women like you," he continued, turning to Alex. "Your reports from the crater were the best eyewitness testimony we've had. And that description of the cylinder—when you went inside the thing! Lady, I'm not sure I could have done that."

"I wish I could have done more," she said sincerely. "Maybe this sample will provide some clues."

"You got that out of a Martian ship?" Duke asked. "You went *inside?*"

"Have her tell you about it sometime," the president encouraged. "And Alex, don't be modest."

"Yes, sir," she replied. "Do you think we'll be able to do an effective analysis?"

"We hope so—the sub's doctor and his staff are anxious to get a look at it. There's a good medical and science lab aboard."

"Good," Alex replied, as there was another knock at the door.

"Ah, that will be the doctor now," said the president, opening the portal to reveal a red-cheeked officer, who stepped inside and eagerly shook Alex's hand. "Commander Rogers, Dr. DeVane."

"You have a sample, I understand—from one of the cylinders?" asked the ruddy-faced man, his eyes bright with enthusiasm. "May I study it?"

"Please," said Alex, handing him the container. "I only hope it will do some good."

"It's the first, the best opportunity we've had to see what makes these fellows tick. I'll get to work on it right away!"

With that, he was gone, and the president put one hand on Alex's, the other on Duke's, shoulder.

"Listen. We're going to be doing a lot of talking, about what you've seen, both of you, and about some ideas that have been cooked up around here." He checked his watch. "That will get under way in two hours. Until then, the captain has offered his cabin to you, for a shower and maybe a change of clothes. They've laid out some Navy duds for you both, as good a fit as they could find. So why don't you make yourselves comfortable, until then?"

"Thank you, sir," they replied together.

A few minutes later a steward ushered them into a small, private cabin. The door closed behind them, and Alex was already thinking:

They could get a lot done in two hours.

SIX

June 20
Delbrook Lake, Wisconsin

I was startled out of a sound sleep by the barking of the dogs, a frenetic and constant baying that indicated real urgency. Sitting up on the couch, where I had been sleeping since the Martian landings, I saw that full daylight was illuminating the world beyond my window shades. In a panic I looked at my watch: 8:15; and I breathed a sigh of relief, since the Wrigley Guerrilla wasn't due to come on the air until nine.

In between the barks and woofs of the agitated dogs I discerned the sound of rumbling automobile engines, tires crunching on gravel—the gravel of my own driveway! The shotgun was in my hand even before I thought about it, and I stepped to the front door, standing to the side of the portal and looking through the narrow slit between the shade and the window frame. I pulled back the shade slightly, enlarging the angle of my view.

An unfamiliar pickup truck rumbled into view, with several similar vehicles coming behind. They were big, with high ground clearance and knobbed tires, and all of them were at least fifteen or twenty years old. One had a camper bed, and they all seemed to have gun racks—complete with guns. The first truck, an old Ford F-150, once blue but now predominantly covered with rust, turned to the side in front of my garage, and I saw that the bed was piled high with equipment, an irregular mound covered with a green tarp. The other trucks stopped a short distance back. I counted at least four in total, but that was about all there was room for out in the open; there could have been more of them still down the hill in the wooded part of my driveway, out of my view. In any event, it was quite a convoy, and I had no idea why these trucks had rumbled into my secluded yard.

In the course of my puzzled speculation, I was not prepared for the sight of my ex-wife getting out of the passenger door of the F-150. A burly fellow in a flannel shirt was watching carefully from behind the steering wheel as she started up toward the front door. The gun rack behind the truck's seat, I couldn't help noticing, contained no fewer than three large rifles or shotguns.

Putting down my own shotgun, I opened the door and stepped outside. The dogs were still barking frantically, so I pulled the door closed behind me, locking them in the house for the time being.

"Hello, Karen," I said. "This is a surprise."

She stopped at the base of my porch steps, shading her eyes as she looked up at me.

"Yeah, well, the world has changed, Mark. Hasn't it?"

I nodded, shrugged. What could I say?

"So you're becoming a dog lover in your old age?" She cocked an eyebrow as she asked the question, and I remembered, for a moment, just how pretty she was.

"Well, they kind of adopted me, I guess. Um . . . do you want to come inside?" I gestured at the convoy, even as I noted that none of the drivers had turned off his engine.

She shook her head. "We only stopped for a minute. I'm here to give you an invitation," she said.

"To what—a gun show?" I asked, surprised. Only after I spoke did I realize that the question had come out more tartly than I intended.

Karen ignored my tone. "We're heading north, up past Baraboo—we're going to find someplace in the country and set up camp, wait this thing out. We have room in the trucks for another person or two, and I told Nick I wanted to see if I could get you to come with us."

I looked at the driver of the pickup, waved rather awkwardly. So that was Nick? He touched a hand to the bill of his baseball cap, then looked away.

"I'm . . . I'm glad you're with someone," I said. "That you made it out of the city okay. . . ."

"It wasn't easy," she said, suddenly tearing up, angrily wiping a hand across her eyes. "I don't suppose you've heard anything about Alex . . . there's no way to know, is there?"

"No, I guess not."

"So. Do you want to throw a few things in a bag and come with us? We'll wait, for a few minutes anyway."

I thought about that, her offer to go away and hide with them. And I felt acutely the vacuum that my life had become, the loss of communication across the world, even from city to city, that we had taken for granted . . . I remembered the Army officer, with his plan to live and breed under-ground, thought of all the legions of people who must be deciding to go somewhere and "wait this thing out." How many pockets of people would there be, each alone and isolated, cut off from all the rest of humankind in a little hiding place somewhere in the world?

"Mark?" Her tone was gentle, caring—as it had been for so many years when she was worried about me, until she just couldn't take it anymore. "Mark, are you all right, really? Are you eating, you know, taking care of yourself?"

"Yes," I replied, strangely touched. "I'm taking care of myself—as well as I can, anyone can, with the world . . . like it is."

"You're not planning to crawl into bed and pull the covers over your head, are you? If you are, dammit, I'm going to drag you along with us!"

Suddenly I knew what I had to do. The laconic voice of the Wrigley Guerrilla, and the word he had enunciated so carefully, came into my mind like a summons.

Comm you nih cate.

"Karen . . . um, thanks, Karen—for thinking of me, for coming here. I really appreciate it. And tell Nick thanks for me, too. No . . . I'm not going to hide, to lie in bed . . . to give up. I wish you both, all of you, good luck. And I hope you find someplace safe, up north. But I can't come with you."

"Why not?" she demanded, suddenly as feisty as I remembered her. "What's so important that you have to stay here, holed up in your house while the world comes to an end?"

"I'm not going to stay here. Not anymore."

"Where are you going, then?" She sounded genuinely curious, con-cerned. I was touched.

"There's someone broadcasting radio out of Chicago. He's called the Wrigley Guerrilla, and he gets on the air now and then. I've been listening to him . . . and I know what I have to do."

"What?" she probed, but there was a hint of softening in the harshness of her tone.

"I have to go and find him," I told her.

June 21
Delbrook Lake, Wisconsin

"Word is, we've dropped a couple of H-bombs on the Martians, in Maryland. It must have taken a helluva recondition, after the Pulse, to get these weapons operable again. Of course, those weapons were shielded against EMP, but I doubt any human ever anticipated the kind of power that was in the Martian weapon. Anyway, I suspect we would have used more of our nukes, if they had still been operable when the cylinders landed. Now, it makes me wonder how many more of them are in the pipeline. I'm not sure I want to find out."

The Guerrilla's morning broadcast, that day, was coming from a location he described as looking like a spaceship that had set down on the shore of the lake. I hadn't been able to decipher that clue, but it wasn't specifically important to me, since I was still at my house.

But the Jeep was packed, and I was nearly ready to set out.

"Well, I'm still making my way around the city and the 'burbs. Driving this old classic would have made Arlo Guthrie feel right at home. Mine's not red, though."

I had already guessed that he was driving a Volkswagen van from the pre–electronic ignition era, but that reference—I still remembered Arlo drawling on about his "red VW Microbus" in "Alice's Restaurant," a song I had enjoyed during my own college days—confirmed my assessment. It was a useful bit of information, since I intended to find him in person. I listened eagerly as he laid out the next set of clues.

"Tonight I'll set up shop on the field named for Butch. The part of it where you might meet a Frenchman or Brazilian. I'll plan to go on the air just in time for the start of a Fourth of July"—he pronounced it JOO-ly— "fireworks show.

"Until then, this is the Wrigley Guerrilla signing off."

He was gone, leaving only the hiss of static crackling from my radio. Normally I would leave the device turned on for a few extra minutes, in case he had a second thought and returned to the airwaves (though he hadn't done so yet). But I had plans, an urgency that I had not felt for a long time.

As I was carrying the radio out to the Jeep, I thought about his most recent clues. The field named for Butch, of course, referred to the WWII ace, Butch O'Hare, whose name had been given to Chicago's massive airport. If I could get there in time, I should obviously look for him at the International Terminal. And the time . . . well, every Fourth of Joo-ly fireworks show started as soon as it got dark, so that was a pretty good guideline.

The dogs were waiting expectantly beside the little vehicle, apparently sensing the portent of the preparations that had occupied me for most of the previous day, after Karen had said farewell, and her convoy continued north. I set the radio in the small niche I had saved for it, between the two seats, and surveyed my packing job.

The rear compartment of the Jeep was basically empty, since the two dogs would ride there. There was a bundle of tow-straps, jumper cables, and a little shovel that Browne had fastened there, and I left it in place reasoning that some or all of it might come in handy. I had added the gas can and siphon hose, lashing them to the roll bar on one side of the back with bungee cords. On the other side, I had carefully arranged a bag of dog food, three empty ice cream buckets that I used as water and food dishes for them, and a jug of water. After packing, I had checked several times to make sure that Klondike and Galahad had enough room, and could still get in and out easily.

My own gear was stowed in front of and on top of the passenger seat. It had taken only a moment's reflection for me to realize that I wouldn't want to break into abandoned houses and sleep in other peoples' beds, so I had packed a small tent and my sleeping bag, as well as a two-burner camping stove with several cans of propane, and a shiny stainless-steel cook kit with pots, a frying pan, plate, bowl, and cup all nested efficiently together. A small duffel bag contained a few changes of clothing for me, as well as a light jacket, hat, and poncho. In the glove compartment I had stashed a flashlight and all the rest of the boxes of shotgun shells Browne had given me, while the gun itself would remain easily accessible on top of the camping supplies.

I had a little bit of food with me, but knew that I would be able to scavenge more food, gasoline, and bottled water as I traveled through the multitude of small towns and cities that lay between my house and my destination. In my pockets I had butane lighters, a Swiss Army knife, and—

though it felt like an anachronism—my wallet with my driver's license and the $300 or so in bills that I had been able to scrounge up from around my house.

The radio was situated so that I could turn it on and listen while I remained behind the wheel. I had detailed road maps of both southern Wisconsin and the Chicago area tucked into a little storage pocket on the driver's door. My final innovation: Since the Jeep had no top, I had bundled a tarp along the roll bar with many bungee cords. In the event of rain, I could stretch it to cover myself, my gear, and the dogs, while still being able to see out the windshield.

"Time to go," I said, popping open the tailgate. Klondike tried to lunge into the Jeep, but Galahad shouldered him aside with a graceful leap. A moment later the Newfoundland scrambled up as well. Both of them stared at me, bright-eyed and panting, as I went around and got behind the wheel.

The Jeep started with the first turn of the key. I took one last look at my house, locked and shuttered and sealed as much as possible. Then I turned down the driveway, rolled with a few lurches through the potholes, and started on my quest for the Wrigley Guerrilla.

SEVEN

June 22
Genoa City, Wisconsin

Klondike's growl pierced the night, a low, rumbling thing, the sound more evocative of a bear or a lion than a big dog. I reached out of my sleeping bag, first to pick up my glasses and put them on, then to push myself up to a sitting position. My mind groped for memory, for a context: I was in a city park in a small town, just a few miles north of the Illinois border. I was sleeping under the open sky, since there had seemed like no threat of rain, and there had been a nice breeze to keep the mosquitoes at bay.

What time was it? Somewhere in the middle of the night was all I could tell, all that really mattered. But why was the dog growling? I tried to put everything into context: I had made it about halfway to Chicago before making camp on this, my first night outside of my house in a very long time. I wrestled with acute disorientation, an almost dizzy sense of vertigo, of broad space and acute vulnerability. Not knowing what was out there, in the darkness, I found myself wishing for the security of walls and a roof, of a securely locked door.

Without even thinking about it, I grabbed the shotgun, clicked the safety off, and pumped a round into the chamber. Both dogs started to bark, standing side by side, bristling against something in the darkness. By then I was fully alert, looking around, trying to see what had alarmed the animals.

"Whoa, there, friend," said a male voice. "Get hold of your dogs. We don't mean you no trouble."

My campfire had faded to a mound of embers, but there was enough of a glow that I could see two men at the very fringe of the illumination, hands held up placatingly. The two dogs stood flanking the remnant of my fire, facing the strangers and growling, hackles raised.

"Klondike—Galahad. Sit!" I barked, and they both did so, though they remained alert. Every few seconds one or the other would utter another menace grumble of sound. "Sorry," I said. "We haven't seen any people over the last day—I think you took them by surprise."

"Hey, I got no problem with a good watchdog," the first speaker said. "I just don't want to get bit." He was a man about middle age, shaggy with unshaven whiskers, wearing blue jeans, a work shirt, and a baseball cap. His companion, who stayed a step or two back, looked a little younger, fidgeted nervously, looking like he was on the verge of running away.

I felt a bit awkward about it, but continued to hold the shotgun across my lap, feeling acutely vulnerable. There was something about these men, their manner and words, that made me very uncomfortable. Was it just my imagination, or was there something really *wrong* about them? I couldn't know.

They were the first people I had seen since leaving my house, and I was unwilling to assume that they had ill intentions toward me. Nevertheless, I felt at an acute disadvantage, half-inside my bedroll, sitting flat on the ground while they loomed over my camp.

"Where are you headed?" I asked, squirming out of the sleeping bag, rising to my feet. The shotgun was pointed toward the ground, cradled easily in my right hand.

"No place in partic'ler. Just saw your fire, came over to check it out."

"Here, let me throw a few logs on." I knelt, tossed some of the kindling I had piled nearby onto the embers, and the dry wood quickly sparked and flared with growing flames.

"Have a seat," I suggested, indicating the park bench near my fire. I remained kneeling beside the blaze, the shotgun still resting casually on my leg.

"You look like an outlaw with that danged piece," said the younger man, speaking for the first time. "Whatcha think—we're gonna rob you or something?"

"No." Shaking my head, I reflected on his question. They certainly did make me nervous. "I guess a fellow can't be too careful these days, though. Right?"

The older man seemed to be the boss. He replied with a nervous laugh. "Guess so. There's troubles all over the place, that's fer sure."

"Are you guys from around here? Is there anyone else in town?" I asked. "I just got here myself . . . passing through."

"We came up from McHenry after the tripods come through," the fellow answered. "We only met one other person on the way."

"Yeah," chorused the young man, with a chuckle that, this time, was truly frightening. "She was a *lot* friendlier 'n you are."

"Sorry. I guess you startled me, waking me up and all. But I don't have anything anyone would want," I suggested.

"That Jeep must run," said the younger man. "You wasn't here yesterday." He leaned forward, his manner aggressive enough that Klondike growled again. "You said 'passing through.' Where you headed?"

"Look," I said, standing up. Adrenaline pumped through my veins, and I was growing more wary of this pair with every passing second. "What do you want?"

Galahad suddenly spun to the side, barking furiously, then charging into the darkness. I had the vague image of a man there—a man with a gun!—and then I heard a stunningly loud report, saw a flash of flame, and smelled the acrid smoke of gunpowder. The white dog, apparently uninjured, ignored the shot and tore into the stranger. Klondike lumbered after the big poodle, his normally benign woofs somehow swelling into savage roars.

My own gun was up and I whirled back at the original pair, who had leaped to their feet when Galahad charged. The young one had a pistol in his hand, was raising it toward me. I pulled the trigger and the shotgun jumped in my hand, the blast of pellets striking the ground at the gunman's feet. He cried out and fell back onto the picnic table, kicking one of his feet frantically, like it was on fire, and he was trying to douse the flames.

"Drop it! Drop your gun!" I shouted, my voice on the edge of hysteria, raising the barrel to line up with the younger man's face. The gun fell from his fingers.

"Get the hell away from here, or I'll kill you!" I remembered only then to pump the gun to chamber another round, but that gesture seemed to be enough to convince the pair—they turned and disappeared into the darkness, the older man running, the younger limping along, favoring his injured foot.

I ran over to the third man, who was thrashing around, trying to push the dogs off of him. He had Galahad's neck in his hands while the powerful dog, snarling lustily, strained to bite his face. Klondike's large jaws were clamped around one of the fellow's forearms, and he was screaming in pain as the Newfoundland shook his massive head, jerking the whole bundle of combatants from side to side.

I stepped over the man and aimed the shotgun down at his fear-maddened face. "Let go of my dog!" I ordered, taking Galahad's collar with my free hand. Seeing another shotgun on the ground beside him, I put my foot on it, then nudged Klondike away. When he was freed, the man scrambled to his feet and sprinted off into the night.

I knelt and checked out the white poodle. There were streaks of blood on his left side, and he whimpered as I probed them. I got a handkerchief and wiped at the wound, relieved that there wasn't a great deal of bleeding. He had been grazed by the blast, but apparently not seriously injured. Galahad pulled away from my ministrations and curled up beside the fire, where he started licking at the places where the shotgun pellets had scored his skin.

Klondike was still growling, but I could hear something else, another unnatural sound in the darkness. My first thought was that it was the three men, but I immediately discarded that notion—this noise was softer, somehow muffled and urgent at the same time.

Looking at the nearby Jeep, the flickering fire, I was torn between wanting to stay right where I was, racing out of this town, or going out to check the strange sound. Were the three men lurking out there in the darkness, waiting to creep in again? They had lost one shotgun in their first attempt, and gotten a firsthand look at the alertness of my dogs, so I allowed myself to hope that they weren't coming back. But they still had that pistol and the advantage of being able to hide in the darkness while my position was known to them. I shivered at the thought that I was being watched.

Again I heard that soft, whimpering sound, and I knew what I had to do.

Taking my shotgun and flashlight, Klondike pacing at my side, I moved toward the noise. I kept the light off, not want to reveal my position, crossing the soft grass of the park. The sounds were coming from a small, square building I discerned, identifying it as a picnic pavilion, roofed but open to the sides, as I got closer.

"Hello?" I said finally. "Who's there?"

The cries came with renewed urgency as I spoke, frantic moaning in obvious response to my question. But there was no articulation, no sense of words. Still, I was pretty sure it was a woman's voice, and I turned on the flashlight and stepped under the eave of the overhanging roof, playing the beam around the small interior.

I spotted her immediately. She was tied up, with a cloth tightly bound around her mouth, left like a bundle on the floor of the pavilion. Her eyes, wide and terrified, bulged from her face above the dirty cotton of the gag, reflecting brightly in the light of my flashlight, and I quickly swept the beam away from her. I saw a few odds and ends—sleeping bags, a camping stove—and guessed that the outlaws had been using the place as a shelter.

Klondike paced and sniffed without becoming overly alarmed, so I felt reasonably certain that the men weren't in the immediate area. I set down my gun and went about untying the gag. It came free and the woman uttered a sobbing gasp of relief, drawing deep breaths. When I turned my attention to the rope binding her wrists, however, I found the knots too tight for my fingers.

"There's a knife over there, by the stove—you can cut the rope," she said urgently. "Let's get out of here!"

I found the blade and did as she suggested, noticing that she was wearing military fatigues. She was young, barely twenty I guessed, with tangled blond hair and a lot of dirt caked on her face and hands. As she rubbed her chafed wrists, I did the same for her ankles.

"I'm ready to move," she said. "If you'll give me a hand."

She leaned on my shoulder, limping, as I awkwardly made my way back to the Jeep, carrying both the shotgun and flashlight in my free hand. She saw my humble little camp and looked around wildly.

"Where did they go?" she asked.

"I don't know," I admitted. "I scared them off—well, my dogs did, mainly. But if that's their stuff in the pavilion, I suppose they didn't go far."

"Can we get away from here right now?" she said. "Please?"

"Sure—here, hop in."

She scrambled onto the pile of my gear in the passenger seat, and I loaded the dogs in the back, then dumped my sleeping bag unceremoniously on top of them. Feeling more anxious with every second, I hopped behind the wheel, started the Jeep, and sped away, the tires spinning slightly on the soft turf of the park's grass until I reached the road. Paying no attention to direction, I careened down a narrow street and made my way out of town.

"Thanks for coming," the young woman said. "I'm Carrie Page—um, Specialist, Illinois National Guard."

"Markus Devane," I replied. "Who were those guys?"

"Three bastards I met in McHenry. That whole town is like Dodge City in the old west—mobs roaming all over, fighting each other, looting. It's like every thug went there after the Martians moved on. Those three jumped me as I was passing through, and brought me along with them as they moved north. I guess they would have killed me, after . . ." She shook her head bitterly, looked away from me.

"You're safe, now," I said, then recognized how lame that sounded. "I mean, from them. I don't know how safe anyplace is, these days."

"Are you heading north?" she asked.

"No. I'm on my way to Chicago. You're going the other way?"

She looked lost, a little forlorn. "I don't know. I was thinking I would get away from here, away from the city. There's nothing . . ." Her voice trailed off.

"What's your story?" I asked, as gently as I could.

She drew a breath, seemed to focus on the question. After a moment she started to talk. "My family lived in Palatine. I was living at home, taking some classes and working when my Guard unit was called up. We were manning a portable radar station, out near Rockford. Directing fire support as the Martians closed in. They must have sensed our signal, cuz the tripods made a beeline for our unit. Burned it up, killed everyone except me."

"I'm sorry," I said. "I understand that they are homing in on radio signals, going for any source of broadcast." Radar, no doubt, made an irresistible beacon for them.

"Well, I made it back to Palatine on foot, and found the whole place deserted. The Martians had already been through. My folks made it out of there, left a note that they were going to try to get to my aunt's, near Green Bay. So I was going to try to get there, too."

"That's a helluva long way," I said. "Were you planning to walk?"

"I didn't see that I had much choice," she said. "So if you're going the other way, you can let me out anyplace along here, and I'll keep going. Thanks for getting me out of there."

Even as she made the statement, I knew that I couldn't just drop her off. I felt responsible for her. Maybe because she reminded me of Alex, or perhaps it was just that she was a person who could actually use my help. But neither was I willing to abandon my quest. "Look, let's find a place to hole up for the rest of the night. There are a lot of vehicles, and no people, around Lake Geneva. Tomorrow we'll see if we can't find you something you can drive, that will get you up north as far as Green Bay."

She looked at me, a startlingly mature expression of appraisal on her features. Finally, she nodded. Within a few miles I came upon a small roadside motel with lots of individual rooms. Like everyplace else, it was abandoned, but I broke into the office and pulled a couple of room keys off the Peg-Board behind the desk. "You get three, I'll take four," I said. "And trust me—things will look better in the morning."

June 23
Lake Geneva, Wisconsin

The daylight did make things look better, not the least of those things being Specialist Carrie Page. She had washed up—the motel had gravity-powered running water, though there was no electricity of course—and combed her hair. She looked remarkably pretty as she emerged to share the coffee that I had percolated in the parking lot over my camp stove.

"Look, I don't want to hold you up," she said, inhaling the rich aroma before taking a careful sip. "I appreciate all you've done, but—"

"But I'm not done," I said insistently. "Think of it like this: You look a lot like my daughter did, when she was your age. I don't know what's happened to her, or even if she's alive. I can't help her, but if I help you, it will let me feel like I'm doing *something*."

She smiled at my earnestness. "Well, if you put it that way, sure. And thanks, again."

We shared a breakfast of toast and rehydrated eggs, and I saw her looking at me curiously. There was something strangely speculative in her expression.

"What?" I asked, a little defensively.

"It's just . . . well, I told you my story. Why I'm here, where I'm going. But, what's yours? I know your daughter is far away, but don't you have someone to go to, to be with?"

I blinked, nonplussed. Then I started to consider her question, and realized that she—and I—deserved an answer.

"No, I don't," I replied. "It wasn't always like this . . . I was a teacher, full professor with tenure, the works. I was friends with colleagues, with TAs, with my students. I had a wife, and things were pretty good. But something happened to me . . . I don't know what it was. I came to be afraid of everything, couldn't face any of those people. The university had to let me go when I stopped coming in to work. Then, I just went to bed. Didn't want to do anything, see anyone. My wife—she tried to help, to take care of me. But I couldn't give her any encouragement. Finally, she got tired of it."

"Sounds like depression," Carrie said, not unkindly.

"Well, that's what they called it, yeah," I said. I shrugged, remembering that feeling of helplessness. "It didn't do me any good to have a name for it."

"But . . . you don't seem like a depressed person," she said. "I mean . . . I'm glad, *really* glad, you found me."

I chuckled wryly. "Me too. Maybe now you see why I need to feel like I'm doing something, trying to make a difference. I have a lot to make up for."

She didn't say anything more, and I appreciated her for that. After eating, we packed up the Jeep and started right out. I suggested we stick to the high ground around the city, because I was reluctant to enter that deep valley, with its legions of crows and ravens, the grisly remnants of the lethal black gas. She agreed, so we followed country roads to remote farms, explored subdivisions of mansion-sized homes, driving slowly, investigating any places where we saw a likely—that is, older—vehicle.

It took most of the day, investigating more than a hundred houses and farms around the outskirts of Lake Geneva, before I found a working pickup truck behind a farmhouse. The keys, predictably enough, were hanging on a hook just inside the back door. It had plenty of gas, and Carrie scrounged some canned goods, a sleeping bag, and some spare clothes from around the house.

"Look," she said. "I've heard there are still Martians in Chicago. Are you sure you want to go there?"

"I'm sure," I said. I had told her about the Wrigley Guerrilla, and she didn't try to dissuade me again.

"What about them?" She looked at the two dogs who, having made themselves thoroughly familiar with the environs of the farmhouse, had settled near the Jeep and the pickup, and were watching us curiously. "You mentioned that they were your neighbor's dogs, that you took them in cuz they needed someone to look after them. I could take them north, if you want. It might be safer than taking them with you into Chicago."

The thought of sending the dogs away was surprisingly distressing to me, but I had to admit that she had a point. I hadn't thought about it that way, but it seemed pretty selfish to drag the dogs along, almost certainly putting them in harm's way. I knew she was right.

"Would you be willing to do that? See that they get fed, and all?" I asked slowly.

"Sure. I like dogs."

"Okay," I said. The idea made too much sense not to do it—why should I risk both of their lives on my own quixotic quest? "All right. Thanks."

"You be careful, Mark." She stood on tiptoes and kissed me on the cheek. "And send word out from this Wrigley Guerilla, if you make it, okay? As soon as I get ahold of a working radio, I'll start listening for him—and you."

"Sure will. And you be careful, too."

The dogs hopped into the front of the pickup when she opened the door and called them. I felt strangely alone, even forlorn, as I watched her drive down the shaded driveway, turn onto the north road away from town. After she had gone a hundred meters, however, she stopped, and got out.

Both dogs bounded out the door of the pickup and came streaking toward me, ears and tongues trailing in the wind. Galahad swiftly outdistanced his lumbering companion, but within seconds they were both back to the Jeep, surging around my legs, looking at me with expressions of unmistakable reproach.

"They didn't want to go north!" Carrie shouted, waving. "They would have clawed through the windows if I hadn't let them out! They're your dogs, now, for better or worse."

"Thanks!" I shouted back, too choked up to say any more. Side by side with the panting dogs, I watched her get back in the truck and drive away. I waved again as she rolled out of sight. Then I opened the tailgate of the Jeep, and Galahad and Klondike scrambled in.

"Okay, fellows," I said, grinning like a fool, blinking back tears. "Partners for life, is that it? Well, let's get going. The big city awaits."

EIGHT

June 23
SSN21 Seawolf
Atlantic Ocean (20 Miles East of Virginia Beach)

The initial conference with the president, the sub's commander—Captain Ricketts—and with General McCanders and a half dozen other high-ranking officers was primarily a debriefing of Duke and Alex by the assembled brass. The pilot had been questioned closely about the nuclear mission, and after they found out that she had been an eyewitness the men had also sought Alex's impressions. Then she related her experiences around the Richmond Crater and described the desolation in abandoned Washington, DC. In response to her question, she learned that, as yet, there was no report of a Martian machine being destroyed, or a Martian injured, by any of humankind's conventional armaments.

After they adjourned, the routine aboard *Seawolf* evolved into what Alex guessed was more or less normal submarine operations. Every few hours the craft would surface to receive radio reports from the mainland. One of the communications officers told Alex that all of the information was being passed from Norfolk Naval Base, through a ruse to divert the Martians' attention from that key installation. The broadcasts originating at Norfolk were first sent by a secure telephone line to a remote radio antenna somewhere in Virginia, or across the bay in Maryland or Delaware. Thus, the actual transmission originated at someplace far from the base, and no location was used more than once. Martian tripods still roamed the area around Chesapeake Bay, and invariably raced toward the site of the broadcast, but they had not yet been able to break the chain of communication. The officer had concluded, a little glumly, that it was too bad they didn't have anything more encouraging to communicate.

Alexandria was getting used to the close quarters aboard the submarine, but she was keenly aware that she was the only female in the midst of a hundred or so men. Also, following the brief loan of the captain's cabin when they first came aboard, she had come to realize that there was absolutely no place that offered any hint of privacy aboard the entire boat. (She had made the mistake of calling it a "ship" at first, but six or eight sailors had hastily corrected her.)

She spent most of her time in one of the small office cubicles, reading about nuclear weapons and the effects of nuclear war, consulting sources in the ship's vast online library. The more she read, the more frightened she became. Finally, she snapped off the monitor in distress, realizing that she was breathing hard, sweating clammy perspiration, just from the terrifying results of her research.

Duke found her still sitting in front of the blank screen. "Hey, they're getting ready for another powwow," he said. "They want us in on it. Are you okay?"

"Yes," she said. "As okay as anyone can be these days."

She was not surprised to be called in for another conference, but it was still a bit of a shock to come through the hatch into the wardroom and see the president of the United States in a T-shirt and blue jeans squeezed in elbow to elbow with a half dozen Navy officers at a little wardroom table. The president wore an old officer's cap pulled down low on his brow, and smiled as Alex and Duke came into the very small conference room.

"SRO, I'm afraid," he said.

"No problem, sir," the pair replied in unison, standing against the wall, squeezing as tightly as they could into a corner as several more officers came in. When the room contained more people than Alex would ever have imagined possible—about fourteen, all told—the door was shut.

The president began without formalities. "We are losing this war, people. Our forces have suffered devastating losses in the air and on the ground. Even our ships, when they have tried to take on the tripods with direct fire, have been damaged or sunk by those damned lasers. The enemy is moving out across the country from its initial conquests—from Saint Louis, both north and south along the Mississippi Valley. Just this morning we lost western Pennsylvania, with the Army conducting a fighting retreat into West Virginia and Kentucky. At best, our troops have been able to delay the tripods a little bit, or lure them away from populations with feints and withdrawals. All of these tactics have resulted in heavy losses and offer only temporary respite, at best.

"Florida has been invaded, from the north. In one day the tripods have swept as far south as Orlando. I have ordered the evacuation of Kennedy Space Center, but I don't have to tell you that there isn't a lot of real estate to the south of the peninsula. They have scoured the entire West Coast, and now appear to be moving inland, focusing on the major population centers. Texas has been overrun.

"Despite the widespread effects of this invasion, we still know terribly little about the enemy we face. Admiral Schaeffer has been assembling all the analysis about the nature of our enemy that the Pentagon has been able to gather." The president indicated a thin, bookish man in a rumpled dress uniform. "Admiral, can you fill us in?"

"Yes, sir." Admiral Schaeffer cleared his throat. "The tripods seemed to be armored with some sort of composite material that is made out of carbon—more like diamonds than anything else known to us on Earth, and has proven impenetrable to everything from heavy guns to armor-piercing rounds fired by our most powerful antitank weaponry.

"In short, we are facing one hell of a problem here. The only way, so far, that we have been able to knock out any of these Martian tripods is with nuclear weapons. Given that our current stockpile, post-Pulse, of these weapons is quite a bit smaller than the number of Martian tripods currently marching around on American soil, this is a tactic insufficient to win the war."

The president nodded grimly and resumed speaking. "It is also less than a slam-dunk decision to authorize these attacks when a bomb is available, and a target ID'ed." He drew a breath and rubbed a hand across his forehead. "We do have, on this submarine alone, a dozen fully operable nuclear weapons. These can be launched via cruise missiles at targets hundreds of miles away. Because *Seawolf* was submerged at the time of the Pulse, the guidance systems and computerization in those weapons was not affected.

"But nuclear-armed cruise missiles are a hell of a scattershot way to try and take out small, moving targets. Not to mention—if we nuke half the landscape to get these things, what kind of country are we going to have to live in if we manage to win the war?"

"Not a very livable one, Mr. President," Alex offered. Though she sensed the question might have been rhetorical, she felt that it needed a clearer answer. The memory of that looming, poisonous cloud over Maryland was a vision that would stay with her for the rest of her life. Other than Duke, she was the only person in the room who had witnessed that attack firsthand, and she knew that she needed to talk about it, to impress upon the president the scope of devastation that would inevitably follow the further use of nuclear arms.

She took a breath, and forged ahead.

"Radioactivity will render the blast zones uninhabitable, probably for decades. This is not just at ground zero, but probably for miles in every direction of the actual explosion. And fallout, carried by wind and rain, might come close to sterilizing the rest of the country. Even if we don't take nuclear winter into account—and it's not a sure thing, but there's reason to put credence in it as a theory—we will quite possibly be responsible for the near extinction of all mammalian life on the continent. The blast in Maryland a few days ago, for example, might drop enough fallout on Washington, DC, and Baltimore to render them uninhabitable for the rest of our lives."

"Begging your pardon Doctor, Mr. President," said one of the sub's science officers. "But the initial reports from Norfolk are not quite that bad. Sure, there's more than a normal amount of radiation falling from the skies, but it's not enough to poison the landscape. There's reason to hope that the amounts will not prove overly deadly."

Is there such a thing as *underly* deadly? Alex didn't ask the question that rose into her mind. Instead, she countered: "Norfolk is five times as far from the blast as DC. And it's too early to know for sure what kind of totals will be eventually be strewn around, even across Virginia and New Jersey."

"Thank you, Dr. DeVane, and Lieutenant Douglas, for that clarity," the president replied. "I have in fact reached a conclusion on the matter. We won't be launching any more nuclear attacks unless there is a clear chance to save human lives by such a strike, or an opportunity to get a lot of these damned tripods without doing a huge amount of collateral damage. That means we'll be holding them in reserve until, and if, the Martians get into the more desolate reaches of the western states."

"But, sir—if I may?" The speaker was Captain Ricketts, *Seawolf*'s commanding officer.

"Yes, of course, Captain. Go ahead."

"It's just that we've got so many of the bastards dead to rights right now. We have a score of good, solid targets confirmed in New Jersey and lower New York alone. Just think—if we take them all out at once, that might be the setback that really turns the tide!"

Alex was appalled. Such an attack would poison a huge section of the East Coast just with the initial bursts. As to the fallout, nobody could predict the long-term effects with any specificity. But she bit her lip, watching tensely as the president nodded, thoughtfully.

"I understand, Rick. But we're not going to take that chance, right now. It's my decision that the cost outweighs the benefits."

The captain nodded, compressing his lips into a white line. But he made no further argument. Alex found herself amazed, and a considerably relieved, that even then, under such unprecedented stress, the premise of civilian control over the country's military remained intact. She allowed herself to draw a deep breath of relief.

"We have to do *something!*" The outburst came from another Navy man, one of the sub's crew—Alex thought she remembered that he was the fire control officer. "Sir," he added lamely. "I'm sorry, but we can't just *take* this shit!"

"No, Jimmy, we can't take this shit. I agree with you there. There is one other tactic worth discussing—a tactic that is, in fact, the reason for this meeting. Commander Rogers has performed some interesting research with the sample of alien tissue Dr. DeVane brought on board. Commander, why don't you tell us what you have in mind?"

Alex's heart quickened with hope. The cheerful medical officer flashed her a wink and began to talk. "Thanks to the sample provided by Dr. DeVane, I have been able to do a little studying. As you suspected, it was a piece of organic material. I concur with your hypothesis—that it was some kind of outer skin, possibly to protect the creature from the environment of space, or maybe simply a shell that it was able to shed as it grew. If I had to choose, I would bet that it was part of an outer epidermis cloaking one of the Martians for interplanetary travel. It suggests, strongly, that the alien bodies require water to sustain life, and that their vital systems are based upon a carbon molecule, much the same as with any of our Terran organisms.

"However, one thing was distinctly different, and it just might be that these alien slime have a weakness," he said, the seriousness of his tone belying the hope implicit in his words. "Microscopic examination immediately revealed something very interesting.

To judge from their flesh, these creatures are absolutely rife with bacteria—virtually every kind of germ that grows in rot or decay was having a happy picnic in those pieces of membrane."

"So they aren't going to catch colds and die?" the president said. The attempt at levity brought forced laughs from all in attendance, of course, though the medical officer seemed to find the remark genuinely amusing.

"No, sir. It's like they already have colds, and the flu, and infections galore. So it might be that what would do them serious harm—I most sincerely hope—is a good dose of medicine."

Looking very pleased with himself, the doctor pulled a basic pill bottle out of his shirt pocket and set it on the table. "Gentlemen—and lady," he said, with a twinkle in his eye. "I suggest a prescription of penicillin. About fifty pounds of it would be ideal for the initial test."

The president was watching intently—clearly he had already been briefed about the theory—and though it might be said that he was smiling, his expression was fierce, more like the leer of a hungry, frustrated wolf that has just caught the scent of blood.

June 24
Norfolk Naval Base, Virginia

The Warthog was fueled up, the two ungainly canisters of the antibiotic bombs tucked neatly underneath, one at the base of each wing. Duke and Alex stood a just inside the hangar, having been back on land for all of twenty minutes.

"You *had* to volunteer for this mission, didn't you?" she said helplessly. She didn't know whether to feel proud of him or sock him in the eye.

He shrugged. "Of course."

"I know," she whispered, taking his hand and squeezing it.

In the hours since the meeting, every medical supply cabinet on the base, as well as the *Seawolf*'s limited stores, had been plundered of penicillin, Amoxicyllin, and every other common antibiotic stocked there. Sailors had opened hundreds of tiny capsules, pouring the white powder on a mixture of shredded cheesecloth and water. A bomb specialist had formulated small, specialized explosives in the middle of each canister so that, when they struck the ground, they would spread a fine cloud of dust through a radius of twenty or thirty meters.

If Commander Rogers was right, any Martian in that area of effect might be expected to suffer serious and deleterious effects. And if he was wrong . . .

Alex tried to avoid thinking about that, but the memory of the mushroom cloud remained in the forefront of her mind.

"You'll be careful, I hope," she said, giving Duke a hug. "I didn't find you again, just to let you go off on another of your wild adventures!"

He kissed her, hard, while the sailors of the ground crew looked awkwardly away—or gawked, appreciatively. "Don't worry, Doc," he said. "I have the nicest harborview table reserved at the Mussel Inn for dinner tonight. The maître d' assures me that we'll have the place to ourselves. Wear something sexy."

She had a powerful lump in her throat as she watched the A10, twin engines blazing, roar down the landing strip and take to the air. She knew that several tripods had been reported on the outskirts of Richmond, and these were his targets. She also knew how deadly those lasers had been to other bombers, and—though he hadn't spelled it out—she guessed that his unique weaponry would require a low, precise bomb run.

"Dr. DeVane?" It was a young petty officer, the same man who had met the A10 when she and Duke had first arrived here. "The president suggested you might want to follow the radio traffic. I can take you to the signals shack."

"Thanks, yes. I'd appreciate that."

The signals "shack" proved to be an underground bunker the size of a high school gymnasium, lit by hundreds of fluorescent lights, and manned by dozens of male and female sailors. They all sat at consoles, wearing headphones, working a variety of dials and knobs.

She was welcomed by a young lieutenant (j.g) named Robinson, who provided her with a seat, and a pair of headphones.

"The pilot will be under radio silence until he completes his run—that's what we've been told, anyway," he explained. "But you might be able to catch some other broadcasts while we're waiting. When it's time for the attack, we'll go dedicated to his circuit. Until then, we will monitor his frequency continually and switch to that channel if there is any change of plan."

She donned the headphones, and at first all she could hear was the pounding of her heart. She played with the dial for a bit, but heard only static. When Lieutenant Robinson tapped her on the shoulder, she lifted one earphone to hear him.

"This is an interesting fellow," he said, reaching over to turn a dial on her console. "Calls himself the Wrigley Guerrilla. Been broadcasting solo out of Chicago for the last week or so—he moves around a lot, so the Martians can't catch up to him."

"Thanks," she said, turning her attention to the low, calm voice in her speakers.

"—what I said about the Twin Cities a couple of days ago, overtaken by events. I hear that the tripods have been up and down the Father of Waters on both banks, taken out everything from New Orleans to Saint Paul. All that great history, flowin' away with the tide. Poor ol' Memphis. . . ."

Alex felt the speaker's melancholy in more than his words—it was as if the loss was something he took personally, but he was determined to hold the emotion close to his vest. For some reason, she thought of her father.

"Well, that's enough sad comment for one day—and besides, I'd best be packin' up my troubles in my ol' kit bag, so to speak, and movin' on from here. Tomorrow, let's have a gatherin' at the place where the Navy might dock a ship, if those sailors wanted to find a nice bar. I'll come on the air at the same time you used to catch your first fix of Matt and Katie."

Alex was puzzled by the cryptic references, though she immediately thought of Chicago's Navy Pier, and the major personalities of the *Today* show. She was about to ask the lieutenant if this was usual when the broadcaster added another note.

"Peoples? This is gettin' to be a right lonely gig. Is there anyone listenin'? Anyone at all? Come by and say hello if you can. Anyway, I'll be back atcha in the AM.

"For June 24, this is the Wrigley Guerrilla, signing off."

"He always does that," Robinson explained, in response to her question. "Gives some sort of cryptic clues as to where and when he'll make his next broadcast. I guess he wonders if the Martians might have translated our speech. They close in on his mobile unit every day, but so far he's stayed one jump ahead of them."

"Are there others like him? Broadcasting from various places in the country, or the world?" Alex found some hope in that thought.

"A few," Robinson said. "Some people come on the air and broadcast until the Martians catch up to them. It never takes too long—they make a beeline right for the source of any broadcast. Others come on sporadically, for a short period of time. There's a sense of community, kind of like the old ham radio days, but these folks are taking big risks. The Wrigley Guerrilla has stayed alive by moving around constantly and keeping his broadcasts short."

They scanned the dial for a few more minutes, heard only snippets of signals, too distant or distorted to make out. By then it was nearing the time of Duke's bomb run, so they turned their attention to the channel that had been dedicated to his mission. For interminable minutes there was nothing there, until, suddenly, the pilot's voice broke through the airwaves. In contrast to his dispassionate report after dropping the fusion bomb, his voice was excited, almost frantic.

"Direct hit! I bounced one right off the motherfucker's dome—came up on him so fast he never knew I was there until it was too late. The bomb exploded and there was a big cloud of powder in the air, covered both Martians."

"Where are you?" Alex asked aloud, though he couldn't hear her.

"I'm due south of Hopewell," he came back, more calmly. "Twelve or thirteen miles, bearing one-four-zero. I've been hit, lost both engines. Still have rudder and a reasonable amount of speed, so no problem. I'm going to ditch in the James. Should be able to make it in—the water is nice and smooth."

"Wait! What . . . ?" She heard the words, but couldn't put a real picture to their meaning. Only when she saw Lieutenant Robinson's face, deathly pale, did she understand what Duke was telling them. His voice came back, the tone clipped and utterly professional, with no trace of fear.

"Alex, if you're there, I love you."

And then he was gone. Only the crackling hiss of static remained.

NINE

The bridge over the Fox River was completely blocked, probably had been that way since the time of the Pulse. I reconstructed what had happened as I parked the Jeep at the western terminus of the two-lane span, studying the obstacle. Two big SUVs had collided in the middle of the bridge, the vehicles pivoting in the crash so that they were wedged between the concrete railings on either side of the roadway. One lay on its side, blocking one and a half lanes, while the other was canted between the first wreck and the bridge railing.

I pounded my fist on the steering wheel in frustration. The nearest adjacent bridge, to the north, meant a lot of backtracking, over the same roads I had painstakingly followed for most of the morning. And if I continued south, I would roll right into McHenry, which—after Carrie Page's description of it—I was in no way curious to investigate.

Needing some time to regroup, I got out of the Jeep and opened the tailgate so that the dogs, too, could stretch their legs. They immediately went to work sniffing the pillars of the bridge railing, marking them hastily, trotting down off the road to check out some trees in a small wood lot at the riverbank. Arms akimbo, I glared at the huge wrecked vehicles. There was no way to squeeze so much as a bicycle between them, let alone a car.

Next I studied the Jeep, trying to decide how much space I would need. My eyes were drawn to the contraption on the front bumper, the winch that Browne had mentioned. I knew that, in theory, it was a powerful motor with a very high mechanical advantage, designed to move heavy objects or to pull the Jeep itself up steep or slippery inclines. Looking at the size of the wrecked SUVs—an Expedition and a Suburban—I had a hard time believing that my little vehicle could even budge one of them, much less move it out of the way.

Angrily, I forced thoughts of defeat aside, trying to reason with myself. After all, I wouldn't need a lot of room to squeeze through. And the Expedition, which was nearest to my end of the bridge, was at least upright, though positioned sideways to the way I would have to move it. But what else did I have to do that morning?

"Klondike! Galahad!" I called loudly, and the dogs came racing back from the small woods. "Sit. Stay." I ordered, posting them at the end of the bridge. Somewhat to my surprise, they obeyed immediately, and continued to stay as I went back to the Jeep and tried to decide what to do next.

"Let's see. . . ." I leaned over the half door and examined the controls, quickly figuring out that the winch was operated by a switch on the dashboard. The electric motor hummed when I flipped it. After a little trial and error, I adjusted the motor direction so that it slowly paid out the impressively stout cable, which had a solid hook on the end. With about ten meters of cable freed, I was able to strap the hook around the rear wheel spring of the SUV—my first thought was the bumper, but I figured that the winch would just pull the strip of metal off without moving the Expedition.

Getting back in the Jeep, I flipped the switch to start the winch rolling and slowly took up the slack of the cable. I clenched my teeth, let the motor rumble away, heard the creaking of metal, the straining, almost musical tautness of the cable. The powerful gears engaged, and I felt a momentary excitement as tires started to slide across the pavement. Then I perceived that the SUV wasn't moving—instead, the winch was pulling the little Jeep closer to the wreck. Of course, it was a simple matter of physics: Other things being equal, the heavier vehicle would move the lighter one.

"Damn!" I shut off the motor in an almost trembling rage. I wanted to quit, to go go home, go to bed. But it was too late for that.

Instead, I tried to think, to approach the problem on a scientific basis. The winch seemed plenty powerful, the cable strong, but I had to prevent the Jeep from moving. I remembered the tow strap in the back. Getting it out, I examined my options. The concrete sidewall of the bridge was a railing supported by several sturdy-looking pillars. If I fastened the tow strap to a pillar, and used it to anchor the Jeep, perhaps the little car would stay put, while the big one slid out of the way. It was worth a try.

The hooks on the strap were fairly straightforward, and the ball of a trailer hitch on the back of the Jeep offered a promising and accessible anchor spot. Carefully, I inspected the nearest pillar of the bridge rail, checking to make sure that it wasn't cracked. It seemed solid, so I wrapped the tow strap around it, circling it three times for extra security, then hooked the other end of the strap to the hitch. It was fairly taut, would be tight if the Jeep moved a few inches forward.

Putting the plan into action, I tried the winch motor again, with a surprisingly high state of excitement. I felt the Jeep lurch a bit, moving until the tow strap was tightly connected to the bridge. The motor thrummed and whined, and I could feel the vehicle vibrating underneath me. Belatedly I realized that if either the strap or the cable snapped, I would be lashed pretty hard by the recoil. I ducked, but was unwilling to give up my perch on the driver's seat.

Then, slowly, I saw the wrecked SUV start to move! Tires screeched sideways across the pavement as the Expedition slid closer to the Jeep, the rear of the vehicle swinging out from the railing, opening a small passage. After a short time it was being pulled straight toward me, and I quickly realized that no matter how long I ran the winch I wouldn't be able to move it any farther from the railing from my present position. The gap wasn't yet wide enough, but I knew what to do. Unhooking the cable and strap, I jockeyed the Jeep back and forth until I was parked in the other lane. Next I strapped my car to the left side of the bridge. Reattaching the cable, it was but a few minutes' work to pull the SUV well away from the wall, leaving a passage wide enough for me to drive without even scraping the sides.

The dogs had watched the whole procedure with expressions ranging from concern to bemusement. After I coiled up the cable and strap, they happily leaped into the back of the Jeep. Once again I started off—it was barely past noon, and Chicago lay just over the horizon.

June 24
Norfolk Naval Base, Virginia

The engines of the three helicopters, all Coast Guard Black Hawks, roared lustily as the four military trucks from the communications shack pulled up to the airstrip. By the time Alex and the detachment of two dozen Marines in full Kevlar and field gear debarked from the vehicles, the blades of the choppers had begun to rotate, slicing faster and faster circles through the air.

Eight Marines climbed into each helicopter, with Alex joining one group. The choppers shook and rattled as they lifted off, skimming low over the water as they made their way toward the mouth of the James River. Alex tried to avoid thinking of Duke in that water, wouldn't allow herself to imagine him bailing out or ditching. Instead, she pictured him waiting in safety somewhere along the bank, with a flare pistol or piece of bright parachute silk, ready to signal his survival, his health, his desire for a quick rescue and a flight back to the base.

The helicopters flew low, widely dispersed to cover the maximum area visually. But there was no sign of the A10 in all that dark river. They chattered their way up the James, closer and closer to Hopewell, Virginia, where Duke had bombed the tripod. In an earlier era, they could have homed in on the downed plane by its built-in radio-location device. That was yet another piece of equipment that had been disabled by the Pulse. Since it would have attracted Martians as well as humans, it had not yet been repaired.

So they would have to resort to their eyeballs. Unfortunately, the murky waters proved impossible to see through, and the plane had apparently gone down without leaving any telltale piece sticking up above the surface.

"We're getting near the target area," the crew chief announced, leaning close to shout into Alex's ear. "We'll go in for BDA and let the other two ships continue the search."

She nodded, understanding that—however much she wanted to throw every other thought to the side and look for Duke—her role was to assess the damage done by the antibiotic bomb. Soon enough they were away from the river, flying over subdivisions and rural woodlands. A swath of blackened ground spread before them, and the pilot slowed the Black Hawk, dropping lower. Alex still hadn't caught sight of any tripod when the pilot set the ship down just behind a thick line of pine trees.

The Marines debarked smoothly, quickly spreading out and dropped prone as Alex and a young lieutenant came after. He led her in a spring toward the tree line, a hundred meters away from the still-spinning blades of the chopper, and the helicopter was rattling into the air and withdrawing by the time the scientist and the officer reached the cover of the pines.

"The pilot spotted what looked like a tripod, on the other side of this woods," the officer said. "We'll get as close as we can on foot."

She followed him at a sprint, ducking under the overhanging limbs, conscious of the armed Marines slipping silently through the greenery to either side of them. Finally, they reached the other side of the wooded line, and crawled the last few feet to look out between the mossy, dense trunks.

She saw the grayish dome of the tripod, resting on the ground. There was no sign of the three light-beam legs, nor were the two tentacles moving, or displaying any rigidity. It looked as close to "dead" as she could imagine any such deadly and animated machine looking.

"Can we move in for a closer look?" she asked the lieutenant.

"Just a sec," he said, gesturing down the valley. "Look."

Alex did, watching as another tripod came into view, striding purposefully toward the disabled machine. It paused nearby, raising the twin tentacles into the air, waving them in menacing fashion back and forth. She caught the carrion stink of the Martian's flesh and, for the first time, heard a low, dull droning noise as the dome came nearer. Resisting the urge to gag, she instead kept her head up and followed the hateful invader with her eyes.

The two humans remained immobile, bellies pressed against the soggy ground. Alex was grateful for the screen of vegetation around them and hoped fervently that the aliens didn't have some IR-imaging process that might reveal them by their body heat. Even so, she was unwilling to leave her vantage point.

As she watched, a second tripod came from the north, moving with unmistakable urgency toward the stricken machine. Only when that one was on the scene, taking over the role of sentry, did the first relax its vigilance. It loped toward the disabled machine, striding on those inexplicable legs, until it loomed directly over its comrade.

Slowly the dome started to lower, its legs growing shorter. When it was barely a couple of feet off the ground, the two tentacle-like appendages reached toward the top of the immobile machine. Alex noted that they had discarded, presumably stowed, their weapons packages—the steely tendrils were like nimble, dexterous limbs, manipulating something on the neighboring machine.

Abruptly, a hatch opened, lifted out of the way by the manipulations of the active machine. Those two tentacles reached into the aperture thus revealed, and slowly, gingerly lifted out the grotesque body within.

Alexandria felt the same wave of revulsion she had felt at the Richmond crater. She saw the bloblike shape, with its trailing tentacles—there must be at least a dozen of the long, supple limbs, she guessed—dangling. But the body pulsed and writhed, and the tentacles wiggled with unmistakable signs of life.

Yet it was clearly weak, and enfeebled. She watched as the second machine lifted the writhing body up, tucked it inside, and started away. The third one remained on station, tentacles waving.

It was time to get away from there and report what they had seen.

TEN

June 25
The Loop
Chicago, Illinois

Just a few months earlier Michigan Avenue in downtown Chicago had been the premier shopping locale in the Midwest, the closest thing that the flyover states could offer to compare to the glitzier sections of Manhattan or LA. There was a Bloomingdale's department store there, and a host of five-star restaurants and hotels, trendy nightclubs, and chic bistros. An array of fabulous museums and art galleries lined the street and its environs, while great stretches of parkland made the Lake Michigan shoreline a delightful draw—at least, on a pleasant summer day such as this. Some of the tallest buildings in the world loomed overhead, and a modern mass-transit system had allowed tens of thousands of people to come and go with relative ease.

I had been here on a few occasions, taking trips with my wife and daughter. Karen and Alex had particularly liked the upscale elegance, ambience, and live music at a French restaurant called Fleur de Lis; I had been partial to the crusty bread and garlic sauce. During the Christmas season, the Loop was really something else, alive with colors, music, vitality. No matter what the time of year, this was a mercantile district that had throbbed with energy, with shoppers and commuters and bums and cops all going every which way. There would be hundreds, even thousands of people visible wherever you looked.

When I was a young man I had found Chicago, and Michigan Avenue in particular, exciting and exotic. But by the time I was entering middle age it was the kind of place that used to make me want to curl up into a ball, to hurry back to my hotel room, close and lock the door, turn out the lights, pull down the shades. Even when I was still teaching, when I was forcing myself to control my breathing, to enter a lecture hall and confront a roomful of students, I had avoided coming to places like downtown Chicago. The traffic alone was enough to bring on a panic attack.

Not that the city had changed that much over those years, but I had. Even before I had become frightened of my own students, of my lecture hall in Madison, it had been easy to find excuses to avoid this great city. There were too many people there—cars would line up for a half an hour just to pass through the toll booths on the highways leading into Chicago. As long as twenty years ago I had begun to use that relentless traffic as an excuse to avoid so much as crossing the state line.

Now I was back, and everyone else was gone.

Literally, as I stood in the very middle of that once-vital street, I couldn't see another living person. There were plenty of cars parked haphazardly along the wide lanes, the usual detritus left by the Pulse. The tracks of the El, the city's famous elevated trains, were visible down one of the side streets. The summer sun was high, brilliant light spilling down into the canyonlike passage of the avenue, illuminating the classic facade of the Art Institute as I walked past, with the two dogs snuffling at my heels. The shotgun was slung easily from my right arm—I had grown so used to carrying it that it was like a part of me, an extra limb.

I had left the Jeep a few streets back, backed into a narrow alley near an intersection where I could drive it quickly out, then speed away in any one of four directions if I needed to. For some reason that I didn't clearly understand, I did not want to drive down this street; it was important to traverse it on foot. Perhaps I was worried that the Martians would find me more easily if I was in a vehicle than if I walked. More likely, however, it was that the vast sense of quiet and stillness around me seemed almost sacrosanct, that to destroy that serenity with a single rumbling vehicle would almost be a desecration.

So I strolled along, looking around, relying on the dogs to alert me of any threats I didn't immediately see with my own eyes. Tall skyscrapers, with massive facades of smoky windows, loomed over me. Was there anyone behind that glass? I couldn't know, and if they were there, those persons weren't doing anything to attract my attention. I was forced to conclude that every one of those great office towers had been abandoned, presumably days earlier.

Beyond the Art Institute, the vast green space of Grant Park opened to my left, breaking the illusion of a canyonlike enclosure. Now, instead, it was as though I walked along at the base of a massive cliff, the precipice of architecture to my right, with a sweep of wooded land on the left extending to eastward to the lakeshore. The trees were impressively verdant and lush, the tall branches waving serenely in the summer breeze. Many gardens in the huge, spectacular park were bright with blossoms, and if the landscaping was a little unkempt, the grass a little long, those facts didn't detract from the pastoral splendor.

Klondike raised his head and growled, his floppy black ears perked upward in a parody of canine alertness. He was staring into the park, sniffing the air. Galahad paused and then he, too, growled, one foreleg raised in an instinctive pointer's pose. I raised the gun, a finger on the trigger—safety off—as I strained to look into the shadows between the trees, to see what had attracted the dogs' attention.

I saw them immediately: gray shadows slipping between the trunks, racing down the park's winding lanes, milling around an ornate pavilion. A pack of them moved past, lupine and stealthy, pausing to look at us with pointed ears upraised. The coyotes had come that far, I realized, and were prowling even into the heart of the region's greatest city. I raised the shotgun slightly, not to start shooting but just to enhance my own sense of security. The animals were cautious and made no move to close in on the dogs and me, but neither did I sense that they were afraid.

Their presence only made me feel more alone. I paced along the middle of the wide street, where a lane had been plowed between the stalled cars, probably right after the Pulse. From there, I could see that the city was remarkably unscathed, at least on the surface. Most buildings were undamaged, and there was even an orderliness to all the stalled cars, as if they had been nudged toward the curbs in an only slightly jumbled pattern of angled parking. Delbrook Lake had suffered far more overt damage from Martian weaponry than had Chicago, but the metropolis seemed more emblematic of the shocking blow that had been delivered to our civilization. How much killing had the black gas done there? How many people had escaped? Where had they gone?

To be sure, the tops of the two tallest structures, the Hancock Building and the Sears Tower, had been burned away with almost surgical precision, no doubt by the lasers; and the tops of those roofless pinnacles canted at steeply sloping angles, as if a crazed architect had gone to work with a giant chain saw. From the proper angle I could see the edges of offices, restaurants, and other once-interior spaces, high above me and exposed to the atmosphere. No doubt there would be wreckage around the bases of those towers, but I had not gone close enough to be obstructed by it.

Down one side street I saw an elevated train that had somehow been knocked off of its track, lying crumpled and forlorn on the street below, having crushed trucks, cars, and pedestrians in its fall. But I walked on, and a corner quickly blocked it from my view so that, once again, the city looked peaceful, more like it was slumbering than that it had been scoured of population by ruthless invaders.

In all the vast loneliness, I knew that there was at least one other person here, somewhere. I hoped that the Guerrilla would be broadcasting in another few hours, and I planned to be back at my radio soon to hear what he had to say. In the course of finding a vehicle for Carrie, I had missed any broadcast that he might have made the previous day, but felt reasonably certain that I would be able to hear him soon if I was only patient about it.

I made my way back to the Jeep, eventually, and drove it down side streets, looking for a place to settle in for a listening session. Finally, I stopped the vehicle, and wandered back into that wide, green park. I waited in a clearing, with my radio on, and I listened for many hours.

But nobody spoke.

June 25
Norfolk Naval Base, Virginia

As soon as they landed and Alex got a look at the face of the communications officer, she knew that Duke hadn't been found. Her heart lurched, but she forced herself to set her concern aside as she climbed into the passenger seat of the waiting truck.

"They're still looking for him," the lieutenant said, trying to be reassuring. "Even that chopper that brought you in, it's heading back out as soon as it can take on more fuel. They'll do everything humanly possible—"

"I know," she snapped, more curtly than she had intended.

"You know, he musta got out of the plane," continued the officer, ignoring her tone. "The water was still, like he said. Probably went in real easy, and floated to shore. He'll probably come walking in any day—that is, if the Marines don't find him first."

Alex sensed that he was groping around, looking for more hollow assurances to offer, and she was relieved when they pulled up in front of the radio bunker. "Go on in," he said, as she was already out the door.

A petty officer was waiting for her and handed her a microphone as soon as she reached the radio.

"*Seawolf* is already surfaced, waiting for our transmission," he said. "The president is at the other end."

"Mr. President?"

She recognized the voice in his confirmation, and forced herself to speak calmly. "We can confirm that antibiotic attack is effective. While not immediately lethal, it induced gradual paralysis and significant disability over the course of three hours. One machine was disabled, two more approached very cautiously."

Alex was broadcasting the message, via a remote antenna, without bothering with any kind of code. If there was any news that she wanted to disseminate over the whole world, this was it. "Repeat: Antibiotics administered against the outside of a tripod appear to have a disabling effect."

"That's the best news we've had since the invasion," replied the president. "Good work."

"Thank you, sir," she replied. Her voice, in spite of her determination, choked.

"And Alex," the commander in chief said, his tone gentle, even fatherly, "they're out there looking—they'll find him. In the meantime, why don't you keep broadcasting. The signal is going out over a remote antenna, remember, so the base at Norfolk is safe. But I want you to get this message out to anyone who can hear."

"Yes, Mr. President. I'll do that. And . . . thank you, sir."

"No, Alexandria," replied the chief executive, still speaking in that familial tone. "Thank *you*."

He was gone, but the petty officer nodded at her, and she started the report again, hoping against hope that people all over the world would be listening.

"This is Dr. Alexandria DeVane. I'm an official with NASA, and I am reporting about a tactic that has been used against the Martians with some success. . . ."

Even as she spoke, disseminating her message of hope, her thoughts and fears were far away, trying without success to push through the murky waters of the James.

June 26
Marshall Fields' Department Store
Michigan Avenue, Chicago

The display window of the huge department store, a convex bay extending out onto the sidewalk, gave me a good view up and down the street. I lay behind a makeshift barricade I had constructed of lingerie-clad manikins, watching the empty avenue. Nearby, my radio was turned low, but I kept my attention on it, waiting for the Guerrilla's next broadcast. It had been two days since I had last heard him, but I refused to acknowledge even the possibility that something had caused him to cease his reports.

Instead, I had made a camp for myself and the dogs inside the elegant store. Klondike and Galahad were snoozing nearby, on soft beds I had made for them out of loosely piled mink coats. I had a stash of food, drink, and batteries that I had scrounged from various stores in the downtown area. Most importantly, I stayed beside the radio or, on those occasions when I walked around, carried the radio with me. I was determined to catch the next broadcast.

And, indeed, my confidence was proved well-founded an hour later. The day had dwindled into twilight, and stars were beginning to pop into view when the Wrigley Guerrilla came back on. I sensed immediately that there was a certain breathless, excited quality underlying his usual laid-back delivery.

"Folks, I have been monitoring some broadcasts from the East Coast. Seems the Martians might have a weakness, after all. There's a report that they've been bombed with a dust of antibiotics—good ol' penicillin, and stuff like that. Some docs and military types apparently opened up a bunch of capsules and loaded all the powder into a bomb, and they got an Air Force pilot to drop it on one of the suckers.

"Well, it sure seemed to slow him down. The eyewitness was none other than a scientist with NASA, a Dr. DeVane . . . she reports that the Martian tripod went dead, sank right down to the ground. A couple more of them came along, and pulled a really sick-lookin' bastard outta there.

"Remember, those hard-shelled tripods that do all the nasty shit, those are *machines*. The Martians are ugly, tentacled buggers, riding *inside* those tripods.

"I'm going to have to cut out, now—there's a few of those tripods roaming around the Windy City these days, and they're getting faster about closing in on my broadcasts. But I'll be coming at you again—let's make it right at the time of that good ol' Gary Cooper movie. I won't forsake you, darling—I'll be broadcasting from a place where you can see the stars, even in the middle of the day.

"Remember, people—keep the faith! We can beat these suckers, if we don't all run away and hide, and wait for someone else to do the job. This is the Wrigley Guerrilla, signing off."

I didn't even notice when he went off the air. My mind was churning with hope, with possibilities, and—for the first time in very many days—joy!

Alex was alive!

ELEVEN

I was up and out of my hiding place, pacing the departments of the store with uncontainable exuberance. Not only was Alex alive, but it seemed clear that she had participated in the most significant breakthrough about the nature and weaknesses of the enemy that threatened to annihilate our entire species. It was almost like I could hear her myself.

As I thought about it, all of the facts started to make sense. Of course, there was that pervasive stench, the stink of rot, that hovered around the Martians. Clearly it was caused by the bacteria that apparently thrived on their flesh. Indeed, not only did germs thrive, but they seemed to be necessary to their very survival. No doubt it was that discovery that had suggested the attack tactic, using antibiotics. It was brilliant! Furthermore, Alex's story gave me a specific idea as to how I could strike a blow against the Martians on my own behalf.

As to the Wrigley Guerrilla, his clues were easy to decipher. I knew that he would be broadcasting from the Chicago Planetarium the next day at noon, so I didn't have much time. Fortunately, that site was only a few blocks from my current location—I wouldn't even have to drive to get over there. But I had some preparations to make before the broadcast.

I remembered a drugstore just a block away from my makeshift nest in the department store, and had no reservations about leading the dogs over there and breaking in by smashing one of the big windows fronting the street. The back of the store, where the drugs were kept, was a little more solidly secured, but in the end I simply blasted the lock on the door with the shotgun, and found myself—ears ringing—in the storage room. Quickly I located an entire series of shelves stocked with penicillin and other antibiotics.

Next I confronted a decision: how to deliver the stuff to the Martians. That, too, did not seem like a terribly vexing problem. In the end, I simply broke open capsule after capsule of antibiotic, and dumped the contents into pint-sized glass jars, then screwed a cap onto each jar. Working all night, I had four of the crude grenades made by midmorning, and decided that would have to do—I had an appointment at the planetarium. Putting the jars in a small backpack I had brought with me from the department store, I carried my radio in one hand. After a moment's doubt, I decided to leave the shotgun behind—the glass jars made far more promising armament, considering the nature of my enemy.

I decided to continue on foot since I would be better able employ the cover of Grant Park and the underpasses around the planetarium than if I was in the Jeep. The dogs didn't enhance my concealment, certainly, but I gave no thought to leaving them behind.

It was only a short walk from the drugstore to the site of the Guerrilla's next broadcast, but I walked fast, feeling a sense of energy that was a refreshing memory of happier times. My original plan had been merely to communicate—to find the man, identify myself as a listener and ally—and then see if there was some way I could offer him assistance. Now, my plan took on a more practical and inherently aggressive nature.

I knew that the Martian tripods were drawn to the sites of his broadcasts, and suspected that the next sending would have the same result. I decided that, instead of seeking out the Guerrilla himself, I would conceal myself in the general vicinity of his transmitter and wait for one or more of the alien machines to come along. Although I was no athlete, I felt reasonably—perhaps foolishly—confident in my ability to throw the pint-sized jar against one of the tripods, smashing the glass to release a cloud of antibiotic.

The planetarium was a huge, classical-looking building on the lakefront, with approaches limited to a couple of obvious paths. There was a pedestrian underpass located right between the two streets, so I decided to take shelter there—or rather, in the small, fenced-in niche just outside the entrance to the underpass. I bade the dogs sit and stay, out of sight below me, and took up my station just before noon. The radio was nearby, turned low, and I tried to divide my senses between watching and listening for any sign of movement.

Time passed slowly, and I fidgeted around, looking this way and that, trying to be ready. Even so I was startled to hear the rattle of a small engine. Moments later I saw him rolling past, a block or so away. He was driving a VW microbus of vintage make, surprisingly free of rust, painted in a nondescript gray. The vehicle halted in a wide parking bay, like a loading dock, near the back of the planetarium. I was tingling with excitement as I watched a radio antenna crank upward, like a manually operated mast. Almost immediately I heard the telltale crackle on the speakers of my radio, knew he was on the air.

I knelt, watching the van as I hunched over my little boom box, turning the volume up just a little. Right on schedule, he was on the air but, for the first time during a Guerrilla broadcast, I really paid little attention to what he was saying. Instead, I kept my eyes open, scanning the surrounding vicinity.

I noted that he was, again, appealing for feedback from listeners, if any, but I was too preoccupied to go over and talk to him directly. He repeated the news about the antibiotic effects on the Martians, and I fervently hoped that there were many others listening, planning for action along the same lines as myself. After a few minutes he announced that his next broadcast would be just past the ivy in the Cubs' den. The time of that broadcast would be the same as the first of the clues I had heard from him—that is, he would go on the air at the starting time of a night game.

He would be at Wrigley Field around seven that night, and I planned to meet him, to talk to him, then. For the moment, my purpose remained focused: I wanted to spot the Martian tripods when they came my way. I would wait for them to be drawn to his transmission, like moths to light, and I would attack.

Looking around, I felt nervous and jittery as the time passed. I didn't even hear him conclude his report, signing off at the end of his broadcast. I was surprised to hear the motor of the van start, and when I turned to look I saw that he had already dropped his mast. With a cloud of gray exhaust and a rattle of that old engine, he drove away. Just like that it was over.

Raising my head, with my belly tingling in fear and excitement, I looked around. Two of the jars were in my pack, and the other two were in my hands. Would I have the chance to use them?

And then I saw the tripod. It came striding through Grant Park, moving smoothly on those three mysterious legs. The Guerrilla started up Lake Shore Drive, and the alien machine accelerated, closing in from the side.

Never did I expect that the tripod could move so damned fast. By the time I charged from my hiding place it was already past, chasing after the speeding van. The dogs were with me, barking furiously. Clutching one of my homemade antibiotic bombs, I cocked back my arm and threw it with all my strength—and then I cried out my frustration as the missile fell to the pavement and shattered, far short of its mark.

But it did not go unnoticed. Without missing a forward stride, the tripod spun the tentacle-mounted laser around. Panic seized me and I reflexively hurled myself off the walkway, down behind the concrete ledge at the edge of the underpass. I tumbled behind the barrier, Galahad at my heels, as the laser snapped off a lethal spear of light.

Klondike, big and clumsy and never too quick to figure out what was happening, didn't move fast enough.

The laser hit the big black dog and he yelped once, loudly and very briefly before the sound was cut off. I smelled burning hair, saw the Newfoundland lying still in the street. He was horribly burned, though his head was untouched—I could see his dark eyes, no longer shining, the pink tongue draped lifelessly on the ground.

"You bastard!" I screamed, pitching another of my bottles mindlessly, as the tripod had already moved out of range. The jar hit the pavement and shattered with a cloud of white dust.

Then the tripod paused, swiveling, turning both of its lethal instruments toward me. The van was out of sight, and the blinking box of that deadly laser was raised above the silver dome, as if searching for a new target.

Cold panic possessed me. Still trembling in fury, grieving for the loss of the loyal canine companion, I could only turn and run, sprinting down through the underpass, cutting around a corner, madly making my way along an empty sidewalk. Galahad sprinted along with me, racing ahead, then stopping and barking frenziedly as he waited for me to catch up. I dashed through the park and onto a street between two blocks of tall buildings, offices rising above, abandoned small businesses—a pawnshop, jewelry store, snack bar restaurant—lying dark and dormant behind the sidewalk windows.

Seeing the Martian machine coming after me, I ran for all I was worth, my lungs straining for air as I sprinted around another corner and raced headlong down the street. Galahad was sprinting ahead of me as if he, too, sensed the seriousness of the threat.

The tripod turned the same corner behind me and it was shockingly close, too near to hope to evade. Instead, I threw my last two bottle-bombs one right after the other. The first went wide, but the second one hit the shell right in the middle, shattering with a cloud of white powder. The laser was coming up fast, so I ducked to the side, taking shelter in the alcove doorway of a bakery. I heard a keening groan, like a turbine winding down, but I was too weak to move. I could only draw frantic, ragged gasps of breath, and wait for the appearance of that lethal ray.

A minute passed, then another, and I heard only silence. Hesitantly, I leaned out of the doorway alcove, risked a glance down the street.

My first impression was encouraging: The machine struck by the antibiotics did indeed seem to be disabled. The light-beam legs had vanished, leaving the silver dome resting on the ground. The tentacles flailed with some energy, but apparently without purpose or control. As I watched, their movements grew ever more feeble, more like reflexive twitching than any purposeful gesture.

Then came the bad news: Another tripod moved out of the side streets behind the disabled machine. It strode past its stricken comrade and started down the street toward my hiding place. I spun, starting to flee, but froze at the sight of still a third tripod coming from the opposite direction. Each stood at one end of a closed city block, effectively trapping me in the middle.

Frantically, I turned around and kicked at the reinforced glass door of the bakery. My third kick crashed the pane inward with a shower of sharp fragments. With Galahad at my heels, I charged inside, looking around frantically for an escape route. I was confronted by a huge display case that had apparently been filled with baked goods at the time the shop was abandoned.

Now the trays in and on top of the case were mounded with objects in the shapes of breads, cakes, and other products—all of them buried under a frenzied growth of mold. Whole trays looked like nothing but green or brown dust, vaguely humped in the shape of loaves or cakes. Wide racks of cookies, long shelves loaded with French bread, had all been taken over by the powdered growth.

The dog and I raced behind the counter. I saw only one door leading into the back of the store and, in a frenzy I grabbed the handle, turned, and groaned in frustration. It was solidly locked. Furthermore, it was a heavy steel barrier, and my initial tug convinced me I would never batter it down. Fear was strangling me as I whirled around frantically, wildly eyeing the deceptively pastoral daylight outside. Galahad sprinted frantically around the room, knocking over a stand that contained rounded green humps that had apparently been hamburger buns; the spoiled food fell to the ground, the dusty mold puffing into the air, swirling colorfully in the angled sunlight coming through the front windows.

That illumination immediately fell into shadow as one of the tripods loomed right in front of the large windows of the bakery. Crumpling behind the counter, I pulled Galahad tightly to my chest, praying to the God I had ignored since my teenage years, fervently hoping that the monster would not follow me there. When I heard the cascade of shattering windows, I knew those prayers were futile. I stared through the glass display case, watching in horror as the tripod burst right through the front of the small neighborhood store.

That foul stink, the carrion stench of the Martian itself, surrounded me, swelling with suffocating force in the confined space as the machine filled the shop. The light-beam legs held the tripod so high that it knocked light fixtures from the ceiling, while flailing tentacles smashed counters and punctured walls to the right and left. The display case shattered, sending glass and moldy pastry crumbling down around me.

The tripod was right overhead, and panic forced me to move. I released Galahad, who bolted for the broken door, and tried to stand, but found myself underneath a large tray weighted down with a hundred moldy shapes. Pushing frantically, I hurled that tray upward with all of my strength, banging it off of the thing's underbelly as I raced directly below the tripod. I tumbled through the shattered window, rolling onto the sidewalk and cutting myself on countless shards of broken glass. Still driven by mindless fear, I tried to get up in the midst of a cloud of greenish dust that clogged my nostrils, nearly choking and blinding me. It was mold, filling the air in and around the bakery, whirling in a blossoming cloud up from the pavement, surrounding the Martian machine inside the bakery, billowing up and around the other tripod standing sentinel in the street.

My legs gave out and I knelt in the broken glass, unable to move, to run. I wanted to weep as Galahad refused to flee but, instead, stood loyally before me, snarling and barking at the looming silver dome. Barely aware of anything except impending and inevitable doom, I vaguely sensed a loud crash beside me. Somehow I made myself roll to the side, out of the way as the tripod within the bakery came sliding out. The machine's movements were unsteady, and I watched in disbelief as the illuminated legs seemed to vanish, bringing the silver dome smashing down to the ground.

The other tripod, in the street, was backing away, making a shrill metallic shriek. It weaved unsteadily, veered wildly to the side, staggering like a drunk, crashing through the plate-glass windows of an exclusive garment store. The tentacle with the laser weapon thrashed, flailing and bouncing, but it did not bring the weapon to bear. In a few seconds that tendril straightened reflexively and flopped limply to the ground.

The hum of machinery, the steady drone that accompanied the tripod's motion, took on an irregular sound. A moment later the noise faded, and by the time I caught my breath, rose to my feet, both machines were silent, inert, apparently helpless. Still bristling, the white dog approached the nearest dome, growling a little, no longer barking. Ready to run, I hesitated instead.

Looking from one to the other, the proof was clear. They were not just inert, but they were utterly disabled, silent . . .

Dead.

James River, Virginia

Duke pulled himself out of the deep water and lay in the weeds along the shallow bank. His ankle was badly sprained, smashed when his A10 had impacted the water. Inflating his life jacket as he released the canopy, he had barely managed to escape the flooding cockpit before the tripods had closed in. A Martian machine had quickly incinerated the tail of his Warthog, the part that had remained visible above the water after he had ditched, and the pilot had drifted motionlessly away, leaving only his face above the surface of the water.

A few hours after the crash, he had heard the chatter of helicopters, knew that they would be searching for him. The silver dome of a Martian tripod glided above the scrub pines on the shore, and the pilot silently willed the rescue choppers to stay away. Alex! God, she'd insist on going along for the search! Holding utterly still, he slowly relaxed as the noise made by the sturdy Black Hawk faded and then vanished entirely, swallowed by the mists along another branch of the river.

For more then a day he bobbed in his life jacket, concealed amid a tangle of flotsam, unwilling to move as a pair of tripods probed the area. One of them stalked right out onto the water, extending a tentacle under the surface to dig around the wreckage of the crashed Warthog. The Martians had continued to investigate through the night and into the next day, roaming through a wider and wider area but inevitably returning to the site of the crash. Every so often one of them fired its weapon, lasers probing here and there with stark red flashes of light.

Finally, they moved on, and the pilot had gamely pulled his way to shore—swimming with his arms, since his throbbing ankle sent waves of pain shooting through him every time he tried to move his leg. For hours he had lain in the shallows, watching, making sure that the tripods were gone before pulling himself onto land.

When he thought he could do so unobserved, he scrambled away from the bank, into the tangle of a dense thicket of evergreens, pulling himself along on his hands and knees. His ankle throbbed, and he had no way to get in touch with anyone. Grimly, he pulled his service revolver from its holster, holding the weapon in his hands.

If the Martians found him there, he would make damn sure that they didn't take him alive.

TWELVE

"This is the Wrigley Guerrilla, coming to you with the most encouraging news I've ever been able to broadcast. There have been some dramatic developments, occurring right here in Chicago, which give us some real hope for the future—*some* kind of future!—for the human race. I hope to heck you can hear me, people, cuz I sure as hell have something to say!"

The Wrigley Guerrilla flashed me a wink. He was a surprisingly old and short man, with wrinkled features, a gray beard, and an almost completely bald head; he'd told me that his real name was Jim Patrick, and he'd been a sportscaster before . . . that's how he put it: just "before." I had found him only a few minutes ago, and he was going on the air with my story that very evening. He told me that his transmitter could get a signal out to places as far away as the coasts, weather permitting. In any event, he promised to keep sending the news out, until everybody in the world knew. There was a growing network of broadcasters like him, men and women getting stories on the air, staying one hop ahead of the Martians. He seemed confident that, once he got the word out, the story of my discovery would spread fast.

Now he spoke again, and I could only hope the message would be heard around the world.

"I'm here with a man, a survivor, named Mark DeVane. He killed a Martian this afternoon with a sort of antibiotic Molotov cocktail—a glass jar filled with the powder he had taken from lots of little pill capsules he took from the back of a drugstore. But that's not the heart of the story. I would ask him to tell you about it, but he's kind of a shy fellow, and says he would rather have me do the talking."

I nodded, encouraging and eager.

"So here it is, people: it seems the Martians can be killed not just by antibiotics, but by the ordinary mold that grows on bread and, presumably, other stale food. Mr. DeVane discovered this by accident, while running for his life and hiding out in a bakery downtown. He says that two tripods were disabled by the stuff, and that both Martians died. It was just moldy bread, with that fuzzy powdery gunk that blew all up in the air when the shit hit the fan—or the Martian hit the display counter, as the case may be—that killed the bastards.

"Anyway, he stuck around—him and his big white dog—to get confirmation, and sure enough, the Martians were toast. Then he came up to Wrigleyville to fill me in. Seems he's a regular listener, and he wanted me to share the story with y'all. This is the news we've been waiting for, people— let's get out there and hit these suckers back, *hard*. I'll broadcast this news again, every hour on the hour. In the meantime, I'm going to hunt me up some moldy bread. . . ."

June 27
General Staff Command Center
Islamabad, Pakistan

The tripods that had ravaged India were advancing to the north and west, approaching the frontier with Pakistan. There were dozens of the deadly machines, and they had been ravaging the populous subcontinent for many days. All of them seemed to be intent upon invading the mountainous country that had thus far been spared the worst effects of the invasion.

General Parvez felt the pressure of a terrible quandary. Every instinct told him that he needed to strike before the invaders crossed into his country. He had the tools: working nonstop since shortly after the Pulse, his dedicated scientists had restored nearly a dozen of the nation's nuclear rockets to working condition. Each was tipped with a potent fusion bomb.

The missiles had ranges approaching a thousand miles, and the tripods were already much closer than that.

It was really no decision, but simply duty. He ordered the launch of the nuclear arsenal at 0500 hours, when all of the targets were well within striking distance. The military telephone net, also fully restored, carried word to his strategic forces. Eleven rockets were launched almost simultaneously, in direct obedience to his order.

The missiles targeted the three main axes of Martian advance: near the coast, at Ahmadabad; across the great desert plain between Jodhpur and Jaipur; and through the stretch of country extending from Delhi/New Delhi almost up to Kashmir and the Pakistani border. He knew that he was bombing a neighboring country, but he reasoned that India had been shattered by the Martian invasion, that his rival's nuclear arsenal was either expended, or destroyed.

With that certainty, and a few fervent prayers to Allah, the rockets flew, carrying their deadly cargo toward the alien machines and the landscape they had so remorselessly conquered.

Indian Army Emergency Command Bunker
Outside New Delhi, India

"They have launched! There has already been an explosion south of Kashmir, and we are tracking more rockets into the midlands!" cried the terrified radar officer. "I have the tracks of nine missiles still active and in flight."

"The fools!" spat General Suresh, shaking his head in despair. "It's not enough that the aliens are ravaging our world—but now we have to fight each other?"

The radar officer made no reply, merely continued to track the blips on his screen. "One more impact, and another," he said. "Ground sensors confirm nuclear explosions."

"How many of our rockets are restored?" Suresh demanded of General Nelev, his strategic attack commander.

"Six, as of now. With two more expected in the next hour."

"Very well," said the Army commander. "Let them fly."

Tradewind Airport
Amarillo, Texas

The Commemorative Air Force was a group of amateur fliers, private citizens of at least moderate means who owned beautifully restored, classic military aircraft. They had once been called the Confederate Air Force, and—to judge by the prominent displays of the "stars and bars" of the Rebel flag—most of the fliers had reclaimed that politically incorrect label. By far the largest branch of the group came from the state of Texas. As many of these machines as could fly were gathered at the small airport on the Panhandle, planning their first combat mission of the new millennium.

Most of their planes were World War II vintage, and included many trainers, as well as several snazzily painted P-51 Mustangs and a couple of P-47 Thunderbolts. There were even some bombers, including the last remaining B-29 still airworthy, as well as a B-25, B-26, and a couple of Navy dive-bombers. None of the aircraft employed any computerization or complicated electronics as essential components, so they had remained flyable after the Pulse.

More than fifty of the vintage aircraft were lined up on the taxiways of this small airport, in a part of the vast state that had not yet felt the string of direct Martian assault. A stream of pickup trucks and old farm tractors lumbered through the gates, dispersing to approach each of the waiting airplanes. In the back of each truck was a pile, mounded high, of moldy food—food that had been scavenged from abandoned commercial bakeries and food-processing plants.

Tom "Tex" McCarthy owned and flew a T-4 trainer, an aircraft he had personally restored—albeit, at the cost of his marriage. Still, the plane meant everything to him. Previously, those annual jaunts to the fly-in at Oshkosh with the other Warbirds had been the high points of his life. On this day he had an even more meaningful mission to accomplish.

His plane, like all the others, was armed by the simple expedient of reinforced garbage bags slung under the belly, or the wings—or, in the case of the B-29 and other multiengine bombers, filling up the bomb bay. With a few minutes of careful installation, Tex's trainer was armed with three large bags slung under the fuselage, all rigged to drop simultaneously when he pulled his bomb release lever—the lever he had never pulled for anything other than a drill.

A young Amarillo cop handed him a map, with several spots marked in red. "We want you to go after these buggers, just north of Dallas," he said. "They've burned out Houston and everything as far north as Fort Worth, and they're heading this way. Remember to come in low—them lasers 're damned fast."

"You bet," Tex replied, grinning fiercely. "I'm as ready as I'm ever gonna be."

"Good luck—if this crazy idea works, you might just save the world," said the cop, offering a firm handshake.

Two minutes later Tex McCarthy and his trainer rumbled down the runway and into the hazy dawn sky. He spotted a half dozen other aircraft with him, all single-engine trainers like his own T-4. They flew in loose formation, no more than five hundred feet above the ground, dispersed over a mile or more to make themselves less vulnerable to a single enemy weapon.

An hour into the flight, Tex saw smoke on the horizon. The whole formation banked to come at the murk directly, dropping so that they were at no more than hundred feet of altitude. His hands tightened on the wheel, and he double-checked his bomb release lever, making sure he could reach it and pull with an instant's thought. He did not expect to have much time.

Then he spotted the enemy, silver domes glinting in the morning sun. The Martian tripods loped along, three of them in a broad line. He drew a bead on the nearest one and opened his throttle all the way, coming in as fast as he could. The other trainers split up, two veering toward each target without any need for communication.

He saw the tentacles waving above the domes, knew that those held the lethal lasers he had been warned about. A spot of red winked from one of them and the airplane to Tex's port instantly began to burn, plummeting the short distance to the ground and cartwheeling in a fiery explosion.

The spot of red light seemed so harmless, yet Tex felt a chill of terror as he saw it swing toward his own plane. As soon as it passed his engine quit, and smoke billowed from underneath the cowl. The prop froze and the plane shuddered, gliding sluggishly.

He was going in.

"What the hell," he thought. He could still steer a little bit. Ignoring the bomb release lever, he put both hands on the stick and pushed the T-4 into a steeper dive. His target was only a hundred yards away.

Direct hit.

Norfolk Naval Base, Virginia

Alex met the choppers as they came in, and once again the drawn, dejected faces of the Marines as they debarked confirmed her worst fears. She knew the light was fading, and it was hard to keep hoping. A young sergeant put his hand on her shoulder, patted reassuringly.

"We're just going to fuel up, ma'am, then head out again. We'll look for a signal fire or something. Might even be easier to spot him in the dark."

"Yes . . . thank you," she said, biting back tears.

"Dr. DeVane?" It was the young communications officer who seemed to follow her everywhere she went.

"What is it?" she snapped impatiently.

"There's a report that came in from that Wrigley Guerrilla. The guy from Chicago you were listening to the other day. He had some real interesting news— you'll want to check it out. We have it on tape."

She took another look at the Black Hawks, as an old fuel truck lumbered onto the flight line. In a few minutes they would be off again.

"Okay—back to the shack, then?"

"Sure. And tell me—I mean, it's maybe just a coincidence, the same last name and all—but do you know a guy named Mark DeVane? Who could be in Chicago now?"

She didn't know whether to laugh, or to cry.

East Los Angeles, California

Rafael Fernandez was known as *Araño* for his spidery quickness and, he liked to think, his lethal sting. Now he would put that to the test. He had been listening to the radio for the past day, hearing about victories scored against the Martians in places like Chicago, Texas, and Virginia. So he had gathered his boys to him, and they had all collected flour sacks filled with moldy peppers, tortillas, and cheese from the back rooms of several of the neighborhood *bodegas*.

The tripod was striding down the center of Whittier Boulevard, the Martian presuming itself master of all it surveyed. Smoke rose from the miles and miles of ruined neighborhoods beyond, and most of East LA had long been abandoned.

But not by *Araño,* and his friends. He had been waiting for this chance, and he was not afraid to act.

Rafael gave the signal, and his posse moved out of the shadows to the attack. The tripod seemed to take no note of them—perhaps it was concerned with grander prey, with machines and metal weaponry. In any event, a dozen young men raced close to it, flinging the plastic bags with inherent skill, releasing an all-encompassing barrage that all but buried the tripod in a cloud of moldy dust.

Only then did the laser snap up and blink. Just like that Jose and Carlos went down, screaming and bloody. But already the missiles had struck home. The laser fired again, this time wildly, as if the Martian within the dome was convulsing in pain or terror. More bags of moldy food flew, smashing and bursting against the hard metal skin of the tripod's dome.

It was only a second later that the Martian machine careened wildly away, slipping along the embankment of a dry canal, crashing into the bottom, where it started to burn. The two dying men had to be left—after they were put out of their misery—but the rest of the gang took off. They had plenty of ammunition, and knew that it wouldn't be hard to find another Martian or two.

James River, Virginia

"Look—there's a fire!" shouted the observer, tapping the Marine pilot on the shoulder. "Three of them, in a triangle—that's got to be a signal!"

"Got it!" The helicopter veered, circling the bright blazes, as the pilot looked for a place to descend.

"There—you can land there!" the observer called, indicating a flat green expanse near the trees bordering the river.

The Black Hawk settled onto a tobacco field a hundred yards away from the smoking fires, which looked like they were fueled by a mixture of gasoline and old tires. Almost immediately a gaunt-looking man in a flight suit came stumbling forward, leaning on a makeshift crutch.

"That's him—that's Duke Hayes!" cried the Marine spotter, as four of his buddies scrambled onto the ground and helped the downed flier back to the helicopter.

Duke Hayes was smoking a huge cigar, and he immediately handed out a dozen more to his rescuers, explaining that he had liberated them from a nearby tobacco shop. His ankle had swollen to the size of a cantaloupe, but he didn't seem aware of any pain.

"Nice to see you guys," he remarked to the crewmen, as they hoisted him aboard. "Care to give a fellow flyboy a ride?"

EPILOGUE

July 3
O'Hare Airport
Chicago, Illinois

Galahad and I were sitting in the Jeep as the A10 Warthog growled over the airport, banked through a long turn, and came in for a landing on a distant runway. I didn't know how or why Alex could be coming in what I knew to be a single-seat tactical bomber, but this was the only plane to arrive in the last three days. It had to be her!

I started the Jeep and raced across taxiways and gate areas that had once been home to hundreds of commercial flights every day. Perhaps they would be again—already the reports were highly encouraging, as all over the country and world humans were taking the war to the enemy, striking the tripods wherever they could be located with the surprisingly virulent, and exceptionally common, weapon of natural food-based mold. In Chicago alone, we few survivors had gathered a massive amount of the stuff, rendered into hand-thrown bombs, and cleared the whole area of tripods in only a matter of days.

Then, a few days ago, I'd received miraculous news: In an amazing radio conversation, arranged by the Wrigley Guerrilla and some Navy technician at Norfolk, I had talked to Alex. She had told me that the Martians had been defeated across almost the full extent of the East Coast and that she was on her way to Chicago.

I stepped on the gas, wheeling across taxiways and connecting roads, so that I was rolling to a stop as the jet engines wound down. The mystery of her choice of aircraft was solved when I saw the double canopy, realized that this Warthog had an extra seat. The bubble of glass popped open, and my daughter was waving, smiling down at me, scrambling out.

And then Alex was on the ground, wrapping me in a hug as a limping Duke Hayes—who looked startlingly like his brother—came slowly down the ladder after her.

"They made a couple of two-seater Warthogs for training purposes," Alex explained delightedly. "One of them was at a base just outside of Washington, and the president authorized Duke to take it for a ride. Dad—can you believe it? We're here! We're alive—and we're going to win this war!"

It was a sunny morning, but I had trouble seeing her through the tears that ran, uncontrolled, from my eyes.